CHRISTMAS MAGIC IN HEATHERDALE

BY
ABIGAIL GORDON

THE MOTHERHOOD MIX-UP

BY
JENNIFER TAYLOR

Dear Reader

Would you like to come with me to a small and enchanting market town to read about the lives and loves of a charismatic man who thinks he has all his priorities right—until he meets a beautiful woman whose life has become a hurtful catastrophe due to the unkindness of others?

If so, do please read on.

With best wishes

Abigail Gordon

Dear Reader

One of the questions I am asked most frequently is where do I get my ideas for a book? I usually reply that they come from conversations I've overheard or from something I have read in the newspapers and this book is the perfect example of that. I was having coffee in town when I overheard two women talking about IVF. One of their daughters was undergoing IVF treatment and this lady was worried in case something went wrong. As she said to her friend, wouldn't it be awful if the wrong embryo was implanted? It immediately piqued my interest.

I kept thinking about what would happen if a woman discovered that the child she had given birth to wasn't actually hers. Of course these things rarely happen, but what an intriguing scenario for a story…

On the surface, Mia and Leo are poles apart. Mia was brought up in care and has had to work hard to earn her living, whereas Leo comes from a wealthy family and has always enjoyed the finer things in life. What unites them is the fact that each is determined to protect their child. Discovering that Harry and Noah were born to the wrong mothers is a huge shock for them both but they are determined not to let it affect the boys. They intend to do all they can to help the children cope with a very difficult situation and make their plans accordingly. What they don't plan on happening is that they will fall in love in the process. Dare they follow their hearts? Or could they end up upsetting the boys even more? It's another dilemma they need to resolve.

I hope you enjoy Mia and Leo's story as much as I enjoyed writing it. If you would like to learn more about my books then do visit my blog: Jennifertaylorauthor.wordpress.com. I love hearing from readers so pop in and leave a message.

Best wishes

Jennifer

CHRISTMAS MAGIC
IN HEATHERDALE

BY
ABIGAIL GORDON

MILLS
BOON

First published in Great Britain 2013
by Mills & Boon, an imprint of Harlequin (UK) Limited.
Harlequin (UK) Limited, Eton House, 18-24 Paradise Road,
Richmond, Surrey TW9 1SR

© Abigail Gordon 2013

ISBN: 978 0 263 89917 7

Harlequin (UK) policy is to use papers that are natural, renewable and recyclable products and made from wood grown in sustainable forests. The logging and manufacturing process conform to the legal environmental regulations of the country of origin.

Printed and bound in Spain
by Blackprint CPI, Barcelona

Abigail Gordon loves to write about the fascinating combination of medicine and romance from her home in a Cheshire village. She is active in local affairs, and is even called upon to write the script for the annual village pantomime! Her eldest son is a hospital manager, and helps with all her medical research. As part of a close-knit family, she treasures having two of her sons living close by, and the third one not too far away. This also gives her the added pleasure of being able to watch her delightful grandchildren growing up.

Recent titles by the same author:

SWALLOWBROOK'S WEDDING OF THE YEAR
MARRIAGE MIRACLE IN SWALLOWBROOK**
SPRING PROPOSAL IN SWALLOWBROOK**
SWALLOWBROOK'S WINTER BRIDE**
SUMMER SEASIDE WEDDING†
VILLIAGE NURSE'S HAPPY-EVER-AFTER†
WEDDING BELLS FOR THE VILLAGE NURSE†
CHRISTMAS IN BLUEBELL COVE†
COUNTRY MIDWIFE, CHRISTMAS BRIDE*

**The Doctors of Swallowbrook Farm*
The Willowmere Village Stories
†*Bluebell Cove*

For Robert Bonar, a good friend and the kindest of men.

CHAPTER ONE

EMPLOYED AS A paediatric consultant at Heatherdale Children's Hospital, Ryan Ferguson was used to the demands of the job, but today had been in a class of its own. Relieved to finally be away from work he pulled up outside the elegant town house that was home to him and his two small daughters.

Rhianna and Martha would be fast asleep at this late hour, but he was grateful that they would have been tucked up for the night by Mollie, his kindly house-keeper, who in spite of the time would have a meal waiting for him.

Ryan's work centred mainly on children with neurological illnesses and injuries and his dedication to his calling was an accepted fact by all who knew him. His intention to bring up his children as a single father was more of a surprise, as there were many women who would be only too willing to fill the gap in his life.

Today's non-stop problems had been serious and in some cases rare, with almost a certainty that the dreaded meningitis would be lurking somewhere amongst his young patients and the battle to overthrow it would begin.

With the workload as heavy as it was, it was becoming obvious that they needed another registrar on the neuro unit to assist him and Julian Tindall, his second-in-command.

A rare shortage of nursing staff due to a bug that had been going round hadn't helped, and as he'd performed his daily miracles the hours had galloped past. Now he was ready to put the day's stresses to the back of his mind and enjoy the warmth and peace of his home for a few hours. Home was in the delightful small spa town of Heatherdale, tucked away amongst the rugged peaks and smooth green dales of the countryside, with Manchester being the nearest big city.

The moment he was out of the car and had collected his briefcase from the back seat he moved swiftly towards where warmth and hot food would be waiting for him, casting a brief glance in the direction of the property next to it as he did so, and his step slowed.

A town house like his own, it had been empty for years and he was amazed to see a car parked outside and a flicker of light coming from inside, as if from a torch or a candle. He frowned. He doubted it was thieves, as there would be nothing in there to steal. Could be squatters, though, and the thought was not appealing.

When his housekeeper opened the door to him she couldn't wait to tell him the latest neighbourhood news. When she'd returned from picking the children up from school there had been the car parked outside, and shortly afterwards a bed had been delivered from a nearby furniture store.

'Wow!' he exclaimed as he closed the door behind him. 'Surely they've had it cleaned first? It must be filthy after being empty for so many years. The amount of lighting inside has to mean that they've not had the electricity switched on and are using candles or a torch. It seems an odd state of affairs. Once I've changed into something less formal, I'll do the neighbourly thing and go and introduce myself, ask if there is anything I can assist them with.'

When he knocked on the door of the run-down house that was a blight in the crescent of much-admired Victorian town houses there was no sound for a moment. Then the door swung open slowly and his jaw dropped at the sight of a slender stranger with long dark hair that swung gently against her shoulders and a face blotched with weeping.

'They haven't been,' she cried desperately as he was on the point of introducing himself. 'The cleaners haven't been and the place is full of spiders' webs and the dust of years. I will have to find a hotel for the night.'

'Are you alone here?' he asked carefully. 'I'm Ryan Ferguson, and my family and I are your new neighbours.' He held out his hand in greeting. The tearful stranger shook it limply but didn't volunteer any information about herself. She seemed extremely distracted, which was no wonder considering the situation.

He got the impression that she wanted him gone but he could hardly go back to his own comfortable home and leave her in such a state.

'Can you recommend a hotel not too far away?' she asked. 'I just can't spend the night in here. I've had a bed delivered but haven't taken the wrappings off it so it should come to no harm for the present.'

Ryan was still standing in the doorway and would have liked to see just what a mess the inside of the house was in, but he could hardly go barging in without an invite.

'You must be exhausted. I'll take you to a hotel if you would like to lock up. My car is parked out front like yours, so I will lead the way and you can follow.'

'Thank you,' she said unsteadily. 'I do apologise for breaking into your evening. I shall be onto the cleaners first thing in the morning.'

'I'm only too pleased to be of assistance,' he told her. 'If you will just give me a moment, I'll go and get my car keys.'

When Mollie opened the door to him again he explained, 'This is our new neighbour, Mollie. I'm taking her to a hotel as the house isn't quite ready to move into.'

'Oh, you poor dear,' Mollie said, observing the strange woman standing hesitantly at the kerb edge. 'What a horrible thing to happen, and on a cold, dark night like this.' She turned to Ryan. 'I'm just about to dish up your meal before I go home for the day. There's plenty to spare, so can we not offer the young lady some hospitality?'

'Yes, of course, by all means,' he said, forgetting his weariness for a moment.

Their new neighbour shrank back.

'I couldn't possibly intrude into your evening any more than I am doing,' she said.

Ignoring her reluctance, Ryan insisted. 'You are most welcome. How long is it since you last had something to eat?'

'I can't remember.'

'If that's the case, you need food now.' He stepped back to let her past him to where Mollie was hovering near the kitchen door. 'If you want to wash your hands you'll find anything you need in the cloakroom at the end of the hall. Mollie will have the food on the table when you're done.'

'Thank you,' she croaked meekly, and disappeared.

Mollie was ready to go by the time his unexpected guest had removed the day's surface grime and once they were alone silence descended in what was a tastefully furnished dining room.

When they'd finished eating Ryan said, 'There's a fire in the sitting room. Make yourself comfortable while I make coffee.'

She nodded and said uncomfortably, 'The food was lovely. Thank you so much.'

He was observing her gravely. 'Are you going to tell me who you are? The house next door has been unoccupied for many years so it was a surprise to find signs of life there when I came home. Are you actually planning to live there?'

'Er, yes,' she told him hesitantly. 'My name is Melissa Redmond. The house was left to me by my grandmother when she died some years ago. I've had no interest in living out here in the backwoods until a short time ago when my circumstances changed dramatically.

'I'd arranged for a firm of cleaners to come in and make it liveable, and for the power to be connected, but when I got here late this afternoon nothing had been done and I was frantic.'

'Yes, I can understand that,' Ryan said slowly. Melissa didn't look quite as bedraggled in the warm glow of the lamps in his sitting room as she had when she'd opened the door of the mausoleum next door. The colour had returned to her cheeks and she seemed a lot calmer. His curiosity about his new neighbour had definitely been piqued. He wanted to know more.

When he came back with the coffee cups she was asleep, overcome by the comforting warmth of the fire. So it looked as if he wasn't going to find out any more about her for now.

An hour passed and Melissa hadn't stirred out of the deep sleep of exhaustion that had claimed her. There was no way she could be allowed to go back to the chill of the house that had been empty for so long, neither did Ryan want to rouse her to go to a hotel at that hour. Instead, he went and found a soft fleece, laid it gently over her, and went up to bed with the intention of checking on her at regular intervals. That turned out to be a wise precaution as the first time he went downstairs, she was awake and about to disappear through the front door.

'Melissa, wait!' he cried. 'You can't stay in that place tonight. I have a spare room that is always kept ready for visitors. I insist you stay in it. I won't be able to sleep knowing that you're not somewhere safe, *and* I've had a very exhausting day that I need to recover from before the next one is upon me.'

'My nightwear is in my case next door,' she protested faintly.

'I'll find you some,' he offered. Was he going insane to let a strange woman wear something that had belonged to Beth?

He pointed to a gracious curved staircase and said, 'If you would like to go up, I'll show you to the guest room. While you are settling in there I'll find something for you to wear.'

Ryan dug out one of Beth's plain cotton nightshirts to lend to Melissa. He avoided taking out any of the prettier nightgowns that Beth had favoured.

Melissa took it from him with a subdued smile and said with tears threatening, 'I hope that one day I'll be able to repay your kindness, Ryan.'

He smiled. 'Don't concern yourself about that. Tomorrow is another day and it just has to be better than this one has been for you.'

With that brief word of comfort he left her and went to a room across the landing. Closing the door behind him, he looked down at his sleeping daughters and wondered just what Rhianna and Martha would think when they saw there was a visitor for breakfast.

As she lay sleeplessly under the covers of the bed in the spare room, Melissa's thoughts were in overdrive. The future that had looked so bleak seemed slightly less so because of the kindness of a stranger who had taken her in, fed her, and offered her a bed for the night.

So much for keeping a low profile in her new surroundings! The hurts she had suffered over recent months had made her long for privacy, for somewhere to hide. But her meeting with a man with the golden fairness of a Viking and eyes as blue as a summer sky had put an end to those sorts of plans.

It seemed Ryan had children who no doubt were fast asleep, and was in sole charge of them, so where was their mother? Wherever it might be, it was not her business. She had to fix her thoughts on tomorrow and the cleaners, the electricity people, and accepting the delivery of her few remaining belongings some time during the day. With those thoughts in mind she drifted into an uneasy sleep.

The sound of children's voices on the landing mingling with her host's deeper tones brought Melissa into instant wakefulness in the darkness of a winter morning. She dressed quickly in yesterday's clothes and prepared to go down to where she could hear the sounds of breakfast-time coming from the kitchen.

Pausing in the doorway, she saw that Ryan was at the grill, keeping an eye on sizzling bacon, and two little girls were seated at the table with bowls of cereal in front of them, observing her with wide eyes of surprise as she said, 'Thank you so much for last night. I feel a different person this morning after the meal and the rest. I'm off to find out what happened to the cleaners and the electricity services.'

He smiled across at her. 'Not before you've eaten. You have no facilities for preparing food next door, so take a seat.'

Rhianna, at seven years old and the elder of his two young daughters, was not a shy child, and burst out, 'Who is this lady, Daddy? She wasn't here when we went to bed.'

'No, she wasn't,' Martha, two years younger, chirped beside her. At that point Ryan took charge of the conversation.

'Her name is Melissa and she's going to live next door to us,' he explained. 'Melissa, these are my daughters, Rhianna and Martha.'

'She can't!' Rhianna protested.

'Why not?' he asked.

'It's haunted!'

'No way,' he said laughingly as he pulled out a chair for Melissa to be seated, as if there had been no hesitation in joining them on her part. 'There aren't any ghosts in Heatherdale, I promise you that, Rhianna. Now, who would like a bacon roll?'

'Me!' the children both cried.

With the day ahead momentarily forgotten, Melissa smiled as the memory surfaced of how, when she'd been at junior school, she and her friends used to pass a creepy-looking empty house on the way there. They had been convinced that there was a human hand on the inside window ledge. It had only been when one of their fathers had gone to investigate that it had been discovered that the 'hand' had been a pink plastic glove. There had been much disappointment amongst the children.

She had done as Ryan requested and seated herself opposite him. As she smiled across at his children she saw that they both had the same golden fairness as their father, but their eyes were different—big and brown and fixed on her.

Making her second contribution to the occasion, Martha asked, 'Are you some children's mummy? We haven't got one any more. Ours was hurt by a tree.'

Ryan had just put cereal and a bacon sandwich in front of Melissa and was about to join them at the table. He stilled, and she saw dismay in his expression.

'Just get on with your breakfast, Martha,' he said gravely, 'and no more questions.'

'It's all right,' Melissa told him. 'I don't mind. They are delightful.' She turned to his small daughter.

'No, Martha, I'm not a mummy, but I do love children. My job is all about making them well when they are sick.'

Their interest was waning to find that she didn't fit their requirements, but not their father's. The stranger at their table was full of surprises. What kind of a job was it that she'd referred to?

Bringing his mind back to their morning routine on school days, when the children had finished eating he told them to go and put their school uniforms on and have their satchels ready for when Mollie came to take them to school.

'Will Melissa be here when we come home?' Rhianna asked.

She answered for Ryan. 'I'm afraid not, Rhianna. My house needs cleaning and sorting. But once that's done everything will be fine and you can come to see me whenever you like.'

Rhianna seemed happy with that answer and she and Martha hopped off to get ready for school.

'Your daughters are adorable, Ryan,' she said with a warm smile.

'They're the light of my life. A life that would not be easy if Mollie wasn't around,' Ryan replied. 'She's a good friend as well as my housekeeper. I have a very demanding job but it's totally rewarding and somehow I manage to give it my best, while organising things at this end to make sure that Rhianna and Martha are happy, though the result is not always how I want it to be. Still, I mustn't delay you. We both have busy days ahead of us.'

She couldn't have agreed more. As she looked around

her at his delightful home, the gloom of yesterday came back. Dreading what the day would hold for her, she wished Ryan a stilted goodbye and went to ring the cleaning firm and the electricity company.

As Melissa waited for the cleaners to arrive, her mind drifted back over her recent past. She recalled how only yesterday, stony-faced behind the wheel of her car, she had driven away from the house that had always been her home in a select area of a Cheshire green belt without looking back.

The doors had been locked, the windows shut fast, and as a last knife thrust she'd put flowers in the hallway, a huge bunch of them that would be the first thing that the new owners saw when they arrived to take over their recently acquired property.

The purchase had been completed early that morning, the money was already in her bank account, but the thought of it brought no joy. It would be a matter of here today and gone tomorrow.

'I'm sorry, sweetheart,' her father had said as the last few moments of his life had ebbed away. 'So sorry to be going like this before I'd sorted things.'

'You have nothing to be sorry for,' she'd told him gently, thinking that he must be delirious. 'You have always been there for me, making me laugh, indulging me, keeping me safe, and David will do the same. I know he will.'

He'd tried to speak again but the mists had been closing in and the nurse at the other side of the bed had said a few seconds later, 'He's gone, Melissa. His injuries were too severe for him to overcome. There will be no more pain for your father.'

Max Redmond had been a charmer, and a wealthy one at that. Melissa had lost her mother to heart failure when she had been eleven and Max had given her everything she could possibly have wanted to make up for the loss. He'd taken her on fantastic holidays, bought her the kind of car that most young people could only dream of when she had been old enough to drive, and had given her a generous allowance that had been more than some families had had to feed their children and pay the mortgage.

The two of them had lived in a smart detached house amongst the rich and famous, not far from the city, and when she'd gone to fulfil a dream and enrolled as a medical student, it had been at a university in nearby Manchester so that her father wouldn't be lonely, although it hadn't seemed likely.

Max had never remarried, but he'd made lots of women friends in the circles in which he'd moved, where wining and dining was the order of the day. However, he had always cancelled any arrangements he'd made if his daughter had been free to socialise with him.

That had been until she'd got engaged to David Lowson, the son of one of her father's women friends. After that, he'd watched benignly as most of Melissa's time away from her career had been taken up with the delights of being in love.

She'd qualified as a doctor in paediatrics in the summer, and on receiving her degree had been employed at a nearby hospital. Life had been good in every way, with all of it centred around the big city that she knew so well and would never have wanted to leave, until her father had walked in front of a speeding car on a road not far from where they lived after a lively lunch in a nearby hotel, and had died from his injuries.

Since then Melissa had experienced all of life's worst emotions: grief at the sudden tragic loss of the man who had loved her so much; sick horror to discover that his last words to her had been referring to a huge mountain of gambling debts that he had accumulated.

There had also been the aching hurt of betrayal from an engagement that had fizzled out when her fiancé had discovered that she was no longer the wealthy heiress that his mother had urged him to propose to, and was going to be poorer than a church mouse by the time she'd sorted out Max's frightening legacy.

Everything Melissa could lay her hands on had been sold, and most of her salary each month had gone into the bottomless pit, with the sale of the house as the final heartbreaking humiliation.

During the time that the sale had been going through, those who knew her had seen little of her. Grief stricken and panicked about the future, Melissa had chosen to hide away from her friends.

Her father had given no inkling that he'd had money problems. Always a man about town, as generous host to all his friends, he hadn't been able to admit to his failings, and she now understood fully his weak apology as he'd lain dying.

Incredibly, there'd been no life insurance to fall back on, or other safeguards that were usually in place regarding the death of a person, but thankfully the money from the sale of the house would clear the last of the debts.

She supposed it would have been sensible to rent herself a small apartment in Manchester and bring the shattered remnants of her life together again somehow. But with her father now resting with her mother in a nearby cemetery, and an ex-fiancé who had cast her aside living not far away, she had been intent on moving to some place where she wasn't known.

Having left the hospital where she'd been employed, she'd headed for the small market town of Heatherdale, where her paternal grandmother had lived and where her house, which had been empty for a long time, was there for her if she wanted it.

The old lady had willed it to her and, though grateful for the thought, it was the last place she would ever have contemplated moving to in the past, but the present was proving to be a different matter. Alone and lost, she'd needed somewhere to hide from the pitying looks she'd received from her father's friends and acquaintances when the news had got around that she was penniless. She'd wanted somewhere to avoid the mocking smiles of those who had witnessed the plight of the 'golden girl' and thought it would do her good to see how the other half lived. But the thing that had hurt most had been the speed with which her ex had found another woman to replace her.

She had found the keys to her grandmother's house in a chest of drawers in her father's bedroom, and as she'd gazed down at the heavy ornate bunch of them it had been as if a means of escape was being offered to her.

There had been receipts with them for payments that her father had made to the local authorities on her behalf over the years to comply with the law regarding the ownership of unoccupied housing, and she'd decided that the paperwork and the keys were heaven sent.

She'd felt as if she never wanted to see the city that she'd loved so much, with its familiar shops, smart restaurants and green parks, ever again. She'd decided to make a fresh start in a place that she'd never cared for much on the rare occasions she'd been there.

With no job, no money, and no family, she had to hope that she could find a future for herself in Heatherdale. First she had to get the house straight. Next on her agenda was finding a job. The obvious choice would be its famous hospital, but if there were no vacancies there for a newly qualified paediatrician then she'd simply have to find something to tide her over.

The internet had come up with the name and address of a firm of domestic cleaners in the Heatherdale area and she'd hired them to give the house a thorough cleaning from top to bottom before she arrived.

Apart from ordering a bed to be delivered later in the day, when she would be there to accept it, the rest of her belongings would arrive the following afternoon, when she was satisfied that the house was ready to take delivery of them.

It wasn't the best time of year to be moving into a strange house in a strange place, she'd thought achingly as the miles had flashed past. The last leaves of autumn had been scattered at the roadside or hanging limply on trees, and a cold wind had been nipping at her while she'd been taking a last walk around the gardens of what had been her home.

During her early childhood she and her parents had visited her grandmother occasionally, but there hadn't been any real closeness between them because the old lady had disapproved of her son's attitude to life in general. She hadn't liked the way he'd been such a spend-thrift, although at that time he hadn't reached retirement and had been making big money in the stock markets.

'When I die I'm leaving the house to the child,' she'd told him. 'There might come a day when she'll need a roof over her head.' As the lights of Heatherdale had appeared on the horizon, Melissa had reflected that the grandmother she'd rarely seen had turned out to be her only friend.

Martha's innocent question about the stranger who had joined them for breakfast was uppermost in Ryan's mind as he drove the short distance to the hospital. It had brought painful memories with it that he only allowed himself to think about when he was alone, but in that moment in the kitchen they had been starkly clear and he'd been extra-loving with the children while they'd waited for Mollie to arrive.

His youngest daughter had described them as being without a mother because theirs had been hurt by a tree. It wouldn't have been the easiest description of her death for Melissa Redmond to understand, but did that matter? She was just a stranger who had joined them for breakfast.

He and Beth had attended the same school in Heatherdale, had both chosen medicine as a career, he in paediatrics and she in midwifery. It had always been there, the love that had blossomed in their late teens and taken them to the altar of a church in the small market town where they lived.

Heatherdale boasted a famous spa that people came from far and wide to take advantage of, and beautiful Victorian architecture built from local stone that he never wearied of. There were spacious parks and elegant shops and restaurants. Everything that he loved was here except for the wife he had adored.

When she'd died he had wanted to die too as life had lost its meaning, but there had been two small children, unhappy and confused because their mother hadn't been there any more, so he'd pulled himself together for their sakes. In the last three years his life had been entirely taken up with his children and the health problems of those belonging to others.

If it meant that he never had time to do his own thing, at least there was the comfort of knowing that his young daughters were safe and happy, and that he was serving a vital purpose in the Heatherdale Children's Hospital where he was a senior paediatric consultant.

He knew that folks found him irritating at times because he never socialised, was always too busy when asked out to dine, even though he had Mollie, who would always take on the role of childminder if needed and who checked out every available woman she met as a possible new wife for him, without actually saying so openly.

As Melissa looked around her house in the cold light of day she was hoping that today would not be quite as horrendous as yesterday. However, every day since she'd lost her father and discovered what he had been involved in had been dreadful.

For the past few weeks she'd felt lost and alone, like

some sort of outcast. Ryan's kindness had been a brief relief from what had been a nightmare for her, but at the same time getting involved with anyone at the moment was the last thing she wanted to do. Especially with the man who lived next door.

All she craved for was solitude, somewhere to hide while her hurts healed, but the die was cast. She wasn't going to get the chance to be just a stranger who nodded briefly during her comings and goings job-seeking and then went in and closed the door.

But, as if to balance the scales, there were those two lovely children and it would be a pleasure to babysit them if ever Ryan felt he could trust her.

She'd also contacted the electricity people. She was informed that they were on their way with a new meter and were going to check all the primitive services and appliances in the house while they were there.

They arrived within minutes and as light began to appear in her darkness, in more ways than one, Melissa rolled up her sleeves and looked around her for what had to be her first task of the day. The guy who had just fixed the electricity meter decided it for her by pointing to an ancient but solid-looking gas fire and asking if she'd contacted the gas services yet as both the fire and an ancient cooker were gas powered.

She needed no second telling as having the fire working meant warmth and the cooker hot food, when she'd cleaned the grime off it and had the chance to shop.

The most pressing mission for Ryan, on his arrival at the hospital, was to start the search in earnest for the new registrar for their department.

The procedure with staff vacancies at the hospital was to advertise them internally first, but so far there had been no joy for the two consultants and the vacancy would soon be advertised locally

Today he had two clinics arranged for consultations, plus a slot in Theatre in the late afternoon. With all of that ahead of him he hadn't had time to check on how his new neighbour was coping at her house.

There'd been an electricity van outside and a plumber's vehicle pulling up alongside it as he'd driven past. He decided he owed her one more visit to check she was managing okay then he would step back and let her get on with her life while he got on with his.

The surgery he was committed to in the afternoon was minor compared to some of the operations he performed on unfortunate little ones and hopefully he would be home in time to have a quick word with Melissa before his special time with his children began.

As Ryan was preparing to put in an appearance at his first clinic of the day his assistant, Julian, appeared and commented breezily, 'Still no sign of a saviour in terms of over-booking, I see. Personnel need to pull their finger out and get us another doctor. I've got a list as long as my arm for today and I'm not used to it.'

Julian Tindall, with his dark attractiveness, was every woman's dream man, until they got to know him better!

Inclined to be lazy, but on the ball in an emergency, Julian was a paediatric consultant like himself and could go places if he stopped fooling around with every attractive woman he met and got his act together.

Ryan held the paediatric unit together with the kind

of steadfastness that he applied to every aspect of his daily life, and if the nights spent without Beth by his side were long and lonely, only he knew that.

CHAPTER TWO

MELISSA'S SECOND DAY in Heatherdale was progressing and she was beginning to feel calmer. The neglected house was starting to come out of its murky cocoon, though not enough for her to rejoice totally. There was going to be mammoth amount of decorating and refurbishing to be done.

But the electricity was on, the plumber she'd asked to come had switched on the water and checked for leaks, and, joy of joys, the cleaners were hard at work, getting rid of the grime and mustiness of years.

Her clothes and the few belongings she had salvaged from the sale of the Cheshire house had arrived in the late afternoon. They included a couple of carpets, an expensive wardrobe and dressing table, a dining table and two easy chairs, but there was no kitchen equipment, which meant that for the time being she was going to have to manage with a solid-looking but unattractive gas cooker that was so old it would qualify as an antique.

Yet it had lit at the first attempt and as soon as the cleaners had finished for the day with a promise to come back in the morning, she began to clean it, and was on her knees in front of it when a knock came on the door. She raised herself slowly upright.

With hair held back with a shoelace and dressed in an old pair of jeans and a much-washed jumper that the Cheshire set would never associate her with, she went slowly to answer the knock. He was there again, the Viking from next door, observing her with a reluctant sort of neighbourliness.

'I've called to see how you've fared today,' he said. 'I see that you've got lighting, but have you got heat and water?'

'Yes,' she replied, stepping back reluctantly for him to enter.

'I have light, and heat in the form of an old gas fire. A plumber has been to turn on the water. The cleaners have removed most of the dust and grime and are coming back in the morning to finish the job.'

'And I see that your belongings have arrived,' he said easily, as if she now had a house full of furniture instead of a few oddments. Unable to resist, he went on to ask, 'Do you have family who will be coming to join you?'

'No. Nothing like that,' she said in a low voice, without meeting his glance. She wished that he would go and leave her in peace. She'd seen the inside of his house and it was delightful, with décor and furniture that was just right for the age and design of the property, all obviously chosen with great care.

No doubt he was thinking that hers was going to lower the tone of the neighbourhood and for the first time since she'd arrived in Heatherdale the grim pride and determination that had helped her to stagger through recent months surfaced.

As if he sensed that she wanted him gone, Ryan moved towards the door but paused with his hand on the handle and said, 'I'm sure that you will like it here once you have made the house look how you want it to be.' He would have to be blind not to realise that she wasn't happy about coming to live in Heatherdale.

He almost asked if she would like to eat with them again but sensed the same reluctance as the night before. He bade her goodbye and, determined to put Melissa Redmond to the back of his mind, he went to join his daughters and the faithful Mollie, without whom he would be harassed full time.

'I saw you call at the house next door,' she said when he appeared. 'Is she all right? It has been all systems go in there today.'

'Yes, it would seem so,' he told her. 'I felt she was relieved that I didn't linger. I get a distinct feeling that Melissa Redmond wants to be left alone.'

'Give her time,' she said. 'The lass looked totally traumatised when we saw her last night. Something isn't right in her life. It stands out a mile, or she wouldn't have come here to live in a house that hasn't been touched for years. Don't forget the couple of times that you've seen her she won't have been at her best.'

'Yes, I suppose you're right,' he said absently, as Rhianna and Martha came running down the stairs at that moment, and as he hugged them to him the stranger next door was forgotten in the pleasure of the moment.

When Ryan had gone, Melissa sank down onto the bottom step of the stairs. The cooker and its requirements temporarily forgotten, she gazed into space.

She wondered what Ryan did for a living. When she'd joined them for breakfast it had been plain to see that he was a loving father in the absence of a mother who wasn't around any more, yet he would have to earn a living somehow or other.

There was an air of authority about him that was noticeable and, much as she was not eager to be involved in the lives of those around her, she couldn't help wondering about him.

Still, there were more important priorities than getting to know the neighbours in this town, which would fit in a corner of Manchester. Such as turning her grandmother's house into a home and finding a job. Dared she intrude on the man next door once again by asking him for information about the famous hospital that she would love to be part of, and the local job centre in that order, so that tomorrow she would have a head start on the employment scene? No sooner had the thought occurred to her than she was acting on it.

Changing her working clothes for a stylish cashmere top, which belonged to happier days, and skinny jeans, Melissa was pressing his doorbell seconds later. When the door opened and he was framed there, looking not the least surprised, she said awkwardly, 'I wondered if you might be able to tell me anything about Heatherdale Hospital? Also, can you let me know where the job centre is? I'm going to go looking for employment tomorrow.'

'In that case, hadn't you better come in?'

She nodded awkwardly and stepped past him into the hall with its beautiful staircase, aware from the surprise in his glance that it was the first time he had seen her looking even the least bit attractive. As she waited for him to say something she felt herself reddening.

'Are you aware that Heatherdale Hospital is for children only?' he asked, breaking into the moment. 'If you feel that you need some sort of hospital treatment, you will have to go to Manchester.'

She was smiling. 'I need the information about the hospital because I would just die for the chance to work there.'

'Doing what?' he asked, with raised brows.

'I've got a degree in paediatrics. When I qualified in the summer I was offered a position at a big Manchester hospital and loved it, but that came to an end when my life fell apart. I had to resign because I intended to leave the area due to my family circumstances.'

So that was what she'd meant when she'd said she had a job making sick children well again. At the time Ryan had wondered if she was employed by some sort of charity, but it seemed she was much more hands on than that, and incredibly he and Julian needed someone like her. Melissa Redmond might be heaven sent!

Obviously he'd never seen her in action. The offer he was going to make her at this moment would be a temporary one until he had her measure, and aware that they were still standing in the hall as she had meant it to be just a brief call on her part, he said, 'Come through to the sitting room, while I make *my* contribution to this night of surprises.'

When they were seated with her eyes fixed on him questioningly he said, 'How would you like to work with me at Heatherdale Children's Hospital?'

'What?' she gasped. 'I don't understand.'

'I'm the paediatric consultant for the neurology wards there and my assistant and I need another registrar to help with the workload. It would be on probationary terms at first but with the opportunity of permanency for the right person. What do you say? Do you want to give it a try?'

'Of course I do!' she breathed, her eyes shining. 'I had no idea that was what you did for a living.'

'I don't mean to pry, Melissa, but can you tell me something about what brought you to Heatherdale? I need to know if it would have any effect on your work and position at the hospital.'

She nodded mutely, took a deep breath. 'My father died six months ago as a result of a road accident when he'd had quite a lot of alcohol. From having a life of luxury and pampering I became penniless because, unbeknown to me, he'd accumulated huge gambling debts over the last couple of years.

'I was engaged to be married at the time and fully expected that my future husband would be there to support me as I dealt with bailiffs and demands for payment from those that my father owed money to, but I was mistaken.

'My fiancé couldn't break off the engagement fast enough, and once I'd paid all my father's debts, which meant selling the fabulous house we'd lived in, all I could think of was leaving the area and finding a bolt hole, somewhere to lick my wounds. The only answer to that was my grandmother's house, which is a far cry from the property I'd lived in before but is mine and isn't tainted. So there you have it, a sorry story worthy of a reality TV show.'

'Thanks for telling me,' Ryan said. 'We all have our nightmares to face at one time or another and you have certainly faced up to yours. Can you come to the hospital some time tomorrow and I'll show you round and introduce you to people, including Personnel, who will need you to fill out endless forms.'

'Yes, of course,' she breathed. 'Thank you for giving me the opportunity to get back into paediatrics. I love working with children and hope to have some of my own one day.'

He nodded as the memory of Rhianna and Martha's approval of their breakfast guest resurfaced. The stranger who had come to Heatherdale in the dark of a winter night would make some child a loving mother one day in every sense of the word, he imagined, just as Beth had been to their children.

'What time do you want me to come to the hospital?' she asked.

'Some time in the afternoon when my clinics are over and I'm not in Theatre, around three—unless you have something else planned at that time?'

'No, I haven't,' she told him firmly.

She'd intended spending the afternoon looking for a washing machine that would fit in with her budget but that could wait, everything could wait. He was offering her the chance to be back where she wanted to be, and if Ryan Ferguson was willing to take a chance on her she was not going to disappoint him.

Later that night, for the first time in months sleep came like a healing balm.

A wintry sun was shining overhead as Melissa drove to the famous children's hospital the next afternoon, and although her mind was full of what lay ahead she couldn't help but notice the beautiful architecture of some of the buildings she was passing.

Maybe the market town of Heatherdale wasn't going to be as dreary as she had expected it to be. Life was beginning to feel worth living again.

Walking away from her parked car, she looked around her. The hospital was another apparently ageless building, built from the beautiful local stone that seemed to be everywhere she looked. She hoped that its interior would not lack the trappings of the latest in modern medicine for the sake of its young patients.

There was no cause to be concerned about that. The inside was bright, cheerful and immaculate, with sunshine colours on the walls and lots of pictures of things that children would like.

As she followed the directions to the neuro wards Melissa's heart was beating faster. She was on home ground, within reach of being back on the job she loved once again.

She found Ryan at the bedside of a small girl, who had been brought in by an ambulance with sirens wailing, with what might be meningitis. It was a road he'd been down more times than he could count and it was never any less horrendous to have to tell a family that one of their little ones had succumbed to the dreadful illness.

There was a fellow doctor standing beside him, but his presence barely registered. Melissa's glance was fixed on the man who in a short space of time had brought some zest into her life. Not only had Ryan taken her in out of the cold that first night but he was going to be the means of finding her employment in the very place where she wanted to be.

He glanced up then, saw her standing in the doorway, and sent his assistant over to suggest that she join them as an observer of the emergency. With her adrenaline quickening, she was beside him in a flash.

'It seemed that the child had become very drowsy during the lunch hour. It had been then that her parents had noticed the tell-tale rash and it had become panic stations. While the ambulance had been speeding to the hospital the little girl had lapsed into unconsciousness.'

Ryan turned to the anxious couple at the other side of the bed and began to explain what would happen to their daughter next—blood tests and a lumbar puncture to test for bacterial meningitis.

When the parents and their sick little one had been taken with all speed for the tests, Ryan's colleague asked. 'So, are you going to introduce me, Ryan?'

'Yes, of course,' he said. 'Julian, meet my new neighbour, Melissa Redmond, recently employed in paediatrics in the Manchester area and now about to join us here on a probationary basis with a view to a permanent position. Melissa, this is Julian Tindall.'

Ryan noticed that she was looking a different person altogether today, dressed in smart clothes and with her hair and make-up perfect. She was quite beautiful in a restrained sort of way.

As Melissa shook hands with Julian she was aware of him sizing her up and immediately had him pegged as an attractive, dark-eyed flirt.

'So when do you want to start?' Ryan asked, 'Tomorrow perhaps?'

'Er, yes, if that's all right with you.'

'Certainly, if you're available,' he replied.

She had never felt more 'available' in her life. He knew she was out on a limb here in Heatherdale, that apart from getting her house in order there was no one who cared a jot about her. Why wait to begin this job of a lifetime?

Melissa wished that there was someone to share her good news with, but the days were gone when she'd had a loving father, an attentive fiancé, and lots of friends to communicate with.

Her glance rested briefly on the house next door where she'd been welcomed into the home of a stranger and had been reluctant to accept his hospitality on a dark and lonely night. Ryan Ferguson must have thought her some sort of ungracious oddball.

The lights were on, which was not surprising as his children would be home from school by now and being looked after by his housekeeper. Melissa wondered again what had happened to their mother.

Whatever it was, the two of them had seemed happy enough until they'd discovered she was coming to live next door. Then had come the protest about it being haunted and she'd tried not to smile at their childish imaginings.

As afternoon turned into evening she saw there was no car outside so obviously Ryan wasn't home yet, and as she began to prepare a snack sort of meal, which was becoming the norm since life had become so drab and disillusioning, she hugged herself at the thought of tomorrow.

* * *

Ryan had phoned home to tell Mollie he would be late due to a seriously ill child with bacterial meningitis that he wanted to try to get stabilised before he left her in the care of the night staff.

It wasn't the first time he'd been late home because of his job and it wouldn't be the last, and on such occasions he was very grateful for Mollie's presence in their lives. She lived alone just down the road from them, having lost her husband from heart failure some years previously and was happy to be of use to him and his children to such an extent.

The girls were in bed by the time he arrived and after a brief chat and a cuddle he left them sleepy and contented to go downstairs to have the meal that Mollie had kept warm for him.

She wished that his life was less stressful, but knew it had been his choice to parent single-handedly after his wife's death. She admired him for the way he cared for his children. Yet she couldn't help wishing that someone would come along who would make Ryan realise what he was missing, that Beth would not have wanted him to be alone for the rest of his life, always involved with work or family when it came to the social life of the town and its hospital.

'I've found a new registrar to lighten our load at the hospital,' he told her as she placed the food in front of him.

'That's good!' she exclaimed. 'Another man, is it?'

'No, it's a woman. Actually, someone you know.'

'That I know?'

'Yes, it's Melissa from next door. She has a degree

in paediatrics and she joins us tomorrow. What do you think of that?'

'I'm amazed, but what a good thing for both of you that she has found employment so quickly and that your stresses will be lighter. It's as if her coming to live in Heatherdale was meant to be.'

Ryan smiled. 'Don't get too carried away, Mollie. I only found out about her qualifications last night and offered her the job on condition that she fits the bill, so it will be probationary to begin with.'

'Yes, of course,' Mollie agreed, thankful that something was going right for him for once.

The blood tests and lumbar puncture had shown that little Georgia had indeed got bacterial meningitis and he'd explained to her distraught parents that she was going to be given large doses of antibiotics that he'd arranged for her to have intravenously in the hope of preventing the dreaded illness increasing its hold on her.

When he'd eventually left the hospital it had been with the determination to ring the ward later for a report on her progress as the next few hours would be crucial.

The answer was what he'd hoped for when he did. His small patient was regaining consciousness and her horrendously high temperature was coming down, so with Mollie having returned home and Rhianna and Martha asleep, Ryan decided to spend the rest of the evening with a medical journal that had been languishing on the back seat of his car for a few days.

When he went out to get it he saw that the house next door was in darkness and he observed it thoughtfully. What was the bet that Melissa was having an early night so that she would be bright-eyed and bushy-tailed tomorrow?

He supposed it could be said that it hadn't been a good idea to offer her a job working with him most of the time, but discovering that she was in paediatrics had been too good a chance to miss in his busy working life. He went back into the house in a thoughtful mood and with the feeling that maybe he needed to cool it where she was concerned.

It was an eight o'clock start for day staff on the wards and the next morning Melissa watched as Ryan kissed his children goodbye with Mollie in attendance, and drove off.

As the taillights of his car disappeared she followed him at a distance, having no wish to be on the last minute on her first day at the hospital.

Today could or could not be the beginning of a new life. A life on a lower level than before maybe, when the envious had called her 'golden girl', but at least she would have some dignity, wouldn't be an object of pity or sly smirks.

In the short time that she'd been in the house she had been aware that something strange was happening. The children next door had said it was haunted and she wasn't going to go along with *that*, but one thing she did feel was that the grandmother she had never really known was somewhere near, content that the one person she had always wanted to live in her house had arrived.

Miserable and lonely she may be, but she was there in the house that had been bequeathed to her all those years ago because the old lady had foreseen what the future might hold for her pleasure-loving son's child. Today Melissa was about to take the first step towards becoming a working member of the community.

CHAPTER THREE

RYAN HAD SEEN Melissa arrive from the window of his office, which overlooked the car park. She was so different from the woman he had been confronted with just a couple of nights ago, it was unbelievable. Her hair, her clothes, the newfound calm had altered her totally.

She was still the stranger who had erupted into his life from nowhere but she was no longer nondescript. Yesterday, when she'd come to the hospital to have a look round and meet Julian and any of the nurses who were present, he'd thought that she was beautiful and still did. Not in a voluptuous sort of way but fine-boned and slender.

Still, there was the promise he had made to himself to cool it with regard to Melissa Redmond. The absence of a woman in his life in the true sense meant that never again would there be the agony of loss such as he'd suffered when he'd lost Beth.

With that in mind he wished Melissa a cool good morning when they met at the entrance to the wards and suggested that she find herself a white hospital coat.

'I've brought one with me from my last job,' she told

him, and wondered who had rubbed Ryan up the wrong way so early in the day.

It wasn't likely to be Julian as so far there was no sign of him having arrived, though on the other hand that might be the reason for Ryan's abrupt manner. Whatever it was, she was determined that nothing was going to blight this day of all days.

Julian came strolling down the corridor towards them at that moment and she flashed him a smile, and after putting on the white hospital coat followed them into the ward.

'I'd like you to do the ward rounds with Julian today,' Ryan told her. 'Watch and learn and you'll soon get the hang of things. Little Georgia is in one of the side wards where she is making a good recovery, and her parents are with her most of the time.

'We also have a ten-year-old boy with us who is a new admission. He suffered a head injury when he fell off his bike. It's quite serious, but at the moment does not require surgery.'

Then Ryan looked straight at Melissa.

'Some time this afternoon I'd like a brief word with you. In the meantime, when the two of you have finished rounds, Julian will direct you to Personnel so that you can get the processing of a new employee over and done with.'

'Yes, fine,' she said, having decided that she was being given the hint that being neighbours didn't mean any special treatment. As if she would expect anything of that kind.

Maybe it was Ryan's way of letting her see that his efforts on her behalf since arriving in Heatherdale were now at an end, and if that *was* the case it would have no effect on the deep gratitude she felt for the kindness he had shown her.

'I wonder what's upset the boss?' Julian mused when Ryan had gone. 'He was rather abrupt. Ryan needs some light relief in his life. He's all work and no play.'

Melissa didn't comment. There was no way she would discuss Ryan with Julian, who, from the sound of it, hadn't a care in the world.

Back in his office Ryan reminded himself that from now on he would be able to relax at the thought of Melissa in the house next door with her few belongings. If she could turn up looking like she had the last two days he need not concern himself about her any more, and that being so he would find it easier to have a good working relationship with her instead of behaving like he just had.

Ryan's crustiness forgotten, Melissa enjoyed every moment of her first morning on the wards with Julian. She would have much preferred it to be with 'the boss', as his laid-back assistant called him, but it was sufficient that she was working in a hospital once more. She read the records of every young patient's treatment and progress thoroughly when they stopped by their beds and asked Julian questions if she wasn't clear about anything.

That afternoon Ryan requested her presence for the brief chat that he'd mentioned earlier in the day, and she went to his office expecting a repeat of the brisk instructions of the morning. She was surprised to see him smiling. She was unaware that he had decided that now there was no longer any need of his help as far as she was concerned, he could relax and return to what life had been like before she'd appeared in it.

'I just wanted to ask how your first day is going,' he said. 'I know how much you wanted to be back in paediatrics.'

'Fantastic,' she told him, 'The chance to work here is the best thing that has happened to me in years and it is all due to you.' She didn't want to give him the wrong impression.

'I'll be fine from now on, Ryan, with the house that I'm going to make as delightful as yours one day, and working here with Julian and yourself, I'm back to the self-reliant person I used to be.'

Still on a high on her way home, she stopped to collect colour charts for paints and some wallpaper samples and once she'd eaten she sat considering them thoughtfully. Renovating the house that was now her home would have to be carefully budgeted, but it also had to be right for the property.

She'd seen the interior design of the house next door and had been aware of how right it was for that kind of house, and though having no wish to copy it, she felt that she needed to keep to a similar kind of décor.

The first room to be transformed was going to be the sitting room so she decided on a heavily embossed wallpaper of red and gold to match the big ornate fireplace that, along with large leaded windows, dominated the room. She sat back in the chair and imagined what it would look like and excitement spiralled at the thought.

Her second day at the hospital felt less strange now she'd adjusted to the fact that Ryan was going to be around most of the time while she was working as well as living next door, but as it was she saw little of him.

His car was there so he was around somewhere, but apart from a glimpse of him at the end of the corridor, talking sombrely to the parents of a patient, he never appeared, and when she queried his absence Julian explained that he had meetings scheduled all day with the hospital hierarchy. He added that she couldn't have joined them at a better time.

On her way home that evening she ventured into the main shopping area of Heatherdale and bought a long ladder that would reach way up towards the ceiling, a large can of white emulsion paint, and the paper that she had chosen for the walls, along with the paste that would be needed to fix it.

An obliging shopkeeper offered to drop off her purchases on his way home after closing the place and he delivered them shortly after she arrived at the house.

She'd never done any decorating before, but of late that had applied to a lot of things that she'd had to face up to, and as soon as she'd had her usual scrappy meal Melissa put on the old clothes she'd worn on the day of moving in and began to climb the ladder with the can of emulsion paint and the roller she was going to use while she painted the ceiling.

Ryan had arrived home shortly after Melissa and as he'd pulled up in front of their two houses had observed the delivery of the decorating materials and the stepladder, and been amazed at the size of it. He'd sighed. What was she up to now? Whatever it might be, he wasn't going to get involved, at least not until he'd eaten the meal that Mollie had prepared for him and the children.

Melissa was getting the hang of it. The roller went back and forth across the age-old ceiling with her standing firmly on her lofty perch. As long as she didn't look down, she would be fine.

At that moment the doorbell rang and as the heavy oak door was on the latch it swung open. As she turned quickly to see who was there, the stepladder swung backwards and sent her flying through the air with a terrified scream.

Ryan caught her just before she hit the floor, absorbing the impact of her fall.

'I am so sorry to be such a nuisance.' She gasped.

He was still holding her close and made no reply, just kept looking down at her. It was the first time he'd held a woman like this since he'd lost Beth and it was gut-wrenching. He'd always known it would be and had made sure that it never happened for his sanity's sake, but with Melissa it was as if he just couldn't avoid her—she was everywhere he turned and he didn't want it to be like that.

Putting her carefully back onto her feet, he said abruptly, 'Whatever possessed you to try something as dangerous as painting this high ceiling? You should have hired a decorator.'

'It would be too expensive,' she replied, wishing those moments in his arms had affected him as much as they'd affected her. She'd felt safe and protected as he'd held her close and it seemed like a lifetime since she'd last had those sorts of feelings.

But she'd sensed tension in him as he'd held her in his arms, a reluctance to have her in such close contact, and her morale had been low enough of late without another putdown, in more ways than one.

'That's because you're new to the area. I know someone who would do this place up for you at a very reasonable rate and make an excellent job of it. Why don't you let me give him a buzz and ask him to come round to give you a quote? You wouldn't be under any obligation.'

'Er, yes, all right,' she agreed reluctantly, 'and thank you on both counts, for catching me and breaking my fall, *and* for offering to put me in touch with someone I can trust to do some decorating. I've had cause to discover recently that people I thought I could trust were not like that at all, far from it. Still, that's in the past. For now I suppose I'd better start cleaning up.'

'I guess so,' he agreed, 'and I'd better get back to my place. Mollie will be getting ready to go home and my children will be waiting to play their favourite game, "Hospitals". They've both got a nurse's uniform.'

He was smiling at the thought and went on to amaze himself by saying, 'Their mother was a midwife. She went out on a late-night call in the middle of a raging storm to supervise an imminent birth, and a tree that was rotten at the roots fell across the car. She didn't survive the injuries it caused.'

'Oh! How awful!' she breathed. 'You must miss her very much.'

'Yes,' he said flatly. 'I do. More than words can say. The newborn was a girl and they called her Beth after the midwife who had been true to her calling in spite of a horrendous storm.'

On that bombshell, Ryan wished Melissa a brief goodnight, and unable to believe that he had actually talked about the worst time of his life to a stranger of all people, he went back to where his motherless children were waiting for him.

When he'd gone Melissa began to clean up the mess but her mind wasn't on it. She had her answer now to the questions about the loss of his wife.

But surely Ryan wasn't intending to spend the rest of his life alone and loveless? Yet wasn't she intending to do something similar? To have been cast aside because her cash value had dropped suddenly had made her realise what a farce her engagement had been, had made her see how gullible and trusting she'd been.

She shuddered every time she thought that someone as shallow as David Lowson could have been the father of any children she might have had. What a contrast between him and the man next door who had put himself out of circulation for the sake of his children, *and in memory of the woman he had loved.*

She really would have to stop being such an intrusion in his life. It wasn't intentional, no one needed to be solitary more than she did, having lost her faith in love and friendship. If Ryan was regretting having got involved with her again about the decorating and on second thoughts decided to let it lapse, she would understand.

When the bell rang a second time an hour later Melissa was expecting it to be Ryan, fobbing her off with an excuse about being unable to find her a decorator.

It was not so. A man in his sixties stood on the doorstep, and as she eyed him questioningly he said, 'Ryan has just phoned to say that you have some decorating that you want doing.'

'Er, yes, I have,' she told him. 'Do come in. I've just moved in and the whole place has been neglected. I tried to paint the ceiling and fell off the ladder.'

'I'm not surprised,' he commented. 'These are very high ceilings.

'Tell me what you want done and I'll call back tomorrow with an estimate. If you agree to it I'll start right away. I wonder if you realise how lucky you are to be the owner of a town house in a place like Heatherdale?'

'I'm afraid I haven't seen it in that light so far,' she told him wryly.

'You will' was the reply. 'We have a well that supplies our very own spa water all the time and is available to all comers, and the most beautiful gardens and historical buildings.'

He held out a capable-looking hand for her to shake and said, 'The name is Smethurst. I'll be round tomorrow with a price if you'll tell me what you want doing. Is it just this sitting room, or the whole place?'

'Just this room to begin with,' she told him, 'but I'm sure that by the time you've done it I will be wanting you to do more.'

'Fair enough,' he agreed. 'See you tomorrow, then,' and went striding off into the dark winter night.

When he'd gone she felt ashamed for presuming that Ryan would have wanted to back out of his offer to find her a decorator, and at the risk of making a further nuisance of herself she went next door to thank him for his prompt attention to her needs.

The children were asleep and Ryan had just settled down to what was going to be his first free time of the day when the doorbell rang. He sighed and, getting to his feet, turned the television down low and went to answer it.

When he saw Melissa standing there his first thought was that it was getting to be too much of a habit, them toing and froing between each other's houses. He'd done what he'd said he would do and phoned Jack Smethurst. What more did she want from him?

'Hello again,' he said observing her unsmilingly. 'What can I do for you this time? I hope you haven't been up the ladder again. I did tell you I would phone the decorator.'

'Yes, I know you did,' she replied with a sinking feeling that she should have waited until morning to express her thanks. 'That's why I'm here. He has been and—'

'What? Already!' he exclaimed. Regretting his churlishness, he added, 'Do come in out of the cold.'

She shook her head. The night *was* cold, but his greeting had been colder. 'No, thank you. I don't want to disturb you any further. Mr Smethurst is letting me have an estimate tomorrow and I just wanted to thank you for putting me in touch with him.'

As she turned to go she gave a gasp of pain and he stepped towards her. 'What's wrong?'

'It's nothing,' she told him hurriedly. 'Just a pulled neck muscle from when I fell off the ladder. I'll take a painkiller when I get in. Goodnight, Ryan.' And before he could reply she was gone, hurrying towards her own front door in the dark night and wishing that she'd stayed put instead of making a nuisance of herself again.

When Melissa had gone, Ryan sat deep in thought with the memory of the mixture of emotions that had gripped him when he'd held her in his arms. There had been shock at the suddenness of it, relief that he'd been able to break her fall, and uppermost there had been a combined feeling of loss and longing that had broken down the barriers of the celibate life that he had chosen for himself.

Once back in his own house he had calmed down, telling himself that the episode had just been a one off, it could have happened with anyone, and would not be referred to tomorrow as far as he was concerned.

But when he'd answered the ring on the doorbell it had seemed that the day was not yet over where he and Melissa Redmond were concerned and he'd been off-hand and unwelcoming, afraid to become too closely involved in her life.

The next morning Ryan waited beside his car until Melissa appeared. He asked if she was experiencing any after-effects of the fall, knowing that it must have jarred every bone in her body.

Dredging up a smile, she told him, 'Just one or two minor aches and pains, that's all.'

She *was* experiencing after-effects but they were mental rather than physical and had kept her awake most of the night, so she was not in the mood to start mellowing at the sight of him. She'd be polite, yes, he was her boss who had saved her from what could have been serious injuries, but afterwards he had let her see that enough was enough.

Ryan changed the subject. 'I've got some catching up to do today. Meetings are a bind when there is work to be done and yesterday's seemed to drag on for ever. Julian reports that you are a natural on the job, manna from heaven, so that's good.'

He didn't say any more, just jumped into his car and drove off, with her following once again. She didn't know what to make of Ryan's mood swings but, then, she was unaware that he had also slept fitfully with the memory of her in his arms sweet torment.

As the long hours of the night had dragged by Melissa had told herself that his manner when she'd gone to thank him for sorting out a decorator would have told even the most unobservant of people that he felt he was seeing too much of her, that she was forever at his elbow.

But the realisation had been there that as far as she was concerned it was a case of *her* not seeing enough of *him*. That was the real reason for her seeking him out again, and having those sorts of feelings for him was the last thing she wanted to happen. Since her father's death her hurts had been many and she had no wish to add to them. Being rejected by one man was enough to be going on with.

When Melissa arrived home that evening the estimate from the decorator was on the doormat and she could have wept with relief at the amount he was asking for decorating the sitting room. She phoned him immediately to tell him to go ahead as soon as possible and did a little dance around the room in question when she'd made the call.

'I'll be round in the morning,' Jack Smethurst had said. 'Mollie next door will let me in if you give her a key.' And that was that. Ryan had turned one of her most urgent needs into something simple and it would be difficult not to do a repeat of last night's display of gratitude.

But she had got the message loud and clear from his manner on that occasion, that just because he'd done her a good turn he didn't want her to disturb him further.

Mollie had gone. Ryan and the children had finished their evening meal and after stacking the dishwasher he did what he'd been wanting to do ever since arriving home. He rang Jack Smethurst to enquire if Melissa had accepted his estimate.

'She has indeed' was the reply. 'I'll be starting in the morning. I've asked the young lady to leave a key with Mollie. Hope you don't mind.'

'No, not at all,' Ryan told him. When Melissa dropped the key in later Ryan was determined that he wouldn't be so surly when he opened the door to her this time.

But it was eleven o'clock and she still hadn't been with the key. He'd been listening for her to ring the doorbell all evening and when he went into the hall to see if her lights were still on he saw the key on the mat with a note beside it to say that she hoped he wouldn't mind passing the key on to Mollie as Mr Smethurst had assured her that it would be all right.

He groaned. The night before he'd made sure that

Melissa had got the message that he wasn't to be contacted out of working hours, and she hadn't forgotten.

Of course Mollie would give the decorator the key when he came. Jack Smethurst and Mollie were dating. If they decided to tie the knot at some future date he might have to find himself another housekeeper, but he had learned to live one day at a time since he'd lost Beth. His children and the job were his lifelines, as he was theirs, and any further than that he wasn't going to contemplate.

As he went slowly up to bed the thought came that Christmas would soon begin to spread its mantle over the ancient market town that was so dear to his heart. He wondered what his new neighbour would have planned for that. She might surprise him and have a house full of relatives turn up.

It would be his third one without Beth and an ordeal to be got through, just as the two previous ones had been, but he would cope for Rhianna and Martha's sakes.

The first sign of the coming festivities would be in a couple of weeks' time when the town's brass band would play a selection of carols outside the old pump room.

There would be mulled wine and mince pies on offer with presents for the children from a bran tub, and the residents of Heatherdale and folk from far and wide would be there, keeping up the traditions of a bygone age.

But before that there would be what there always was, young lives needing a gift of another kind, that of a healthy body, and Ryan was forever thankful that he could help towards that end in his clinic, on the wards and in the operating theatre.

As he pulled back the curtains to let the light of a winter moon into his bedroom and lay back against the pillows Ryan wondered just how close Melissa was to him at the other side of the wall.

The next morning Ryan had already left when Melissa sallied forth. She'd been waved off by Mollie and the children, who were still in their nightdresses at that early hour.

It wasn't until she and Ryan met on the wards that he had a chance to speak to Melissa, and his first words were, 'Good news about the decorating. I've given Mollie your key to pass on to Jack.'

'Yes, I can't wait to see it,' she said wistfully, with a vision of the furnishings in the house she'd had to sell coming to mind, but why was Ryan suddenly so chatty? Could it be that he had decided that there was no cause for unease, that she posed no threat to his organised existence?

When Rhianna and Martha had waved her off that morning she had felt a lump come up in her throat. Ryan may have lost his wife but he still had his children to cherish, safe and happy, while she had no one.

As if to emphasise that fact, Julian had caught her up in the car park and looking around him had said, 'I see that the boss is here before us, needless to say. He's always first on the job, as if he hasn't a moment to spare.'

'If you mean Dr Ferguson, maybe he hasn't,' she'd said dryly. 'I think he's amazing.'

'So do a lot of other women,' he'd told her, 'but

sooner or later they have to accept that he is a one-woman man, even though the woman in question isn't around any more. If he ever decided to get married again, they would be queuing up.'

'Really!' she'd commented, and had left it at that. There was no way she was going to discuss with Julian the man who had been her saviour at one of the darkest times of her life.

After their brief chat about the decorating the day began satisfactorily from a medical point of view. Ryan dished out instructions. 'We have two clinics today, Melissa. I'm taking one and Julian the other. I want you to sit in at mine as joining me whenever you can will be a big part of your duties until you are ready to take a clinic of your own.'

She was smiling. The job, the wonderful job, was like balm to her soul. Even if Ryan never ever did her another good turn she would bless him for ever for this chance to use the skills that she'd had to put to one side.

As adults with children appeared before them, one lot after another, he turned to her frequently and asked her advice, explaining to them that she was a doctor from a Manchester hospital who they were pleased to have as a new member of staff at Heatherdale.

The courtesy of his introduction brought the sting of tears after dealing with debt collectors and bailiffs for months, with the added pain of missing friends and an ex-fiancé.

When the clinic was over he said briskly, 'Well done. You are going to be a big help to me. When you've had a break go back on the wards with Julian for a late-morning round.' When Melissa didn't immediately answer he asked, 'Are you all right?'

'Yes,' she breathed. 'Oh, yes!'

She was, from a job point of view, but Julian's comments about Ryan earlier had taken her into uncharted territory, and she knew that of all things she must be careful where he was concerned. The last thing she would want was to become one of the hopefuls waiting in the wings.

Ryan was very pleased. It wouldn't be long before Melissa was taking a clinic of her own. Maybe an extra doctor on the unit would give him more time with the children, as well as it being the answer to some of her problems. Further than that he was not going to think. A good relationship on the unit was enough to be going on with and as he hadn't given her any cause to think otherwise it should work all right.

CHAPTER FOUR

THE DECORATING OF the sitting room was finished and Melissa was delighted with it, so much so that when she arrived home and saw it on the evening of the third day of the transformation she had to restrain herself from going to the house next door to invite Ryan and his children to come and see it.

When she'd been on the point of leaving for the hospital that morning, Jack Smethurst had asked, 'Do I take it that the roll of pale gold carpet is for in here?'

'Yes,' she'd told him, and had wondered if Ryan was also acquainted with a carpet fitter. He'd found her a decorator so maybe he was.

It was one of the two lengths of carpet that the buyers of the Cheshire house hadn't insisted be included in the sale and she'd chosen the red-and-gold wallpaper with it in mind.

And now she saw that she needn't have concerned herself about the fitting of it as the carpet had been laid and was the perfect finishing touch to the room. She could have wept with thankfulness.

On observing that no charge had been made for it on the account that had been left for her, she vowed that the first thing she would do when the decorator came for payment would be to ask how much she owed him for the extra work.

What Melissa couldn't know was that the night before Ryan had said to Jack Smethurst, 'I saw the wallpaper that time when Melissa fell off the ladder and presume that the gold carpet is to go with it. If she says that it is, will you fit it and let me have the bill? And don't tell Mollie or she'll be shopping around for a wedding outfit. Although she never puts it into words, I know she worries about my solitary state.'

Jack had laughed. 'She's already looking for an outfit but it's not for your wedding, it's for ours, so be warned, but don't worry. She loves the three of you too much to stay away from you for long, and, yes, I'll see to the carpet, but tell me, why are you doing this? You hardly know the woman.'

'I met Melissa on the night she came to live in Heatherdale and she was in a dreadful state. The house was filthy and she'd been let down by the cleaners, but it wasn't just that. I felt that something had happened to her beyond bearing. She was like a lost soul and I can't forget it, even though she is so different now, employed at the hospital, making her house fit to live in, and doesn't seem so alone as she did then.

'But there is still something about her that worries me, that's why I want her to have the pleasure of seeing the carpet fitted and the room finished when she comes home tomorrow. So do we have a deal? And don't forget, Jack, not a word to Melissa about it...ever.'

'Yes, if you say so' had been the reply.

* * *

It was no use, Melissa decided. Whether Ryan approved or not, she just had to go and tell him how thrilled she was to have at least one room fit to live in. Surely he wouldn't object to what he usually saw as an intrusion because he was the one who had caught her when she'd fallen off the ladder and found her a decorator.

His car was outside so he was home, but she was going to restrain herself until he and his family had finished their evening meal. It wouldn't be fair to butt in before that and so she made herself a sandwich and spent the next half-hour gazing rapturously around her.

She was about to venture forth when the phone rang and she was spared having to seek him out.

'I hope you don't mind me ringing,' he said, 'If you remember, I asked for your phone number when you started at the hospital in case I had to get in touch with you regarding an emergency of some kind on our patch.'

'No, not at all,' she replied, relieved that it was Ryan's turn to cross the privacy line. 'What can I do for you?'

'You can tell me how the room looks. Are you happy with it?'

'Over the moon,' she told him with a lift to her voice. 'And guess what, Ryan? Your decorator friend has fitted the carpet for me and it looks dreamy.'

He was smiling and carried away by her delight. 'So is it all right if I bring a bottle of champagne to celebrate the occasion and the girls and I come to admire the transformation?'

'Yes, of course,' she said eagerly, and went on to tell him laughingly, 'Just as long as Rhianna and Martha won't be expecting to see a ghost. The only person here who is a shadow of their former self is me!'

When they arrived shortly afterwards Ryan was carrying the champagne and his daughters were on either side of him. He saw that Melissa was wrapped around with delight and hoped she would not discover his part in the fitting of the carpet.

While he was thinking those sorts of thoughts Melissa had been into the kitchen and had come back with the champagne in two flutes out of boxes of oddments that had survived the removal, and with glasses of fruit juice for the children.

Ryan raised his glass. 'So, now that you have an elegant sitting room, does it mean that you are going to stay here in Heatherdale and make the rest of the house as attractive as this room?'

'Yes,' she said. 'The place is growing on me. When I went into the centre the other day I was entranced by the beauty of the architecture and the pump room with the well beside it forever providing the famous spa waters. I think I might get to like Heatherdale. I am already over the moon with its hospital, and in any case I can't afford to buy or even rent another property elsewhere.'

The conversation was about to take an awkward turn. Martha had come to stand by her side and looking up at her said, 'Do you know any mummies? When you came to breakfast you said that *you* weren't a mummy, but we thought you might know where there is one.'

Although her glance was fixed on the small questioner, Melissa could feel Ryan's tension so keenly it was as if he was glued to her side, and she said with great gentleness, 'I'm afraid I don't, Martha, but you have got a lovely daddy, haven't you?'

'Yes,' Rhianna chipped in, 'but lots of our friends have a mummy as well as a daddy.'

Ryan was cringing. 'That is enough from both of you. We came here to look at Melissa's house, not to be impolite and nosey.'

'It's all right,' she assured him. 'I understand.' And to take the sting out of what he'd said to them, she went on, 'They are lovely children, Ryan, a credit to you.'

He was not to be humoured. 'I'm not looking for "credit" and now I think we shall go. Say goodnight to Melissa,' he told his daughters and as they wished her a subdued farewell, unable to help herself, she bent and kissed them both, holding them close just for a second.

In return they clung to her and when she looked up she saw pain in Ryan's expression and was immediately sorry for causing a situation that would have no joy in it for him. Ryan marched to the door, opened it, and waited for Rhianna and Martha to leave her side.

When they'd stepped out on to the drive he said in a low voice that was for her ears only, 'It would seem that I am not very successful with regard to my children's contentment, although it is only since they met you that this kind of thing has kept cropping up.'

'I'm sorry,' she said. 'I meant no harm, Ryan. They're both so appealing I couldn't resist holding them close for a moment.'

He nodded. 'I suppose that's fair enough.' And taking them by the hand he went with a brief goodbye.

When Rhianna and Martha were asleep he stood looking down at them with the feeling that he'd behaved like a complete moron by objecting to a moment's affection for them from Melissa.

Martha had never fretted about not having Beth around before. He doubted that her fixation with the subject was because Melissa reminded her of her mother as she was not like her in any way. Maybe she sensed something about her that she and Rhianna needed, something that he couldn't see but which the eyes of a child saw, and he was just going to have to live with the disruption in their lives that it was causing until it had passed. He'd felt sick inside as he'd watched them lift up their faces to be kissed. His heart broke for them all.

They left their respective houses the next morning with the same thought in mind. Whatever had been in their minds the night before, today they both had jobs to do. His far more important than hers, and as tomorrow was Saturday Melissa hoped that the weekend would give them the chance to avoid any further uncomfortable meetings.

The trouble was that Ryan knew only the brief details of her past that she'd told him on the day when she'd first gone to the hospital. Was it any wonder he was wary of his children getting too close to a virtual stranger?

Thankfully their positions at the hospital had an impersonal approach that gave them some degree of separation otherwise it could be awkward, to say the least.

Having made a good recovery from the meningitis, young Georgia was due to go home and, as was sometimes the case, her grateful parents had brought a bottle of something for the doctor who had saved her life and chocolates for the nurses. As they were ready to leave, Georgia's father said to Melissa, 'We are having a party next Saturday to celebrate having our little daughter back with us and would like Dr Ferguson to be there, but he tells us that he has other commitments. Can you not persuade him to change his mind?'

As if! she thought. She was the last person Ryan would take note of, and in any case he was certain to have something planned with Rhianna and Martha, so she smiled and said that she had no authority over him.

She didn't see Ryan again during the rest of the morning. He and Julian were both taking clinics and she'd been left to do the rounds while they were absent.

When she was taking a short lunch break in the staff restaurant Julian appeared and for once his expression was grave. 'What's wrong?' she questioned.

'Two young lads and their respective parents were at the clinic this morning,' he informed her, 'and both of the youngsters have been diagnosed with muscular dystrophy, which, as you know, is caused by a faulty inherited gene from somewhere back in their families. Ryan had the ghastly job of telling them.'

'Not telling the children surely?' she questioned.

'No, of course not,' Julian replied. 'Just the parents. It is at their discretion what they tell the youngsters.'

'There have been some huge steps forward with regard to muscular dystrophy over the years,' she reminded him. 'Diagnosis and treatment have advanced a great deal.'

'You seem to be well informed,' a voice said from behind her, and Ryan was there, the golden Viking who was just as fierce as men of old when it came to protecting those who belonged to him.

She didn't deny it. 'Yes, I am. I've been on a course about the illness.'

Julian had been to the counter and was coming back with sandwiches and coffee for the two of them. Having no wish to intrude into their lunch break, Melissa got to her feet and left them to it.

The rest of the day passed uneventfully and so did the evening, with the only interruption the arrival of the decorator to enquire if she was satisfied with the room now that it was finished.

'It's perfect,' she told him, 'and I can't thank you enough for fitting the carpet. Do you want to add it on to the original account, or give me a separate one? Either way will be fine, but I would like to pay for all the work that you've done while you're here.'

'The fitting of the carpet is included in the first figure I quoted,' Jack Smethurst said awkwardly, with the memory clear of Ryan's stipulation that Melissa must not know about his being involved in it.

'But you didn't know then that I was going to have it put down in the sitting room,' she persisted.

'I suppose I guessed,' he replied, and thought that Ryan's concern for her was complicating what should be a simple payment for a job well done.

Still unconvinced, Melissa wrote out a cheque for the original quote and when he'd gone decided that if she asked him to do any more work for her she would insist at the time of asking that he give her a separate price for the laying of any carpets, or carpet, as she'd only brought the two pieces with her.

As it was, she could only feel that Ryan had done her a really good turn by recommending Mollie's man friend to do the job, and when he had gone she sat unmoving with the thought of the coming weekend on her own bringing no joy.

She'd seen the signs of Christmastime appearing on the wards and in the corridors of the hospital while she'd been there today, and it had been the same when she'd driven home along the quiet lanes where high in the trees there had been the rare sight of mistletoe, and down below every so often a bright red flash of holly, but there had been no joy in it. Christmas was just going to be something to be endured this year.

She'd thought of volunteering to work along with others over the Christmas weekend so that staff on the neuro unit with children could be with them, but the thought came that Ryan was one of them, and if he was caught up in any emergencies that couldn't be avoided, it would be catastrophic unless Mollie could be there for the children.

Saturday morning brought with it wintry sunshine, a chill wind, and the opportunity for her to carry on organising her new home as best she could with whatever was available in the form of resources.

She'd seen Ryan and the children go out on foot in the direction of the town centre, which was only a short walk away, while she had been putting curtains up at the dining-room window. She wished there was someone as close to her as his children were to him in spite of Martha's yearning for a mother.

Her own mother was long gone, her father had followed her just a short time ago, and she'd been an only child. As for her friends and the man she'd thought she was going to marry, none of them knew where she was and that was how she intended it to stay.

Having seen Ryan and the children strolling along happily had made her feel restless, and the chores that she'd had lined up were something that could be left for another day, so after showering and dressing carefully she ventured forth into the town centre.

It was a beautiful town, with its pump room and the well that produced the spa water from underground close by. There were hotels built out of weathered limestone that had a stately magnificence, gardens that stretched as far as the eye could see, and all around the small market town were the high peaks and green dales.

She came across Ryan and the girls on the pavement outside one of the toy shops and before she had a chance to backtrack Rhianna saw her so she had to stop.

'Hello, there,' he said easily, as if they were on the best of terms. 'Are you out Christmas shopping, too?' He then whispered, 'I've brought the children to have a look around the toy shop to get some ideas from what they show interest in, and then we're going to look for a wedding present for Mollie.'

'No,' she said in reply to his question. 'I haven't given Christmas a thought, or at least if I have they've been negative ones.'

He would have liked to ask her what she meant by that, but refrained with the children close by, and guessed that it would be something to do with her solitariness, which he supposed he could do something about if he was so inclined.

The children would love it if he asked Melissa to spend Christmas Day with them but what about him? Would having her there make the occasion a bigger ordeal or a lesser one?

Bringing his thoughts back to the present, he asked, 'Could you possibly stay here with the children for a moment while I go into the shop to check on how long delivery might be on some of the items they have on display?'

'Yes, of course,' she said, determined that there would be no repetition of the last time she'd been with them.

'We liked your sitting room, didn't we, Martha? But we think the rest of your house is ugly.' Rhianna piped up.

'Yes,' her sister agreed.

Melissa hid a smile. She was with them on that. It *was* ugly, but not for long, if not in time for Christmas maybe soon after.

'It was Daddy who told Mr Smethurst to put the carpet down on the floor for you,' Rhianna continued, and Melissa frowned. What was that supposed to mean?

'He told him not to tell you.'

'And why do you think that was?' Melissa asked gently.

'He said he would give him some money.'

So that was why the decorator hadn't wanted any extra payment for laying the carpet. Light was dawning.

Ryan stepped out of the shop at that moment, and leaving the children engrossed in what was in the window Melissa stepped quickly towards him and took him to one side.

'You paid for the carpet to be fitted, didn't you?' she choked out. 'I wondered why I wasn't charged any extra for it. It was very kind of you, Ryan, but please don't treat me as a charity case.'

'That is not how I see you,' he said levelly. 'I meant no offence. It was just a thought that it would give you pleasure to see the room finished when you came home, that's all.'

With that Ryan went to where the children were still observing the toy display and said, 'Say goodbye to Melissa.' And not allowing time for kisses and hugs this time, he walked them away from her and disappeared from sight.

There was a coffee shop nearby and Melissa went inside on leaden feet. As she stirred the drink in front of her unseeingly she was ashamed of her reaction to his kindness in one way but hurt that Ryan hadn't thought that he might have embarrassed her with his act of generosity.

He was the most attractive, amazing man she'd ever met, as well *as a paediatric surgeon* who was bringing up two motherless children with a totally selfless kind of love, and she'd dared to berate him for what to him had been just an act of thoughtfulness.

The urge for sightseeing was gone. She drank up quickly and made her way back to the crescent of town houses where they lived, feeling so ashamed of her behaviour she wouldn't be able to rest until she'd apologised. Ryan had shown her nothing but kindness since the day she'd arrived in Heatherdale and that was how she'd repaid him?

She would pop a note through his door so it was there when he and the children arrived home from their Christmas shopping. For her part she intended to be nowhere to be seen. It would be time enough to face him when they met up on Monday morning at the hospital.

With every passing day she was becoming more aware of him and didn't want it to be like that because she knew that to him she was just someone he was allowing briefly into his busy life.

Ryan groaned when he read the note that was on his doormat when they got home. Their relationship, if it could be called that, was like a see-saw, up and down, but more down than up, and if he had any sense he ought to let it stay that way.

He had never met anyone to make him change his mind about marrying again, and if he ever did he hoped that it would be someone he knew something about. The children were his first consideration in everything he did because they were small and vulnerable, and if he was doing them no favours by not providing them with a new mother figure, at least he wasn't blotting out what little they remembered of Beth.

Tomorrow he would clear the air with Melissa, tell her that in future he would never again interfere in her affairs, and if the promise made life less liveable he would have to stick with it.

She wasn't around on the Sunday, as he'd been expecting, and he felt frustrated and on edge, eager to say his piece and clarify the situation between them knowing that he wasn't going to rest until he'd said it.

But short of talking into thin air he was going to have to wait until she reappeared.

He wasn't to know that she was at the last place he would have expected. She'd seen a notice in the hospital announcing that there was to be a children's Christmas party for past and present young patients on Sunday and that volunteers to assist from staff and friends were needed.

On impulse she'd given her name to the organisers during the week and after Saturday's upset was grateful to have somewhere to go where she could be lost in a crowd, instead of being isolated in her grandmother's house.

She'd checked to make sure that Ryan wouldn't be there and been told that consultants didn't usually take part on such occasions, that it was organised by the nurses and social workers based at the hospital. It would start mid-morning and finish halfway through the afternoon.

The party was a yearly event that was held in the run-up to Christmas, and when she arrived Melissa felt as if she belonged for the first time since she'd come to Heatherdale.

For the children who were confined to bed there was special attention to their needs and she was perched on the side of the bed of a small girl who'd had surgery a few days previously after a fall that had resulted in bleeding inside her head.

They were playing one of the fun games that had been provided and the little one was forgetting her tears and fears in the excitement of the party when Melissa looked up and her eyes widened. Ryan and his children had just arrived and he was chatting to one of the nurses.

He hadn't seen her, but Rhianna and Martha had. They'd left their father's side and were coming across the ward to her.

Ryan looked up at that moment and surprise showed on his face.

This was the last place he would have expected to find Melissa. Weekdays yes, but not on a Sunday. He wouldn't be here himself if it hadn't been that just an hour ago he'd had some bad news that could affect the neurology unit during coming days. He'd driven to the hospital to check on what his clinics and surgery arrangements were for the coming week.

A phone call had come through from Julian's parents to inform him that their son had been involved in a riding accident the previous day and was in a Manchester hospital with spinal injuries.

'It looks as if it might be a long job,' Julian's father had told Ryan and he'd thought that Melissa had arrived in the unit in the nick of time. She was going to be heaven sent in his working life—*and could be the same out of it if he would only let her.*

There was no use denying it. Melissa was never out of his mind no matter how much he told himself that she was just a passing fancy. His children loved her and who could blame them? There was a gentleness about her when she was with them that pulled at his heartstrings, but did she feel the same about him? He doubted it. She seemed to have enough emotional dramas of her own to worry about, without taking on those of a bereaved father!

The phone call had brought him to the hospital to check what was on their agenda in the unit for the coming week with Julian missing, and here *she* was, conveniently already on hospital premises.

'Will you excuse me for a moment?' he asked the nurse beside him. 'I see my colleague over there, chatting to my daughters, and I need to speak to her. Dr Tindall has had a serious riding accident and we need to check what we have ahead of us in the coming week.

'Can you look after Elfrida for a few moments while I talk to Melissa?' he asked Rhianna and Martha, indicating the small girl in the bed, and when they nodded he told her in a low voice, 'Julian isn't going to be around for some time. He's been seriously injured in a riding accident so it is going to be all systems go here next week and for some time to come.

'I'm here because I need to know what I'm down for in the clinics and theatre and I can get that information from my secretary's computer, so I'm going to have a quick look. Finding you here has saved me having to disturb you at home so can I leave the children with you for a little while?'

'Yes, of course,' she told him. She had listened to what he'd had to say in stunned silence, aghast to hear what had happened to Julian, with her first thought for the hospital's Romeo. Then it dawned on her that it was going to be just the two of them working together for the foreseeable future until a temporary replacement could be found.

They were going to be in each other's company

workwise much more than she'd expected. How was she going to cope with that? How was she going to keep a hold on the attraction he had for her, being near him so much in the neuro unit and only a few yards away from him at home?

But most importantly, would Ryan want her around him so much? He might feel that living next door to her was enough, especially after her having been so ungrateful about the carpet-laying incident.

After flicking through his appointment list on the computer, he returned to Melissa and the girls.

'So what do you think about Julian? What a shame, eh?' he commented.

'Yes, it is,' she said in a low voice. 'I have had no wish to go back to Manchester since I moved here, but will put all that to one side and go to visit him when I get the chance.'

'Me too,' he agreed. 'I'm going to have plenty to keep me occupied for some time to come, but will find time for that.' He looked around him. 'How long are you planning on staying at the party?'

'I'm not sure,' she told him. 'It depends on how long I'm needed.'

'Right, we'll be off, then,' he said, and with a child on either side of him he went.

Melissa could tell that Rhianna and Martha were disappointed that she wasn't leaving at the same time as them, but she knew the rules now and number one was '*no fussing please*', so she waved them off with a bright smile that faded as soon as they'd disappeared.

* * *

Outside in the hospital corridor Ryan hesitated. He was going to take the children for a meal somewhere and was tempted to ask Melissa to join them. He wanted to make amends for their exchange of words outside the toy shop. Turning, he took the children back into the ward and saw that the party was practically over. Relatives of the children were helping nursing staff to tidy the place and Melissa was ready for the off, expecting that he would have gone by now.

'What's wrong, Ryan? I thought you'd gone.'

'We're going for a meal in the children's favourite restaurant,' he explained, 'and I wondered if you would like to join us.' It was a spur-of-the-moment invitation and he expected her to refuse.

'Yes, I would like to very much,' she told him, 'just as long as you are sure you want me there.'

'I wouldn't have asked you otherwise,' he said easily. 'I'll lead the way in my car, with you following, if that's all right?'

'Yes,' she replied.

She noticed that his expression didn't alter when Rhianna cried, 'Goody! Melissa is coming with us, Martha!'

When they were seated at a table in a bright modern restaurant with the children tucking in to fish fingers and chips and the adults something more spectacular, Ryan amazed her by commenting in a low voice, 'This is what I miss, family outings. We used to do this a lot when Beth was with us, but it all feels like a charade now.'

'Maybe it does,' Melissa said carefully, 'but you are

the only one who can put that right, Ryan. You are a fantastic father, holding down a very responsible job, but you must feel the loss of your wife a great deal. What was she like? Tell me about her.'

'Beth was just Beth, medium height, slim and very active, with brown eyes like the children's and light brown hair. She was a loving mother and dedicated to bringing babies safely into the world. Wouldn't hear of it when I tried to persuade her not to go out in the storm, and that was how she lost her life.'

When he lapsed into silence Melissa asked gently, 'And would she not want you to have the joys of family life again with someone else?'

'Maybe' was the answer. 'But so far there has been no one that I've wanted enough to be ready to take that step.' Until now, maybe? But he was far from sure that it would be a good idea to give Melissa any signals that he might regret afterwards.

Even though today had shown an affinity between them that hadn't been there before. Maybe it was because this was his loneliest time of the year, and whatever her Christmastimes had been like in the past, this one looked as if it was going to be a non-event.

The waitress was at his elbow, waiting to take orders for dessert, and the conversation became general again until they were leaving the place and Rhianna spotted mistletoe above the doorway.

'Look, Daddy!' she cried, and lifted her face to be kissed beneath the white berries. When he'd bent to oblige it was Martha's turn, and as he straightened up she cried, 'Melissa hasn't had a kiss! She must have one too!'

As Melissa shook her head laughingly, Ryan stepped towards her and took her in his arms. He wished the moment could go on for ever because the feel of her mouth under his and the closeness of her was like coming in out of the cold.

When he let her go there was a round of applause from the other diners and taking her hand, with Rhianna on one side and Martha on the other, they left the restaurant with not a word between them and went to their separate cars.

On arriving home, Ryan unlocked the door to let the children in. Before going inside himself, he walked over to where Melissa stood at her own front door.

'Do I have to say sorry for what happened?'

'No,' she said lightly, 'not at all. It was only a Christmas kiss, wasn't it?'

'Yes, of course,' he replied with a tight smile, and was gone. After his door had closed behind him, Melissa went inside and sank down onto the nearest chair. She relived the moments in his arms again. Beyond that she couldn't think.

CHAPTER FIVE

IT HAD BEEN the strangest of weekends as far as Melissa was concerned. She wasn't sure what to think as she drove to the hospital on the Monday morning. First there'd been her exchange of words with Ryan outside the toy shop about the carpet-laying, and the consequent remorse on her part for being so ungracious when she'd tackled him about it.

Then, thinking she had been well away from him when she'd gone to help with the party, he had turned up there with the bad news about Julian and had left her uneasy about what it could mean for them both. Finally there had been that surprise dinner invitation, culminating in an unexpectedly passionate kiss!

Monday morning was always Ryan's first clinic of the week and even though Melissa was early he was there before her and observed her keenly for a second when she appeared.

'If you do the ward rounds, I'll get going with the clinic earlier than usual,' he said briskly. So much for their kiss under the mistletoe. He was finished before her and came to join her as she moved from bed to bed, where often anxious parents were hovering, seeking reassurance.

Ryan was impressed with what he saw. Melissa was a natural with patients and parents. Obviously he'd seen her in this mode before and was satisfied with the way she performed, but today his awareness of her was heightened. He'd spent the night tossing and turning, the memory of their kiss haunting him. It should have been a peck on the cheek and it hadn't been. It had opened a floodgate of longing that he wanted to hold back, but the more he observed her the harder it became.

Unaware of how his mind was working, Melissa was concentrating on the young occupants of the beds in the two wards. She was confident that it was here that she belonged, amongst children who were sick and needed all the help they could get to become well again.

As the young ones and the parents hovering around their beds saw her approaching they felt her reaching out to them. No matter how worrying the diagnosis they had been given previously or might be receiving, she made them feel that their child was special.

'So,' Ryan said when the rounds were over. 'Now we'll leave the wards in the care of the nursing staff and have a quick lunch. This afternoon you can watch and learn while I operate on a child with a cleft lip and palate, just as long as there aren't any emergencies brought into A and E that our unit have to deal with.'

She was expecting Ryan to lunch in his office as he'd done on other days since she'd joined the staff of the neuro unit, but when she moved in the direction of the staff restaurant he fell into step beside her and when they'd queued and been served he said, 'Do you mind if I join you?'

'No, of course not,' she told him. She hoped he wasn't going to refer to the mistletoe incident while they were eating. It would be just too embarrassing if he did as she hadn't been entirely unresponsive while he'd been kissing her.

She needn't have concerned herself. He made no mention of it. He was probably regretting it and had decided to act as if it had never happened.

When they'd finished eating, Ryan got to his feet and said, 'I usually have a quick chat with Mollie in the lunch hour to check that the children got off to school all right, so will you excuse me? They were chattering non-stop about yesterday at breakfast-time.'

Before she could ask what part of the day before he was referring to, he was wending his way towards the restaurant exit.

He was an exceptional man. Strong and caring when it came to those he loved, and professionally a doctor of complete dedication to his calling. When she compared him to the man she'd been going to marry she felt grateful now instead of bitter that David had called off their engagement. It was all because of the man who'd taken her under his wing when she'd come crawling to Heatherdale like a lost soul.

She still had no idea what Ryan really thought about her, of course. However delightful he was to work with, nothing had changed back at the town houses where they lived. When he came home from the hospital each night she didn't see him until the following morning and so she had to be satisfied with that. However, she did wish she had the chance to see the children more often, even if their father was still guarding his private life just as much as before.

On the Saturday of her second week on the neuro unit, Melissa planned to visit Julian at the hospital where he was recovering. It was against the vow she'd made never to return to Manchester, but she felt so sorry that Julian's career and future had been put at risk by such a dreadful accident that the least she could do was take him some magazines, nice things to eat, and give him a few hours of her time.

She was undecided whether to tell Ryan what she was intending, or just proceed with her arrangements. In the end decided to just go and tell him afterwards.

'Wow!' Julian said when he saw Melissa approaching his bedside and to his parents who were present.

'This is a surprise! Mum, Dad, may I introduce Melissa? She's a doctor on my neuro unit.'

They smiled across at her.

'So, how are you coping without my charm and expertise?' he teased.

She had to smile at the question. Only Julian would be so chirpy while flat on his back with a spinal injury.

'Everyone is hoping that it won't be long before you are back amongst us.'

She could hear footsteps on the polished floor behind her and children's voices, and when Julian exclaimed, 'Look who's here now!' she turned slowly and saw Ryan coming towards them with Rhianna and Martha in tow.

When the children saw her they ran to her side, and Martha asked, 'How did you know we were coming?'

'I didn't,' she told her gently, 'but it's a lovely surprise.'

'We knocked on your door to ask you if you wanted to come with us,' Rhianna explained, 'but you weren't there. Why are you never there when we want you, Melissa?'

Ryan was chatting to Julian after greeting his parents and wasn't a part of her conversation with the children, but Melissa knew he'd heard what Rhianna had said, although he was still smiling at the chirpy patient on the bed.

'I'm hungry, Melissa,' Martha said pleadingly, taking Melissa's hand.

'I'll take them to the snack bar near the main entrance for something to eat while you talk to Julian,' she told Ryan. 'And I promise not to lose them,' she teased gently. Before he had time to reply they were off with smiles from her two young companions and a level look in her direction from their father.

As Ryan watched Melissa and the girls walk away, he was filled with mixed emotions. On the one hand, it was heart-warming to see how easily and openly his girls responded to her. On the other, it made him feel things he wasn't yet ready to feel. Was he attracted to her? He thought he probably was, but was he ready to do anything about that attraction? And what about letting the girls get too close? He was on dangerous ground.

'So where are you off to when you leave here?' Julian asked, breaking into his thoughts. His parents had gone to do some shopping while he had someone to talk to and Ryan brought his thoughts back to the present as Julian continued to chat.

'They tell me that the Christmas lights are on everywhere in the city centre and that there are Father Christmases appearing in all the big stores. Your children will want to visit him, won't they?'

'Yes, I'm sure they will,' he agreed. 'I hope that you will soon be mobile again, Julian. If our hospital wasn't just for children, we could have had you recovering in Heatherdale.'

'I'll do my best,' he promised. 'Besides, you'll be all right with Melissa filling my slot. How lucky can you get?'

Ryan's smile was twisted. 'I don't know. It's debatable.'

Melissa's appearance in his life had brought chaos rather than tranquillity into the ordered existence that was the only way he could survive his many responsibilities of family and work. But at night, in the darkness, in his lonely bedroom, when all the house was still, visions of her came to mind.

The long dark mane of her hair, the mouth that was never anything but tender when she was with his children, but buttoned up if *he* ever tried to get to know her better, and the dark hazel eyes that were full of hurt and loneliness.

She was in his line of vision at the top of the ward, bringing the children back from the snack bar, and as he was going to take Rhianna and Martha to see Santa Claus in one of the big stores it seemed only fitting that he should invite her to go with them rather than let Melissa make the train journey home on her own.

'Do you want to come with us to tell Santa Claus what you want for Christmas?' he asked her as the three of them drew level.

Julian had just been taken for a scan and as Melissa surveyed the empty bed she had a question of her own. 'Where's Julian?' she asked anxiously.

'Gone for a scan. He said to pass on his goodbyes,' he replied laconically. So much for his invitation. Could it possibly be that Melissa was attracted in another direction?

Melissa smiled, the moment of anxiety past. 'Yes, I'd love to see Santa.' There were a few things she would like for her first Christmas in Heatherdale, top of the list a better understanding with her independent neighbour.

As they left the hospital, Ryan's thoughts were running on a different track. He was remembering that Mollie wouldn't be around to cook the Christmas dinner for them as she usually did. She and Jack were getting married on the morning of Christmas Eve and they were off to Italy later in the day for their honeymoon. He was going to have to polish up his cooking skills.

He was still doubtful about asking Melissa to share the most festive day of the year with them as he knew she would pick up on his sadness and see his tension. Yet for all he knew she might have plans of her own on how to spend the day. Although she hadn't exactly been bubbling with joy when Christmas had first been mentioned. But spending it in a house that had only one presentable room was not a tempting prospect.

* * *

They found a jovial Santa in the first of the big stores that they came to amongst the busy city throng. Excitedly, Rhianna couldn't wait to tell him exactly what she wanted this Christmas.

'There are lots of things we would like,' she told him, 'but most of all we want a mummy.'

Santa's white brows lifted. It was obvious he wasn't too sure how to react to that one!

'Why don't you make a list and send it to me?' he said. 'One of my fairies will give you my address.'

Rhianna seemed satisfied with that and the small party made their way from the store.

'I'm sorry that you had to be involved in yet another awkward moment,' Ryan said. His tone was casual, as if it had been something and nothing.

Melissa was unaware that, inside, Ryan was cringing at another plea from his children for someone to take Beth's place. She smiled.

'Think nothing of it,' she told him. 'What the children are asking for is quite understandable, but anyone can see how well cared for and happy they are. You are a man in a million.'

'Most folks think I'm a fool,' he replied dryly. 'Struggling on alone.'

She was the fool for imagining that one day he might turn to her.

They worked together, doing what they'd been trained for, and it was a joy. They lived next door to each other, and if they weren't always communicating under those circumstances she was always conscious of his nearness.

Any imaginings of what it might be like to have him beside her in the night were kept under control. Ryan was a man who was travelling along a road of his own making and didn't want company on the way. What about herself? Hadn't she vowed to steer clear of the opposite sex too?

Unaware of Melissa's thoughts, Ryan was wishing that those few moments in the store when Rhianna had turned a happy occasion into a depressing one had never happened, but as they had the atmosphere between Melissa and himself needed lightening.

'Shall we go for a meal before we go for the train, somewhere bright and festive?'

'That would be lovely,' she replied. Her glance held his for a precious moment and he smiled.

'Let's go, then,' he said briskly, and with Martha holding Melissa's hand tightly amongst the crowds, and Rhianna clinging to her father, they went to find a place to eat.

'You know the city better than I do, so you choose,' he suggested as they moved along. 'How far are we from where you used to live?' He saw the brightness fade from her face.

'Not far enough,' she replied flatly, and pointed to a restaurant that had an attractive menu displayed. 'I think that your young ones will like this place.'

So much for Melissa telling him anything about herself that he didn't already know. Yet why should she tell him about her life before Heatherdale if she didn't want to? It didn't make him feel any less curious.

'Melissa!' a voice exclaimed from nearby. 'I've been

wondering where you'd got to.' When Ryan looked up he saw an expensively dressed older woman looking down at them.

'And now you know,' Melissa replied coolly. 'How are you, Monica?'

'Er, I'm fine, busy getting ready for David's big day. It's going to be the wedding of the year in our set.' The other woman's glance went over Ryan and the girls. 'I see you haven't been moping.'

'Dr Ferguson is my boss, and these are his children.'

'Ah. I see,' Monica said with a meaningful smile that belied the words.

'I don't think you do,' Melissa told her. Her face was drained of colour but she remained totally calm.

Ryan was curious about the identity of this woman who was interrupting their meal. She was going, thank goodness!

'It has been nice to meet you, Dr…er… And what lovely children.'

Uninterested, Rhianna and Martha tucked into the food that had just arrived, but as the other woman floated off, Melissa's calm deserted her and she bent her head as a flood of painful memories came back of the weeks and months before she'd moved to Heatherdale.

As he watched her Ryan felt like following that Monica woman and throttling her. He didn't know who she was to Melissa, but it was clear that she was bad news as far as she was concerned.

'I wouldn't mind knowing who that was,' he said gently, and this time Melissa didn't hesitate to reply.

'She was going to be my mother-in-law until her son broke off our engagement.'

'Of course, I remember you telling me that you were escaping a broken engagement. I hope you don't think that all men are that shallow, Melissa? He obviously didn't deserve you.'

'No, of course I don't think that.' she said quickly. 'It's very kind of you to take my side so readily.'

If she didn't feel that the new rapport that the day had brought between them might be spoilt, she would have told him that if she *had* felt like that, getting to know him would have made her think again. She couldn't help but admire the choices he'd made when he'd lost his wife, and she was deeply moved by his gentleness with sick children. She felt privileged to know him.

They finished their meal quickly, the girls' excited chatter filling any potentially uncomfortable silences between Melissa and Ryan.

On the train journey home the two of them were again silent, but the children continued to make up for it. Used to being in the car, the novelty of a journey by train or bus caused great excitement and Melissa had to smile.

She'd been brought up with expensive cars and still used that form of transport, but now it was a small second-hand car. Where at first it had been a wrench to see them go, now it didn't seem to matter as long as she arrived at her destination.

She would have liked to invite the three of them in for some supper when they arrived back in Heatherdale, basic as her accommodation was, but she knew if Ryan came up with a reason not to accept the invitation it would take the edge off the brief closeness.

As they parked their respective cars and approached their own doors, Ryan was reluctant for the day to end.

'Would you like to come in for a coffee?'

'Are you sure?' she asked in surprise. 'I'd considered asking you the same thing but didn't want to cause embarrassment if you refused for some reason.'

He *wasn't* sure, far from it! As she'd walked along level with him he'd watched the dark swathe of her hair swing gently against her shoulders and had wanted to hold her close, tell her that she had no need to be so alone any more.

If she needed someone he would be there, next door, ready to help. Yet would he be able to fulfil that promise on a purely friendly basis and not begin to want more? If he had any sense he would let Melissa get on with her own life now that she was settled here and was no longer unemployed. He should take a back seat and take pleasure from working with her.

She was excellent at her job, quick to learn, efficient in every aspect of paediatrics, and their young patients responded well to her, without alarm, but he hadn't answered her question.

He could tell her glibly that, yes, he was sure, because he didn't want the day to end just yet. Their relationship had moved on, he'd felt it in every word she'd said, in her every movement, but he wasn't sure that he was ready to let Beth be just a beautiful memory, instead of keeping to the vows he'd made on the day she'd been lowered gently into a grave in the churchyard.

Melissa watched him, wondering when his thoughts were going to come back from where they'd gone. He'd opened the front door to let the children into the house and for what seemed like an eternity she'd been waiting for him to say something as she had a strong feeling that he was regretting his impulsive invitation.

Sure enough, he turned to face her.

'Maybe we *should* call it a day, Melissa. The children are usually tucked up in bed by this time. But I want you to know that if ever you have a problem I'll always be only too pleased to help if needed.'

'I can cope, Ryan,' she told him levelly. 'The past few months have taught me a lot about myself and I feel stronger than ever. I'm hoping that most of my problems will be over once I've got the house how I want it. So please don't feel that you need to increase your commitments by adding me to the list.'

On that comment she opened her own door and went inside, and as he watched it close behind her Ryan's heart sank. What was he playing at? He'd invited her to have coffee and then gone back on it, and had been extremely patronising with his offer of help.

He was the one in need, content on the outside unhappy on the inside. Mollie had ventured to tell him a few times that Beth would not want him to live like this and he'd just ignored her advice and let it pass.

But on those occasions he hadn't known that there was such a person as Melissa Redmond and now he did. Not only was she one of the best registrars he'd ever worked with, she was his neighbour. Were the fates telling him something? Not if they knew that once he made up his mind regarding something important he rarely changed it!

CHAPTER SIX

IT WAS SUNDAY again. This was the day that Melissa always felt was long and empty. Well, not empty—she had plenty of chores she could get to. Still, her life did feel empty of family and friends because there was no one to phone her, or come to her door, except Ryan, of course, and after her cool reception of his change of mind the night before she wasn't expecting that. Part of her was almost dreading seeing him at work in the morning, too.

What had he expected her to do once the children had fallen asleep and they had been alone? Strip off and do the dance of the seven veils? One thing was sure, he would be keeping a low profile today after her chilly acceptance of his speedy change of mind.

She was wrong. He phoned at midday.

'Have you ever done any knitting, Melissa?'

'Not since I was about twelve,' she informed him. 'Why do you ask? Are you short of something to do in your spare time?'

'Hardly! Explain to me, what is spare time?'

'I've heard it described as the time you wish you had but never get. So tell me more about the knitting.'

'Rhianna wants to knit her doll a wetsuit. But first she has to learn how to knit.'

'Has she got a pattern, wool, and needles?'

'Er…no.'

'Right, so if you will entrust her to me, the two of us will go to the shops today and sort that out, if any of those kinds of places are open on a Sunday.'

'No problem regarding that,' he told her. 'Heatherdale is a popular tourist centre. They come from miles around to see the spa, the well and the rest. Sunday is one of the busiest days for the shops, but are you sure you can spare the time to take Rhianna for the wool and stuff?'

Could she spare the time? Of course she could. Ryan was actually willing to let Rhianna out of his sight for a while *and into her keeping*!

'Yes,' she told him, 'but a wetsuit is rather ambitious for a first attempt. Beginners usually start with something simple, like maybe a scarf for their doll?'

He was laughing. 'We Fergusons always aim high— in endeavour that is.'

She didn't join in. Was he referring to his dedication to his job or his celibate life or both?

'So shall I send Rhianna round?'

'Yes, but, Ryan, what about Martha? Won't she want to come?'

'No, she's all right, watching a children's film on TV at the moment.

'Thanks for offering to take Rhianna for whatever she needs to get started, and being willing to spend some time with her.'

'Thanks are not necessary,' she told him. 'It will be a pleasure, *not a chore*,' she continued coolly.

'Yes, of course,' Ryan said hastily. He'd phoned her with the request about the knitting because he'd been desperate to hear her voice after his bungled invitation. He was getting the kind of reception he deserved, though, looking on the bright side, Melissa hadn't hesitated when she'd heard what he'd rung for. He said a brief goodbye and went to tell Rhianna the good news.

As he watched the two of them walking along the pavement in the direction of the town centre, Ryan swallowed hard. They looked so right together, with Rhianna chattering away to Melissa and doing a little skip every few steps, but not as right as if it had been Beth taking her daughter to the shops. Would that feeling of loss ever go away?

They weren't gone long and then they were back. Melissa phoned to say that she was giving Rhianna her first knitting lesson and would send her back shortly. She'd also managed to talk Rhianna out of the wetsuit and into the idea of knitting her doll a scarf for starters.

'Sounds great,' he said. He wished Melissa was there beside him so that he could have the pleasure of her company, instead of having only her voice to listen to, but thankfully there was still tomorrow to look forward to at the hospital, where they had no hang-ups around each other.

Melissa saw Mollie arrive earlier than usual while she was having her breakfast the next morning, and within minutes Ryan was on the phone.

'Emergency Services are bringing in two youngsters with serious head injuries from a pile-up on the motorway. Eleven-year-old twin boys who were in the back seat of the family car without seat belts. They were thrown forward like rag dolls when the car behind them in the pile-up connected with the back of theirs. It's the tail end of the night shift so they're hanging on for the moment. Needless to say, I want to be there when they bring them in, so I'm off now. Can you follow as soon as possible? If surgery is required, I'll want you to assist.'

'Yes, of course,' she told him, already stepping out of her nightdress on her way to the bathroom. The adrenaline was kicking in. This was what she'd trained for, and it was going to be under the guidance of Ryan Ferguson. Did anything else matter?

If he was going to throw a fit every time she was near enough for the other kind of physical contact that had nothing to do with medicine and everything to do with sexual chemistry, at least she would have these kinds of moments to treasure.

Ryan was in Theatre, scrubbed up and masked, when she got there. He pointed to a motionless young figure on the operating table.

'Both twins have frontal fractures of the skull due to the force with which they were thrown forward, but this young guy is the most serious so I'm going to operate on him first. The other lad is next door, being watched over by theatre staff. The anaesthetist is at the ready so get gowned up and then we'll begin.

'The two boys had arrived and been scanned by the time I got here. It has shown there's a subdural haemorrhage to deal with for this youngster. He has been barely conscious since it happened, so I don't want to delay as there's bleeding between the inner surface of the skull and the outer layer of the meninges. Have you been involved with anything like this before?'

'Only once, but I remember it clearly,' Melissa told him. 'Just tell me what to do and I'll do it.'

As she scrubbed up, in what could not have been a more unexpected moment, Melissa realised that she was falling for Ryan, the golden-haired consultant who had burst into her life like a breath of clean fresh air. She loved his integrity, his devotion to his children, and to those belonging to others who came into his care, and above all his loyalty to his dead wife.

Would he ever feel the same way about her? There was a spark between them that would soon become a flame given the chance.

Ryan was waiting. The theatre nurses were in position, the anaesthetist poised for action at the head of the operating table and everything became centred on saving the life of an injured child.

Later in the morning the process was repeated for the second boy with the same sort of injury as his brother.

It seemed that they'd been on their way to school, with their mother driving, and with the carelessness of youth had skipped fastening their seat belts, which had caused not only devastation for themselves but a nightmare for her too.

Just before three o'clock in the afternoon the theatre staff were having a welcome late lunch in the staff restaurant after the traumas of the morning. It wasn't unusual, they often had to eat when they got the chance. Ryan had chosen to have a bite in his office as he wanted to make his regular call home to check that Mollie had coped all right with the Monday morning rush for the children.

The two boys had been transferred to the high-dependency unit, where they were being monitored all the time by nursing staff and watched over by their horrified parents, whose normal Monday morning had turned into a nightmare.

When Ryan had spoken to Mollie he went to seek out Melissa, who was in the middle of a late ward round. He found her sitting by the side of the cot of a tearful two-year-old whose mother had just taken an older child to the toilet. She was holding his hand and soothing him gently. Melissa was fantastic, either on the job or off it. So why couldn't he act on that delightful thought and do something about it, instead of holding on to the past so tightly?

'When you've finished rounds, I'd like a quick word in my office,' he said briskly to conceal the effect she was having on him.

She smiled up at him. 'Yes, of course, Dr Ferguson.' She pointed to the toddler who was now asleep, still holding her hand. 'I'll just let Oscar settle into a deeper sleep before I move away.'

'Of course.' When a nurse approached with the medicines trolley he went.

The nurse was middle-aged, plump with a smiley face, and as she observed his departing straight-backed and purposeful figure, she said with comic wistfulness, 'Isn't he something to make any woman's heart beat faster?

'I keep telling my husband that if he doesn't stop

watching football on the television instead of taking me out, I'm going to run off with Dr Ferguson. Which might not be so easy as our doctor friend is reluctant to put any woman in place of that nice wife of his.'

The nurse went on her way, moving from bed to bed with whatever medication its young occupant might be requiring. Melissa was despondent. To be told what she had already worked out for herself had put a blight on the day.

When she went to Ryan's office the first thing she saw was a florist's delivery of beautiful flowers of the season on a side table. Picking up the bouquet, he got to his feet and came round to her side of his desk and handed them to her.

'Just to say thanks for putting Rhianna on the right track with the knitting. There wasn't a sound out of her last night. She was working away at it until the very last moment before going to bed and at breakfast before I left the house. So thanks, Melissa.'

She looked down at the flowers and swallowed hard. It was the moment to tell him that she would do lots more for his children and *him* if he would let her, that she was falling in love with him, he was in her every waking thought *and in her dreams*, but something held her back.

She was letting a nice gesture mean more than had been meant by it. Her dealings with her ex-fiancé had shown her that humiliation was a hard pill to swallow if she should be mistaken, and hadn't the medicines nurse just confirmed Ryan's devotion to his wife's memory?

'You didn't have to do this, Ryan. I enjoyed the time spent with your daughter, but thanks, anyway.'

As she turned to go he stopped her.

'There is one other thing.'

She swivelled round to face him once more.

'You were good in Theatre this morning. We work well together. Keep it up and you will have a great future before you in paediatrics.'

'Maybe,' she told him gravely, 'but somewhere along the way I want to be a wife and mother, too.'

She watched him flinch.

'Yes, of course,' he agreed stiffly, and went back to the paperwork on his desk, leaving her to make an undignified exit. Once out of his office she went through a side door that led to the car park and put the flowers in her car out of sight. There was no way she wanted questions asked about them by other staff that might set rumours off that were not true.

The twin boys from the motorway accident had regained consciousness when she returned to the neuro unit and were looking pale, drowsy, and rather the worse for wear. Unless anything unforeseen occurred, they should, however, make full recoveries.

During their separate operations they'd had burr holes drilled into their skulls and blood clots drained away, followed by repair of damaged blood vessels.

As she checked them over their father said sombrely, 'Somehow I don't think they'll forget to fasten their seat belts again.'

When Melissa went to her car at the end of the day Ryan was about to drive off in his and he rolled the window down.

'You know that Mollie is getting married to Jack on

the morning of Christmas Eve and that Rhianna and Martha are to be her attendants? She was saying the other day that she wondered if you would be willing to help in the choosing of their dresses.'

'Me!' she exclaimed. 'But I hardly know your house-keeper.'

'She may not be that for much longer, I fear, certainly not in the same capacity. Come the new year I might have to find a substitute, but that's a few weeks away yet. So, getting back to the wedding and the children, Mollie would be glad of your advice as you wear such attractive clothes yourself.'

She smiled. How ironic.

'My clothes belong to a time when I was a pampered pet and I haven't been able to afford anything new since, but while I've come to live in Heatherdale I've forgiven my father. In a strange sort of way he did me a favour when I had to sell the place we had in Cheshire and come to live in my grandmother's house.' *Because if it hadn't happened I would never have met you,* she wanted to tell him, but she was still too cautious. The dread of being hurt again was like a dark shadow hanging over her

'It's good to know that you're happy here!' he exclaimed. 'I've had my doubts about that once or twice. I have always felt that this is a magical place, but I don't expect everyone to feel the same as I do.'

With an unmistakeable lift to his voice he continued, 'Getting back to the matter of Mollie's wedding, can I tell her that you'll go with her to choose the children's dresses? She is concerned that they should have something really pretty but also warm and cosy for this time of year. I can usually manage to choose their clothes myself, while giving them some degree of choice, but not when it is something like this, and in winter.'

'Yes, of course. I'll help in any way I can,' she said. Was she in her right mind, surrounding herself with the trappings of motherhood when their father ran a mile if she came within touching distance?

'Thanks, Melissa, that's wonderful. I am most grateful,' he told her, still smiling, and added jokingly, 'I've got my name down for a knitted pullover when Rhianna is more accomplished in the art.'

She smiled back at him. 'Don't tease her, Ryan. She is more like you than you realise, not to be defeated by anything, but she is only seven years old.'

He didn't reply, just gave her a long level look, and she wondered if he thought her interfering. He brought the subject back to Mollie's wedding.

'The way things are going, we Fergusons are going to be well represented on the day as not only are the girls going to be Mollie's young attendants, she has asked me to give her away as she has no close family. Her husband died a few years ago and she has no sons or daughters to do the honours, so it will be my pleasure.

'Her invitation was addressed to Ryan Ferguson, family, and friend, so if you want to tag along with us, Melissa, feel free. You will be most welcome.'

'Thanks just the same but no,' she said levelly, not enamoured by the phrasing of his invitation. 'I am not a tag-along sort of person. My life has scraped the bottom of the barrel over recent months and one of the things it has taught me is not to accept being merely tolerated by anyone.'

She watched his eyes widen and his jaw tighten. She drove off before he had a chance to comment. If he had, Ryan would have told her that he'd phrased the invitation in such a manner because he didn't know what Melissa thought of him, and a casual approach had seemed like the best idea at this stage of their relationship.

What would she have said if he'd worded it along the lines that she was the best thing that had happened to him in years and he would be proud to have her by his side in front of Mollie and her wedding guests?

The rest of the week dragged by on leaden feet.

On the day that Ryan was holding one of his clinics Melissa asked, 'Is there a chance that I could sit in with you as I did when I first came onto the ward? I learned such a lot.'

'I'm glad to hear it,' he said with a dry smile, 'but I think not at present. If Julian was here there would be no problem, but as it is I need you on the wards while I'm taking the clinic so that all aspects of the job are covered. I don't know if he will ever be mobile enough to come back to us but if he eventually does...'

'What?' she asked. '*What* if he eventually does? Are you going to tell me I might be out of a job? Do you want me gone?'

'Now you are being ridiculous,' he told her, and almost laughed.

As if!

She was the best registrar he'd ever had. How could Melissa ever think that he would pass her over because of a few wrongly chosen words in the car park the other night? He just had the feeling that he needed to cool it for a while. After all, their small patients came first.

It was Saturday. The small town was buzzing with Christmas shoppers and a local brass band played carols in the centre of the town square beside the huge Christmas tree.

As she heard the music in the distance, Melissa remembered Ryan telling her about the musical event some time previously. When she saw the three of them come out of the house next door and move off in that direction, she decided to go to the special yearly happening herself, but from another direction to avoid being invited to *tag along.*

It wasn't likely, of course, not after the reception the wording of his invitation had received that evening in the hospital car park, but she wasn't taking any chances. She was relieved that Ryan wasn't going to be present later in the afternoon when the promised shopping trip with Mollie and his children was to take place.

There were lots of the townsfolk gathered around the tree and as the band played the familiar music and those there sang the equally familiar words, she looked around her at the beautiful setting and sent up a prayer of thanks to the fates that had brought her here.

It was as if Manchester, the place that had been so familiar to her with its smart stores and many famous restaurants, didn't exist, and neither did the millionaire's row where she had lived with her father on money owed to others.

For the first time in ages she was beginning to feel in control of her life. That the house was still dark and dismal except for her delightful sitting room didn't matter—she would get that sorted eventually. She had the job she'd always longed for in pleasant surroundings and had met a man who made all others seem nondescript.

The only cloud in her sky was that she doubted he saw her in the same light, though why should he when he was still in love with the wife who had been taken from him so tragically?

A child's voice calling her name broke into her thoughts and when she looked up there was Ryan with his girls, all three smiling their surprise at seeing her amongst the festive crowd.

'Hello, there,' Ryan said. 'I nearly phoned to remind you of the band playing carols before we left the house as I wasn't sure if you remembered me mentioning it a couple of weeks ago.'

Unable to disguise her pleasure at meeting them, she told him, 'I'd forgotten but when the sound of the music came drifting over I realised where it was coming from and came to see what was going on.'

She turned to Rhianna and Martha.

'Are you ready for us going shopping this afternoon for your dresses for Mollie's wedding?'

'Yes,' they chorused excitedly.

Martha added, 'We already know what kind we want, Melissa.'

'Really!' she said in mock surprise.

'So be prepared,' Ryan warned laughingly, and followed it by saying, 'We are about to go for a hot drink somewhere. Dare I ask if you'd like to join us?'

There was no mention of her 'tagging along', she noticed as their glances met, but she knew he wouldn't have forgotten and she wished she hadn't been so snappy the other night in the car park.

'I'd love to,' she told him, letting the joy of being with the three of them take over. It diminished somewhat as they strolled along the high street in the direction of a café in one of the parks.

She had forgotten how well known Ryan must be in the town as a paediatric surgeon and a very attractive single father, and every time someone called across to him in greeting, she was observed with unconcealed curiosity.

In keeping with the frosty winter morning she was wearing a designer winter coat, elegant knee-high boots with high heels, and on her head was a fake fur hat the same colour as the coat. She wondered if the interest she was arousing in passersby was due to Ryan being seen with a woman, and an expensively dressed one at that.

Those observing them couldn't be expected to know that she had a wardrobe full of expensive clothes in a house that was like something out of the Dark Ages except for one room. Before leaving it, she'd stood in front of the mirror in the dressing table that had been one of the few things she'd managed to salvage from the onslaught of the bailiffs, and thought that if she sold some of her clothes, the money would buy wallpaper and paint.

Ryan had also noticed the stares and buzz of interest they were causing and suggested they go down the next side turning, but she shook her head and told him she was fine. She wished it was true.

While they drank coffee and the children sipped hot fruit drinks, Melissa and Ryan were silent. The girls, unaware of any tension in the atmosphere, chatted happily about their role in the upcoming wedding and Rhianna asked, 'Will you help us to get dressed that morning, Melissa?'

'Er, yes, of course I will, if you want me to,' she answered, somewhat dazed at the way she was being involved in their lives once more. She wasn't sure how Ryan would feel about her stepping into the mother role once again, so having offered to do as Rhianna had asked she needed to know what his opinion was.

'Would that be all right with you? I don't want to intrude on such a special day.'

'Of course. I would be greatly obliged if you would help the girls to get dressed, but only if you come to the wedding as my guest.'

'All right, I'll come!' she said levelly. 'Are you sure you want me at the wedding as your guest, though? It always feels like treading on eggshells when we are together outside the hospital. When we're there it's so different, more like being on safe ground.

'I've got to go, Ryan. I'll come for the children at the arranged time this afternoon.' And after kissing them both lightly on the cheek, she left the café.

Ryan sighed. Melissa had kisses in plenty for his children, but no tender gestures came his way.

They worked together as if they were joined at the hip, but once away from Heatherdale Children's Hospital the spark that he'd thought was there never seemed to burst into flame. She was right to point out that things were far from easy between them outside work.

Her outfit today had been stunning but he'd hesitated to tell her so as he seemed to have developed a talent for saying the wrong thing where Melissa was concerned. His mind went back to the night when she'd opened the door of the cold, grim house next door to his, looking on the point of collapse, and had burst into tears. He hadn't known in those few seconds that his life was about to change. It was something he was finding hard to accept and until he did there would be no peace in him.

Now that Melissa had gone, the children were fidgeting, ready to go. He paid for the drinks and they set off in the same direction as Melissa. He was hoping they might draw level with her, but she was nowhere to be seen and he wondered how she could move so fast on those heels.

Melissa enjoyed the afternoon spent with Mollie and the children immensely.

Melissa liked Ryan's middle-aged housekeeper and had not forgotten how she had suggested to him that they invite her to eat with them in her distressed state on that dreadful night when she'd been so much out on a limb she'd been on the verge of collapse.

It was easy to see that the children were fond of her, which was not surprising with Mollie being the only womanly figure in their lives.

As they walked the short distance to the high street she wasn't surprised when Mollie said, 'Rhianna and Martha are staying at my house tonight. They have a sleepover every few weeks. We have a lovely time and as it's always on a Saturday night there is no rush to get them to school the next morning. It gives Ryan a few hours of freedom to do whatever he pleases, which is rarely connected with socialising, I'm afraid.

'Before he lost Beth they had lots of friends and a lovely social life. During the first twelve months after she was gone there were some of the unmarried women that they knew who would willingly have stepped into her place if he'd asked them, but there was nothing further from his mind, and as far as I can see there still isn't.'

They had stopped outside a small but select department store and while Melissa would have liked Mollie to carry on talking about Ryan for ever, the older woman's thoughts had switched to dresses for her attendants.

'They have a delightful children's clothes section in this place, shall we see what is on show?'

A display of pretty long dresses in pastel colours, obviously aimed at Christmas partying for the young, immediately attracted the attention of all four of them. And after some degree of trying on, the small attendants-to-be were fitted out with dresses in a soft turquoise fabric with matching under-slips to help keep out the cold.

As they left the store Mollie asked, 'What do you think they should carry, Melissa, posies?'

'What about if they keep their hands tucked into little furry white muffs decorated with snowdrops?' she suggested.

The bride-to-be was smiling. 'Yes, indeed. They will keep their hands warm.'

'And what are you going to wear?' Melissa asked.

'I've bought a lovely dress and jacket in apricot silk.' Mollie's face took on a dreamy expression. 'And I'm delighted to say that Ryan is going to give me away. It won't be an easy day for him, with Beth not being there beside him, but I've invited him to bring a friend.'

'Yes, he's asked me to fill the gap.'

'That *is* good news! And are you going to?'

'Er, yes. I think so,' she replied. Mollie might not be so pleased if she knew the circumstances of her agreeing to be his partner for the occasion.

When they'd completed their shopping by buying soft white satin shoes for the children, Mollie said, 'Would you mind dropping off what we've bought at Ryan's house so that I can take the girls straight to my place?'

'Yes, of course,' Melissa said, and as the three of them set off in the opposite direction she heard Martha say, 'Melissa is going to help us get dressed for your wedding, Mollie.'

And Rhianna chipped in with, 'She's going to make us beautiful.'

Melissa considered Ryan's daughters beautiful already. With a slightly aching heart she set off to deliver the afternoon's shopping into their father's keeping.

CHAPTER SEVEN

WHEN HE OPENED the door to her Ryan stepped forward to take the shopping from her and then stood back to allow her to pass.

Noticing Melissa hesitate, he said, 'I've just finished catching up on a back log of paperwork from the hospital and am about to relax over a mug of tea. Can I persuade you to join me?'

She stepped inside, knowing that she wouldn't have refused the invitation if it had been a mug of castor oil he was offering.

He saw she was wearing the same outdoor clothes as she had that morning.

'Can I take your coat and your hat?'

Melissa nodded, and he stepped forward and slid the coat off her shoulders with one hand, gently removed her hat with the other and hung them carefully on a nearby coat hook.

She had become very still while he was taking off her hat and coat and when their glances held the dormant spark suddenly became a flame and instead of ushering her into the sitting room he led her slowly upstairs into his bedroom. As they faced each other beside the bed, which to him was the loneliest place on earth, she still hadn't spoken.

'Say something, do something, Melissa, please,' he said softly. 'Show me that you want me as much as I want you, or we'll let this moment pass.'

As he waited to see what she would do, Melissa began to take off her clothes, and as the dress that she'd been wearing beneath the coat slid to the floor and flimsy underwear and tights followed, she was smiling.

When she stood before him naked she spoke for the first time. 'Now *you* show me,' she said softly.

Without a second asking he stripped off and lifted Melissa onto the bed. His mouth caressed hers and the soft stem of her neck before dropping to the firm mounds of her breasts. She gave herself to him in a huge wave of wantonness, crying out as longing was appeased and delight filled her being.

But as she lay content in Ryan's arms afterwards Melissa realised that he hadn't spoken since he'd asked her to show him that she wanted him to make love to her. Raising herself up on to one elbow, she looked down at him and saw that his expression was no longer that of the man who had just possessed her, adored her and made her feel wanted. It was as if he'd pulled down the shutters.

'Ryan, what's wrong?' she asked with deadly calm. 'Clearly what has just happened between us didn't mean as much to you as it did to me.'

He didn't deny it and it was like a knife in her heart. Instead, he put her away from him gently.

'I am so sorry, Melissa. I would never willingly hurt you. I let my guard down, sought solace from you, and should not have done. It was unforgivable. When Beth was taken from me I chose a path to follow and have never diverted from it until a few moments ago. I hope you understand.'

She understood all right. What had made her think that the magic of Heatherdale had brought the man she would love for ever into her life when he had his own agenda? Was this how Ryan coped, a brief liaison with some willing member of her sex when the strain got to be too much, and then back to the life he had chosen?

The thought brought with it the urge to be gone, back to the house of horrors next door. It propelled her to her feet and in a matter of seconds she was dressed again in the clothes she had shed so willingly. Ryan made no protest, just threw on a robe and left her to it.

When she went down the curving staircase he was waiting in the hall, and lifting her coat and the fur hat off the hook where he had hung them she walked past him and out into the winter dark.

If it wasn't for her commitment to the sick children who came into their care at the hospital and the fact that she had nowhere else to go, she would be gone. Melissa drew the curtains to shut out the night of her humiliation.

She'd convinced herself that she understood Ryan's loyalty to the memory of his dead wife, even though it did seem an awful waste of another life…*his*. But to-night he'd taken the first step towards letting the memories be just that, and as he'd made love to her she'd rejoiced at the thought, until she'd looked down at him amongst the tangled sheets of his bed, seen the look on his face, and thought she should have known better.

After a miserable night she slept late on Sunday morning. She was brought out of sleep by the bedside phone ringing. She hoped it wasn't Ryan. He was the last person she wanted to speak to.

It wasn't, but the call *was* from next door. It was Rhianna to say that Mollie had brought them back home. They wanted to try on their dresses and the rest of their outfits to show their father, so would she come and help them to dress up for him?

She'd been finding a glimmer of comfort in the thought that she would have today to gather her wits before facing him on Monday morning, but the children were unwittingly turning that into a vain hope as there was no way she would refuse their plea.

'I'll come round in twenty minutes, Rhianna.'

After showering and dressing quickly, she skipped breakfast until later and went next door. Thankfully it was Martha who answered her knock.

'Daddy is under the shower and says he will wait until we are ready before coming down.'

Was that because he wanted to get the full effect of their outfits or because he was in no rush to see her again so soon? If that was the case, he need have no worries. If it hadn't been for the affection she had for his children he wouldn't have seen a blink of her today.

They looked delightful in the long turquoise dresses with their hands inside the pretty muffs and their feet in the satin pumps, and when Rhianna called up to Ryan from the hall that they were ready, Melissa felt her mouth go dry.

The children were standing at the bottom of the curving staircase as Melissa hovered near the front door. The longing to open it and be gone was strong, but the two small girls wanted her there and there she was going to stay no matter what, until he'd seen them dressed how they would be at the wedding.

He came slowly down the stairs towards them and she swallowed hard. Her mouth felt dry, her body weak and wilting at the sight of him with the golden thatch of his hair damp against his head from the shower and the rest of him covered by a cotton shirt and shorts. Though dry-mouthed and weak at the knees, beneath it she was in control. Last night had been humiliation time once again and she'd walked right into it, but it was not going to happen again.

On the third step from the bottom, Ryan paused and, observing her standing behind the children, stony-faced said, 'Thanks for finding the time to assist in the dressing-up parade, Melissa, they needed your help.'

'Think nothing of it,' she said levelly. 'It's nice to know that I'm needed by someone.' She placed her arms around their shoulders. 'We have two pretty bridesmaids waiting to hear what you have to say about their outfits.'

He was smiling as he came down the last steps of the staircase, giving no sign of having got the message in her first comment.

'The two of you are always beautiful to me, but in these lovely dresses, with the sweet little muffs to keep your hands warm, and the dainty shoes on your feet, you will be more beautiful than ever. What do you say to Melissa for helping you to choose them and dress up in them this morning?'

'Thank you,' they chorused, and hugged her close, then went slowly up the stairs to take off their finery.

When they'd gone Ryan said, 'I imagine that coming here this morning was the last thing you wanted to do.'

'Yes, it was,' she told him, 'and now I'm going to go and have some breakfast. I won't be available for the rest of the day.'

'Of course,' he said, and after waving to the children, who were looking down at them from the upstairs landing, she left, without another look in his direction.

The thought of spending her working day doing the job she loved had always been a pleasure to contemplate each morning as she drove the short distance to the hospital, and with Ryan nearby most of the time on the wards and in surgery it had been blissful, but not so on the Monday morning after the events of the weekend. Melissa was dreading being in his presence for any length of time.

But any awkwardness between them was avoided when she arrived because, amazingly, Julian was back in circulation, still as darkly attractive as ever but thinner, looking drawn and on crutches. She came across the two men chatting beside their cars in the staff parking area.

When Julian saw her he leant against his car and waved a crutch in her direction and she went to join them.

'This is a very pleasant surprise. It's lovely to see

you. Are you just visiting, or here to take up where you left off?'

'Just visiting today,' he said breezily, with his usual aplomb, 'but I'm hoping to come back on a part-time arrangement soon. The spinal unit in Manchester have worked wonders for me. The boss says he'll have me back whenever, so we will be a happy threesome once more.'

Melissa very much doubted it!

'When I'm back in harness, maybe we could have a night out together, the three of us,' Julian continued.

Melissa just smiled and didn't let it falter when Ryan spoke for the first time to comment, 'It would have to be a twosome, I'm afraid. All my time away from here is spoken for.'

On that downbeat comment he turned in the direction of the nearest entrance to the hospital and they followed him inside. Melissa took care to stay level with Julian's slow progress on his crutches and vowed that Ryan was not going to dampen her spirits or Julian's on his totally unexpected appearance.

He didn't stay long, just enough to say hello to everyone, and when the night shift were ready to go and day staff about to take over she walked with him to his car. On the way he stopped and, leaning forward between his supports, kissed her lingeringly while they were opposite the window of Ryan's office.

Taken aback, she didn't push him away, just told him laughingly, 'It's clear that your cheek wasn't affected in the accident. You will be getting me the sack.'

'That was for the benefit of a mutual friend of ours,' he said, serious for once, 'as I guess that nothing of that nature has been happening in those quarters while I've been away.'

'The answer is *yes* and *no*,' she told him, 'but how did you pick up on that?'

'By observing you both when the two of you came to visit me in the spinal unit.'

'Oh!' she said blankly, and before he could comment further waved him off and hurried back inside.

Ryan was in the secretary's office by the time she reached the corridor, having paused briefly to remind the tranquil middle-aged woman that an urgent appointment was needed for a child who had been diagnosed with epilepsy.

The family had missed the first appointment after the diagnosis when they would have discussed the illness in detail with the parents and explained to them what treatment was going to be given their daughter to control the symptoms and seriousness of it. Ryan caught Melissa up at the entrance to the wards.

Julian's ploy had worked. He'd seen the kiss from the window of his office. His colleague had some nerve, yet why shouldn't he come on to Melissa if he was so inclined? She hadn't exactly pushed him away.

They were both free to fraternise with whoever they liked, had no family ties or emotional hang-ups from painful memories that wouldn't go away, so it made perfect sense to Ryan that Julian and Melissa would get together. It didn't make him feel any happier, though!

'The results have been back a couple of weeks from the scan I requested for a child we saw at one of the clinics with suspected epilepsy. We gave the parents a date for an early appointment as soon as we knew what it was, but they didn't keep it. So I've just been asking my secretary to phone them.' He glanced at a clock on the wall above their heads. 'So now maybe we can get the day under way.'

'Yes, of course,' she said flatly, avoiding making a fool of herself again by explaining what had been behind Julian kissing her outside his office window. There was always the chance that Ryan had been relieved to see her turning her attention to someone else after him bringing her down to earth so abruptly when he'd just taken her to the stars, so maybe explanations were not needed.

'I was called here late last night to observe a five-year-old boy who had been brought in as an emergency,' Ryan said. 'I want him to be our first priority this morning.'

He led the way towards a small side ward that was used for seriously ill children or any who might have something contagious.

'So what time was it when you got the call?' she asked.

'Half past nine.'

'And what did you do about Rhianna and Martha?'

'Er, brought them with me.'

'You got them out of bed to come here when I was next door?' she said in an angry whisper. 'I would have thought that their welfare was more important than you not wanting to have anything to do with me again.'

He ignored the last part of her protest and assured her, 'The children weren't asleep and they were well wrapped up with cosy dressing-gowns over their night-dresses and warm boots on their feet.

'Both of them were concerned about the sick little boy and also as I was already in the dog house where you were concerned I didn't want to damage my image any further. If you remember, you had said that you wouldn't be available for the rest of the day when you were leaving us after the girls' modelling session.

'We are not here to question each other's motives in any shape or form, Melissa. We have a very sick child here. His name is Alexander.'

They approached the small figure on the bed.

'His parents have been here all night and I've suggested that they go for some breakfast while we check if the procedure I started then is working.'

At that moment the door behind them opened and Alexander's parents appeared, followed by a porter with a trolley, and while nursing staff were lifting the small boy carefully onto the trolley Ryan said to them, 'Has Alexander had anything in the nature of a cold sore recently?'

'He had one a couple of weeks ago,' his mother told him tearfully. 'An aunt of mine who is subject to cold sores had been hugging and kissing him when she called round, and it was shortly afterwards that a big blister appeared on his lip. The chemist told us what to use and it finally healed over.'

'Let's go,' his father said impatiently, with his arm around his wife. 'There is no time to lose, is there, Dr Ferguson?' When Ryan nodded sombrely they went, one on either side of the trolley that carried their small son.

In those moments Melissa's admiration for the doctor who had even put his own children second to a very sick child belonging to someone else reached new heights.

She'd had no right to criticise him for bringing Rhianna and Martha out late at night for once if Mollie hadn't been able to babysit for him, which had to have been the case.

Had she been so desperate for family and friends that she'd coveted his children? Was she now hurting because he didn't want her intruding into the life he had planned for himself and his daughters? If that *was* the case, it would not happen again.

By late afternoon their small patient was showing signs of responding to the anti-viral treatment after a second intravenous infusion. It wasn't mind-blowing, just a slight improvement, but it showed there was a chance that he might be able to fight off the serious infection, and it brought tremulous smiles to the faces of his parents that hadn't been there before.

The phone call to the family of the small girl with epilepsy had worked. A slapdash sort of young mother had brought the child to Outpatients in the late afternoon and had been forced to sit up and take notice when Ryan broke the news to her that the fits that her child had been having were due to epilepsy.

'That is the bad news,' he told her, as Melissa sat in with them. 'The good news is that young children often grow out of it as they get older. The word "epilepsy" refers to abnormalities of electrical activity in the brain that can be sometimes brief, which is how you described your daughter's seizures. Any longer and it could be a more serious matter.

'You must remember never to try to bring her out of

it when she has a seizure. Just make her comfortable and she will recover of her own accord. The same if she occasionally has periods of drowsiness or doesn't answer when spoken to. Don't make a fuss, just let her come back to normality in her own time.

'A couple of things to bear in mind are to try to prevent her getting overtired or upset about anything, as those are situations that can trigger a seizure. Make sure that the staff at the school she attends are aware of the problem in case something of that kind occurs while she's in their care.

'I'm going to prescribe an anticonvulsant medicine that will help to reduce the number of seizures and in time they might disappear altogether,' he said reassuringly.

The young girl's mother had listened to what he'd had to say without interruption but now she was finding her voice and the first thing she did was apologise. 'I'm sorry we didn't keep that other appointment. I had no idea that a few funny moments in a child's life could be so serious.'

'We're hoping the episodes will decrease once your daughter starts taking the medication that I'm prescribing,' he told her.

When they'd gone Ryan said wryly, 'So what do you think the chances are that the mother will remember what I've said?'

'I'm not sure,' Melissa told him. 'She sounded sincere enough when she actually had something to say.'

'I hope you're right, for the child's sake' was the reply. 'I'm going to have a word with Alexander's parents to answer any questions they might have, and if the

improvement is being sustained try to persuade them
to go home and rest for a while.'

At the end of the day Ryan sought her out.

'Alexander seems to be stabilising now he's on the
treatment, but in case I get called back here this evening, can we call a truce?'

'In what way?' she asked.

'Can I ask if you will stay with the girls if that should
occur?'

'Yes, of course,' she said immediately. 'Just give me
a buzz if you need me.' He might need her help with
the girls but his requirements for her didn't seem to ex-
tend beyond that.

Ryan arrived home shortly after Melissa, and after an
evening that was dominated by listening for the phone
to ring into the silence, and frequently checking that
his car was still where he'd parked it, Melissa went
slowly up to bed.

It would seem that there had so far been no setbacks
in Alexander's recovery, which was good, and also good
was the thought that she and Ryan had found an uneasy
kind of peace. If nothing else was ever forthcoming between them, she would have to live with the memory
of being naked in his arms, matching his passion with
her own, and for a few blissful moments seeing a future
of living and loving together with Rhianna and Martha
and maybe children of their own one day. She should
have known better.

Ryan was not mercenary like David, or a shallow
charmer like Julian. He was a man whose life had been
changed drastically on a stormy night and he'd taken it

on himself to stay faithful to his wife's memory while he brought up their children.

His life was rich and meaningful. Small wonder that he didn't need any more strings to his bow, so why did she feel that she had been guided to Heatherdale for a purpose more important than having a roof over her head?

Her grandmother had been a far-seeing woman. She'd known that one day Melissa would come to the small market town that was weaving its magic around her as it did with many others. Had the old lady foreseen her finding there the man who would be her heart's desire, while she was living in the drab town house that one day she was going to turn into a dream home?

As sleep began to claim her, her last thought was that she would seek out the place where her grandmother was buried. She recalled her father once saying that it was in the graveyard of the nearest church. When she found it she would make it beautiful, as she was doing to the house after years of neglect.

On Saturday morning Melissa set forth to find her grandmother's grave.

It was a cold and clear morning with the feeling of Christmas everywhere. The large tree that the council had erected dominated the centre of the town and shops and restaurants were in full festive mode as she walked the short distance to where she'd noticed a gracious stone building not far away from where she lived.

Older by far than the town houses, it stood on a large mound high off the roadside with a tall spire pointing upwards and was surrounded by a tranquil graveyard.

It took some time to find what she sought and her surmise that she was going to find long neglect there was proved correct. Overgrown and dirty, what had once been an attractive resting place was crying out to be cleaned, and once she'd found the spot where her grandmother was buried it would be just a short journey with cleaning materials and some hard work to make it beautiful once more. With all the weeds and brambles dug out of the ancient plot, it would be one way of offering her thanks to the person whose foresight had been her only hope to cling to in recent times.

After a quick lunch Melissa was back with all the necessary tools for the job and as she walked slowly along a side path in a sheltered place next to one of the stone walls of the church her eyes widened. There was a grave of gleaming white marble there with beautiful roses on it, but it was the inscription that caught her eye.

HERE LIES ELIZABETH (BETH) FERGUSON
CHERISHED WIFE OF RYAN
LOVING MOTHER OF RHIANNA AND MARTHA
MAY SHE REST IN PEACE

Melissa put the bucket she was carrying down slowly and laid the spade beside it. On returning to the grave-yard, she'd gone down a different path to reach her grandmother's grave. If she hadn't she wouldn't have seen this. It was almost as if it had been meant, but in what way?

Yet even as she asked herself the question the answer was there. 'I don't want to take your place,' she said softly. 'I just want to love Ryan and Rhianna and Martha and help them to keep your memory alive.'

At that moment the sun broke through cloud high above and as Melissa took a last look at the beautiful memorial to a midwife who had risked her life and lost it to the elements when she'd put an imminent birth before her own safety, she bent to pick up the spade and bucket, and the rest of the things she'd brought, and at the same moment heard the crunch of feet on the gravel path in the deserted church yard.

When she looked up Ryan was coming towards her, and crazy as it was she felt as if he had caught her out in some misdemeanour as he observed what she'd brought with her in astonishment.

'What on earth?' he exclaimed, with a sideways glance at his wife's grave. 'You've not taken on an extra job at weekends as a grave-cleaner, have you? Only I'm in charge of this one.'

'That's not funny,' she said stiffly. 'The things I've brought with me are to clean up my grandmother's grave. I feel it is the least I can do after her leaving me her house.

'I came earlier to inspect it and of course after years of neglect it was how I thought it would be, so I went home to collect some things to help clean it up. I must have taken the wrong path. They all look alike.

'Your wife's grave is beautiful. I'm sure that she must have been the same, Ryan.' Melissa turned to go.

'Wait!' he called. 'Give me the spade and the bucket and anything else that is heavy. Did you honestly think I was going to let you stagger off like a pack mule?'

She didn't reply, just did as he'd asked and led the

way to her grandmother's overgrown grave. 'Ugh!' he said when he saw it. 'That is too much for you to tackle. Perch on the seat over there while I give it a go.'

He was taking off his jacket and rolling up his sleeves and she said, 'Before you do, I have a couple of questions.'

'What are they?' he asked.

'Where are the children? And did you follow me here?'

'Rhianna and Martha are at a birthday party that won't be over for a couple of hours. I didn't follow you here. It was an opportunity to spend some quiet moments with Beth, to feel her near in the midst of my restricted life. I came because the future was becoming unclear and I hoped that I might see the way ahead better after some quiet time with her.'

'And I've butted into that, haven't I?' she said. 'Sallying forth with my grave-cleaning equipment. I'm sorry, Ryan.'

'You don't have to be,' he told her. 'You've done nothing wrong since the moment of your arrival in Heatherdale, except perhaps make me doubt some of my decisions. Maybe I needed someone or something to take the blinkers off my eyes.

'With regard to today and us meeting like this, I can always come again as this place is so near where I live. However, before I start cleaning the grime of ages off this imposing headstone, I have a question for you.'

'What is it?'

'Are you going to partner me, as you promised, to Mollie's wedding? Only you didn't sound too sure the last time it was mentioned.'

'Yes, I suppose so,' she told him flatly. 'If you recall the occasion of my lack of enthusiasm it was when only hours before we'd made love and I was unsure whether you had just used me because I was there or if I hadn't made the grade when it came to your sex life.'

He threw the spade down with a clatter. 'I don't have a "sex life", Melissa!

'The kind of life I live doesn't allow for that. I made love to you because you were and still are totally desirable, and you are the only woman I have wanted to make love with since I lost Beth.

'The way I behaved afterwards was because I felt guilty. Because that kind of magic didn't fit in with the vows I made when I lost her, not because I didn't want you like crazy.'

He picked up the spade. 'And now, as nothing has changed, can I proceed with the job in hand? It is going to take some time, so I will have to keep an eye on the graveyard clock with regard to the birthday party.'

So Ryan *had* wanted her. To hear that was joy untold, or at least it would be if he hadn't finished what he'd had to say with a reminder that nothing had changed with regard to his commitment.

'Don't be late on my account,' she told him, bringing the moment back to reality. 'There's no rush with this. I shall persist until my grandmother's grave is returned to its original splendour. With regard to the party, I could pick the children up if you want me to.'

'It would be good if you could,' he replied. 'They will be pleased to see you and I can carry on here until the light fades. The party is at the house of one of Rhianna's school friends and Martha was included in the invitation.'

'What time do you want me to pick them up?' she questioned. 'I'll need directions on how to get there, not being a native of this beautiful place. I can't believe what I ever saw in life in the big city.'

He rested on the spade for a moment and with his vivid blue gaze observing her said, 'So you have no regrets at finding yourself living in Heatherdale?'

'No,' she said gravely. 'I am employed in the kind of work I've always wanted to do, with a first-class paediatric consultant to learn from in the process of healing sick children, and have a house that has twice as much character even in its present state as the over-the-top expensive showpiece that was in keeping with my father's vision of an ideal home.'

She didn't mention that she might also have found the man of her dreams living just next door, too.

Ryan's glance was still on her in the silence that followed and she brought herself back down to earth by saying, 'So, when do you want me to pick up the children and where? It will be dark soon so it would be better to go now, I feel. I'd rather to be too early than too late.'

'Yes,' he agreed, and gave her the address where the party was being held and directions to get there.

'I'll take your tools home with me and see you back there later.'

As he watched her go, snug against the cold in a warm jacket and leggings with a woolly hat covering her head, he saw a different vision of her in his mind's eye, looking up at him from the covers of his bed, beautiful, wanton, adoring. What had he done?

Spoilt it, made her feel cheap because of the self-sacrificing dogma that he lived his life by. The children had more sense than he had. They already loved Melissa without any reserve. But their life with their mother had been short, while his love for Beth had been there since his early teens and it had deepened with every passing day. Never once had he expected that they wouldn't grow old together.

CHAPTER EIGHT

WHEN RHIANNA AND Martha came tripping out of the party with all the other young guests their faces lit up when they saw her, and as Melissa hugged them to her it was a moment of unexpected pleasure in the approaching dusk of a winter afternoon.

'Where's Daddy?' Martha wanted to know, and when Melissa had explained they climbed into the back of the car and talked about the party, Mollie's wedding, and Christmas all the way home. Melissa wished that *she* could visualise some joy coming her way in the weeks to come.

When they arrived back at home, Ryan had returned and had hot drinks waiting for the three of them. With the children perched one on either side of him, he was listening intently to their excited account of the party while Melissa observed the three of them bleakly.

They had something that she was not likely to ever have, a loving family bond, because she had fallen in love with Rhianna and Martha's father. He was the only man she would ever want to give her a child and as the chances of that were not good, childless she would stay.

'You look very serious,' Ryan said suddenly from

beside her. 'If it's about the grave, a few more hours the first chance I get we'll have it sorted.'

The grave was the last thing on her mind but thanks were due for his assistance.

'I'm most grateful for you taking over,' she told him stiltedly. 'Any improvement will be better than it was and, now, if you will excuse me, I need to change out of these clothes into something less drab than my grave-cleaning outfit.'

'Yes, sure,' he agreed, and it was there again, the memory of when he'd made love to her, taunting him, reproving him for how he'd treated her afterwards.

The hospital was already full of Christmas cheer, with a beautifully decorated spruce in the grounds and another in the entrance hall, and for the staff there was a ball arranged to take place a couple of weeks before.

Julian was hoping to be mobile enough to attend and was expecting an enthusiastic response from Melissa at the news, but as far as she was concerned if Ryan wasn't going to be there because of his domestic duties, or for any other reason, it would put a blight on the occasion.

With Christmas being so near, Melissa was turning her thoughts to presents for the children next door and a wedding gift for the bride-to-be. With regard to Ryan it would be like trespassing into his privacy to buy a personal gift, so it would have to be something basic that didn't give off any messages other than Christmas good wishes.

From his manner after those never-to-be-forgotten moments when he'd made love to her it had been clear that he'd felt it vital to point out that it had been just a moment of hunger for her that had been the cause of it. With the hurt of that forever in her mind he need have no concern that she was going to use the magic and romance of Christmas to tempt him again.

She smiled a wintry smile. What were the least personal of gifts for the opposite sex? Socks, scarf, handkerchiefs, toiletries, book token?

What about a romp with a junior doctor? From the way he'd described it, there had been nothing personal about *that*, either.

On the Friday night before the staff ball Melissa went shopping, and as she walked past the house next door on her way to the town centre it was ablaze with light. The curtains were drawn back and she could see Ryan and children seated at the dining table, having their meal. Longing swept over her in a painful tide as any impetus to shop drained away at the sight.

For a moment she almost turned back, but returning to her empty house would make the evening seem even more desolate. Better to be among the crowds of late-night Christmas shoppers than cooped up on her own.

It turned out to be the right thing to do. The shops were ablaze with all the reminders of the time of year they could think of, and inside them the public were buying gifts that would be brought out into the open only on the day.

Choosing a present for Mollie was no problem. A wedding gift voucher from the elegant department store where they'd chosen the girl's dresses didn't take long, and neither did a talking teddy bear each for Rhianna and Martha.

About to take the escalator to the floor above that to Menswear, she stopped, her eyes widening.

Ryan and the children had been on the point of finishing their meal when Melissa had passed the house earlier looking less than happy, and he had immediately gone into the kitchen where Mollie was tidying up and said, 'I've just seen Melissa go past looking lost and lonely. Could you hang on here for a little while longer, so that I can go after her to make sure that she's all right?'

'Yes, of course,' she said immediately. 'That lovely girl has nobody else to care about her except us. Take as long as you like.'

'All right, no need to push it, Mollie. I *have* got eyes in my head, you know.' He opened the front door. 'I'm presuming she was off to do some late-night shopping, would you agree?'

'Almost certainly' was the reply. 'The shops are open late tonight. Try the department store where we shopped for the girls' outfits. It's classy and so is she!'

Groaning at Mollie's second plug in favour of the only woman he'd ever cared about since Beth had been taken from him, he went, heading off towards the town centre.

There was only one man that she knew with hair like gold and eyes as blue as a summer sky. Melissa watched Ryan making his way towards her through the crowds. But how could that be? It was only a short time since she'd seen Ryan and his children having their evening meal.

He was beside her in seconds, relieved to have found her so quickly. Taking her arm he drew her to one side. Observing him anxiously, she asked, 'What's wrong? I saw you eating at home not long ago.'

He was smiling. 'That was then, this is now. I saw you pass and thought you looked lost and lonely so I followed you to make sure that you were all right.'

She felt tears prickle her eyes. He cared enough to come chasing after her from just a fleeting glance through the window, but not enough to want her in his home, his bed and his heart. *She* knew where she belonged but he didn't.

'I'm fine,' she told him with a brittle smile. 'I came to do my Christmas shopping for the only people I know as I'm short on family and friends. I also came to get a wedding gift for Mollie and Jack. I take it she's with Rhianna and Martha?'

'Yes, of course,' he told her evenly, and wondered if Julian was on her list. If what he'd seen outside his office window that day was anything to go by, he might have graduated to the top of it. But for the present the moment was his. He'd found Melissa, and Mollie had said there was no need for him to rush back.

'Let me take you for a coffee,' he suggested, 'or we could be more upmarket and go to a wine bar. I'm not too pushed for time.'

She was wearing the fake fur hat and coat again and was very much the elegant shopper, but there was strain in her expression, her dark hazel gaze was asking for answers to the questions that filled her mind and without setting too much store on his importance in her life he knew that he was most likely the cause of it.

'Yes, all right,' she agreed, to his surprise. 'Whatever you decide will be fine.'

'We'll go to a new place that has just opened near the pump room. I was there the other night and it is quite something.'

He'd seen her expression and said, 'It was on a private consultation. The guy and his wife who own the place are the son and daughter-in-law of the chairman of the hospital board and they'd asked for a visit to their small daughter in their apartment above the wine bar. So, you see, I wasn't living it up,' he said dryly. 'Mollie was doing the honours once again and I nearly asked you to go with me for the experience…and the company.'

'But you didn't,' she commented, as they made their way out of the store amongst the jostling crowds.

'No, I didn't. It was Tuesday night and it had been an exhausting day for us both, if you remember. It hardly seemed fair to ask you to work on into the evening.'

It was only half-true. It had been on his mind to ask her to accompany him ever since the chairman's urgent phone call that morning. He only felt alive in her presence, and when she wasn't there he lived on the memory of her in his arms, giving herself to him trustingly, completely, only to be rejected when his sanity had returned.

And then, hoping to lessen the hurt he'd caused her, he'd got himself involved in the task of cleaning up that filthy grave with Beth's beautiful white marble gleaming not far away in a wintry sun. He doubted it was enough to earn her forgiveness.

He was steering her across the busy main street with his hand beneath her elbow and as she looked up at him questioningly he said, 'What?'

'The little girl you went to see, what was the problem?'

'I'm not sure until I get the results back from tests that I've arranged. There was something rather puzzling about her condition.'

'So are you going to tell me what you think it might be?'

'No. This is the two of us spending a short time together away from everything else in our lives.'

'We won't be away from everything if the little girl's parents are at the wine bar,' she pointed out.

He shook his head. 'They won't be. They're staying the weekend at the grandparents' place, the chairman's house. Otherwise I wouldn't be taking you there as it would seem rather tasteless, don't you think?'

'Yes, I do,' she agreed, and thought it would also be tasteless if Ryan was using their meeting in the department store as an opportunity to spare her some of his precious time, with the get-away excuse, whenever he chose to use it, of Mollie waiting to be relieved from childminding.

He had stopped outside what had to be the wine bar. Soft lights were spreading their glow onto the pavement outside another of Heatherdale's attractive stone buildings and she hoped that it wasn't going to be one of those places with low lighting and intimate corners.

It wasn't. When they went inside it was warm, well lit, and crowded. He saw her smile and thought that at least one of them was pleased.

When he'd gone through the bar area on the Tuesday night to get to the apartment above, it had been deserted, but tonight was Friday of course. 'Shall we go somewhere else?' he suggested, not wanting to forego the pleasure of some quiet time together that they weren't going to get in that place.

'No,' she told him. 'Maybe just the one drink and then home.' She glanced at the shopping that he'd been carrying for her. 'We're not exactly dressed for Friday night on the town and Mollie needs to be relieved. I'll stay with the children while you take her home.'

He almost groaned out loud. Having got her to himself for once, Melissa was all for rushing back home. She'd been wary of being alone with him ever since they'd made love. Was there ever going to be any clarity in their lives away from the hospital?

Workwise they were in complete harmony, both with the same dedication, but away from that there was nothing to hold on to. He wasn't going to let the opportunity to talk about themselves go by, even if only for a short time, and when they'd found a table and he'd been to the bar Ryan asked, 'Would you like to spend Christmas Day with us, Melissa? The children would love it, if you haven't already made other arrangements.'

She smiled a twisted smile. What other arrangements could she have made in a place where she knew no one and had no connections other than those she worked with? The alternative would be booking a solitary meal at some restaurant.

'It's very kind of you to invite me,' she said stiffly, 'and I would love to be with the children on such a special day, but I wouldn't want the invitation to be a drag on you personally at a time that will have painful memories.'

'Having you with us will help to put them into the right perspective,' he told her, and was amazed how much he meant it. 'So what do you say?' He smiled. 'Would you be willing to sample my cooking?'

'Yes, I would,' she said. 'I really would. I'd love to spend Christmas Day with your children.'

She hadn't mentioned looking forward to spending the day with him but between now and then he would work on it, just as long as he didn't allow himself to be sidetracked by responsibilities that he was hesitant about sharing with anyone else.

With a lighter heart than when he'd found her in the department store he said, 'Maybe we should make tracks. As you so rightly pointed out, we ought to be relieving Mollie.'

As they walked the short distance to their respective houses there was new harmony between them that Melissa prayed would last, and that she wasn't setting herself up for more heartache.

They found the children asleep and Mollie painstakingly retrieving dropped stitches in Rhianna's knitting when they got back. On seeing their expressions, the older woman thought thankfully that the short time they'd spent together seemed to have brought them closer.

When he came back after seeing Mollie safely home, Melissa was ready to leave, and he protested, 'Surely you have time for a coffee?'

She was turning to go and shook her head. 'I have things to do, Ryan.'

'I'm still not forgiven for what happened between us, am I? Our working relationship is second to none, but our private lives are lagging behind, and I'm to blame but, Melissa, I *am* working on it.'

She was weakening. 'It isn't your fault that you lost the wife that you loved so much, and your devotion to her memory is very special. But what about your children's needs? Do you remember what Rhianna asked Santa for?'

'Yes. I am hardly likely to forget that. She asked for a *mummy*, which was not the first time since you came into our lives, but I'm not going to fill the gap for the sake of my small daughter's request to Santa. It is the agony of such a loss that I couldn't face again that makes me hesitate. *Do you understand?*'

She was across the room and holding him in her arms. 'Yes, I do,' she told him softly. 'It would be so much easier if I didn't, but I do.'

Brushing her lips gently across his cheek, she held him closer and when he turned his head the kisses were there and everything became a blur of aching need until he eased himself out of her arms.

Looking down at her gravely, he said, 'I don't want to hurt you any more, Melissa. I'm going to make that coffee and afterwards I'll see you safely back to your place.'

She nodded, unable to speak because her heart was racing and her bones melting as he disappeared into the kitchen.

When he came back with the drinks Ryan said surprisingly, 'Am I right in thinking that our friend Julian lusts after you? I saw that kiss out there in the hospital car park and let's face it, *he* wouldn't bring any baggage with him, would he?'

'That was Julian trying his hand at matchmaking between the two of *us*, instead of his usual womanising,' she informed him with the euphoria of previous moments disappearing. 'I do not sleep around with the likes of him, neither do I like to be described as husband-hunting, and if ever you decide that we do have a future together I would feel blessed to have Rhianna and Martha to love and care for, just in case you have any issues about that.'

She was on her feet and placing the coffee cup carefully on to a nearby table when she said, 'I can see myself out.' As he came towards her she shook her head and before he could protest she was gone.

Saturday dragged by with the thought of the ball in the evening bringing no feeling of anticipation. If it wasn't for the fact that Julian was to be there and expecting a fuss from everyone at his reappearance, Melissa would have given it a miss. She couldn't even muster the enthusiasm to come up with an outfit for the evening ahead.

One thing she wasn't short of was clothes, expensive ones that she'd been loath to part with when settling her father's debts. Her smart car, her jewellery had all gone into the seemingly bottomless pit, but her clothes she'd managed to save and somewhere amongst them were a couple of evening dresses carefully protected against the chill that was ever present in her grandmother's house.

They hadn't discussed the ball since his put-down after they'd made love. When it had been mentioned before then it had seemed that it was one occasion when he was prepared to socialise and let his children do one of their favourite things—spend the night at Mollie's.

So she had half expected that they would go together for the sake of convenience if nothing else, but things had changed between them since then and if he suggested they go together now she would refuse. There was no point in starting hospital gossip when there was nothing to comment about.

She was going to go use a taxi to transport her there and back. That way her arrangements could be best controlled. The thought of an early departure might seem tempting as the evening wore on.

When she tried on the dresses the choice wasn't easy. A black low-cut number that fitted the smooth lines of her body like a glove or a high-necked sleeveless dress of pale cream silk that accentuated the dark sheen of her hair and luminous hazel eyes were the choices before her.

She was drawn towards the black with an urge to show her neighbour that she was more than the drab girl next door, much more.

But the jewellery sold to help clear the debt had left her without the kind of relief that the black dress would need, whereas the cream number's high neck needed no such adornments.

So putting the thought of sophistication to one side, when the time came to dress for the evening ahead her choice was going to be that with long elbow-length gloves to match the dress and conceal her lack of finery.

* * *

After the rebuff of the night before, Ryan had spent the day cleaning the car in the morning and then taking the girls to the cinema to see a children's Christmas movie in the afternoon. Mollie had been to collect them and a brooding silence lay over the house.

There had been no sightings of Melissa all day and as the minutes dragged past he knew that he could not let her make her own way to something like the ball in the town centre when she hardly knew the place.

It would be churlish not to offer to take her. If she refused, so be it, but at least he would have offered, and if she preferred to spend the evening with Julian and his cronies he would have to endure it because she must be weary of him forever bleating about his responsibilities.

When she opened the door to him his eyes widened. He had yet to shower and change into a dinner suit, but she was ready, beautiful, and desirable in a fantastic dress.

'I came to ask how you intend to get to the ball,' he said levelly.

'Why? I'm going by taxi. I was just about to ring for one,' she replied, hiding her dismay at the sight of him showing no sign of being ready himself. Was Ryan not going because she was?

'Forget the taxi,' he said. 'I'll take you.'

'No, thanks.' As his jaw tightened, she continued, 'You might cramp my style while I'm giving all the men with no baggage the benefit of my company, and in any case if you are driving it will stop you from drinking a toast or any other kind of alcohol.'

'So why don't we share a taxi, if you don't mind waiting until I'm ready?' he persisted.

'Yes, all right,' she agreed, relieved to know that he hadn't changed his mind about the evening ahead, that he still had every intention of attending the ball.

When he called for her half an hour later her mouth went dry at the sight of him, as it always did. Scrubbed clean with his golden fairness accentuated by a dark dinner jacket and pristine white shirt, he was every woman's dream man yet didn't seem to realise it, and if he did, he didn't care.

In that moment it was there again. The certainty that she would never want any man but Ryan, and if he didn't feel the same about her she was either going to have to stand by and watch him live his life without her or leave Heatherdale and endure a second new beginning where he wasn't forever so near but so unattainable. With that thought came the vision of a grave of beautiful white marble in a secluded corner of a nearby churchyard.

'I rang for a taxi before I left the house so it should be on its way,' he informed her, conscious that her thoughts were somewhere else, though he would have been surprised to discover where.

They sat facing each other on the drive to the hospital, each of them so conscious of the other they needed the space between them to quell the longings they sparked off in each other.

When they arrived at their destination, Melissa stood by hesitantly while Ryan paid the taxi driver. She was the one who should have given the ball a miss. It would have been so much easier for them both if she had.

He belonged there, was highly respected at the hospital, and had lived in Heatherdale all his life. She was a newcomer, also a doctor dedicated to child care but way behind him in experience, and with a past that when she looked back on it seemed so empty and fruitless she couldn't believe how she had existed without what she had found here.

As the taxi began to pull away, Julian's car stopped beside them at the kerb edge en route for the hotel car park. 'Wow!' he said when he saw her. 'Aren't you the lucky one, Ryan? I'm no longer on crutches but still need two sticks so I can't offer any competition.' With that he drove off to find a parking space.

'One can't help but admire that guy's impudence,' Ryan said laughingly when he'd gone. 'Can we stand having him back when he's well again, do you think? Julian has already been sounding me out with regard to some part-time hours, but I don't relish the idea of him hovering over you all the time to make me jealous.'

Melissa hadn't spoken since they'd arrived. Julian's appearance had lifted her out of the doldrums, but she was still not in a party mood and had no answer forthcoming to what Ryan had just said.

Instead, she led the way into the foyer and when they separated to go to their respective cloakrooms to hand over their coats she realised that this must be a rare occasion for Ryan, out on the town probably for the first time in ages.

She was wrong not to understand his lifestyle, and wrong to present such a miserable face. Tonight she would forget everything except that she loved him more than life itself, and if she possibly could was going to make it a night for him to remember.

When she appeared back in the foyer he was chatting to an older couple she identified as the chairman of the board and his wife.

As she hesitated Ryan beckoned her across.

'Dr Redmond is a colleague who has recently joined us and is proving to be a lifesaver in every sense of the word. She will be working with me as I treat your granddaughter.'

Ryan must have received the results of the test he'd ordered. She was keen to discuss the findings, but other guests were hovering, waiting to speak to the chairman of the hospital board, and as the two of them moved on she asked, 'So what is it that is wrong with their granddaughter?'

'I only got a phone call with the results of the tests a few moments before I left the house tonight,' he explained, 'and have just been informing the grandparents of what has come up in them before I told you. Are you sure that you want to talk work at a time like this?'

'Yes, if you do.'

'Then let's find somewhere where we won't be overheard. This is a private consultation that I'm dealing with, don't forget.'

'I won't forget,' she promised. Their work with children with neurological problems was the one area of their relationship that brought no personal heartache.

'Have you heard of von Recklinghausen's disease?' he asked when they were seated at a table at the far end of the ballroom. 'Or to give it its medical title neurofibromatosis?'

'Only vaguely.'

'I'm not surprised with a name like that. It's an inherited disorder diagnosed from numerous soft fibrous swellings of nerves on the trunk and pelvis in the first instance. They can be of any size and are pale brown in colour.'

'And that is what the little girl has got?'

'Yes. Fortunately they are not present in the central nervous system, which could cause problems such as epilepsy. They will not require surgery unless they begin to look unsightly.

'When I said I was confused as to whether I was right in suspecting the von Recklinghausen's disease it was because no one in either of the child's parents' families has ever had it, so little Carly seems to be what could be the first of others who might inherit it from *her* if she has any children.

'Her grandparents have been extremely worried about her and even now with a diagnosis that might have been much worse they're apprehensive. I've told them that we will see her regularly and keep a keen eye open for any signs of the illness affecting the central nervous system in the future, and there you have it.'

At that moment an announcement was made asking those present to take their places for the meal that was part of the evening, and as they seated themselves with the rest of the neurology staff Julian appeared on the other side of her.

'I saw the two of you wrapped up in each other at the far table,' he murmured conspiratorially.

'We were discussing a patient, if you want to know,' she told him. 'Don't jump to conclusions.'

CHAPTER NINE

As the night wore on Melissa was conscious of the festive atmosphere amongst the staff of the renowned children's hospital. It was an opportunity that came once each year for them to socialise with those who, like themselves, worked endlessly towards the healing of the young.

Obviously a few were missing because the wards and emergency sections needed to be staffed, as well as having a small nucleus of theatre staff available should the need arise, but the bulk of them were there to enjoy the Christmas ball that the authorities held for them each year.

It had been noted by most of them that Ryan Ferguson, head of the neuro unit, had arrived in the company of his new registrar, and there were those there who were curious as to the meaning of it. But when she was swept in turn onto the dance floor by a couple of young medics, with an amicable smile from the man himself, their interest waned.

Fortunately, they were not able to read his thoughts, which were a jumble of not wanting to be seen to be monopolising Melissa and the longing to hold her close and dance every moment of the night away with her. But she'd reminded him about his tactless comment regarding men with no baggage and he was giving her the chance to get to know some of them.

For her part, she'd felt sick inside at being handed over to the young hopefuls like some sort of raffle prize, and when they had each returned her to where Ryan was chatting to other staff members, she was already debating whether to go and keep a subdued-looking Julian company to make up for his lack of mobility.

No sooner had the thought occurred to her than she acted on it and as Ryan watched her cross the now deserted dance floor in that direction he groaned inwardly.

He wanted her in *his* arms, not those of someone else, to be able to forget his hangs-ups and frustrations for a while. So why wasn't he doing just that, letting Melissa's nearness banish the aching feeling of loss that was there whenever they were apart?

'So what's new?' Julian asked, when Melissa seated herself beside him. 'Is the boss blind or what?'

'I'm competing against a beautiful memory,' she told him, 'and I don't want it to be like that. I want Ryan to see me as an opportunity to move into a new relationship without causing any hurt to the past, but of all things he is a man of honour and integrity. He was the first person I met when I came to Heatherdale and he took my breath away.'

'That was because you hadn't met me first,' he teased, and as she laughed at his cheek he went on, 'Watch out, here he comes.'

The band had started to play again, smooth, languorous music to warm the blood and create desire. When

Ryan stopped in front of them he held out his hand, and when she took it in hers he raised her to her feet and said, 'My turn, I think.'

It would always be his turn if he could only see the rightness of it. More likely he was only dancing with her out of some sense of duty.

She was wrong about *that*! Ryan stayed by her side for the rest of the evening. Every time the music filled the ballroom they danced and his nearness was fantastic, his touch a delight. She wondered how the night would end for them, with the children safely tucked up at Mollie's.

It wasn't going to be her in his bed, that was for sure. The pain of his rejection after they'd made love still gnawed at her. So what did it leave them, a peck on the cheek and goodnight?

Unaware of her confusion, Ryan was smiling down at her. They were being watched, talked about, and he didn't give a damn. He could imagine them gossiping about him and Melissa, but for once Ryan didn't mind.

He had gone to the bar to get them drinks and while he was waiting to be served amongst many others Melissa's unease increased regarding what was going to happen when they arrived back home with only themselves to be concerned about.

They'd danced almost every dance together; the attraction between them was at its peak. Would they be able to separate each to their own property with just a brief farewell?

She wouldn't be able to face another putdown if they made love, only for Ryan to have regrets again afterwards. It was a ghastly situation to be in, never sure whether one day he would ask her to marry him, or would keep her on the edge of his life for ever.

There was the memory of the other day when they'd met unexpectedly by his wife's grave and he'd made no secret of how much Beth still meant to him. Would *she* ever mean so much to him that he could accept her in Beth's place?

The uncertainties of the moment were crowding in on her and aware that it would still be a few minutes before Ryan was served, she rose to her feet. Moving swiftly in the direction of the cloakroom, she collected her coat and keeping out of sight went into the hotel foyer and out into the night where taxis were lined up in readiness for transporting homeward-bound revellers. It took only seconds to give directions to the driver of the first one in the queue and she was gone.

When Ryan arrived back at the table and she wasn't there he expected her to reappear any moment, but as the minutes ticked by and eyes were on him it began to register that Melissa was no longer in the building.

Julian stopped by the table and said, 'I think she's gone, boss.'

Ryan got slowly to his feet and made his way towards the taxi rank.

Was she insane? Leaving the warmth and safety of the hotel to go out into the dark winter night alone? Surely Melissa wasn't so wary of him that she was concerned that he might want a repeat of that last time when Rhianna and Martha had been at Mollie's?

All he had wanted was to have her with him at the ball, to dance with her, delighting in her nearness that always kept the loneliness he lived with at bay, and to see her safely home when it was over. Any other desires would have been kept tightly under control, but it would seem that she saw him as someone who would want it all his way and she'd panicked and gone.

When the taxi driver pulled up at the bottom of his drive Ryan saw that Melissa's house, gaunt and unpainted, was in darkness, and as the man drove off he wondered what to do next. How was he going to find out if Melissa was safely home or elsewhere without creating a disturbance?

One thing was sure: he was not going to put his key into the lock of his front door until he was sure that she was warm and safe behind hers. So first a phone call and if there was no answer it was going to be a case of hammering on it until Melissa appeared, and if she didn't he shuddered to think what he would do.

Melissa was huddled under the bedcovers when he rang and cringed at the sound, but when it continued she reached for the bedside phone and managed a weak 'Hello?'

'So you're back safely,' he said flatly, as relief washed over him. 'What was behind the sneaky Cinderella performance? You could at least have let me know that you wanted to leave so that I could have seen you safely home.'

'I didn't want you to have to do that,' she explained awkwardly. 'It wasn't as if I was your partner for the evening, even though we'd danced a lot. We'd just shared a taxi to take us there, that was all. I'm sorry if

I caused you any anxiety, it was just that…' Her voice trailed away and into the silence that followed he let her see that he read her mind.

'You didn't want to risk a repeat of the last time the children stayed at Mollie's?'

'Yes, that was it, and now will you please leave me alone?'

'If that is what you want, yes,' he said coolly, and rang off.

Melissa turned her face into the pillows and wept.

She awoke the next morning with head aching and face red and blotchy from weeping, but with a decision made to leave Heatherdale, to find somewhere where she could live without hurt and insecurity and where there was a position in paediatrics.

Estate agents were open on Sundays for a few hours in the town, so she decided that later in the morning she would make an appointment for one of them to come round to value the house and set things in motion. She just hoped that Ryan wouldn't make a fuss about her departure from Heatherdale when the time came.

A move in February or early March was not far away and wouldn't leave it too long before she went. In the meantime she wouldn't get any closer to Rhianna and Martha so that they weren't too upset when Santa didn't bring them a new mummy, or at least the promise of one.

And what of their father? She knew Ryan wanted her but in what role in his life? She'd been betrayed by her own father, discarded with all speed by a shallow fiancé, and in the wonder of meeting a man like Ryan had hoped that he might feel the same about her. Maybe a part of him did, but there were side issues, grief of long standing and children to consider. Would he ever feel ready to put someone in Beth's place?

Mollie brought the children back in the middle of Sunday morning and immediately cottoned onto an atmosphere of gloom around their father.

'So, how was the ball?' she asked. 'Did the two of you enjoy yourselves?'

'Er…yes,' he replied unconvincingly and she didn't pursue the subject.

There was no sign of anyone from next door when Melissa set off for the centre of the town at midday. Mollie's car was nowhere in sight so she concluded that Ryan must have taken the children out for Sunday lunch. If that was the case she was grateful for it. The last thing she wanted was to meet them on her way to the estate agent's.

The place was empty of customers when she got there and a smart-suited middle-aged man sprang to attention when she went inside and asked if someone could come to value a property that she wished to put on the market as soon as possible.

'I can come now if you like,' he offered. 'As you can see, we are quiet at the moment.'

On the point of taking him up on the offer she decided that it would be better if he came some time early the following day while Ryan was at the hospital, the children at school, and Mollie wasn't around, and with that in mind left a key with him.

By the time she arrived back at the house her determination was dwindling. Was she crazy to be cutting herself off from Ryan and the children in such a hurry? Suppose no one wanted to buy the house when the 'For Sale' sign went up. It could hardly be described as a desirable residence in its present state, and what about her grandmother's wish that she should live there, and the grave that she was going to sort out?

They were things that belonged to the past, she reasoned miserably. It was the present that she was running away from.

Monday was a weird day, working with Ryan in assumed harmony when she longed to be somewhere else where there was no heartache. But the children in their care had to come first and no matter what was going on in their lives away from the hospital, when they were there it took priority over everything.

When they'd come face-to-face in the corridor on arriving he'd said, unsmilingly, 'I'm told that we have had some intakes over the weekend that are going to keep us busy, so when you're ready...'

'Yes, of course,' she'd said coolly, and presented herself on the wards within minutes to find him already examining a twelve-year-old girl who had been rushed in over the weekend after drinking some kind of noxious substance and had had to have her stomach washed out.

'Do we know what it was?' she asked.

'Not at the moment,' he replied. 'Apparently the youngster was partying at a friend's house and was given a drink that caused her to start vomiting and lose consciousness temporarily. The inside of her mouth and throat is very inflamed so she's been given something to ease that, and as you see she's now sleeping normally after the ordeal of the stomach wash-out.

'Her mother is here. She thinks that one of the lads at the party thought he was playing a harmless trick on her daughter and gave her some concoction in the drink that he'd got out of the chemistry lab at school. He is now being questioned by the police.'

His voice was brisk and businesslike, as it always was when they were on the wards or in the clinics, but there was a remoteness about it that wasn't usually there, as if he was talking to a stranger. Whatever was between them was now over.

It confirmed to Melissa that she was doing the right thing in leaving Heatherdale, and when the estate agent rang in the early afternoon with a valuation figure that was better than she'd expected she told him to go ahead with the sale.

'How about a board outside?' he questioned. 'Not everyone wants that, but it is a good way of advertising.'

'Yes, please,' she told him. It would be easier for Ryan to find out what she was planning that way, instead of having to face him herself with the news.

When she'd arrived at the hospital that morning everyone except her had chatted about the ball. There'd been no sign of Ryan and she'd gone to the secretary's office to check on what the day had in store for them to avoid being involved in the small talk when they came face-to-face.

He was still annoyed by her conduct of Saturday night, when she'd left the hotel without telling him, and if his manner was remote his feelings weren't. He'd been so wrapped up in his safe lifestyle he'd given no thought to hers, living alone without friends or family in that ghastly house. Tonight he would make amends, go round to see Melissa and ask her to forgive him for his selfishness.

That determination lasted until he pulled up in front of their two houses in the evening and saw the 'For Sale' sign. 'Oh, no!' he exclaimed. Were his eyes deceiving him?

Melissa must have really meant it when she'd told him to stay away from her. Where on earth was she planning to go? She'd told him how she loved Heatherdale. Had it been a short-lived attraction and the same applied to him? She was writing him off like a ship that had passed in the night.

And what about Mollie's wedding? He'd asked Melissa to partner him for the occasion and be there for the children while he was performing his duties during the service. Rhianna and Martha loved her and she loved them. It was just him who was the problem.

There was no sign of her car so maybe she was avoiding him. She would have to face him sooner or later and until then he was going to keep a low profile, for her sake if nothing else.

'What do you think is going on next door?' Mollie questioned when he went inside. 'Doesn't Melissa like us any more?'

'I don't think she has any problems with you and the girls,' he told her wryly, 'but she's not too thrilled with me.'

'She won't be gone before Christmas, will she?' she asked anxiously, without commenting on his remark about himself.

'I very much doubt it' was the reply. 'She won't want to miss your wedding and also hopefully the children's excitement on Christmas morning.'

He was rallying from the shock of seeing the sale board. House buying always took a few weeks at least, sometimes months, and if she got a buyer who was in no rush it could take for ever. Melissa would be around for Christmas, unless she'd got any other dreadful surprises planned.

Melissa had called in at the estate agent's just before they closed to sign any necessary paperwork and to avoid arriving home at the same time as Ryan. When she eventually turned up she breathed a sigh of relief because there was no sign of him, which would give her a few hours' respite before having to face him the following day.

Once she'd eaten she phoned Mollie, who was back home, to assure her that she would be there for her wedding and if she needed any help with anything she had only to ask. The last thing she wanted was to cause any hassle for either the bride or her two small attendants.

'I'm sorry to see that you're intending leaving us, Melissa,' the older woman said. 'Ryan and the children need you, and I feel that you need them.'

'I can't compete with his devotion to his wife's memory,' she told her. 'He is happy as he is, Mollie.'

'Not all the time.'

'Maybe, but that is how it seems to me,' she replied, and changed the subject. 'I will see to the children getting ready on the morning of the wedding so have no worries on that score, and will be in touch before then to check if you need me for anything else. If Ryan still wants me to partner him, that's okay, too, though I have my doubts about whether he will.'

After saying goodbye to the motherly housekeeper, she settled down to browse over the day's events, aware that so far there had been no feedback from Ryan. Maybe he was just relieved that she was removing temptation out of his way.

Ryan was far from relieved about the state of affairs. If Melissa had wanted to make him realise how much she meant to him, she was succeeding. Mollie had called to say that the two of them had spoken on the phone and that Melissa was still available to assist on the morning of the wedding and that she would still partner him on that occasion if he wanted her to.

So there was going to be time for her to change her mind over Christmas and afterwards while she was waiting for a buyer. In the meantime, he would be his normal self when they were in each other's company, without referring to her wanting to move.

The next morning on the wards Ryan talked only about their patients, which was not unusual on a normal day, but Melissa had been expecting at least some mention of her putting the house up for sale and concluded that he must see it as something of minor interest. If that was the case, she wasn't going to refer to it, either.

The days leading up to Christmas and Mollie's wedding were some of the strangest Melissa had ever known. On the last Saturday before the two events there was a knock on her door and she opened it to find a van from a local tree nursery parked in front. When he saw her the driver said, 'I've got a tree here for you.'

'There must be a mistake,' she told him. 'I haven't ordered anything from you.'

'Well, somebody has,' he told her. 'Two trees were ordered and paid for to be delivered to these two houses.' When she looked across, Melissa saw that he had already deposited a tree on Ryan's drive. 'Your neighbours are out,' he explained, and without further comment went to his truck and hoisted a fresh green spruce tree from the top of a pile and carried it to her door and through into the hall.

'Have a nice Christmas, lady,' he said, after resting it upright against the wall, and went on his way.

Where she hadn't done anything regarding decorations so far, Ryan's house already had a festive look about it, with fairy lights around the door and Christmas lanterns glowing in the garden as soon as darkness fell. No doubt the delivery of the tree would create a focal point for the children's presents to be placed around.

All of that was perfectly understandable but why go to the trouble of providing her with a tree too? Was it another example of the way he was ignoring her decision to leave him to his restricted existence?

Later the same morning, on her way to buy ornaments for the tree, she stopped off at the cemetery to put Christmas flowers on her grandmother's grave, and observed it in amazement when she got there. It was immaculate. Ryan had said he would clean it and had kept his word, but how when it was dark in the evenings

and late afternoons and there would be no time before
he went to the hospital each morning?

It was only the previous Saturday that they'd met
there and he'd made the offer. Had it been in his
thoughts that he wanted her to have peace of mind regarding it when she was gone and had wasted no time
in cleaning it up?

Before continuing on her way, she stopped in front
of Beth's grave. She would try to make up for their
mother not being there over Christmas for the children,
but couldn't promise any joy with regard to their father
because he didn't want her to take their mother's place
and she would have to accept that.

Ryan had gone to have a haircut in readiness for his role
at the wedding and had gone to a unisex hairdresser so
that Rhianna and Martha could have theirs made especially beautiful at the same time in preparation for the
occasion. Only a week to go and it would be upon them.

When they arrived back at the house the tree was
there on the drive, but there was no sign of Melissa's.
He hoped that she'd accepted it in the spirit it had been
given. Whatever happened in the new year, he was determined that her decision to leave Heatherdale was not
going to put the blight on Christmas.

He saw her go past on her return from the shops and
within minutes she was on the phone, thanking him for
the tree and asking how he'd managed to find time to
finish the cleaning of the grave.

'It was just as easy to order two as one, and no way
would the children want you not to have a tree when
they come to see you over Christmas. As to the clean-

ing up of the grave, I'm afraid I haven't been performing miracles. The church has a facility where they will
maintain a grave on a regular basis, so you have your
answer to that.'

'Well, thanks, anyway,' she told him. 'If you pass
the contract on to me, I'll see that it gets paid when
due.' And without further comment she rang off with
the thought in mind that she was supposed to be keeping a low profile with Rhianna and Martha instead of
spending most of Christmas with them. But it wasn't
going to be easy with the wedding and Christmas morning and everything else that gave the young excitement
and delight at such a time of year.

If the morning had brought surprises with it in the form
of the unexpected delivery of the tree and the immaculate gravestone, the afternoon's surprise was in a class
of its own.

The estate agent phoned to say that they had a buyer
for the house. 'What, already?' she croaked, as her legs
felt as if they would give way under her. Yet wasn't it
what she wanted, to be off as soon as Christmas was
over?

'Those houses where you live are always soon
snapped up,' he said, 'so don't be surprised. It amazes
me that they're not listed, like a lot of the buildings in
the town. The buyer's bankers are in charge of the sale
as he is some busy professional guy, so we'll be dealing with them.'

'When did you show him around?' she asked, still
stunned.

'We didn't. He asked for a brochure to be sent to his

bank, saw that it was what he's looking for, and wants to buy it. Could be a developer, I suppose,' the voice at the other end of the line was saying, and as she listened it was all so unreal, like Ryan's calm acceptance of her leaving Heatherdale with no sign of dismay.

If anything should make her feel confident that she was doing the right thing, it was that, but if she'd been lost and lonely when she'd come to this place that had captured her heart, what she was going to feel like when she left it didn't bear thinking of.

In the early evening she went upstairs and went through her clothes to decide what was going to be the most attractive outfit she possessed to wear at Mollie's wedding.

A pale blue dress of fine wool with a matching jacket and high-heeled shoes seemed a good choice, but she had no large wedding-type hat to go with it and settled for an inexpensive fascinator that was modern and youthful and shaped to show off the dark sheen of her hair.

When she observed herself in the mirror she was smiling. She was 'poor' and 'needy', she thought, but could manage a show of prosperity when the need arose and hoped that Ryan would approve of her outfit.

The following day the 'Sold' notice went up outside the house and if Melissa was expecting any revealing comments from Ryan regarding it she was disappointed. He merely commented as they arrived home simultaneously at the end of a busy day at the hospital that someone had wasted no time and left it at that, leaving her once

again with the sick feeling that she was a poor judge
when it came to the men in her life.

Especially when his next comment was to remind her
that he would be cooking Christmas dinner and hoped
she realised how much Rhianna and Martha were looking forward to her spending the day with them. There
was again no mention of *his* feelings about the invitation, and she told him levelly if that was the case with
regard to the children, she would be there.

But first there was the ordeal of the wedding to get
through.

It was the day of Christmas Eve, and as Ryan drove
the four of them through town to the church where the
wedding was to take place it was thronged with last-
minute shoppers and sightseers come to share in the
magic of Heatherdale at a special time of year.

When she'd gone next door earlier in the morning,
in good time to help Rhianna and Martha into their
pretty outfits, Ryan's heart had ached when the children had run up to her and hugged her, and he'd felt
the familiar longing take hold of him, as it always did
when she was near.

'You look very swish,' he'd commented.

'So do you,' she'd told him, taking in the vision of
the tall figure in morning suit and smart white shirt.
Would she ever be able to put him out of her mind when
he was no longer only feet away from her all the time
at the hospital, and almost within touching distance in
the house next to hers? Lots of women would be happy
with that arrangement, if only to have him in their lives,
but not her. The pain of always being an onlooker would
be too much to bear.

The children had been tugging at her, eager to get dressed, and she'd given them her full attention for the next half-hour, then presented them to him and had to watch the pain in his expression that had to be at the thought of what their mother was missing.

She'd wanted to go to him and hold him close again, but it had been a moment that had belonged to Ryan and his children only and she'd gone into the next room and stood gazing out of the window until his voice had come from behind asking, 'So are we ready to leave, then?'

Feeling that she would be relieved when the day was over, she'd nodded and when the children had come trooping in and had stood one on either side of her she'd taken them by the hand and followed him out to the car.

The church was full of well-wishers as both Mollie and Jack were well respected in the area. Once Melissa had positioned the children behind the bride, who was holding Ryan's arm for support, the organist struck up the wedding march and the ceremony got under way, with her hurrying to find a seat near the front.

It was like the night of the ball, curious glances in her direction. Unless they'd had cause to meet her at the hospital for some reason, she was a stranger to most of them, but it would seem not so to Ryan and his children.

When she would have seated herself at a small table amongst others at the reception that followed, Ryan went to her and raising her to her feet took her to the top table to sit beside him and the children, with Mollie beaming her approval.

The bridal pair intended honeymooning in Italy for two weeks and were leaving on a flight later that evening. Ryan was taking leave due to him from the hospital to cover the time that Mollie would be away.

Fortunately she was intending to stay on in the role of his housekeeper but Melissa thought there would always be times when there was the problem of someone to be there for Rhianna and Martha when he was working. If things had been different they could have shared those kinds of responsibilities between the two of them, but he hadn't wanted to let her into his cloistered life.

No point in wishing for the moon. She had made her decision to leave behind the feeling of being surplus to Ryan's requirements, and soon would have to decide what direction to take for yet another new beginning.

CHAPTER TEN

IT WAS LATE afternoon when they arrived home from the wedding and as Melissa wished the children goodbye, with a promise to see them the next day when Santa had been, the evening stretched ahead like an empty void.

She had no wish for a continuation of the day's awkwardness between Ryan and herself, and when he'd asked her what she had planned for the evening she'd told him hurriedly that she was meeting friends in the town.

He'd eyed her dubiously and explained that he would be spending the time preparing for the Christmas dinner that he was going to cook for them the next day. She was welcome to join him if she wanted to, and if she didn't and still persisted in going into town, she must be sure to get a taxi home and to ring him if she had any problems.

'I won't be doing that,' she protested hotly, 'expecting you to leave the children on my account.'

'I wouldn't be. I would bring them with me.'

'Yes, well, that isn't going to happen because I won't need you,' she said firmly.

Under any other circumstances she would have been more than willing to be with him in the kitchen, but the thought of being alone with Ryan for any length of time, as the children would be in bed early on such a night, was not to be faced.

Never once had he said he was sorry she was leaving, that he wanted her to stay, and if that wasn't a guideline for her own attitude towards *him*, *she* didn't know what was.

He was using her fondness for his children as a lever to achieve his own ends and she couldn't believe it of him. Once Christmas was over she would be on the outside of his life, as she'd been before. Without further comment she left him to his preparations for a meal that she felt would choke her.

Melissa hadn't had any intention of going into town for Christmas Eve, but her quick-as-a-flash excuse for not spending any more time that day with Ryan was making her feel that she had to justify what she'd told him, and she *had* been invited to join a group from the hospital who were intending to wine and dine the evening away in one of the local restaurants, so maybe she would take them up on it and try to chase away the blues that way.

It didn't work. She kept thinking of Ryan and his ever-changing moods. How he hadn't wanted her to come into town, and how he'd fussed about her getting home safely, *and the rest*. Had it been that he'd felt guilty because it was because of him that she was leaving Heatherdale?

She excused herself from the gathering early and did as he had ordered and used a taxi for the return journey. She would have called to let him know she was home except that his house was in darkness and she didn't want to disturb him.

She wouldn't have done. The house lights had fused when he'd plugged the tree in and he'd been searching for a torch when the taxi had stopped in front, but he'd seen its headlamps shining in the darkness and had thought thankfully that she was back.

He had a gift for Melissa, a Christmas surprise that he would give her in the morning and hope it would last for ever, and with the lights back on, the turkey cooking slowly, and all the trimmings that went with it sorted, he went to bed, and in what seemed like no time at all the children were tugging at him to get up because Santa had been.

They'd had their breakfast and were upstairs surrounded by all the things they'd asked for when he phoned Melissa. The lights were on in the house next door, smoke was curling out of the chimney, and it was now a reasonable hour to get in touch.

When she answered he said, 'Merry Christmas. Are you up and about?'

'Er, yes' was the reply. 'I'll be over shortly. I've got presents for you and the children.' Ryan would hardly be jumping for joy when he opened his to find a book token!

'Fine,' he said, 'but I'm not phoning about anything like that. It's to tell you that the guy who is buying your house is outside and he wants a word. I think he wants to introduce himself.'

'What?' she gasped. 'It's Christmas Day, for heaven's sake.'

'So goodwill to all men, yes?'

'Mmm, I suppose so. Where exactly is he?'

'Waiting on the drive.'

'All right, thanks for letting me know.' She went to greet the stranger at her door.

But when she opened it there was only Ryan there, and looking around her she questioned, 'So where is he?'

'Quite close' was the reply. 'In fact, very close. If you reach out you can touch him.'

'What? You?' she gasped, holding on to the doorpost. 'How? Why? What do you want with two houses?'

'To make them into a home for the four of us, Melissa. Did you really think that I was going to let you go out of my life now that I've found you? Now, is it all right if I step inside? I don't want to propose to you on the doorstep,' he said gently.

Speechless, Melissa stepped aside to let Ryan in.

'When you appeared in my life on a dark autumn night, distraught and dishevelled, the last thing I felt like was having to offer you food and find you accommodation. It had been a long, busy day at the hospital and all I wanted was to enjoy the meal that Mollie had cooked and then spend some special time with my children. But for ever kind and thoughtful about others, Mollie wanted to see you fed and warm before I took you to find a hotel, and I remember that I agreed to whatever she suggested with a reluctance that must have been obvious to you.

'I little knew that I would fall in love with the stranger at my door and that the way of life I had set for myself was going to be thrown into chaos. It has taken the thought of losing you to bring me to my senses, and I'm buying your house for two reasons.

'One, because we owe it to your grandmother. Because of her generosity in leaving it to you, you came into my life, and because our two houses made into one will be delightful when the builders have finished with them. So will you marry me, Melissa? Will you let me take you next door to tell the children that their wish has been granted, that Santa has sent them a mummy who will love them always?'

'Yes,' she breathed. 'It is all I've ever wanted for weeks, to be your wife, but why buy my house when it's yours for the asking to be part of our home?'

'Because once you were rich and now are poor,' he said laughingly. 'And now you will be rich again.'

'Having you and the children will be all the riches I need,' she said softly.

'Yes, I know,' he agreed, 'but nevertheless…'

With his arms around her they went to tell Rhianna and Martha their good news, and when they ran to her and held her close Melissa hoped that somewhere not far away their mother would be giving the four of them her blessing.

'Can we phone Mollie and tell her that we're going to have a mummy?' Martha cried

'Yes, but just a quick call,' Ryan warned, as he and Melissa went to check that the food he'd prepared was cooking satisfactorily.

* * *

In a hotel in Italy, the bride of the day before was enjoying a late breakfast with her new husband when her mobile phone rang, and when she'd listened to what the childish voices had to say she cried joyfully, 'Jack! There's going to be another wedding!'

EPILOGUE

WINTER HAD PASSED. It was spring, with new life opening
up in the parks and gardens of the famous market town
and with the outline of the moors that surrounded it taking on a softer green than the bleak shades of winter.

The building work was finished, the two houses had
been made into one, and the result was a gracious family home that was going to be a joy to live in.

Since Melissa had come to live with them, Ryan's
bed was no longer the loneliest place on earth. When
he held her close in the night there was always the joy
of knowing that she was his, always would be, and the
spring wedding that they were planning would tell the
world that it was so.

The children were on cloud nine because they were
going to be bridesmaids again, this time in summery
dresses with pretty posies. Julian, now recovered from
his injuries, was going to be Ryan's best man, and Jack
Smethurst would be giving Melissa away.

Everyone who wasn't on duty at the hospital was
there to celebrate the wedding of two of its doctors, and
the old stone church near the town houses was full of
well-wishers, amongst them grateful parents of patients.

When Melissa arrived in a white wedding gown that was stunning in its simplicity, carrying a small ivory cross that had been her mother's and with two young bridesmaids carrying her train, it felt as if she'd been waiting for this day all her life.

When she stopped for a second, framed in the doorway of the church as the organist began to play the music that announced the arrival of the bride, Ryan turned from his position in front of the altar and as their glances met it was there, the love that each of them had for the other, and like a blessing the scent of roses, Beth's favourite flowers, was all around them.

The photographs had been taken in front of the church and as the guests began to make their way to the reception at an hotel in the town, Melissa and Ryan left the children with Mollie and Jack for a few moments and went into the graveyard. She laid the small white cross she had carried beside the roses that always graced the grave in the quiet corner then, hand in hand, they went to that other grave where Ryan placed the carnation he had worn on its weathered but immaculate surface and after a few moments in the silence that was all around them they returned to where the future was waiting.

* * * * *

THE MOTHERHOOD MIX-UP

BY
JENNIFER TAYLOR

MILLS & BOON

First published in Great Britain 2013
by Mills & Boon, an imprint of Harlequin (UK) Limited.
Harlequin (UK) Limited, Eton House, 18-24 Paradise Road,
Richmond, Surrey TW9 1SR

© Jennifer Taylor 2013

ISBN: 978 0 263 89917 7

Printed and bound in Spain
by Blackprint CPI, Barcelona

Jennifer Taylor lives in the north-west of England, in a small village surrounded by some really beautiful countryside. She has written for several different Mills & Boon® series in the past, but it wasn't until she read her first Medical Romance™ that she truly found her niche. She was so captivated by these heart-warming stories that she set out to write them herself! When she's not writing, or doing research for her latest book, Jennifer's hobbies include reading, gardening, travel, and chatting to friends both on and off-line. She is always delighted to hear from readers, so do visit her website at www.jennifer-taylor.com

Recent titles by the same author:

THE SON THAT CHANGED HIS LIFE†
THE FAMILY WHO MADE HIM WHOLE†
GINA'S LITTLE SECRET
SMALL TOWN MARRIAGE MIRACLE
THE MIDWIFE'S CHRISTMAS MIRACLE
THE DOCTOR'S BABY BOMBSHELL*
THE GP'S MEANT-TO-BE BRIDE*
MARRYING THE RUNAWAY BRIDE*
THE SURGEON'S FATHERHOOD SURPRISE**

†*Bride's Bay Surgery*
**Dalverston Weddings*
***Brides of Penhally Bay*

**These books are also available in eBook format
from www.millsandboon.co.uk**

In memory of Jean and Bob Taylor,
the best parents anyone could have had.

CHAPTER ONE

'DR KHAPUR WILL see you now, Mrs Adams.'

'Thank you.'

Mia Adams stood up and followed the receptionist along the corridor. It had been almost six years since she'd last visited the fertility clinic. Although she had intended to come back after Harry was born, to thank everyone, somehow she had never got round to it. The journey into central London from Kent had seemed too daunting with a baby in tow, plus there'd been Chris to consider.

Although Chris had coped remarkably well with the problems of living his life as a paraplegic, there had been times when he had needed that extra bit of care and attention. Consequently, the months had slipped past before she had realised it. It was doubtful if she would ever have come back, in fact, if she hadn't received that letter.

Mia frowned, wondering once again why Dr Khapur had contacted her. Harry was five now and she couldn't understand why the consultant wanted to see her. It wasn't as if she was hoping to have another child; Chris's death two years ago had ruled out that possibility. So what did Dr Khapur want? Had something happened? Something to do with Harry?

Mia's stomach lurched at the thought. It was an effort to appear composed as the receptionist ushered her into an elegantly appointed office. Dr Khapur rose from his seat, smiling warmly as he came around the desk.

'Mrs Adams! Thank you so much for coming. Please…take a seat, my dear.'

The elderly doctor guided her towards a group of comfortable chairs near the window and Mia felt her unease intensify. Whenever she had visited the clinic in the past, she had sat at one side of that huge mahogany desk and Dr Khapur had sat at the other. Maybe it was silly but this new approach made her feel more nervous than ever so that her hands were shaking as she placed her bag on the floor.

'Did you have a good journey?' Dr Khapur asked solicitously as he sat down. He smiled at her but Mia detected a certain strain about his expression that heightened her feeling that something wasn't right. It was an effort to reply calmly when her nerves seemed to be stretched to breaking point.

'Fine, thank you, Doctor. Chris and I moved to London a few years ago, so I didn't have as far to travel.'

'Ah, I see. Good. Good.'

He rubbed his hands together and Mia had the distinct impression that he was finding it difficult to decide how to continue. She leant forward, knowing that she had to get to the bottom of what was going on. If something was wrong, and if it had anything to do with Harry, she needed to know what it was.

'Dr Khapur, I….'

She got no further when the door suddenly opened. Mia looked round in surprise, frowning when she saw the tall, dark-haired man who had entered the room. Privacy was of the utmost importance to the clinic's clients and she couldn't understand how he had got past the receptionist. That Dr Khapur was less than pleased by the interruption was obvious from the way he jumped to his feet.

'Mr Forester, please! I really cannot allow you to come barging in like this.'

'Is this her?' The man ignored Dr Khapur as he turned to Mia and she shivered when she felt his cold grey eyes sweep over her. Colour rushed to her cheeks as she imagined what he would see. Medium height, medium build, mid-brown hair and regular features didn't add up to all that much in her opinion. Her eyes were her best feature, a pure emerald green that lit up her face when she was happy. However, as she was feeling far from happy at that moment she doubted they would do much to enhance the impression he formed of her.

She stood up, surprised that she should care one way or the other what he thought of her. She had no idea who he was even though it appeared he knew her.

'I'm sorry but what exactly is going on?' She looked away from that searching grey gaze and turned to the doctor. 'I think I deserve an explanation, Dr Khapur.'

'I…ehem…' Dr Khapur began unhappily.

'Of course you do. And if I'd had my way, you would have had that explanation months ago.' The man's voice was hard, edged with an anger that Mia didn't understand, although it still affected her.

'In that case, why don't you explain it all to me, starting with your name and why you're here?' She heard the tremor in her voice and knew that he must have heard it too but it was the least of her worries. She didn't care what he thought about her. She only cared about what he was going to say and if she was right to suspect that it had something to do with Harry.

'My name is Leo Forester.' His tone was still hard but the anger had disappeared now and been replaced by something that sounded very much like compassion. Mia shuddered. She had a feeling that Leo Forester wasn't a man given to feeling compassion very often. She was already steeling herself when he continued but there was no way she could have prepared herself for the shock of his next statement.

'The reason why I am here, Mrs Adams, is quite simple. I am your son's father.'

Leo could feel the tension that had gripped him ever since he had woken up that morning reach breaking point. Just for a second his vision blurred before he ruthlessly brought himself under control. This wasn't the time to weaken. He had to get this sorted out. It wasn't only his life that would be affected by the outcome of this meeting but Noah's as well.

The thought of his son was the boost he needed. Leo ignored the fact that Mia Adams's face had turned the colour of putty. Maybe he should have tried a gentler approach but at the end of the day it wouldn't change anything. He was her son's father even if she was going to find it very hard to accept that.

'If this is some kind of a joke,' she began, but he didn't give her a chance to finish.

'It isn't. Believe me, Mrs Adams, I wouldn't joke about a thing like this.' His tone was harsh and he saw the rest of the colour leach from her face and regretted his bluntness. For a man like him, who made a point of never regretting his actions, it came as a shock, an unpleasant one too. He couldn't afford to make allowances for Mia Adams's feelings or Noah could suffer.

He turned to Dr Kahpur, needing to get back onto a more solid footing. 'Mrs Adams and I need to talk. Is there a room we can use?'

'I'm sorry but I have no intention of going anywhere with you until I know what's going on and why you've made that ridiculous claim.'

Leo could still hear the tremor in Mia Adams's voice but it didn't disguise the steel it held as well. He realised with a start that even though she had suffered a massive shock, she wasn't simply going to accept what he had to say. A flicker of something akin to admiration rose inside him and he nodded, trying to hide his surprise. If he rarely regretted his actions then he was even less likely to form a favourable opinion of a person with such speed.

'Of course. Perhaps Dr Khapur would care to explain the situation to you.'

Leo sat down, waiting while the others resumed their seats. Mia Adams didn't look at him as she smoothed her skirt over her knees. She appeared completely composed as she waited for the elderly doctor to begin and Leo's admiration cranked itself up another notch or two. After dealing with Amanda and her constant histrionics, it was a pleasant change to meet a woman who didn't feel it necessary to create a scene to get her own way.

'This is all very difficult, my dear,' Dr Kahpur began. 'Nothing like it has ever happened before, you understand, so it's been extremely hard to know how to handle things. All I can say is that we shall do everything possible to put matters right.'

Leo forbore to say anything, although how Dr Khapur could make this situation right was beyond him. He waited in silence for the older man to continue, wishing he would get on with it. The sooner Mia Adams was in possession of the facts, the sooner they could decide what they were going to do.

'It would be a lot easier if you'd explain why this gentleman claims he is Harry's father.' Mia Adams's tone was firm. Leaning forward, she looked Dr Khapur straight in the eyes. 'I want to know the truth, Dr Khapur.'

'I… Yes, of course you do.'

Dr Khapur looked more uncomfortable than ever at being asked a direct question and Leo realised that they wouldn't get anywhere if he left it to him to explain what had happened. Time was of the essence and every wasted second was a second too long.

'It appears there was some kind of a mix-up,' he said shortly. He adopted his blandest expression when Mia Adams turned to look at him, the one he used when he needed to break particularly bad news to one of his patients. In his opinion, the absence of emotion helped people cope with even the worst prognosis.

The fact that he knew Mia Adams would consider this the worst thing that could have happened to her made his heart pang in sudden sympathy but he ruthlessly blanked it out. He wasn't interested in her feelings, he reminded himself. It was Noah who mattered, Noah and her child, Harry. His son.

A wave of emotion rose up inside him at the thought. Bearing in mind that he had spent his adult life divesting himself of any hint of emotion, it took him by surprise. It was an effort to continue when he felt so out of control.

'It seems that the embryos were implanted in the wrong women. My ex-wife received the embryo that had been created from your egg and your husband's sperm while you received ours. In short, Mrs Adams, Amanda gave birth to your son and you gave birth to ours.'

'No!' Mia Adams leapt to her feet. She glared at him, twin spots of colour burning in her cheeks. 'I have no idea why you're making up these ridiculous lies but I refuse to sit here and listen to anything else.'

She spun round on her heel, her back rigid as she strode to the door. Dr Khapur stood up as well but Leo didn't give him the chance to intervene as he went after her. Gripping hold of her wrist, he drew her to a halt, feeling a ripple of awareness run through him when he felt the delicacy of the bones beneath his encircling fingers. They felt as fragile as a bird's, so easily crushed that unconsciously he loosened his hold even though he didn't release her.

'I am not lying. Every word I've said is true.' He bent and looked into her eyes, feeling another frisson pass through him when he found himself suddenly enmeshed in that glittering emerald gaze. He had never seen eyes that colour before, he found himself thinking inconsequentially before he brought his mind back to more important matters.

'The child you gave birth to, Mrs Adams, is, in reality, my son. And now we need to decide what we're going to do about it.'

CHAPTER TWO

Mia sank down onto a chair, praying that she wouldn't pass out. Her head was spinning from a combination of shock and fear. It couldn't be true. Harry was *her* son; she knew he was! Maybe a mistake had been made but what proof was there that she'd been involved in the mix-up?

Oh, she could understand Leo Forester's desperation—who couldn't? To discover that the child he had believed to be his wasn't his biological child must have been a terrible shock. But there was no way that he was going to lay claim to Harry!

She looked round when the door opened, feeling her heart contract with fear when she saw Leo Forester come in. Dr Khapur had acceded to his request that they should be allowed some time on their own to talk and this time she hadn't objected. The sooner this was sorted out, the better.

'Mrs Rowlands is making us some coffee. It should be ready in a moment.'

He sat down opposite her, stretching out his long legs under the coffee table. Mia studied him in silence, wondering how it must feel to discover that everything you had believed to be true was no longer certain any more. She knew how she felt, yet there was little sign of the confusion she felt apparent on his face.

How old was he? she wondered suddenly. Late thirties? Older? His hair was very dark with only a few threads of silver shining through. It was expertly cut, too, the crisp dark waves clipped close to his well-shaped head. His features were strong and very masculine—a firm jaw and well-defined cheekbones giving him an aristocratic appearance that befitted his whole bearing. Leo Forester looked like a man who was used to being in charge, a man who rarely took account of other people's opinions. It wasn't the most comforting thought in the circumstances.

A knock on the door roused her from her reverie. Leo Forester got up to answer it, taking the tray from the receptionist and carrying it over to the table. Without bothering to ask, he poured them both coffee, pushing the sugar bowl and milk jug towards her before picking up his cup. Mia added a dash of milk to her coffee, although she didn't feel in the least like drinking it. However, it gave her something to do, a few extra minutes' grace before she had to tell Leo Forester that she was very sorry but he would have to look elsewhere for his missing child. Harry was hers, hers and Chris's, and nobody was going to take him away from her.

'Before we go any further, Mrs Adams, I want to show you something.' Leo Forester put down his cup then reached into his inside pocket and took out his wallet. Flipping it open, he passed it across the table. 'This is Noah.'

Mia reluctantly took the wallet from him and glanced

at the photograph, wishing that he hadn't shown it to her. It seemed wrong to build up his hopes, wrong and unnecessarily cruel. Maybe he did believe that ridiculous claim he'd made but she knew the truth, knew that Harry was her child…

Her breath caught as her eyes alighted on the solemn face of the little boy in the photograph. He had blond hair, so blond that it appeared more silver than gold. His eyes were blue, a deep dark blue framed by thick black lashes that matched the dark slash of his eyebrows and created a startling contrast to his fairness. Just as Chris's had done.

Mia felt the ground roll beneath her feet as she stared at the picture, at the small straight nose, at the determined little chin with that hint of a dimple in it. It was pure coincidence, of course. Maybe the child did look very like her late husband but it didn't prove that he was hers and Chris's child, as Leo Forester claimed.

'I take it from your expression that there's a resemblance between Noah and your husband?'

Leo Forester's voice betrayed very little of what he was feeling and Mia was grateful for that. She seemed to be awash with so many conflicting emotions that she couldn't have coped with his as well. She gave a tiny shrug, needing to hold onto what she *knew* to be the truth. Harry was her son, not this boy.

'Chris was very fair too,' she said quietly, passing the wallet back to him.

'I wondered who Noah favoured.' Leo Forester slid the wallet into his pocket and picked up his coffee cup. His hand was rock steady as he lifted it to his lips and all of a sudden Mia found herself resenting the fact that he could behave this way. Surely any normal person would be torn in two, wondering and worrying about this situation?

'The fact that your son happens to have similar colouring to my husband is hardly proof, Mr Forester.' Scorn dripped from her voice but if she'd hoped to sting him into a reaction she was disappointed. His expression didn't alter as he looked steadily at her over the rim of the cup.

'Of course not. It will need DNA tests to confirm it. I suggest we make arrangements to have them done as soon as possible.'

'I have no intention of allowing Harry to be tested!' She glared at him, feeling a wave of anger wash away the fear that had invaded her ever since he'd made that ridiculous claim. 'I'm very sorry for you, Mr Forester. I'm sure that in your shoes I would do everything possible to get to the bottom of this matter. However, Harry isn't your son. He's mine. Mine and Chris's.'

'And if that is true then the DNA results will prove it.' He shrugged, his broad shoulders moving lightly under his perfectly tailored jacket. That he was a wealthy man wasn't in doubt and Mia felt a fresh rush of fear hit her. Leo Forester obviously had the means to pursue this if he chose. If he decided to take it to the courts, he would be able to hire the very best lawyers to make his case. Even though she was working, she had no hope of fighting him if it came to a lengthy legal battle. She simply didn't have the money. Perhaps it would be wiser to concede this point in case the fight became more desperate in the future?

The thought of what might happen in the future made

her inwardly tremble but she had learned at an early age to hide her feelings. She looked steadily back at him, wishing that she had followed her instincts and never agreed to visit the clinic. She'd had a bad feeling when that letter had arrived out of the blue, although not for a moment had she imagined that something like this would happen.

'If you're determined to go down that route then I shall agree to have Harry tested on one condition.'

'And that is?' Leo Forester raised a dark brow. His expression was as bland as ever but Mia could see a nerve tic in his jaw and realised, with a start, that he was nowhere near as composed as he was pretending to be. The thought was comforting for some reason and her tone softened.

'That Harry isn't told anything about this. He's only five and it will just confuse him if he's told that Chris might not be his daddy.'

'I have no intention of telling him or Noah anything until we get the results of the DNA tests.'

Leo Forester put his cup down with a clatter and Mia realised, with another start that he'd had to put it down because his hands were shaking. Maybe he did prefer to keep a rein on his emotions, but beneath that cool exterior there was definitely passion brewing. It made her wonder what would happen if he ever let himself go.

Mia pushed that thought aside. What Leo Forester did or didn't feel was of no consequence, except where it concerned Harry, of course. She needed to make it clear that any hopes he was harbouring about claiming her son as his own were never going to come to fruition.

'I shall arrange to have a DNA profile done on Harry.

Once I receive the results, I'll contact you. Obviously I'll need an address or telephone number where you can be reached.'

'I'll give you my card.' He took out his wallet again and pulled out an ivory-coloured card. He didn't hand it over immediately, however.

'It seems pointless you having to go to all the trouble of finding someone to carry out the DNA tests, Mrs Adams. Why don't you leave me to make the arrangements?'

'Thank you but I'd prefer to do it myself,' Mia said shortly, and he frowned.

'Because you don't trust me not to pull some sort of a stunt so that the results come back in my favour?'

Mia heard the irritation in his deep voice but it didn't bother her. There was too much at stake to worry about his finer feelings, if he really had any, of course. It was disappointing to wonder if she'd been wrong about him. Maybe what you saw was what you got and in this instance it appeared that the handsome Leo Forester was a very cold fish indeed.

'Yes.' She took the card off him, annoyed that she should waste even a second thinking about him. Leo Forester had come into her life uninvited and definitely unwelcome and the sooner she got rid of him, the better. 'I have no intention of allowing you to pull the wool over my eyes, Mr Forester. Whilst I feel very sorry for the plight you find yourself in, it really isn't my concern. The only person I'm interested in is my son.'

She stood up, picking up her bag and looping the strap over her shoulder. Leo Forester stood up as well and for a moment she thought he was going to stop her again when she tried to leave. However, in the event, he merely stepped aside so she could pass.

'Thank you,' Mia murmured politely. She made her way to the door, curbing the urge to run. She wouldn't give him the satisfaction of knowing how scared she felt, how fearful of the future. *Harry was her son.* She repeated the mantra as she reached for the handle, hoping it would help her maintain her control. For some reason it seemed important that she shouldn't let Leo Forester know how terrified she was.

'Aren't you forgetting something, Mrs Adams?'

Mia had actually opened the door when he spoke and she paused reluctantly, wondering if he had done it deliberately, almost let her escape before calling her back, like a cat playing with a mouse. She glanced round, smoothing her face into a carefully neutral expression. He might enjoy playing games but she had no intention of being party to them.

'I don't think so.' She shrugged. 'What else is there to say until the results of the DNA tests come back?'

'Obviously, I need an address or, at the very least, a phone number where I can contact you.'

'Why would you want to contact me?' Mia countered. 'You and I have nothing further to discuss, Mr Forester. As I'm sure the DNA results will prove.'

Mia walked out of the door, half expecting him to call her back again, but he didn't. She made her way along the corridor, shaking her head when Dr Khapur's secretary jumped up and told her that the doctor wanted to speak to her. She didn't want to speak to him. Not right now, anyway. At some point she would need an explanation as to why she'd been involved in this ridiculous affair but not right now. Right now all she wanted to do was go home and see Harry. *Her* son, not Leo Forester's.

Leo cursed himself as he strode along the corridor. He had made a complete and utter hash of things and ended up making an already difficult situation worse. Wrenching open the door, he stepped out into the street, wondering why he had allowed Mia Adams to get to him that way. He knew what had to be done; he should do because he'd gone over it enough times. However, all the careful arguments he'd rehearsed, the calm and rational statements he had planned, had simply melted away. He had taken one look at the fear on Mia Adam's face and bottled it. Hell!

There was a taxi dropping off a fare at the corner. Leo flagged it down and gave the driver the address of the hospital. He was due in Theatre at two and it was almost that now. The taxi dropped him off outside the main doors and he hurried inside, nodding briefly to the porter.

Although he divided his time between his private practice in Harley Street and his NHS commitments, he was well known at the hospital, if not well liked. He was a hard taskmaster and he knew that the members of his team admired rather than liked him. It had never worried him before but as he made his way up in the lift, he suddenly found himself wishing that he had a better rapport with the people he worked with. If he had taken the trouble to develop his social skills, maybe he would have had better luck convincing Mia Adams to trust him.

Leo's mouth compressed as he stepped out of the lift.
He wasn't given to such foolish thoughts normally and
it was irritating to be beset by them today. The sooner
he got himself in hand, the better. Mia Adams might
be hoping this situation would go away but he knew
it wasn't that simple. This was just the beginning and
there was going to be a lot more upset before this matter
was resolved. It wasn't only him and Mrs Adams who
would suffer either. There were two little boys whose
lives were going to have to change.

Mia was on duty the following morning. She took
Harry to the school's breakfast club and left him happily
demolishing a bowl of cereal then walked to the station.
It was almost three years since she had moved to London. Chris had been offered a job with a leading firm
of accountants and they had decided it was too good
an opportunity to miss. The fact that Chris had been
confined to a wheelchair following a climbing accident
in his twenties had severely restricted his job options;
however, the firm hadn't seen it as a problem.

Chris had loved the job and enjoyed every minute of
his working life. Mia knew that moving to the city had
been the right thing to do but she couldn't help wondering if she should move back to Kent at some point.
Harry would not only benefit from all the fresh air and
open spaces to play in, he'd be able to spend more time
with his grandparents. The downside, of course, was
that she would have to give up her job and she doubted
if she would find another that would allow her to spend
so much time with Harry.

As a senior sister, working as part of the bank of

nurses at The Princess Rose Hospital, she could pick her own hours. She had worked mornings when Harry had been at nursery so she could be home in time to collect him at lunchtime. Now that Harry had started school, she had increased her hours and was thinking about going full time soon—heaven knew they could do with the extra money. However, as it would mean Harry having to stay at the after-school club until she got home, she had decided to leave the decision until after Christmas. Harry would have settled into school by then and she'd feel happier about leaving him for longer.

The train was late as usual and she had to run to reach the hospital in time for her shift. Penny Morrison, who organised the bank nurses, grinned when Mia came panting into the office.

'Either you're in training for the next London Marathon or the train was late. My guess is that it's the second option.'

'You'd be right too.' Mia hung her coat in her locker then took a comb out of her bag and tidied her hair. 'I wish they'd invest in some new trains. I mean, they wouldn't break down as often if they weren't so old, would they?'

'Ah, but new trains cost money and nobody has any these days, or so they claim.'

Penny picked up the spreadsheet she used to sort out where everyone was working. There were fifteen bank nurses and they covered all the departments as and when they were needed. It was a system that worked well and had reduced the high costs of hiring agency nurses to provide cover.

'Right, you're down for Cardiology this week. The ward sister has sprained her ankle and she's off sick. You might end up there a bit longer, in fact.'

'Fine by me. I've not covered Cardiology before so it will be nice to do something different,' Mia agreed. 'Anything I should know beforehand?'

'Not really. Oh, apart from the fact that one of the consultants is a bit of a tartar so watch your back.' Penny rolled her eyes. 'Jackie was there a couple of weeks ago and she's refused to go back if he's on duty.'

'Heavens! He sounds a real sweetheart, I don't think.' Mia grimaced as she took her ID out of her bag and clipped it to the pocket of her navy uniform top. One of the other nurses arrived just then so she left Penny to deal with her and made her way to the third floor where the cardiology unit was situated. Everything looked very peaceful when she arrived and she grinned at the staff nurse who'd been holding the fort until she got there.

'Either all your patients are extremely well behaved or you've sedated them. Which is it?'

'Neither.' The staff nurse grimaced. 'They're simply too scared to kick up a fuss.'

Mia laughed. 'You don't look that scary to me.'

'Oh, it's not me who's terrified them into submission.' The younger woman looked over Mia's shoulder and groaned. 'Here's your culprit now. And that's my cue to beat a hasty retreat. Good luck. You'll need it!'

Mia looked round, the smile still lingering on her lips as she looked at the man walking towards her. He was tall with dark hair lightly threaded with silver and chiselled features...

All of a sudden the room started to whirl, spinning faster and faster until she felt quite giddy. What on earth was Leo Forester doing here?

CHAPTER THREE

'THESE NOTES ARE incomplete, Sister. Make sure the file is updated before I return for my afternoon round. I shouldn't need to remind you that it's your job to ensure that all the information I require is available.'

Leo handed the file to Mia Adams. He turned to the two new F1 students who had joined his team the previous week, ignoring the wary look that passed between them. Maybe he had been rather hard on Sister Adams but he wouldn't tolerate incompetence in any shape or form.

'Mrs Davies will be having bypass surgery tomorrow. What needs to be done beforehand to ensure the operation goes smoothly?' he demanded, ignoring the voice in his head that insisted he was being unreasonable. So what if Mia Adams had taken charge of the unit only that morning? As ward sister, it was her responsibility to ensure that everything was up to date. Far too many errors occurred because staff had omitted some vital piece of information.

The thought reminded him rather too pointedly of the error that had been made over Noah. Finding out that the child he had believed to be his son had no biological connection to him and Amanda had been a terrible shock and he still hadn't got over it. He loved Noah with all his heart and there was no way that he was prepared to give him up, but he still needed to find out the truth, prove that Mia's child—Harry—was his real son. After that, well, he had no idea what would happen. It all depended on what Mia Adams decided.

The thought that so much was hanging on her decision wasn't easy to accept. Leo was used to running his life his own way and rarely made allowances for other people. It was little wonder that his tone was brusquer than ever when the students failed to answer. He didn't want to be beholden to Mia Adams, but he might not have a choice.

'I fail to see why you're finding it so difficult to come up with an answer.' He pinned the unhappy pair with an icy stare. 'This is something you should have covered in your first year as students. If you can't answer a simple question like this then you are of no use to me.'

'May I suggest we take this into the office?'

Leo looked round in surprise when Mia Adams cut in. He wasn't used to being interrupted and didn't appreciate her making suggestions. He opened his mouth to tell her that in no uncertain terms but she had already moved away. Leo frowned as he watched his team follow her to the office. They hadn't waited for his permission; they had simply done her bidding and it was a shock, an unpleasant one, to realise that they preferred to follow her lead rather than his.

'I'll come back to see you later, Mrs Davies,' he said politely, noticing for the first time that the woman was trembling. She gave him a wan smile as he moved away from the bed and Leo found himself wondering what was wrong with her. She'd appeared perfectly composed when he had arrived but obviously something had upset her.

His mouth thinned as he strode towards the office. It was Mia Adams's fault, of course. Mrs Davies had picked up on the tension and reacted accordingly. Well, he intended to take Sister Adams to task and make sure she understood who was in charge before she upset any more of his patients.

'A word, please, Sister Adams,' he began as he entered the office.

'Just a moment, Mr Forester.' She barely glanced at him as she carried on issuing instructions to one of the nurses and Leo felt his temper leap up a couple more notches. He was the consultant and although he didn't consider himself to be next to God in the pecking order, he did expect to be treated with due respect.

'After you've sorted that out, Sally, can you take Mrs Davies a cup of tea? She's a bit upset so sit with her, will you? It will help to calm her down if she has someone to talk to.'

Mia smiled at the younger nurse, giving no sign that she was worried about keeping him waiting, and Leo had to clamp down on the urge he felt to do something drastic, like shake her. Bearing in mind that he wasn't a man given to violence on any level it was a surprise to find himself reacting this way. It was little wonder that he was caught flat-footed when she turned to him.

'There's something you wish to say to me, Mr Forester?'

Her tone was cool in the extreme and he saw several

members of his team glance at each other in amazement. Nobody spoke to him this way. Nobody queried his decisions or interrupted him either. Nobody had ever dared—until now. Leo's temper, which had been hovering just below boiling point, peaked and he glared at her.

'Yes. Let me make this clear, Sister Adams. When I am with a patient I don't expect to be interrupted. Do you understand?'

'Perfectly. However, I think it's only fair that I make my position clear too. The patients are my responsibility while they're on this unit. That means that if I notice that someone is in pain or upset I shall do something about it.' She paused, her emerald-green eyes meeting his across the desk, and if there was any hint of remorse in them Leo certainly couldn't see any sign of it. 'Mrs Davies was becoming increasingly distressed by the way you were speaking to your students. Naturally I took steps to resolve the matter.'

Mia held his gaze, wondering when the heavens were going to fall in on her. That Leo Forester was less than pleased by what she had said was obvious but she didn't care. Nobody should be allowed to speak to people the way he had spoken to those poor students. Maybe other folk were willing to put up with his bad temper but she wasn't, especially not after the havoc he had created in her life.

The claim he had made about Harry being his son had been on her mind constantly for the past twenty-four hours. Although she was sure it was a mistake, she couldn't quite rid herself of the thought, *what if*? What if he was right? What if Harry was his son and what if Noah was hers? What if the DNA tests proved it? Then what would happen? Her mind kept churning it all over but there were never any answers. How could there be? The situation was way beyond anything she'd had to deal with before. It made everything else that had happened in her life pale into insignificance. If Harry wasn't her son, she had no idea what she was going to do.

Thoughts flashed through her mind at the speed of light yet it felt as though a lifetime had passed when she focused on Leo Forester again. That he was furiously angry was obvious and she decided there and then that the only way to deal with him was by fighting fire with fire. Maybe it was wrong to allow their personal issues to spill over into work but she refused to bow down before him on any matter. Harry was her son. She was responsible for the patients on this unit; they were both unassailable facts.

'If you have a problem with the way I run this ward I suggest you take it up with the head of Nursing. I'm sure she will be happy to discuss any issues you care to raise.'

She picked up the file and walked around the desk, pausing when she came level with him. Even though several inches separated them she could feel the power of his anger like a living force and inwardly shuddered. Leo Forester would make a very bad enemy. It was a scary thought in view of what had happened.

'Please feel free to use my office, Mr Forester. I shall make sure you aren't interrupted.'

Mia swept out of the door, half expecting him to call her back, but surprisingly he didn't. She made her way to the nursing station and logged into the patients' records. Leo Forester was right: there was something missing from Anthea Davies's notes. The woman had had an angiogram the previous week and the results needed to be added to her file. Mia made the necessary changes and printed out a fresh sheet and placed it in the file. Contrary to what Leo Forester thought, she was always thorough, always liked to be prepared to prevent any mistakes occurring.

She sighed as she went over to the cabinet and filed the notes in their rightful place. If only the staff at the fertility clinic had been as thorough she and Leo Forester would not be having to face such a potentially life-changing situation.

Leo was tied up in Theatre for the rest of the morning. However, as soon as he'd finished he changed back into his clothes and headed for the cardiology unit. Whilst he hadn't been prepared to make matters worse by causing a scene, he had no intention of letting Mia get away with treating him that way. Maybe they did have issues, issues that none of their colleagues knew about, but he wasn't going to let her make a laughing stock of him.

She was in the men's section of the unit when he arrived, talking to one of his patients, a young man called David Rimmer who had a long history of heart problems. David had been born with several holes in his heart and had been in and out of hospital over the past twenty-two years. Recently, he had started to suffer from cardiac arrhythmia—an abnormal and rapid heartbeat—and he would be having cardioversion that afternoon. His heart would be stopped before an electric current was passed through it, hopefully shocking it back into its proper rhythm. Although Leo knew that David must be in a lot of discomfort, he grinned when he saw Leo approaching.

'Seems you've met your match at last, eh, Doc? The buzz on the ward is that Mia gave you a real rollicking this morning. I only wish I'd been there to see it!'

Leo summoned a smile, not wanting the younger man to think he was at all put out to learn that he was the subject of gossip. 'You shouldn't believe everything you hear, David. It's not always true.'

David laughed. 'You would say that! Still, it's nice to know that you're human after all. It's done wonders for your image.'

Leo frowned. How on earth could his run-in with Mia have improved his image? He glanced around the unit, feeling his surprise intensify when several patients smiled at him. Normally, he found that people were rather reserved around him, but not today. As he looked at the friendly faces turned towards him, he felt a sudden warmth envelop him. It was rather nice to be on the receiving end of smiles for once.

He cleared his throat, refusing to get carried away by such a ridiculous notion. He much preferred it that his patients should value him for his skills as a surgeon rather than as a potential friend. 'I wonder if I might have a word with you, Sister?' he said politely. Maybe he wasn't out to win friends but there didn't seem any harm in observing the niceties.

'Of course.' Mia's tone was icily polite. She turned to the younger man and Leo couldn't help feeling the tiniest bit irked when he heard the warmth in her voice as she wished David good luck. Obviously, *he* didn't rate that level of concern.

The thought was irritating, although Leo was very aware that he was behaving completely out of character. Normally, he wouldn't have cared a jot how people addressed him, as long as they weren't rude, of course. Nevertheless, Mia's distant approach stung. For a second he found himself wondering how it would feel if she addressed him with genuine affection in her voice before he dismissed the idea. It was never going to happen, not after the havoc he was about to create in her life.

He led the way into the office and closed the door. He didn't want any interruptions, nothing and nobody to throw him off course. Maybe they were facing a very difficult situation but he needed to lay down some ground rules. Mia didn't look at him as she walked around the desk and sat down. She appeared perfectly composed but Leo sensed her inner turmoil and for some reason the harsh words he'd been going to say seemed wrong. This was as stressful for her as it was for him; maybe he could afford to lighten up a little.

'Before you say anything I want to apologise. I should never have spoken to you like that this morning.'

The apology caught him on the hop. Leo hadn't expected it and found himself struggling to reply. 'No, you shouldn't,' he said more sharply than he'd intended.

She gave a little shrug, her slender shoulders rising and falling beneath her navy cotton uniform, and he felt a flash of awareness shoot through him. For the first time since they'd met, he *really* looked at her, deliberately taking stock instead of simply forming an overall impression.

Her features were neat and regular: a firm little chin;
a short straight nose; softly rounded cheeks. Her skin
was very pale, almost translucent in the harsh glare of
the fluorescent light overhead. Her hair was a soft mid-
brown, caught neatly back from her face with a plain
black clip. Her eyes were her best feature, a pure emerald green that seemed to glitter with an inner fire that
fascinated him. Some people might have described Mia
Adams as ordinary but not him, he decided. Not when
he looked into those incredible eyes.

Leo took a deep breath, used it to shore up his world,
a world that seemed to be falling apart around him.
First there'd been the shock of discovering that Noah
wasn't his child and now this. He couldn't be attracted
to Mia Adams; he wouldn't allow himself to be! However, as he looked at that ordinary little face and those
extraordinary eyes staring back at him, he realised that
he might not have a choice. There was something about
her that intrigued him, and it had nothing to do with the
fact that she had given birth to his son.

Mia bit her lip, wishing that Leo Forrester would say
something. He was staring at her with the oddest expression on his face...

He suddenly spun round on his heel and strode out
of the room, leaving her staring after him in confusion. She hadn't expected him to let her off so lightly.
Maybe she had apologised, and meant it too, but she'd
been sure he would give her a dressing down. He'd have
been perfectly within his rights to do so because she
had overstepped the mark that morning.

Normally, she wouldn't have dreamt of speaking to

a consultant that way. But she'd not even tried to hold
back as she had told him what she thought. Maybe this
situation was unusual but she would be extremely lucky
if he didn't make a formal complaint about her and
heaven only knew what would happen then. Staff had
been sacked for less and the thought of losing her job
was worrying. She would need every penny she could
earn if it came to a legal battle over Harry.

Somehow Mia got through the rest of the morning
and did the hand-over. It was after two p.m. when she
collected her coat from the staffroom. Penny was at her
desk; she looked up and grinned when Mia went in.

'Well done, you! I hear you sent the redoubtable Leo
Forester away with a flea in his ear.'

'Don't!' Mia grimaced as she shrugged on her coat.
'I suppose it's all round the hospital?'

'Of course. Suffice to say that most folk consider
you to be a real heroine. Leo Forester isn't exactly top
of everyone's Christmas card list,' Penny added dryly.

'I really shouldn't have said what I did,' Mia admitted. 'It was a stupid thing to do.'

'You're only human, love. Which is more than I can
say for the handsome Leo. Heaven only knows how he
ever became a father. Oh, he's gorgeous looking and everything, but he's so *cold*. I mean, can you imagine him
letting go enough to actually make love to a woman?'

Mia felt a tide of heat sweep up her face. She bent
down to retrieve her bag from the locker, not wanting
Penny to witness her reaction to the question. Maybe
Penny couldn't imagine it but she could. Only too well.

Fortunately the phone rang so she was saved from
having to reply. Mia mouthed 'Goodbye' and left hur-

riedly. If the trains were running on time, she should be home just in time to collect Harry from school. She headed out of the main doors, pulling up the hood of her coat when she discovered it was raining. Afternoon visiting was under way and there were cars coming and going from all directions. She paused to allow an expensive sports car to pass through the gates ahead of her, sighing when it stopped and the passenger window rolled down. No doubt someone was going to ask her if she knew where they could park.

'Get in.'

Mia jumped when a deep voice barked out the command. Bending, she peered into the car, feeling her heart leap when she saw Leo Forester behind the wheel. His expression was as bland as ever but she could see a spark of something in his eyes that warned her it would be a mistake to argue with him. Opening the door, she slid into the seat, buckling the seat belt as he pulled out of the gates. They drove in silence for several minutes before he spoke.

'I think it would be best if we agreed to forget what happened today. Neither of us expected to find ourselves working together, but as there's nothing we can do about it, we'll just have to get on with it.'

Mia felt a rush of relief flood through her. 'You don't intend to make a complaint about me, then?'

'Of course not.'

He sounded so surprised that she grimaced. 'I thought you might, that's all.'

'Well, you can stop worrying. I won't be making any complaints, not unless you do it again, of course. I don't think my ego could take another battering.'

The hint of laughter in his voice was so unexpected that Mia stared at him. 'I was sure you'd want to teach me a lesson.'

'I probably would have done if circumstances had been different.' His grey eyes met hers for a second before he returned his attention to the road but it was long enough to make Mia's heart race.

She took a deep breath, calling herself every kind of a fool. Leo wasn't interested in her, not the person she was. He was only interested in Harry. She had to remember that and not allow herself be duped into thinking that he cared about her feelings any more than she must care about his. It was the children who mattered, Harry and his son Noah. And his next words confirmed that.

'I assume that you're going to collect your son from school?' He drew up at the traffic lights and turned to look at her. Mia steeled herself when she saw how solemn he looked. She had a feeling that she wasn't going to like what he had to say.

'Yes, I am. Why?'

'Because I'd like to ask a favour of you.' His eyes held hers fast and for some reason she found that she couldn't look away. 'May I go with you, Mia? And meet Harry?'

CHAPTER FOUR

ONCE, JUST BEFORE he had gone off to university, Leo had made a parachute jump. All his friends had been keen to try it and he'd gone along with them. In the event, most of them had chickened out so there'd been just two of them in the plane and he'd been the first to jump. As he had stood in the doorway, watching the ground rushing past below, he had felt his stomach sink with a mixture of excitement and fear. Although he had never jumped again, he remembered the feeling quite clearly. It was exactly how he felt as he waited to meet Mia's son, scared and elated because he was about to leap into the unknown.

'There he is.'

Mia touched him on the arm and Leo flinched. He looked over to where she was pointing but he couldn't pick out one child from another. There seemed to be a sea of small excited faces staring back at him…

Leo's breath caught as his eyes alighted on a sturdy little boy with dark brown hair standing up in spikes around his head. It had to be Harry; he just knew it was! Even though he would have dismissed the idea that his genes had somehow recognised those of his son if any-one had suggested it, he knew it was true.

Anyway, the boy had his nose as well as his hair. He had his chin too *and* his cheekbones, he realised in astonishment. In fact, the resemblance was so marked that he couldn't understand why Mia hadn't noticed it. Surely she could see how alike they were, he thought as she brought the child over to meet him?

'Harry, this is Leo. He's a doctor and he works at the hospital. He very kindly gave me a lift here so I wouldn't be late.'

Leo had to hand it to her. Even though she must be finding it extremely difficult, there was no hint of un-certainty in her voice as she made the introductions. Her only concern was for her son and his admiration for her increased tenfold, especially when he found himself comparing the way she behaved to the way Amanda would have reacted.

The thought of the scene his ex-wife would have cre-ated was very hard to swallow and his mouth thinned with displeasure. Harry took one look at his grim ex-pression and scooted behind his mother's legs. Leo took a deep breath, cursing himself for allowing thoughts of Amanda to spoil the moment. Amanda had caused enough damage without him allowing her to ruin this too.

'Hello, Harry. It's nice to meet you.' Leo fixed a smile to his mouth but Harry obviously wasn't con-vinced it was genuine. He shrank away when Leo held out his hand.

'He'll come round,' Mia said quietly. 'Just give him a moment.'

She led Harry to the gate, leaving Leo to follow. There were a lot of parents milling about and they soon disappeared from view. Leo experienced a moment of panic as he peered over the crowd because he still had no idea where she lived. Maybe it was selfish but he needed a few more minutes with Harry, a bit more time to get to know his son.

The words seemed to dance in neon-bright letters before his eyes. Harry was his son; he was more certain than ever it was true. But where did that leave Noah? He loved Noah with an intensity he had never believed himself capable of feeling. From the moment he had been handed the wrinkled, bloodied little bundle in the delivery room, he had known that he would lay down his life to protect him. Amanda had got over her longing for a child by then and hadn't even wanted to look at the miracle they had created, but he had been entranced, thrilled, enthralled.

When Amanda had decided after six months of motherhood that it wasn't for her, Leo hadn't argued and he certainly hadn't tried to stop her leaving. He had never actually loved her but she had been sophisticated and worldly and had suited his requirements, as he had suited hers.

Their parting had been amicable enough and he'd been relieved that he'd been left, both physically and metaphorically, holding the baby. It had meant he could bring up Noah the way he wanted, make sure Noah enjoyed a far happier childhood than he'd had. If only Amanda had stayed away none of this would have happened.

The crowd parted and he spotted Mia and Harry

standing by the gates. He hurried to join them, seeing the way the child shrank back as he approached. It grieved him that he had made such a bad impression on the boy and he promised himself that he would do everything possible to rectify it. If he was to be part of Harry's life he wanted the child to feel comfortable around him.

'I'll run you home,' he said, refusing to dwell on the thought that he might not get the chance to play daddy to his son. It all depended on what Mia decided and as he had no idea what that would be, he couldn't go counting his proverbial chickens. Unlocking the car, he flipped forward the passenger seat so Harry could climb into the back. It was a tight squeeze and Leo realised not for the first time that he would have to buy something more suitable. Maybe he did love his car but with two children to consider now, it was hardly the most suitable of vehicles.

Mia made sure that Harry's belt was buckled then slid into the passenger seat. Leo closed the door and went round to the driver's side. He started the engine then glanced at her, seeing the strain that had etched tiny grooves at the sides of her mouth. His hands clenched on the steering wheel because the urge to reach out and smooth them away was almost too strong to resist. However, he had to resist it, had to resist doing anything that might alienate her.

'Where to?' he asked instead, sounding brusque and cold when he had meant to sound warm and approachable for Harry's benefit.

'Straight down the road and left at the junction.'

She glanced over her shoulder and smiled at Harry

and Leo saw the little boy's face immediately brighten as he checked the rear-view mirror before pulling out. That there was a deep and loving bond between the pair was obvious and he found himself wishing with all his heart that Noah could have had that sort of a relationship with Amanda. The problem was that Amanda put herself and her needs first every time. Noah came way down her list of priorities, somewhere below the next designer handbag she coveted or the next exotic holiday.

Leo could feel his mouth tightening again and fought to control it. If he was to win Harry round, he not only needed Mia's co-operation but a major re-think about his own behaviour. He sighed. He had realised from the moment he had discovered that Noah wasn't his biological child that his life was going to undergo a massive upheaval, but only now did he understand how much *he* was going to have to change.

'It's the house with the red door…just there on the left. Yes, that's it.'

Mia gathered up her bag, trying to control the urge to leap out of the car. She wasn't sure why she had agreed to let Leo meet Harry but it had been a mistake. She glanced round, seeing the worry on her son's face. Although Harry was a happy and loving little boy, like most children his age he hated unexpected changes to his routine. Being ferried home by a stranger, even in such a luxurious vehicle as this, was obviously troubling him.

'Thank you again for the lift,' she said politely, turning to Leo. Although she was eager to get Harry into the house, there was no way that she was going to be rude. She summoned a smile when Leo looked at her. 'I hope we haven't taken you too far out of your way.'

'Not at all.' He shrugged. 'I live in Primrose Hill so it's only a short drive from here.'

A short drive maybe, but there was a massive difference in property prices, Mia thought wryly, glancing at the neat little terraced house they were parked in front of. She hurriedly opened the car door, not wanting to go down that route. Continually worrying if Leo intended to use his extensive resources to lay claim to Harry was counterproductive. She got out of the car then turned to unlatch the seat so Harry could get out, frowning when she found herself fumbling with the unfamiliar mechanism.

'Let me do it.'

Leo gently moved her aside and tipped the seat forward. He offered Harry his hand but the child ignored him. Jumping out of the car, he ran up the path to the house and stood there with his back towards them. Mia sighed softly.

'Harry hates it when his routine is changed. He prefers it when he knows exactly what is going to happen and when.'

'It might have helped if I'd made a better impression,' Leo observed, and Mia frowned when she heard the regret in his voice. He hadn't struck her as a man who ever regretted his actions; he came across as far too confident for that. However, it appeared she may have been wrong.

It was worrying to think that she might have misjudged him. Mia cleared her throat, not wanting him to guess how unnerved she felt. 'Children are highly susceptible to people's moods and Harry has become even more sensitive since Chris died. He was only three when it happened so he didn't really understand what was going on, but he saw how upset I was and it made a big impression on him.'

'I see.' Leo frowned. 'I didn't know that you'd lost your husband. I'm very sorry.'

'Thank you.' Mia felt a lump come to her throat when she heard the sympathy in his voice. Although she had come to terms with Chris's death, it touched her that Leo should offer his condolences and mean them too.

'Was it an accident? He couldn't have been very old, I imagine.'

'Indirectly, yes, it was.' She took a quick breath, knowing that she couldn't afford to let his response influence her. Until she was sure that she could trust him with regard to Harry, she needed to be objective.

'Chris was injured in a climbing accident while he was at university. He suffered serious spinal damage and was unable to walk afterwards.' She shrugged, aware of how hard it was going to be to remain dispassionate. Leo wasn't the sort of man one could ignore. 'As you know, being confined to a wheelchair makes people more susceptible to certain conditions and sadly that's what happened with Chris.'

'I'm sorry,' he repeated. 'It must have been a very difficult time for you.'

Mia inclined her head, deciding it was safer not to pursue the matter. Talking about Chris's death always upset her and she couldn't afford to allow her emotions to get the better of her. She quickly changed the subject to one that seemed more fitting.

'I have the address of a lab that does DNA testing. I'll collect the samples tonight and post them off first thing tomorrow morning. I should have the results back by the end of the week.'

'Will there be a problem about providing a sample of your husband's DNA?' he queried, frowning.

'No.' Mia didn't elaborate. She didn't want to explain why she had kept Chris's hairbrush. It was the last link she had to him, the only thing left of the man who had given her so much; however, there was no way she intended to explain that to Leo. She forced a smile to her lips, hating the fact that she felt so emotional. It wasn't just thinking about Chris—it was everything else, Harry and Noah and what would happen if it turned out that she and Leo really did have the wrong children.

'Anyway, I mustn't keep you. You must be anxious to get home,' she said, blanking out the thought. Of course she had the right child! Harry was her son and he couldn't be anyone else's. As the DNA results would prove. She held out her hand, preferring to end the meeting on a note of formality. 'Thank you again for driving us home.'

'It was my pleasure.'

His hand enveloped hers and Mia felt a rush of heat invade her when she felt the strength of his fingers close around hers. She quickly withdrew her hand and hurried up the path. She heard the car start up but she didn't look round. She didn't want to think about Leo Forester any more that day. She just wanted to go inside the house and get on with the evening. She and Harry had a set routine and she intended to stick to it—tea, playtime, bath, story, bed. If she stuck to it her life would feel normal but if she deviated in any way then who knew what could happen.

Mia bit her lip. There was one change to their routine she would have to make. She had promised to collect the DNA samples and she couldn't break her word even if she wanted to. What would happen if the tests proved that Harry wasn't her son? she wondered sickly. How would she cope with having her whole world torn apart?

Having a child of her own had always been her dream. She had been taken into care when her own mother had been unable to cope with looking after her. Her father had been well off the scene by then. Mia had never met him and didn't even know his name so she had spent her childhood being shunted from one foster-home to another.

She had longed for someone to love and care for her, but it hadn't happened. Her mother had refused to allow her to be put up for adoption so Mia had had to make do with temporary placements. Some had been good, others not so good, but the worst thing was that none of them had been permanent.

She had grown up longing for a home and a family of her own, although she had been very choosy about who she had gone out with. She hadn't intended to make the same mistakes her mother had made and had turned down more dates than she had accepted. She had earned herself a reputation for being very stand-offish, in fact, and that in turn had led to the incident that still haunted her.

When the new registrar on the spinal unit where she had worked had invited her out, she had refused at first.

Although Steve Parker had seemed pleasant enough, Mia hadn't been sure if it would be wise to go out with him. Steve was a bit of flirt and she had had no intention of becoming another notch on his bedpost. However, he had persisted and in the end he had worn her down.

They had gone out together several times and Mia had found herself enjoying his company. Steve had been fun and attentive and it had felt good to be on the receiving end of his compliments and feel special. Although she had never slept with a man before, she'd realised that she wanted to sleep with Steve so when he had suggested they should spend the night together, she'd agreed.

It was a complete and utter disaster. Steve was so rough and insensitive, making no allowance for the fact that it was her first time. Mia couldn't wait for it to be over and left as soon as she could. She tried to write it off to experience but it wasn't possible, not after she found out that Steve had been spreading stories about her, claiming that she was frigid and that any man foolish enough to get her into bed would regret it. However, the final humiliation came when she learned that he'd also claimed he had only slept with her to win a bet and that he was sorry he had bothered. As he'd put it, it would have been better if he'd forfeited the money!

Mia was mortified and swore she would never allow anything like it to happen again. She never went out on a date after that and might never have seen her dreams come true if Chris hadn't been admitted to the spinal unit. She nursed him back to health, sat with him while he struggled to come to terms with what had happened, and grew to love him for his humour and his courage.

When he asked her to marry him, she accepted immediately, sure that it was the right decision. And when she had Harry, she knew that she had everything she had ever wanted.

Now it appeared that nothing was certain any more. All she knew was that if she lost Harry, her life would be meaningless.

By the time Friday rolled around, Leo felt as though he was walking on a tightrope. Mia had promised that the DNA results would be back by the end of the week and they should arrive that day. His stomach was churning as he made his way to Theatre because the thought of what they would reveal was mind-blowing. If they proved that Harry was his son, what was he going to do?

He scrubbed up, nodding his thanks when the scrub nurse helped him on with his gown. His team was waiting for him, standing silently in Theatre as he preferred them to do. Some surgeons liked to listen to music while they operated but he liked silence, nothing to distract him, nothing to distract them. Heavy metal or classical—it was all the same to him. Noise.

'How's the patient?' he asked Gerry Carter, his anaesthetist. He knew that the theatre staff drew lots to decide who would work with him, the ones who lost being sent in as part of his team. It had never worried him before that he was so unpopular but for some reason he found it irritating that day. Would it hurt them to smile when he came in, to wish him good morning even? Surely he wasn't that much of an ogre that he not only scared little children but grown men and women as well?

The memory of how Harry had reacted to him had stayed with him and he found himself thinking about it again as the anaesthetist rattled out a summary of their patient's vital signs. He was going to have to do something about his attitude if he hoped to win the boy round, Leo decided for the umpteenth time. He suddenly realised that Gerry had stopped speaking and was staring at him, obviously expecting a response, although for the life of him, Leo couldn't imagine what it should be.

'Sorry. What did you say?' He gave a short laugh, faintly rusty admittedly but a laugh all the same. 'It must be my age. I'm finding it difficult to concentrate these days.'

There was a stunned silence before someone gave a little chuckle, hastily turning it into a cough when they realised what they were doing. Leo felt heat flow up his face as he wondered if he'd made a fool of himself and was grateful for the concealing folds of his mask. He concentrated on what Gerry was saying, nodding when the other man came to the end of his spiel.

'That's great. Thanks. OK, folks, let's get to work.'

Leo grimaced as he took his place at the table. Normally, he would have simply set to work without uttering a word, so why had he felt the need to say that? Surely he wasn't that desperate to improve the image his colleagues had of him? It was Harry he needed to impress, nobody else…except Mia.

Finding out that her husband had died in such tragic circumstances had affected him far more than he would have expected. He had found himself thinking about it all week, imagining how difficult the past few years must have been for her. He had also found it hard to come to terms with the fact that her husband had been wheelchair-bound. Although he knew it had nothing to do with him, he couldn't help speculating about their relationship. Had Mia undergone IVF treatment because she and her husband had been unable to make love?

He swiftly erased that thought. He needed to concentrate and he couldn't do that if he was thinking about issues that didn't concern him. The patient, Hilary Johnson, was undergoing surgery to replace her aortic valve. Leo made the first incision through the sternum then Hilary was placed on a heart-lung machine and her heart was stopped. It was an operation that was only carried out in extreme cases, when a patient was suffering life-threatening symptoms, but he had performed it many times before and worked swiftly, excising the damaged valve and replacing it with a prosthesis. He waited while the woman was removed from the machine, preferring to check for any problems before closing up. He nodded when everything appeared to be functioning normally.

'That all seems fine. Dr Halshaw, perhaps you would like to close up? It will be excellent practice for you.'

He moved aside so that his registrar could step up to the table, ignoring the startled looks that were being exchanged. He rarely invited his juniors to take part so it was a bit of a red-letter day, but maybe it was time he made some changes in work too. After all, the younger doctors were never going to progress if they didn't get any hands-on experience, were they?

'Good. You've made quite a decent job of that,' he said when the younger man had finished. He glanced around, rather enjoying the fact that everyone appeared

slightly stunned to hear him praise one of their number. A sudden and wholly unfamiliar sense of mischief
spurred him on. 'Thank you, everyone, in fact. You all
did extremely well today.'

Leo exited Theatre, smiling to himself when he heard
a babble of conversation break out as the doors swung
to. Maybe it was time he tried a different approach if
it stopped people becoming complacent. It would keep
them on their toes if they weren't sure how he was
going to react.

He showered and changed, then went to the consultants' lounge to write up his notes. Although one of the
juniors would type them up later, he preferred to outline
the procedure while it was fresh in his mind. He had
almost finished when there was a knock on the door.

'Come,' he called, without glancing up from the
screen. He saved the file before he looked up, feeling
his heart give an almighty leap when he saw Mia standing in the doorway. She had an envelope in her hands
and he knew—he just knew!—it contained the results
of the DNA tests.

Leo rose to his feet, his head swimming as thoughts
rushed through it. He wasn't ready for this! He didn't
want to hear what she had to say, didn't want to know
if Harry was his real son. He loved Noah and he didn't
want any other child to supplant him.

'I have the results of the DNA tests.'

Her voice was so calm that it cut through all the turmoil in his head. Leo nodded abruptly. 'And?'

'I haven't opened it yet.' She showed him the envelope with its seal still intact. 'I thought it best if we read
it together. That way there will be no mistake.'

Meaning that he wouldn't be able to accuse her of skewing the results, he thought wryly, although he couldn't blame her for being cautious. Whatever they discovered, it was going to have far-reaching consequences for all of them—him, her and the two boys.

'Right. Do you want me to open it?' he offered, but she shook her head.

'I'll do it.' She slid her finger under the flap and ripped it open. Taking out the single sheet of paper it contained, she read what it said before handing it to him.

Leo glanced sharply at her but he couldn't discern anything from her expression. He took a quick breath then looked at the paper, although the words seemed to dance before his eyes. He, a man who read reports far more complicated than this every day of his life, couldn't make sense of it!

'It appears you were right.'

Mia's voice was still calm, although she couldn't disguise the pain it held. Leo felt a rush of regret hit him when he looked up and saw the anguish in her beautiful eyes. All of a sudden he wished he hadn't started this, that he had just accepted that Noah was his son and carried on the way they'd been. Now it was too late to go back, far too late to take away the pain she was feeling.

'The results are conclusive. Harry isn't mine and Chris's child. We aren't his biological parents.'

CHAPTER FIVE

'DRINK THIS.'

Leo placed a cup of tea in front of her but Mia didn't make any attempt to pick it up. How could she when her hands were shaking so hard that she would only drop it? He muttered something under his breath as he picked it up and raised it to her lips.

'Come on, just a sip. It will help.'

Mia obediently took a sip of the hot liquid, feeling her stomach roil with nausea when she tasted the sweetness of the tea on her tongue. She stumbled to her feet, praying that she wouldn't disgrace herself by throwing up.

'Through here.'

He led her into the consultants' bathroom, guiding her to the basin when she began to retch. Mia bent over the sink, wishing the floor would open up and swallow her. The sheer humiliation of throwing up in front of him was just too much, coming on top of the shock of learning that Harry wasn't her son.

Tears welled in her eyes and she heard Leo sigh as he moved away. She didn't blame him for leaving. Why should he have to deal with this on top of the shock he'd had? Although it hadn't been such a shock for him, of course. He had known from the outset that Harry wasn't her child. He'd simply needed the results of those tests to prove it to her. Now they had to decide what they were going to do. About Harry. And Noah.

'Sit down.'

Mia jumped when Leo reappeared with a towel. He sat her down on the lavatory seat then rinsed the wash-basin. Once it was clean, he soaked the end of the towel in cold water then wiped her hands and face.

Mia shuddered when she felt the coolness of the cloth on her skin. It felt as though the chill was invading her whole body, seeping deeper and deeper into every pore. Maybe the tests had proved that Harry wasn't her bio-logical child but he was still her son and nothing was going to change that!

She pushed Leo's hand away, knowing that she had to make it clear that she wasn't going to give Harry up. Even though she had no idea what she was going to do about Noah, she was sure about that. 'It doesn't make any difference what those results say. Harry is my son and I won't let you take him away from me.'

'And I won't let you take Noah away from me ei-ther.' His tone was flat yet she could hear the emotion rippling beneath the surface. If she was determined to keep Harry then Leo was equally determined to hold onto Noah.

'Then what are we going to do?' She sighed when he didn't answer. 'You must have thought about what you wanted when you started this, Leo. So what did you decide?'

'I didn't.' He ran his hand through his hair and she

could see that it was trembling. Maybe he appeared to be handling the situation far better than she was, but it didn't mean he wasn't affected by it.

'You must have had some idea of what you wanted to achieve,' she insisted, more gently this time. In a way, it made her feel a little better to know that she wasn't alone in having to deal with this situation. Leo was going through the same kind of heartache that she was experiencing.

'Not really.' He gave her a tight smile. 'I acted on instinct more than anything else. Once I discovered that Noah wasn't my biological child, I set out to find out who was.'

'How did you discover that Noah wasn't yours?'

'Noah was involved in a road traffic accident several months ago and needed a blood transfusion. It turns out that he has a fairly rare blood type so I was tested to see if I could be a donor for him.' He shrugged. 'Amanda was driving and she was injured as well so they already knew that she wasn't a suitable match for him.' He laughed shortly. 'The doctor who came to tell me that I wasn't a match either didn't know what to say. I mean, it was obvious from the blood work that neither Amanda nor I were related to Noah.'

'It must have been a terrible shock!' Mia exclaimed.

'It was. I couldn't take it in at first. After all, I'd watched Noah being born and *knew* that he was the child Amanda had given birth to. How could he not be our son? I convinced myself that the hospital had made a mistake somehow.' He sighed. 'It was only when Noah was on the mend that I thought about it properly and realised that if there had been a mistake, it must have happened at the clinic. I contacted Dr Khapur and he agreed, reluctantly, to check their records.'

'So how did you discover that I was involved in the mix-up?'

'Sheer luck. Dr Khapur was very disinclined to discuss the matter from the outset. Every time I phoned to speak to him, he was unavailable.' He shrugged. 'In the end, I took matters into my own hands and went to see him. His secretary tried to fob me off, but I told her that I intended to sit there until Dr Khapur would see me. He must have realised that he had no choice in the matter and invited me into his office. Your file was on his desk along with Amanda's and I asked him, point blank, if you were involved.'

'And he confirmed that I was? So much for patient confidentiality!'

'No. To give him his due, he tried to deny it, but I could tell he was lying and insisted that he told me the truth otherwise I'd go straight to the Human Fertilisation and Embryology Authority and make an official complaint.' He sighed. 'I'm not proud of the fact that I resorted to threats but I needed answers. Anyway, it did the trick because he admitted that it was possible you were the other party and that he had asked you to come and see him. I don't think he meant to let it slip when you were due to visit the clinic but he was very flustered by then. I decided that I needed to speak to you myself and made sure I was there.'

'I see.' Mia frowned. 'That explains how you happened to be there the other day but it doesn't explain how the mix-up occurred. Do you have any idea what happened?'

'Not really. All I can gather is that you and Amanda had embryos transferred on the same day. I can only assume that something went wrong during the process.'

'It's incredible.' Mia shook her head. 'I mean, there are strict guidelines laid down to avoid something like this happening. Chris and I chose that particular clinic because of its excellent reputation, in fact.'

'No doubt we shall find out what went on eventually, but at the moment we have more pressing matters to worry about.'

'Namely two little boys,' Mia agreed sombrely.

'Exactly.'

Leo looked round when he heard voices coming from the other room. It was lunchtime and his colleagues were starting their breaks. He couldn't bear it if people found out about what had happened and started gossiping. Noah went to school with several of the other consultants' children and Leo didn't want him overhearing something he shouldn't, even though he would have to be told at some point.

The thought of how confused Noah was going to be when he found out that Leo wasn't his *real* father was too painful. Noah had been through enough in the past six months and Leo was determined that he was going to protect him from any more unhappiness. He came to a swift decision, hoping that Mia would agree.

'I don't know about you, Mia, but I really don't want people finding out about this. To my mind it's a private matter and we need to deal with it ourselves.'

'I agree, although I shall have to tell Chris's parents, of course.' She shook her head. 'Heaven knows how they'll react. They adore Harry, all the more so because he's their last link to Chris. They'll be devastated when they find out he isn't Chris's son.'

'Obviously, you can't keep it a secret from them,' Leo agreed, although he had no such compunction when it came to his own parents. Sir Iain and Lady Davina Forester weren't exactly doting grandparents, but then they'd never been doting parents either.

He dismissed the thought with an ease that should have worried him, but he'd had years to come to terms with his parents' lack of interest. So long as he had performed well at school and behaved impeccably out of it, they had been perfectly content. However, they had never loved him the way he loved Noah.

No one had ever loved him like that, he thought suddenly. Amanda certainly hadn't, not that he'd wanted her to. That kind of love came with far too many strings attached and he preferred his life to be free of such complications. That's what had attracted him to Amanda in the first place—she hadn't been the clingy type and had been perfectly happy doing her own thing while he did his. It had never worried him that she hadn't loved him so it was a surprise to find himself wondering how it would feel to be loved totally and with an all-consuming passion.

'It's other folk I'm concerned about,' he explained, getting back to what really mattered. 'Noah goes to school with several of the other consultants' children and I don't want him to become the subject of gossip, especially when it will only upset and confuse him.'

'I feel the same about Harry. There's quite a few children at his school whose parents work at the hospital.' Mia shook her head. 'The less everyone knows about this, the better.'

'In that case I think we need to be circumspect.' Leo glanced round when he heard someone rattle the doorhandle. It struck him how odd it would appear if he and Mia were seen leaving the bathroom together. People were so quick to add two and two and come up with the wrong answer.

The thought of the answer they might come up with sent a rush of heat through him and he cleared his throat. He made a point of never being seen alone with any female members of staff. His private life was his concern and not the basis for gossip.

After his divorce had become common knowledge there had been a lot of speculation but he had soon nipped it in the bud. The few relationships he'd had since splitting had been conducted well away from the hospital. They had been brief affairs, based on sexual need rather than anything else, and he had made sure that the women involved had understood that. Thankfully, there were a lot of women in his circle who felt the way he did. They didn't believe in love either and were happy to satisfy their needs on a no-strings basis.

He couldn't imagine Mia agreeing to that kind of a relationship. She would expect more than that. Far more than he could give.

The thought caught him flat-footed so it was a relief when Mia took charge. Standing up, she pointed to the second door that opened into the bathroom. 'Where does that lead?'

'To the consultants' rest room.' Leo gathered his wits, which seemed to be racing in several different directions. He and Mia weren't ever going to have a relationship that was based on anything except their boys. 'There shouldn't be anyone using it right now but let me check to make sure.'

Mia stepped back to let him pass as Leo went to the door. The bathroom was a little too small for two people and he flinched when his hand brushed against her arm. He could feel the silky-soft down on her skin tickling the back of his hand and shuddered. He hadn't touched a woman in any way that wasn't connected to his work since Noah's accident and the speed with which he found himself responding shocked him. He could feel feather-light tingles spreading over his skin, as though each tiny hair had triggered an individual response.

His mouth thinned as he opened the door and checked the room was empty. He wasn't attracted to Mia for the simple reason that he refused to allow himself to be attracted to her. It was Noah who mattered, Noah and Harry, not him and what he did or didn't feel. Mia may have given birth to his son but it had been purely an accident. It didn't mean there was a bond between them.

Opening the door to the corridor, Leo checked there was nobody about then ushered her out. He watched her make her way to the lift, wondering all of a sudden if he was right to write her off. Mia had not only given birth to his son but she had loved and nurtured Harry for the past five years. She had played a major role in Harry's life and nothing could change that. That she was destined to play a role in *his* life from now on was a given too.

Leo took a deep breath as he watched her step into the lift. He couldn't ignore Mia even if he wanted to.

It was raining when Mia woke up on Saturday morning. It had been a miserably wet summer and now it appeared that autumn was repeating the trend. She grimaced as she headed downstairs. She had promised Harry they could go to the park that morning and only hoped the rain would stop. Harry would be so disappointed if the promised trip had to be cancelled.

She gave Harry his breakfast then sent him into the sitting room to play while she tidied up. She had just finished washing the breakfast dishes when the phone rang and she hurried to answer it, hoping it wouldn't be her parents-in-law. She and Harry were going to their house for lunch the following day and she really needed to work out how to break the news to them that Harry wasn't their grandson if she wasn't to give them the most terrible shock. She sighed as she picked up the receiver because no matter how she phrased it, Joyce and Edward were going to be dreadfully upset.

'Mia? It's Leo Forester.'

Mia started when she recognised the deeply assured tones flowing down the line. 'How did you get my number?' she demanded, then pulled a face. It wasn't exactly the friendliest thing to have said, bearing in mind that she and Leo were going to have to work together in the coming weeks…

Or, rather, years, a small voice inside her head amended.

'Directory enquiries,' he replied succinctly, his tone not altering.

Mia rolled her eyes. It would take more than the odd snappy remark she came out with to dent his composure! 'I see.' She took a deep breath to calm herself. She needed to behave as coolly and as rationally as Leo did if they were to sort out this mess. 'Has something happened?'

'If you mean have I heard from the clinic then no. They are maintaining a strategic silence, probably because their lawyers have instructed them to do so.'

'Lawyers!' Mia exclaimed. 'You really think they've taken legal advice?'

'Of course. Apart from the fact that we'd be well within our rights to take them to court and sue for compensation, they have committed a massive error, one that could mean their licence is revoked.'

'But we're not going to sue them, are we?' Mia asked, her heart sinking at the thought of the ensuing publicity if the story came to light.

'I'm not planning to do so and I assume you aren't either. However, the mistake will have to be reported to the HFEA.'

Mia sat down abruptly on the stairs. 'I can't bear the thought of this getting out. We both agreed that we don't want people talking for the boys' sake, but we may not be able to stop it.'

'It won't come to that. This is a private matter, Mia, and I shall make that perfectly clear to all involved. It won't be only the clinic that could find itself facing a lawsuit if details of what has happened gets into the newspapers.'

'Thank you. I can't tell you how relieved I am to hear that. I couldn't bear it if Harry's life was blighted by this.' She took a wobbly breath. 'Obviously, I'll pay half the costs if we do have to go to court, although it may take me some time to raise the money, I'm afraid.'

'Don't worry about that. I shall bear any costs involved.'

'Oh, but I couldn't let you do that! It wouldn't be fair.'

'I suggest we sort it out if and when we need to.' He changed the subject, making it clear that he didn't intend to discuss the matter any further. 'Are you doing anything special today?'

'Not really,' Mia told him, realising that it was pointless arguing. She had a feeling that once Leo made up his mind, it was difficult to get him to change it, although she had no intention of allowing him to foot the bill if they did end up in court. She would start saving towards it and that way she wouldn't be beholden to him.

The thought of being in debt to Leo made her feel more than a little uneasy, although she wasn't sure why. It was an effort to concentrate when he continued.

'Good. I've promised Noah that I'll take him to the park this morning and I was hoping that you'd agree to bring Harry along too. The sooner the boys meet the better, plus I'm sure you must be anxious to see Noah.'

Mia bit her lip, unsure what to answer, unsure how she felt even. Meeting Noah was the next logical step yet the thought scared her. Harry was her son and she didn't want their relationship to change in any way. However, once she met Noah, it would be impossible to maintain the status quo.

'I know how scary it is, Mia. I felt exactly the same the other day when I met Harry, as though I was leaping into the unknown. But you need to meet Noah, not just for your sake but for his.'

Leo's tone was persuasive. It held a concern that she hadn't heard in it before and she shivered. It was hard to deny him anything when he spoke in this winning way.

'You're right, it is scary. I… Well, I don't want to do anything that might upset my relationship with Harry,' she told him honestly, and he sighed.

'I understand. I'm terrified that having Harry around will somehow alter how I feel about Noah. Crazy, isn't it? I mean, there's no basis for thinking such a thing, is there?'

Mia smiled when she heard disgust in his voice this time. 'I don't think we should be too hard on ourselves, Leo. I mean, how many people have to go through something like this? There aren't any rules so we have to rely on our instincts and that's what's so scary.'

'Don't tell me you're a control freak too?' he demanded wryly, and she laughed.

''Fraid so. I like things to be just so and preferably the way I want them to be.'

'Then pity help those two boys, that's all I can say. Having one parent who's a control freak would be bad enough, but to have two? Well!'

Mia chuckled. 'I'm sure they'll survive. Anyway, what about your wife? Surely she isn't as set on having everything done her way as we are?'

'Believe me, my *ex*-wife makes us look like beginners when it comes to being demanding. What Amanda wants takes precedence every time.'

His tone was so cold that Mia shivered. The thought of the other woman having anything to do with her beloved Harry was very hard to accept. 'I see. I'm not sure if I'd be happy at the thought of Harry spending time with her after hearing that,' she told him truthfully.

'There's no need to worry. Amanda isn't the least bit interested in Harry.'

'She knows about the mix-up, though?' Mia queried, wondering if he was telling her the truth. She couldn't imagine any woman not wanting to meet her own child but, there again, why would Leo lie about it?

'Oh, yes. I told her what had happened. Suffice to say that Amanda was more concerned with how it could impact on her rather than on Noah or Harry.'

He didn't say anything else. Although it appeared that his ex-wife wasn't involved, Mia couldn't help feeling uneasy. She simply couldn't accept that any woman, no matter how self-centred, could ignore what had happened. She realised that she needed to find out exactly what she was dealing with and the only way to do that was by asking Leo straight out. She was just about to do so when Harry appeared.

'Can we go to the park now, Mummy?' he demanded plaintively.

'Soon, sweetheart.' She placed the receiver to her ear again as Harry reluctantly went back to the sitting room.

'I take it that you and Harry were planning to go to the park too,' Leo observed. 'Excellent. It'll appear far more natural if we happen to meet up. We don't want to make a big deal of this, do we? The boys will only get suspicious and start worrying that something is going on.'

'Which it is.' Mia sighed. 'I wonder how they'll get

on with each other. That's something else we need to think about.'

'Let's take it a step at a time, shall we?'

They made arrangements to meet in the playground before Mia hung up. She went to tell Harry that they would be leaving shortly and sent him off to find his trainers. He whooped with delight as he tore up the stairs. He was obviously looking forward to the outing and she only hoped it would work out for all of them, Harry, Noah, Leo and herself.

Her heart gave a little jolt when it struck her that she was about to meet her real son. Although she had seen that photo of Noah, she knew nothing about him—what he enjoyed, if he was athletic or musical or neither. As Leo had said, it was like leaping into the unknown so no wonder she found the idea daunting. Still, at least Leo would be there, she consoled herself, and for some reason the thought made her heart leap once more.

CHAPTER SIX

IT HAD STOPPED raining by the time they arrived at the playground. Leo looked around but he couldn't see any sign of Mia. Noah ran off to play on the slide, ignoring the other children as he climbed the slippery steps.

Leo sighed as he watched him. Noah had always been a quiet child and he had become even more withdrawn since the accident. He wasn't sure if it was the prolonged stay in hospital that had affected him or Amanda's disappearance. Amanda hadn't made any attempt to see Noah in the last six months. She hadn't phoned or even emailed to ask how he was either. Discovering that Noah wasn't her biological child had given her the excuse she'd needed to cut him out of her life.

Although she had never been around very much, Leo knew that Noah must miss even the sparse contact he'd had with the woman he believed to be his mother. It made him realise how careful he needed to be when he introduced Noah to Mia. The little boy could resent Mia's sudden intrusion into his life.

It was something else to worry about, one more thing to add to the ever-expanding list. Not for the first time, Leo wished that he had let sleeping dogs lie. What had he hoped to achieve? All right, so he and Mia would get to know their real children but was that enough to justify disrupting Harry's and Noah's lives? Children needed stability but what hope did they have of giving the boys that when they were about to rock the very foundations of their existence?

'Hello! This is a surprise. I didn't expect to see you here.'

Leo looked round when he heard Mia's voice. Fixing a smile to his lips, he went to meet her, trying to ignore the way that Harry shrank away when he approached. It was obvious that the child's initial opinion of him hadn't improved.

'I've brought my son, Noah, here to play,' he explained, refusing to feel hurt. It was his own fault that he'd made such a bad impression on Harry and it was up to him to do something about it. His smile deliberately widened. 'That's him, over there on the slide.'

Leo pointed to Noah, who was surrounded by several other children, a couple of whom also had blond hair. He felt Mia stiffen and instinctively reached for her hand. 'He's the one wearing the red jacket. He's at the top of the slide now.'

'Yes, I can see him.'

Leo heard the tremor in her voice and realised that she was deeply affected by her first actual sighting of Noah. His fingers tightened around hers as a wave of tenderness washed over him. He knew how she felt because he had felt the same when he'd first seen Harry—shocked and amazed by the resemblance the boy bore to him. When Harry ran off to play on the swings, Leo led her over to a bench.

'It knocks you for six, doesn't it?' he said as they sat down. 'I mean, you try to prepare yourself but it's still a shock when you see them for the first time.'

'It is.' She could barely speak and he heard her take a quick little breath. 'He's so like Chris—his hair, his build, the way he tilts his head—everything!'

'I was just as stunned when I saw Harry,' he admitted. 'He has my nose and my chin, the same colour hair.' He gave a self-mocking laugh, trying to lighten the mood in the hope that it would help her. 'His hair even sticks out like mine does if I don't get it cut every couple of weeks!'

Mia turned and stared at him. 'You think Harry looks like you?'

'Of course. Surely you can see the resemblance?'

Leo frowned as she turned and stared at the little boy. He couldn't believe that she hadn't noticed how alike they were. His eyes rested on her as she studied Harry and he saw to the very second when what had been so clear to him from the moment he had laid eyes on the child became clear to her too. Her face was very pale when she turned to him, so pale that he thought she was going to faint and he gripped her hand harder, ruing the fact that he'd felt it necessary to point out the resemblance. The last thing he'd intended was to upset her.

'I can see the resemblance now.' She bit her lip. 'I don't know why I didn't spot it before.'

'Probably because this has been such a shock for you,' Leo said soothingly, surprised that he should feel it necessary to offer comfort. Although it went against the grain to be rude, he wasn't known for being compassionate. In fact, if he was honest, he rarely took account of other people's feelings, mainly because he didn't expect them to take account of his. However, for some reason, he felt a need to soothe her, to comfort her, to make this meeting as easy for her as it could possibly be.

'Do you think so?' Her eyes held his fast and he could see the plea they held. 'Maybe I was deliberately trying not to see how like you Harry is because it would mean those test results are right.'

'They are right, though.' Even though he hated to upset her, Leo knew that he had to make this most important fact absolutely clear. 'You read the letter, Mia. The results prove conclusively that Harry isn't your son.'

'But they don't prove he's yours!' She shot to her feet, her eyes spitting fire at him. 'There was nothing in that report to say that you are his father, Leo. Absolutely nothing!'

'I know.' Leo rose as well, realising they were attracting attention. He lowered his voice, hating the thought of people overhearing their conversation. 'Which is why we need to send off more DNA samples, but from you and me this time as well as from the boys. I'll get it organised and then we'll know for sure what we're dealing with.'

'It's that simple, is it?' She sat down abruptly and Leo saw the anger drain out of her. 'We send off more samples of hair and saliva and they'll send us back another report to say that Child A belongs to this or that parent.'

'No, it isn't simple,' he said sharply. 'Nothing about this situation is simple, Mia. It's a mess, and there's no point pretending that it isn't going to cause a massive upheaval for us as well as for Harry and Noah. However, the only way we'll get through it is by working together. If we start fighting then we'll achieve nothing apart from destroying the lives of two innocent little boys. Is that what you really want?'

'Of course not.'

Mia took a deep breath and tried to get a grip on herself. It wasn't easy but, as Leo had pointed out, nothing about this situation was easy. She looked across the playground, feeling her heart ache when she saw Harry at the top of the slide. He must have sensed she was watching him because he turned and waved, his face breaking into a mischievous grin as he propelled himself at top speed down the slide. He came running over to her, bubbling with excitement.

'Did you see how fast I went, Mummy?'

'I did,' she replied, giving him a hug. 'You're a proper little demon on the slide!'

He laughed happily as he ran off to have another turn. Mia turned to Leo, knowing that she owed him an apology. It wasn't like her to create a scene but there again she'd never had anything like this happen to her before. 'I'm sorry. I'm afraid it all got the better of me but it won't happen again.'

'It's been a shock for both of us,' he said quietly, and she shrugged.

'Yes, but that isn't an excuse.' She paused, not wanting to cause another upset, but she needed to be absolutely sure of the facts. 'I think we should have those tests done as soon as possible. We need to be certain that we know exactly what we're dealing with.'

'I agree. We can't afford to make another mistake, not when it could impact on the boys.' He shrugged. 'Maybe there is a resemblance between Noah and your late husband, and maybe I do think that Harry looks a lot like me, but it isn't proof. It will be safer if we see it written down in black and white before we make any plans.'

'What sort of plans?' Mia said swiftly. 'I made it clear that I won't allow you to take Harry away from me.'

'And I made it equally clear that I am not prepared to give up Noah,' he said curtly, interrupting her.

'Then what exactly are you talking about?'

'I'm not sure.' He frowned. 'The boys are far too young to tell them what has happened—it'll only confuse them. But obviously we each need to maintain contact with our real child or it could cause problems in the future. I don't want Harry to grow up thinking that I wasn't interested in him and I'm sure you don't want Noah thinking that either.'

'Of course not. So what do you suggest?' Mia said slowly. 'That we meet up on a regular basis so we can get to know the boys and they can get to know us?'

Leo looked across the playground. Mia followed his gaze, her heart contracting when she realised that Harry and Noah were on adjoining swings. They had no idea what had happened and it was up to her and Leo to make this is as easy as possible for them.

'Won't they think it strange, though?' she said, turning to him. 'I mean, we can't keep on *bumping* into each other, can we?'

'No. They're bright kids and they'll soon realise something is going on. We have to find another way to go about this and the only thing I can come up with is if we let them think we're going out together.' He

shrugged, ignoring her gasp. 'There are lots of kids at
Noah's school whose parents have split up and are in
new relationships and I imagine it's the same at Harry's
school. If we tell them that we're seeing one another,
they'll think it's quite normal. What do you think?'

What did she think? Mia was lost for words, quite
frankly. It was mind-boggling to imagine herself dating Leo...

Wasn't it?

Heat roared through her veins as she looked at his
handsome face and realised that the idea wasn't so out-
rageous after all. 'I...um...'

She got not further when Harry appeared. 'I'm
thirsty, Mummy. Can I have a drink, please?'

'Of course you can, darling.' Mia shot to her feet
so fast that she almost dropped her bag. She slung the
strap over her shoulder, pinning a smile to her lips as
she turned to Leo. She needed to think about what he'd
suggested, see if she could come up with a better idea.
The last thing she needed was to become even more
involved with him than she already was.

'It was nice to see you again, Leo. Enjoy the rest of
your day.'

'You too,' he replied politely, rising. Noah came running over and he put a protective hand on his shoulder.
'This is Mia, Noah. Say hello to her and Harry, her son.'

'Hello,' Noah muttered, scuffing the toe of his trainer
on the ground.

'Hello, Noah. It's good to meet you.'

Mia felt a rush of emotions overwhelm her as she
studied the child's downbent head. Close to, the resemblance to Chris was even more marked. Not only

did Noah have Chris's ash-blond hair and black brows but his nose was the same shape too. All of a sudden she knew that no matter what it took, she had to get to know him. He was her child, hers and Chris's, and even though she had no idea if she would ever be able to tell him that she was his mother, she couldn't bear the thought of not being involved in his life.

Her head lifted and she looked Leo straight in the eyes. 'I think your suggestion might work. Let's talk about it next time we meet, shall we?'

'Of course.'

Leo didn't say anything else as she led Harry away but he didn't need to when his expression said everything for him. Mia shivered as she and Harry made their way to the café. Maybe Leo had made the suggestion purely to help the boys but they both knew it could have repercussions for them too.

She bit her lip, trying to contain the rush of excitement that filled her as she recalled the way he had looked at her just now. That he was aware of her as a woman wasn't in doubt. However, her feelings for him were far more complicated. Since Chris had died she hadn't dated, hadn't been interested in going out with other men. She never really had been, if she was honest. What had happened with Steve Parker had put her off the idea of dating and if she hadn't met Chris then she doubted it she would have found the courage to try it again.

However, Leo was different. Very different. Pretending that they were seeing one another for the sake of the boys wouldn't be easy. What would be easy was making the pretence real.

* * *

Leo was glad to go into work on Monday morning. At least while he was working he would have less time to worry about what had happened on Saturday. He sighed as he made his way to Theatre. He had spent the remainder of the weekend thinking about his meeting with Mia and what had transpired.

Suggesting that they should pretend to be involved for the sake of the boys had been an off-the-cuff idea. However, as soon as he'd broached it, it had become increasingly attractive. It had been ages since he'd been out with a woman and he would appreciate some female company; however, he knew that it wasn't the reason why he found the idea so appealing. Getting to know Mia seemed as important as getting to know Harry, strangely enough.

Leo cursed softly as he thrust open the door to the scrub room. What in heaven's name was wrong with him? He could have his pick of women, women who were far more beautiful than Mia. This situation was skewing his thinking, making him come up with the craziest ideas. His only interest in Mia was as the mother of his son!

'Oh, please, *please,* don't make me do this! I'll do anything—scrub toilets, wash out sick bowls—anything at all if you'll spare me this. It's Monday and I really can't face the thought of two hours locked up in Theatre with our beloved leader!'

Leo came to a halt when he found Declan Murphy on his knees in front of Janice Lang, the theatre sister. The F2 student was staring beseechingly up at her, his face bearing an expression guaranteed to appeal to even the hardest heart. Janice and the rest of the team were laughing so hard that they didn't notice he had come in. It was only when he approached them that they spotted him. Declan obviously realised something was wrong when everyone hurriedly moved away. He looked round, his freckled face paling when he saw Leo.

'A moving performance, Dr Murphy.' Leo smiled thinly as his errant F2 scrambled to his feet. 'Your talents are obviously wasted working in this particular type of theatre. You should apply to RADA and see if they can offer you a place.'

'I...erm... Thank you,' Declan faltered, then gulped when he realised what he had said.

Leo headed into the shower room, managing to contain his mirth until he had turned on the water. Declan's face had been an absolute picture, he thought as he stepped under the jets. It would be a long time before he pulled a stunt like that again! It made him realise all of a sudden that it wasn't always necessary to play the heavy-handed boss. Sometimes a dash of humour could be far more effective.

Leo frowned as he pulled on fresh scrubs. He was very aware that the idea would never have occurred to him in the past. Was it this situation with Noah and Harry that was making him behave so differently? he wondered. Finding out that Noah wasn't his son had knocked the feet from under him; nothing seemed certain any more, including his own actions. Where once he would have known he was right, now he found himself questioning his decisions.

It was what had happened that weekend. He'd kept thinking about that suggestion he'd made to Mia, wondering if it had been the right thing to do. Normally, he wouldn't have given it a second thought but it had been on his mind, day and night: should they pretend to be dating for the sake of the boys or was it tempting fate?

His mouth thinned as he slid his feet into a pair of rubber clogs. There was no chance of him becoming romantically involved with Mia or any other woman! He had learned his lesson after what had gone on with Amanda and he had no intention of placing himself in the same position again. So maybe his heart hadn't been broken when Amanda had left him but his pride had been dented and that had been enough to put him off forming another long-term relationship. Even if he and Mia did decide to carry through with the idea, their relationship would only ever be make-believe.

He pushed open the door to Theatre, wondering why he still felt so ambivalent. As long as they both understood what they were doing, there wouldn't be a problem.

Would there?

CHAPTER SEVEN

MIA ARRIVED EARLY for work on Monday morning. Amazingly the train had been on time and she'd been spared the usual last-minute dash from the station. At least something was going right, she thought as she made her way to the staffroom.

She sighed as she hung her coat in her locker. Lunch with her in-laws the previous day had been even worse than she had feared. Joyce and Edward had been devastated when she had told them about Harry. They had refused to believe her at first and it was only after she had shown them the results of the DNA tests that they had accepted it was true.

She and Harry had left soon after lunch. Although they usually spent the afternoon with Chris's parents, Mia had realised that the couple had needed time on their own to come to terms with what had happened. Their goodbyes had been stilted, all the more so because Joyce had hurried away in the middle of waving them off. Although Mia sympathised with her mother-in-law, she hoped that Joyce wouldn't allow this development to affect her relationship with Harry. Harry needed his grandparents' love and support more than ever now.

Penny was on holiday that week but she had left the roster pinned to the notice-board. Mia grimaced when she discovered that she was covering Cardiology again. Along with the stress of breaking the news to Chris's parents, she had found herself constantly thinking about Leo's suggestion. Whilst she was still determined to get to know Noah, she was no longer sure if it would be wise to let the boys think she and Leo were involved. Harry, in particular, could find it upsetting to think there was another man in her life, especially when he seemed to have taken such a dislike to Leo.

Mia made her way to the unit and did the hand-over then went to check on the patients. She was surprised to find David Rimmer in the end bay. He had been discharged following his successful cardioversion and she hadn't expected to see him again.

'I'll have to add your name to the coffee list if you're going to be a regular,' she said, smiling at him. She picked up his chart, sighing when she discovered that he had been admitted suffering from the same symptoms as before: a rapid and irregular heartbeat.

'Milk and two sugars, please,' he said chirpily, although Mia could tell the effort it cost him.

'I'll make a note of that.' She gently replaced the oxygen mask over his face and shook an admonishing finger at him. 'Now leave that on or it will be water not coffee for you, my lad.'

'Yes, Mum,' David retorted cheekily. He looked past her and grimaced. 'Is she always this bossy, Doc?'

Mia looked round, feeling her own heart race when she saw Leo standing behind her. He was dressed in theatre scrubs, the soft green fabric outlining the powerful muscles in his chest. He looked so big and over-whelmingly male that she found herself responding in a way that shocked her.

Sex had never been a major issue in her life. She'd only slept with Steve before she had married Chris and it had been a complete disaster. That was why she'd had no qualms about marrying Chris. The fact that they'd been unable to make love because of his injuries hadn't worried her, although Chris had fretted about it.

There had been no reason to revise her opinion either, yet she couldn't pretend that she wasn't affected by Leo's nearness. All of a sudden the doubts that had plagued her all weekend came rushing back. What would happen if she found herself falling for Leo and wanting to turn fiction into fact?

Leo had no idea what Mia was thinking but he could tell there was something troubling her. He had to make a determined effort to concentrate as he replied to David's question. 'I really couldn't say. However, I suggest we focus on you rather than on Sister Adams.'

His tone was chilly and he cursed himself when he saw the younger man's face fall. There really hadn't been any need to speak to David that way but he'd reacted instinctively. The suggestion that he knew Mia well enough to comment on her behaviour had hit a nerve, coming on top of his earlier thoughts.

He deliberately cleared his mind of any more foolishness as he explained to David that he was going to try another round of cardioversion. He wasn't attracted to Mia and he didn't intend to be attracted to her either. He had enough to contend with without complicating matters any more.

'But what's going to happen if it does it again?' David said, anxiously. 'You can't keep on stopping and starting my heart, can you?'

'No,' Leo agreed. 'We've already tried various combinations of drugs and they've been less than successful so it could be that an ICD is the answer.'

'What's that?' David asked him, frowning.

'An implantable cardioverter defibrillator,' Leo explained dryly, and smiled. 'You can see why it's called an ICD for short.'

'Too right!' David rolled his eyes and Mia laughed.

Leo cleared his throat, determined to ignore the effect the sweetly husky sound was having on him. So what if his blood pressure *had* risen a couple of notches and his breathing *did* seem a little more laboured than usual? He was a normal healthy male, with normal healthy appetites—he would have responded the same way to any woman.

'Basically, an ICD is used to treat anyone who has a dangerously abnormal heart rhythm.' Leo made himself focus on what he was saying. It wasn't like him to become distracted when dealing with a patient and he didn't intend to let it to happen again. 'Size-wise, it's slightly bigger than a matchbox and consists of a pulse generator plus one or more electrode leads, which are placed in the heart via a vein.'

'How does it work?' David wanted to know.

'The device constantly monitors your heart rhythm. If it detects a dangerous rhythm it can deliver three different treatments to restore the heart to a normal rhythm. Pacing, which is a series of rapid, low-voltage electrical impulses, cardioversion, which is one or more small electric shocks, or defibrillation which consists of one or more larger electric shocks.'

'I see. How is it fitted, though?' David grimaced. 'You said that the electrode leads are placed in the heart so does that mean I'd need an operation?'

'Yes.' Leo could tell that David wasn't happy at the thought of undergoing more surgery. David had been in and out of Theatre many times and most of the operations he'd had had entailed a lengthy stay in hospital afterwards. He hastened to reassure him.

'However, the device will be inserted under a local anaesthetic, although you will need to be sedated as well. It usually takes about an hour or so and then we will keep you in overnight so we can check it's working properly.' He shrugged. 'After that, you'll need to have it checked occasionally but that's all.'

'Really!' David exclaimed. He turned to Mia and grinned. 'Reckon the doc is telling me the truth or has he missed out the gory bits in case he scares me?'

'I'm sure Mr Forester wouldn't mislead you.' Mia glanced at him and Leo felt his blood pressure perform another of its new tricks, shooting skywards before he could stop it. It was all he could do to maintain a neutral expression as she continued in the same husky tone that was having such a devastating effect on him.

'He strikes me as someone who always tells the truth, no matter how unpalatable it is. I think you can trust him, David. I do.'

Mia wasn't sure why she had said that. Maybe she had wanted to reassure David but she knew it wasn't the only reason. She waited in silence while Leo explained to David that he would be taking him down to Theatre that afternoon. She did trust Leo and it was a surprise to discover she felt this way.

Growing up in care had made her wary of trusting anyone. Every time she'd formed an attachment to one of the care workers, they had either left or she had been sent to yet another foster-home. The experience had made her develop a protective shell and she had never allowed anyone inside it. It wasn't until she had met Chris that she had felt able to lower her defences. She had trusted Chris and now it appeared she trusted Leo too. It was unsettling to admit it.

Mia roused herself when she realised that Leo had finished. Leaning over, she once again fitted the oxygen mask over David's nose and mouth. 'Keep that on and I'll fetch you a cup of coffee. Deal?'

'Deal!' David high-fived her and settled back against the pillows. He looked exhausted as they moved away from the bed.

'I hope the ICD works,' she said quietly as they made their way to the office. 'He looks worn out.'

'No wonder, after what he's been through,' Leo replied in a tone that made her glance at him.

Colour swept up her face when she saw the awareness in his eyes because she knew what lay behind it. It was that comment about trusting him that was causing him to look at her this way. Why in heaven's name had she said it? It had been a stupid thing to say...a stupid thing to *think* in the circumstances. She couldn't afford to trust him until she was sure what his intentions were towards Harry.

Panic shot through her as she went into the office.

Had she allowed herself to be lulled into a false sense of security? What if Leo hadn't been telling her the truth and intended to try and claim Harry? They said that blood was thicker than water and if Harry was his son he could be planning to gain custody. The thought was more than she could bear and she swung round.

'What I said just now was purely for David's benefit.' She carried on when Leo said nothing. 'Whilst I trust you to do whatever is best for your patients, I have reservations when it comes to Harry.'

'You still believe that I might try to gain custody of him?' He sounded so cold that Mia shivered.

'I think it's possible—yes.'

'Then all I can do is repeat what I've already told you. I have no intention of trying to take Harry away from you, neither do I intend to allow you to take Noah away from me.' He pinned her with a cold-eyed stare. 'The old cliché about trust being a two-way street is very true, especially in this instance. I have to trust you, Mia, just as you have to trust me, whether we like the idea or not.'

He didn't say anything else as he turned and walked out of the door. Mia bit her lip, wondering why she felt like crying. There'd been something beneath the ice in Leo's voice, a kind of raw hurt that had touched her. She knew that she had upset him, hurt him, wounded *him*, the person he was, not the man he portrayed to the world. Beneath that coldly aloof exterior was a warm and loving man, a man who was as afraid to open his heart as she had been before she'd met Chris.

Her breath caught. She and Leo had more in common than just the boys, it seemed.

* * *

Leo spent the afternoon seeing patients at the private practice in Harley Street he shared with several other top-notch consultants. They covered a wide range of specialities from cardiology to oncology and were kept incredibly busy even in these straitened times.

People were prepared to spend money on their health and his view was that it was their decision, although, unlike some of his colleagues at the practice, he didn't subscribe to the theory that the service he provided to his private patients should be any better than what he offered to his NHS patients. He put one hundred per cent effort into helping *all* his patients.

His last appointment had phoned to cancel so he had an early finish for once. He drove home, wondering if he should make the most of the time and take Noah out. There was a new animated film showing at the cinema and he was sure that Noah would enjoy it…or at least he *thought* he would.

He sighed as he parked in the driveway. Noah had become so withdrawn since the accident that it was impossible to predict what he liked any more. Whenever he suggested they should do something, Noah always agreed but he never showed any real enthusiasm. He seemed happier at home, playing in his bedroom, in fact. Leo had tried to draw him out but he had failed to get to the root of the problem. Noah just shook his head whenever Leo asked him if he was worried about anything.

He knew that he needed to find out what was wrong but he didn't know how to set about it. Maybe Mia could suggest something?

He frowned as he let himself into the house. It was worrying to realise that he was starting to think of Mia in those terms. She might be Noah's biological mother but she knew absolutely nothing about him. She hadn't walked the floor, night after night, when Noah was a baby, trying to get him off to sleep. She hadn't been there when Noah had chickenpox and cried continuously. She hadn't even been there when Noah was rushed into hospital following the crash, so ill that the doctors had given him only a thirty per cent chance of surviving.

He had gone through all that on his own, walked the floor with him, soothed and comforted him, cried at the thought that he might lose him. So why on earth did he imagine that Mia could offer any advice? Was he looking for a way to create a stronger bond between them, to draw her deeper into his life? And if so, why? Was it really for the sake of the children or for himself?

Leo had no idea what the answers were to any of those questions and it troubled him to feel so unsure. He liked his life to be free of uncertainties but in this instance it wasn't possible. He drove the questions from his mind with a ruthless determination that made him feel a little better. So long as he could master his own thoughts he would be fine.

Noah was in the kitchen, eating his tea. Mrs Davies, their housekeeper, collected him from school each day and stayed with him until Leo got home. She smiled when she saw him coming in.

'You're nice and early for a change, Doctor. Noah's not finished his tea yet.'

'My final appointment cancelled,' Leo explained,

trying not to feel hurt when Noah didn't look up. Before the accident, Noah would have come running to greet him but these days he barely acknowledged him. It was as though the child blamed him for what had happened even though Amanda had been driving. Maybe he *would* mention it to Mia, he decided. If she could shed any light on Noah's behaviour it would be worth the risk.

Leo wasn't sure exactly what risk he was taking and refused to speculate. Drawing out a chair, he sat down beside his son and ruffled his hair. 'Did you have a good day at school?'

Noah nodded as he spooned spaghetti hoops into his mouth and Leo bit back a sigh. It was obviously not one of Noah's better days if he was refusing to talk to him. He persevered, determined to break down the barriers the child had erected between them. He loved Noah with all his heart and he couldn't bear to think there was something wrong with him and not be able to do anything about it.

'I thought we could go and watch that new film that's on the cinema seeing as I managed to get home early. What do you think? It's another one about that panda and you loved the first one, didn't you?'

Noah looked up, his expression betraying the tiniest hint of enthusiasm. 'Do we have to go in the car?'

'Nope.' Leo grinned, determined to make light of Noah's aversion to going anywhere by car. This was something he did understand, only too well. It was an effort to clamp down on the rush of anger at the thought of what Amanda had done but he'd be damned if he would upset Noah when he had finally made a breakthrough. Anyway, presenting a pleasant face to the world was a skill he needed to develop if he wasn't to completely alienate Harry.

Thinking about Harry reminded him of all the upset that was going to happen when Noah found out the truth about who his parents actually were. Not for the first time, Leo wished that he had left well alone and never started this. He and Noah could have carried on the way they'd been, and Mia and Harry could have done the same. They'd have remained oblivious of the true facts and that would have been far better for all of them.

Wouldn't it?

'We'll go on the bus. It stops right outside the cinema so there's no point taking the car and getting stuck in traffic.' Leo adopted a deliberately upbeat tone, not wanting Noah to suspect anything was wrong. So maybe he wasn't sure if it would have been better for him if Mia had never found out about the mix-up but that was his problem. If he and Mia had never met then he would never have felt he was missing out, would he?

He hurried on, refusing to dwell on that thought. 'Tell you what—we'll have an ice cream before the film starts, if you fancy it.'

'Yes!' Noah's face lit up. Pushing his plate away, he shot to his feet and went haring out of the kitchen to get ready.

'He's not finished his tea,' Mrs Davies said, shaking her head.

'Sorry.' Leo grimaced. 'My fault, I'm afraid.'

'Not to worry.' She cleared away the plate. 'It's nice to see him looking more like himself, isn't it?'

'It is.'

Leo felt a lump come to his throat and stood up. The fact that Mrs Davies had noticed the change in Noah only made it worse. As he went to get changed, he promised himself that he would do whatever it took to help Noah get over the accident. And if that meant involving Mia then that's what he would do, no matter what the cost to him personally.

CHAPTER EIGHT

NORMALLY, MIA WOULDN'T have taken Harry out on a school night but she decided to make an exception that night. He'd seemed unusually subdued when she had collected him from school and a little gentle probing had eventually elicited the answer. Harry was upset because he thought that Grandma was cross with him and he didn't know what he'd done wrong.

Mia's heart was heavy as she assured him that he had done nothing wrong and that Grandma had been feeling poorly and that was why she hadn't stayed to wave them off. This was the very thing she had wanted to avoid and she had no idea what she was going to do if Joyce reacted the same way again when they next went to visit her.

Perhaps it would be safer if she left it a couple of weeks and gave Joyce and Edward time to come to terms with what had happened, yet that would probably upset Harry too. He loved his grandparents and he would miss not seeing them, especially when they had always made such a fuss of him in the past. Talk about being stuck between a rock and a hard place!

In an effort to take Harry's mind off it, she suggested

they go out for tea at a fast-food restaurant. It worked as Harry could hardly contain his excitement at the thought of the forthcoming treat. They caught the bus, which was another thing Harry loved doing. Catching a train or taking the bus was far more exciting than travelling by car!

The restaurant was busy and they had to queue up to place their order, Harry, predictably, opting for the meal that came with a free toy.

Mia ordered a chicken wrap, nodding when the young man behind the counter told her he would bring it over. Picking up their tray, she looked for somewhere to sit but every table was taken. It was only when she realised that someone was waving to her that she spotted Leo sitting near the window and her stomach sank. The one thing she had never expected was that he'd be here.

She made her way to his table, forcing a smile when he stood up. 'Thanks for letting us share your table. It's packed in here tonight, isn't it?'

'It is indeed.' He took the tray from her while she slid into the booth, and quickly decanted its contents onto the table. He looked up and frowned. 'Aren't you having anything?'

'A chicken wrap. They said they'd bring it over when it was ready.'

Mia slipped out of her coat, wishing that she'd worn something a bit smarter than the ancient jumper she had changed into after work. The elbows were wearing thin and the front was decidedly bobbly so it could hardly be called flattering. She sighed as she helped Harry unpack his food so he could get at the free toy.

What did matter what she wore? Leo wasn't interested in her; he was only interested in her son.

'I see Harry's opted for the same deal as Noah.'

Leo's voice held a hint of amusement and Mia felt a little shiver run through her. She looked up, feeling her heart jolt when she saw a matching amusement in his eyes. He looked so much more approachable when he let down his defences, she decided, then wondered why the thought worried her so much. She cleared her throat.

'I think it's the free toy that's the big attraction rather than the food.'

'I'm sure you're right. They certainly know how to push all the right buttons when it comes to attracting the kids.'

He laughed and she felt the hair on the back of her neck lift. He really did have the sexiest laugh, deep and soft and as rich as melting chocolate.

'They do. No wonder they make so much money.' Mia's own laughter sounded strained but thankfully Leo didn't appear to notice.

'Pity I don't have shares in the company. I'm sure they're doing a lot better than the ones I do have.'

Mia smiled politely, although she was hard pressed not to let her anxiety show at the reminder that Leo had a lot more resources at his disposal than she had. He had promised that he wouldn't try to gain custody of Harry and she had to believe him. She helped Harry unpack his chicken nuggets, sighing when she realised that she had forgotten to get any tomato sauce to dip them in. She was about to go and fetch some when Leo pushed a small container across the table.

'Is this what you're after? I got way too much. Noah won't eat it all so Harry may as well have it.'

'Oh, right. Thanks.' She passed it to Harry. 'Say thank you to Leo, darling.'

'Thank you,' Harry muttered with a sad lack of grace.

Leo shook his head when Mia went to remonstrate with him. He waited until the child was busily occupied with his meal. 'Leave it. If you tell him off, it will only make matters worse. I'm afraid Harry isn't all that keen on me.'

'That's no excuse for being rude,' Mia countered.

'Normally, I'd agree with you but this situation is difficult for all of us.' His expression was sombre all of a sudden. 'It can only get even more difficult too. Heaven knows how these two will react when we tell them what's happened.'

'Don't.' Mia shivered. 'I can't bear to think about it. Yesterday was bad enough.'

'Yesterday. Why, what happened?'

'We went to visit Chris's parents.' She lowered her voice, although Harry and Noah were playing some sort of complicated game that involved their toys crashing into each other and couldn't possibly hear her. 'My mother-in-law was terribly upset—they both were, although Chris's dad handled it better. It ended up with her disappearing when she was supposed to be waving us off. Poor Harry thought he'd done something wrong and upset her. That's why I brought him out for tea, to take his mind off it.'

'Hell! That's the last thing you need, Mia.' He reached across the table and touched her hand. 'I'm so sorry. It's all my fault. I should never have started this, should I?'

'I don't think you had any choice once you realised there'd been a mix-up at the clinic.'

Mia withdrew her hand simply because it would have been far too easy to leave it where it was. The warm strength of Leo's fingers made her feel safe, secure, protected even, and she knew it was dangerous to feel that way. Leo's only interest in her was as the mother of his son and she mustn't forget that, must never open herself up to that kind of heartache. People could and did let you down; she knew that only too well. Maybe Chris had never failed her but that didn't mean Leo wouldn't.

'No. You're right. I couldn't have ignored it. It wouldn't have been right for any number of reasons. But it's still hard to accept that my actions are going to cause an awful lot of upset for you, Harry and Noah.'

'And for you too,' she pointed out, determined to stick to the subject under discussion. Allowing herself to be sidetracked by how she felt was stupid. 'This is bound to have an effect on you, too, Leo.' She glanced at Noah and bit her lip. 'If you love Noah the way I love Harry then I can imagine what you're going through.'

'I'm terrified that it will be the final straw when he finds out I'm not his real dad.'

Mia frowned. 'What do you mean, the final straw?'

'Just that Noah hasn't been himself since the accident. He's become very withdrawn.' He spread his hands wide open in a gesture that hinted at the frustration he was feeling. 'When I suggested coming out tonight, it was the first time I've seen him show any enthusiasm for ages.'

'He's been through a lot,' Mia observed, feeling a little knot of anxiety gather in her chest as she looked at Noah. Maybe she didn't have any real role in his life, but she did care about him. 'Being injured so badly must have shaken him. He's bound to behave differently for a while.'

'So you think that's what it is? He's still shocked because of the accident?'

Leo's tone was urgent and her frown deepened. 'I think so but what do you think? You know him better than I do.'

'I'm not sure—that's the truthful answer.' He shook his head. 'I've tried everything I can think of to get to the bottom of what's wrong with him. I've tried talking to him about the accident but he just clams up whenever I mention it. I even suggested he should draw me a picture of what happened but he wouldn't do it. Basically, he's shut me out and I don't know how to get through to him.'

'Have you tried counselling?' Mia suggested, feeling more concerned than ever.

'Oh, yes. He simply refused to say anything when I took him so that was that.'

'What about his mother? Will he speak to her?'

'I doubt it even if I knew where she was.' His tone was grim. 'The last I heard, Amanda was holidaying on some yacht in the Caribbean or, rather, *recuperating*, as she put it. She hasn't been in touch for months and I doubt if she'll bother now.'

'Because Noah isn't hers?' Mia said, appalled.

'Yes. Amanda had gone off the idea of motherhood even before Noah was born. In fact, if I hadn't threatened to tell everyone what she was planning, she would have aborted him.'

'No! But why go through all the discomfort of IVF if she wasn't committed to having a child? Did she do it for you?'

'Amanda never does anything for other people,' he said dryly. 'No, all her friends were having babies and she decided that she wanted one as well. I tried to talk her out of it but she was adamant.' He shrugged. 'She became even more determined when she failed to get pregnant. It turned out that her ovaries were blocked and the only way she could have a child was through IVF, so that's what we did.'

'But she changed her mind once she was pregnant?' Mia said, frowning.

'Yes. She hated being pregnant, hated feeling sick, hated being fat, hated everything about it. If I hadn't laid down the law, she would have got rid of Noah without a second thought.' His expression was grim. 'It was no better after Noah was born. Amanda wasn't interested in him and left when he was six months old.'

'How awful! It must have been very difficult for you.'

'Not really. To be frank, it was a relief not to have to put up with her constant complaints. I applied for sole custody of Noah and it was granted, although I did agree to allow her access. However, her visits were infrequent to say the least. She hadn't seen Noah for almost a year when she turned up one day and asked if she could take him out. I wasn't keen but there seemed no reason to refuse so I agreed. And that's when the accident happened.'

His tone was harsh. 'So as far as I'm concerned

Amanda isn't involved in this. It's you and me who need to decide what to do, so if you want out now that you know Noah has problems, you'd better say so, Mia. The last thing I want is him getting hurt any more.'

Leo could feel anger welling up inside him. He wasn't sure what had triggered it, apart from the fact that thinking about Amanda always left him feeling out of sorts. Mia drew back and he could tell that she was offended but so what? He needed to make it clear that once they involved the children there was no going back.

'And the last thing I want is Harry getting hurt either. It seems we agree on something.'

Her tone was sharp. Leo felt his temper leap another notch up the scale. He wasn't used to people speaking to him that way and didn't appreciate it. He glared at her. 'Then we need to formulate some sort of a plan, don't we?'

'Hopefully, something better than the last one you came up with,' she shot back.

'About us pretending to be seeing one another?' His brows rose. 'And what was wrong with that, may I ask?'

'Oh, nothing, except that I'm as likely to agree to go out with you as with Jack the Ripper!'

She turned to Harry, ignoring Leo as she told the child that it was time they left. Leo forced down his anger as he told Noah that it was time they left too if they weren't to miss the start of the film. Noah gathered up his plastic toy and put it carefully in his pocket.

'Can Harry come with us?' he asked, looking beseechingly at Leo.

'I'm not sure if Harry's mummy wants him to stay

out late,' Leo hedged, because it was the last thing he wanted. Oh, not that he didn't want Harry to accompany them, but if Harry came then Mia would have to come too. The thought of being subjected to any more of her pronouncements didn't exactly fill him with joy. Comparing him to Jack the Ripper indeed!

'Can Harry come with us, Mia? Please?' Noah begged, and Leo immediately forgot his injured feelings. Having Harry go with them was obviously important to Noah and that was all that mattered.

He looked at Mia and shrugged. 'It's up to you, but Harry is very welcome if he'd like to come. You too obviously.'

Mia took a deep breath. She wasn't sure why she had gone off at the deep end. Maybe it was because Leo believed that she was no more trustworthy than his ex-wife had been but it had been wrong of her to react that way. They would never deal with this situation if they started quarrelling with each other.

'If Harry wants to go then I can't see that it's a problem.' She dredged up a smile when Harry whooped in delight. 'I think that's a yes.'

Leo laughed and she was relieved to see no trace of annoyance on his face. 'Seems like it. OK, guys, let's go. We'd better get a wriggle on if you want to buy some popcorn before the film starts.'

'Yes!'

The two boys went racing to the door and Mia hurriedly followed them. 'Wait!' she ordered before they had time to go charging outside. She took hold of their hands, bending so she could look from one excited face to the other. 'There are a lot of cars out there so you're to hold my hands and not go running off. Understand?'

They both nodded, holding obediently onto her hands as she led them outside. The cinema was at the far side of the complex and they skipped along beside her, chattering excitedly about the film they were about to see. Mia paused outside the cinema so Leo could catch them up, surprised by the pensive expression on his face as he ushered them inside. She waited until the boys had gone to select their popcorn before she asked him what was wrong.

'Nothing. In fact, everything's better than it's been for a long time.' He looked at the children. 'I was starting to think that I'd never get through to Noah, but tonight he seems so much more like his old self and it's all thanks to you and Harry.'

He turned and Mia's breath caught when she saw the way he was looking at her. Maybe it was gratitude that had prompted it but it felt good to see warmth in his eyes after the chill that had been there earlier. She realised that she wanted him to look at her this way all the time and it was scary to know how vulnerable she was. She mustn't make the mistake of thinking that Leo cared about her for her own sake.

'I'm glad we could help.'

She gave him a quick smile then went to pay for the popcorn. Leo had the tickets when they went back and he shepherded them into the auditorium. The theatre was packed but they had numbered seats right in the middle. The film started almost immediately and the boys were soon engrossed. Mia stared at the screen, although she took in very little of what was happening.

Leo was sitting at one end and she was at the other, with Harry and Noah in between, and she told herself that she was glad. At least it meant she didn't have to sit beside him.

Her breath caught as she found herself imagining how it might have been if they had sat next to each other. She would have felt the warmth of his body, heard him breathing, smelled the scent of his skin, that clean fresh aroma that was such an intrinsic part of him. Feelings she had never experienced before suddenly swamped her and she bit her lip. She could feel her body growing hot and languid, hear own breathing becoming laboured, feel her nose tingling as though the scent that filled her nostrils was real.

Was this how passion felt? she wondered. This awakening of the senses, this heightening of awareness? Although she had loved Chris, they had been unable to make love—his injuries had made it impossible. They had shared kisses and caresses, though, and she had enjoyed them, but she had never been aroused to passion. If she was honest, she had believed that she was incapable of feeling passion but if that were true why did she feel this way?

Mia sat there in the darkness and tried to work it out but it was impossible. Impossible to take these feelings and categorise them, explain them or will them away. All she knew was that she was twenty-nine years old. She had been married. She had borne a child. Yet she had been an innocent, untried, untested, unaroused.

Until now.

Leo stared at the screen. The colours were so vivid that they made his eyes ache but he was afraid to close them. There were thoughts lurking in his head, ones he didn't want to encourage. He needed to concentrate on the film and shut them out, turn his mind away from those tantalising images of him and Mia sitting close together, holding hands, sharing a kiss, sharing more.

He cursed softly, turned it into a cough when Noah glanced at him. He turned and grinned at his son because Noah was his son no matter who his biological parents were. Mia might be Noah's mother but he was Noah's dad and he intended to be his dad for evermore. Nothing was going to get in the way of that, nothing was going to part him from this child he adored, neither Mia nor this crazy attraction he felt for her.

'OK?' he whispered, struggling to get a grip. One thing could lead to another and before he knew it, he'd be in so deep he'd never get out. He had been attracted to other women in the past and had parted company from them when the time had come, but he couldn't do that with Mia, could he? She was part of this whole package, her and Harry, and Noah and him. They were all bound up together so that if you wanted one you had to have the other as well. Mia and Harry came as a pair. Just like him and Noah.

'It's great!'

Noah grinned at him then turned back to the screen and Leo felt his heart overflow. He couldn't describe how wonderful it felt to see the child looking so happy. It had been a long haul to reach this point and there could still be problems ahead, but Noah would get there eventually. He was sure of that, just as he was sure that meeting Mia had been the trigger. Noah had formed a bond with her and Harry and that was what had made the difference. He would always be grateful to her for that.

He glanced along the row, felt his breath catch when he caught sight of her. She was staring at the screen but he knew that she wasn't thinking about the film. There was just something about her expression, a certain set to her features that told him it was the last thing on her mind.

Leo turned away, staring sightlessly ahead. He could no longer see the eye-aching colours flashing across the screen or hear the raucous music. He was being drawn into a world of his own, a world that he really, *really* didn't want to inhabit.

He groaned quietly, unable to fight off temptation any longer. Pictures immediately flooded his mind, pictures of him and Mia touching, kissing, caressing, making love. He knew it was wrong to indulge himself this way. If he followed through on such thoughts it could be a disaster, and not just for him but for Noah and Harry. He had dated enough women both before and after his marriage ended to know that physical attraction didn't last. Oh, it might take a month or two but it always faded, and that would complicate matters even more.

He could deal with the thought of Mia being Noah's real mother, accept that she had given birth to his son. What he couldn't handle was the idea of her once having been his lover. That would be a step too far!

CHAPTER NINE

IT WAS GONE seven by the time the film ended. Mia took hold of Harry's hand and briskly led him outside, wanting to bring the evening to a speedy conclusion. Turning, she smiled politely at Leo, who was in the process of zipping up Noah's coat.

'Thank you for inviting us. We really enjoyed it, didn't we, Harry?'

'It was brilliant!'

Harry grinned at them and she saw Leo's expression soften. It touched her that it so obviously meant a lot to him to have earned Harry's approval, but she hardened her heart. She couldn't afford to let her emotions run away with her again.

Heat rushed up her face as she recalled in vivid detail how she'd felt in the cinema and she turned away, making a great production of fastening Harry's jacket. Maybe she was attracted to Leo but nothing was going to come of it; she would make sure of that. It would be foolish in the extreme to get involved with him when the situation they faced was already so fraught.

'I'm glad you enjoyed it, Harry. Noah enjoyed having you along. Maybe you'd like to come round to our house one day and play with him, if your mummy doesn't mind, of course.'

Mia looked up when she heard the hesitancy in Leo's voice. It wasn't like him to exhibit anything other than supreme confidence, so it came as a surprise. 'Of course I don't mind,' she said quietly, wondering what could have dented his legendary self-assurance.

'Good.' He gave her a quick smile and she realised that she must have imagined it. There was certainly no sign of indecision as he turned to Harry. 'How about if you come round on Saturday? Would you like that? Noah and I can pick you up around ten if you fancy it.'

'Yes!' Harry exclaimed, obviously delighted at the thought of seeing his new friend again.

Mia didn't share his joy, however. Leo had made no mention of her going along and she wasn't sure if she was happy to let Harry go off on his own with Leo just yet. Maybe he was Harry's real father but she knew very little about him apart from the fact that he was a first-rate surgeon.

'Noah's daddy and I need to talk about it first,' she cautioned. She shook her head when Harry's lower lip jutted ominously. 'I'm not saying that you can't go, darling, but Leo and I need to sort out the details.' She gave a forced little laugh, hating the fact that she'd been made to take on the role of the bad guy for spoiling the promised treat. 'Why, I don't even know where Noah lives!'

'You're right,' Leo said with a grimace. 'Sorry, Harry. I should have asked your mummy first before I suggested it.'

'Never mind.' Mia tried to shrug it off as an oversight, although she wasn't happy about his high-handed behaviour. If he thought he could walk all over her, he could think again! She took hold of Harry's hand. 'I'll give you a call and see what we can work out. OK?'

'Fine. You should have my phone number but I'll give it to you again just in case.' He dug in his pocket and came up with a scrap of paper, scribbling down his telephone number before handing it to her. 'We live in Primrose Hill—I should have written the address down as well.' He took the paper from her and wrote down his address then gave it back to her. 'If you do agree to let Harry come I promise I'll take very good care of him, Mia.'

'I'm sure you will,' Mia agreed, wondering if he was deliberately making it appear as though she was fussing. Her smile was strained as she slipped the paper into her pocket. If Leo was planning to play these sorts of games, she had no intention of letting him get away with it. 'Right, it's time we went home. Say goodnight, Harry.'

She led Harry to the bus stop after he'd said goodbye. Fortunately their bus arrived almost immediately so they got on board and climbed the stairs as Harry loved sitting on the top deck. Mia caught a glimpse of Leo and Noah standing at the bus stop before their bus pulled away and had to clamp down on the anger bubbling inside her.

Was Leo trying to gain the upper hand by offering Harry treats? She hoped not. The situation was difficult enough without that sort of added pressure. Harry was her son no matter what the DNA tests said and she wasn't going to allow anyone to lure him away. How would Leo feel if she tried to do the same to Noah?

she wondered, and shivered. She could imagine only too easily how Leo would react.

Leo made his way home, very much aware that he had upset Mia. He got Noah ready for bed then went downstairs, wondering what to do. Normally, he wouldn't have cared two hoots. Although he was never deliberately rude, he did tend to be a little too forthright so there'd been a number of occasions when he had unwittingly hurt someone's feelings. Normally his solution was to ignore it because in his experience folk got over it in the end. However, he couldn't seem to take that approach with Mia. He had upset her and he regretted it. Very much.

He went into his study and picked up the phone then hesitated. Would a phone call be enough or would it be better if he spoke to her face to face? He would hate to think that she didn't believe he was genuinely sorry, especially when it could have a detrimental impact on their future dealings. He needed Mia on his side, although he wasn't prepared to delve too deeply into all the reasons why it was so important to him.

He phoned his housekeeper instead and asked her if she would mind sitting with Noah as he had to go out. As soon as she arrived, he left. He glanced at the dashboard clock as he started the car: half past eight. Not too late to go calling by most people's standards so, hopefully, it wouldn't be too late for Mia. He certainly didn't want to upset her any more than he already had!

Mia had just made herself a cup of tea when there was a knock on the front door. Putting the cup on the table, she went to answer it, wondering who it could be. She rarely had visitors and it was too late for any salespeople to call. Opening the door, she gasped when she found Leo standing outside.

'What are you doing here?'

'I was going to phone but then I decided it would be better if I spoke to you face to face,' he said quietly.

'Really?' Mia replied, hoping he couldn't tell how on edge she felt. Having him turn up like this was a shock and not a pleasant one either after what had happened earlier. She squared her shoulders, determined to stick to her decision not to allow him to ride roughshod over her. If he had come to harass her about allowing Harry to visit his home this weekend, he could think again.

'So, what do you want? Or do I need to ask?' Her smile was tight. 'If you've come to *browbeat* me into agreeing to let Harry come and play with Noah then forget it, Leo. I make the decisions where Harry is concerned, not you.'

'I know. And I'm truly sorry if you thought I was trying to force your hand.' He grimaced, his handsome face filled with contrition. 'I'm so used to getting my own way that it's hard to accept that I need to consult you when it comes to Harry.'

'Oh. I see.' Mia was nonplussed by the apology and had no idea what to say. She bit her lip and heard him sigh.

'I never meant to upset you, Mia. The last thing I want is you and me falling out.'

'Me too. We've enough to contend with without us being at odds.'

'Too right we do.' His tone was wry. It matched the

smile he gave her as he stepped away from the door. 'Anyway, I won't keep you. I just wanted to make my apologies and smooth things over.'

'I appreciate that.' Mia took a quick breath, wondering why she felt so loath to let him leave. She didn't bother trying to work it out as she opened the door wider. 'Would you like a cup of tea, seeing as you're here? I've just made a pot and you're very welcome to share it with me.'

'Thank you. I'd like that.' He smiled at her as he stepped into the tiny vestibule. 'A cup of tea sounds like just the thing to seal a friendship.'

Mia smiled politely as she led the way into the living room, although she couldn't help wondering if they would ever be friends. Necessity had brought them together rather than choice and there was no way of knowing if they would get on in the long term, just as there was no way of knowing if friendship would be enough. She bit her lip. Having Leo as her friend might be good, but having him as her lover would be even better.

'I'll get your tea. Milk and sugar?'

Mia forced the thought aside, terrified that he would pick up on it. She didn't want Leo to be her lover; the idea was ridiculous. It would only complicate matters even more, especially if they fell out as lovers so often did. Imagine how difficult it would be to see and speak to Leo, to have any dealings whatsoever with him if they'd been intimately involved. No, she must forget how she'd felt in the cinema and focus on what really mattered, Harry and Noah. She may not have given birth to Noah but he was still her son and she cared about him.

'Just milk, please.' Leo looked around the room, smiling when he spotted a photo of Harry on the mantelpiece. He picked it up, shaking his head in amazement. 'There's a photo of me at about the same age and we could be two peas in a pod.'

'Really? You must let me see it one day.' Mia went over to the shelves in the alcove next to the chimney breast and picked up the photograph album. 'There's a lot more photos in here if you'd like to have a look at them.'

'I would. Thank you.'

Leo took the album from her and she sucked in her breath when their hands touched. He took it over to the sofa and sat down, opening it at the first page. He seemed engrossed when she left the room and it was a relief. At least Leo hadn't experienced that flash of awareness that had shot through her when their hands had touched. It would be so much harder if he had, so much more difficult to fight her feelings if she knew that he felt the same.

She took a deep breath, forcing down the rush of sensations that had filled her. They were the parents of their two beautiful boys. It was enough of a bond between them and they didn't need anything more.

Leo inhaled sharply as Mia left the room but his heart was racing. He couldn't remember the last time he had felt this way—probably never. Whatever relationships he'd had in the past, he had always been in control. Even when he had asked Amanda to marry him it had been a conscious decision, weighed up and evaluated beforehand. Love hadn't entered into it, desire had been merely a bonus. He had enjoyed sleeping with Amanda enough to overlook her more irritating traits, although even that hadn't lasted much beyond their honeymoon. Desire rarely did last in his experience. So why had he reacted so strongly when his and Mia's hands had touched? Why did he want it to happen again? And, most worrying of all, why did it feel as though his brain was engaged this time and not just his body?

'Here you are.'

Leo jumped when Mia reappeared with a cup of tea for him. He took it from her, taking care not to touch her this time. Once was enough if his current parlous state of mind was anything to go by. 'Thanks.'

He took a sip of the hot liquid then looked for somewhere to put the cup down. Mia hurriedly moved a small table closer to him.

'Use this.'

'Thank you.'

He placed the cup on the table and sat back in his seat, determined to project the right image. Maybe he did feel at sixes and sevens but it would pass and he'd soon be back to his usual self. He frowned, wondering why the idea seemed less appealing than it should have done. He liked his life free of emotional ties, apart from the ties he had to Noah obviously. So why did he find himself wondering if he was missing out?

'Harry really enjoyed the film. He talked about it all the way home.'

'Did he? That's good.'

Leo dredged up a smile. His life was fine and there was nothing he lacked. He had enough money to buy whatever he wanted and go wherever he chose. He enjoyed his work and wouldn't wish to do anything else. If he needed to satisfy his more basic needs then it was easy enough to find an attractive woman to satisfy them with. He had everything he could possibly want.

Except Mia.

The blood rushed to his head so that he missed what else she said. There were reasons why he and Mia could never get involved, important reasons like the effect it could have on the boys, but it didn't make a scrap of difference. Leo realised with a sinking heart that it was what he wanted. Badly. He, Leo Forester, erstwhile master of his own destiny, had no control whatsoever in this instance.

Mia's voice faltered. Leo was staring at her, although she doubted if he'd heard a word she had said. She had no idea what was going through his mind but if his expression was anything to go by, it wasn't pleasant. She cleared her throat and saw him jump. 'Penny for them. You were miles away.'

'Was I? Sorry.'

He turned to the next page in the album, studying a photo of Chris holding Harry on his lap. Harry had been just a few weeks old when it was taken and he was staring at the camera with that intensity that very young babies often displayed. Mia drummed up a laugh. She really didn't want to know what Leo had been thinking. Something warned her it would be too disturbing.

'Harry was about six weeks old when that was taken,' she explained, clamping down on the rush of heat that scorched her veins. To imagine that Leo was experiencing the same kind of uncertainty as she was would be asking for trouble. 'He'd just had a bath and Chris was giving him a cuddle before I put him to bed.'

'He looks very contented.'

'He was. He was such a good baby, ate and slept exactly like the textbooks said he should do.' She smiled reminiscently. 'Chris and I used to say that we'd won the jackpot when we got Harry.'

'Noah was the exact opposite,' Leo said wryly, and she was relieved to hear him sounding more like he normally did.

'Was he?' she said quickly, wanting to keep the conversation on track. It was easier when they focused on the children, less stressful.

'Mmm. He never slept and as for feeding…! We were lucky if we could get a couple of ounces of milk down him.'

'It must have been very difficult for your ex-wife,' she observed, wondering if that explained why Noah's mother had abandoned him. A lot of women suffered from postnatal depression and it could be that Noah's mother had been one of them.

'Amanda had very little to do with looking after him. She hired a nanny to care for him when she left hospital,' Leo said shortly.

'I see,' Mia replied, because there wasn't much else she could say. She had loved looking after Harry and had relished every moment, but maybe she was being uncharitable. After all, she hadn't suffered all those sleepless nights, had she?

Leo didn't say anything else as he turned to the next photo, which happened to be one of her sitting on a rug in the garden, holding Harry. He studied it intently, rather too intently, in fact. Mia gave a nervous little laugh.

'The bags under my eyes were the result of rushing around all over the place. Harry wasn't responsible for them.'

'I never noticed them.' He looked up and his grey eyes seemed to shimmer with silver fire as they rested on her. 'I was just thinking how happy you look, Mia. Happy and fulfilled.'

'I was.' Mia felt a lump come to her throat. It was silly to feel so touched by the observation but she couldn't help it. 'I loved being a mum and to cap it all, Chris was so well at the time too. It was one of those perfect times in your life when everything comes together.'

'You must miss him, your husband, I mean.'

'I do. He was so brave. It doesn't seem fair that after everything he'd been through, he should have died like that.'

'What happened exactly?'

'He developed a DVT. Chris had no idea, of course. He wasn't aware of any pain but I realised something was wrong when I saw how swollen his leg was.' She sighed. 'He was rushed into hospital and given drugs to dissolve the clot but part of it must have broken off. He had a massive heart attack and there was nothing anyone could do.'

'It must have been horrendous for you.'

The sympathy in his voice brought tears to her eyes and she blinked them away. 'It was. Harry had just turned three and all I could think about was that now he would grow up without a father. I know how it feels not to have a family and it broke my heart to think that Harry would miss out on so much.'

'Did your father die when you were young?' Leo asked, and she shook her head.

'No. Or, rather, I don't think he did.' She saw him frown and realised that she would have to explain. Her tone was brisk because she didn't want him to think that she was looking for sympathy. 'I never knew my father. He was well off the scene by the time I was born. I don't know that much about my mother either as I was taken into care when I was eighteen months old and had very little contact with her after that.'

'Good heavens!' Leo exclaimed. 'I had no idea that you'd had it so tough.'

'There's no reason why you should have known,' she countered. 'Anyway, it's all in the past. It doesn't affect me now.'

'Oh, I think it does.' He looked at her and Mia shuddered when she felt the intensity of his gaze envelop her like a physical force. 'The way you were brought up has made you the person you are today, Mia. It's one of the reasons why you're such a good mother, in fact.'

He paused and she steeled herself for what he would say next. 'I only wish that you'd been around when Noah was born. It would have made the world of difference to him, I'm sure.'

CHAPTER TEN

'So, IS THERE anything you'd like to ask me, David?'

Leo waited while the younger man gave it some thought. It was Friday morning and a slot had unexpectedly become vacant in Theatre. As soon as he had found out, he had contacted David Rimmer and offered him the chance to have the ICD fitted. The sooner it was done the better, in his opinion.

'I don't think so.' David frowned as he turned to Mia. 'Is there anything else I need to know, do you think?'

'No. I think Mr Forester has covered everything, David.' She squeezed the young man's hand. 'My advice to you is to let him do what he does best—mend wonky hearts!'

David laughed, obviously relieved to be given such straightforward advice. Leo smiled too, although his own feelings were far more complicated. Ever since Mia had revealed what a difficult time she'd had growing up, his emotions had swung from one extreme to the other.

Whilst he admired her fortitude, he wished with every scrap of his being that she hadn't had to experience so much unhappiness in her life. It made his own upbringing seem like a walk in the park by comparison and he found himself wondering if he was guilty of self-indulgence. Maybe his parents hadn't smothered him in love but they had always been there for him.

It was unsettling to find himself re-evaluating yet another aspect of his life. He pushed the thought aside while he concentrated on David. 'As I explained the other day, you'll be having a local anaesthetic, not a general one. You'll be sedated as well but you will be conscious throughout the procedure.'

'So basically I'll know what's going on but won't be able to kick up a fuss if I don't like it?' David observed wryly.

Leo laughed, very much aware that he wouldn't have laughed a few weeks ago. He would have maintained a strictly professional front rather than encourage a patient to speak to him this way, but that had been before he'd met Mia. Meeting her had changed him. It was another disquieting thought.

'That's right. Once I have you on the table, there's no backing out. Still, look on the bright side. The ICD will mean that you'll see a lot less of me in the future.'

'Bonus!' David declared. 'Although I have to admit that I'll miss Mia. She makes a wicked cup of coffee.'

'Flatterer,' Mia retorted, laughing.

She straightened the sheet then followed Leo to the door. He paused so she could catch him up, thinking how pretty she looked. The navy-blue colour of her uniform suited her, he decided, highlighting the chestnut lights in her hair and bringing out the glorious emerald-green shade of her eyes. His gaze ran over her as he took appreciative stock. She was neither too fat nor too thin but just perfect. It was only when he realised that she was looking expectantly at him that he rallied.

'I'm not anticipating any problems. David should be back on the ward later this morning. Are his parents coming in?'

'Yes. He told them to wait until after the op so it will be nearer to lunchtime before they get here.'

'Good. Right, it looks like we're good to go.' Leo turned to leave, not wanting to linger in case it became a habit. Work was work and they'd agreed to keep it separate from their private lives. A frisson shot through him and he had to remind himself that the only private life he and Mia had revolved around the children.

'Before you go, Leo, I just want to make sure what the arrangements are for tomorrow,' she said, putting her hand on his arm.

Leo sucked in his breath when he felt the hairs all over his body stand to attention. It was just a touch, he told himself sternly, but it was hard to think of it as *just* anything. 'Tomorrow?'

'When Harry comes to play with Noah.' She frowned. 'You are still expecting him? He's talked about nothing else all week and he'll be really disappointed if he can't come.'

'Of course he can come!' Leo exclaimed. 'I didn't think you were keen on the idea, that's all.'

She sighed. 'I wasn't when you first suggested it but now I've accepted that you aren't trying to lure Harry away, I'm fine with it.'

'I would *never* try to lure him away from you, Mia.' He covered her hand with his, feeling his heart leap when he realised how small and delicate it felt compared to his. An unfamiliar rush of tenderness filled him and his tone deepened. 'I give you my word on that.'

'Thank you. I appreciate it more than you can imagine.'

Her voice had softened, the husky tones making all those pesky hairs start saluting again. Leo felt the fledgling tender feelings change to something deeper and drew in his breath. Even though he knew it was inappropriate to behave this way at work, he couldn't help himself. It was only when he heard footsteps coming along the corridor that he managed to get a grip.

He stepped back so that Mia's hand slid from his arm. 'I'll pick Harry up around ten if that's all right with you?'

'Fine. I'll make sure he's ready.'

She smiled but he could see the awareness in her eyes and knew that she felt the same as he did. He turned away, barely acknowledging the greeting as he passed one of the nurses. His head was spinning as thoughts whirled around inside it. He was attracted to Mia and she was attracted to him too but they couldn't act upon their feelings. They had to concentrate on Noah and Harry, on making sure that what had happened at the clinic didn't ruin their young lives.

Leo took a deep breath as he stepped into the lift. He might want Mia but he could never have her. The sooner he accepted that, the easier it would be.

'My, my, you two looked very cosy. Do I detect a hint of romance in the air?'

Mia started when Penny Morrison stopped beside

her. Taking a deep breath, she turned to her. 'Don't be silly. Mr Forester and I were discussing a patient.'

'Really? So that's why you were staring into each other's eyes.' Penny grinned. 'Pull the other one, Mia. That's got umpteen bells on it!'

Mia sighed. She knew it was pointless trying to convince Penny that she was telling the truth. After all, she and Leo had been staring at each other. She ditched that thought because she couldn't deal with it right then. Maybe later she would be able to make sense of what had happened but not now.

'You're adding two and two and coming up with five hundred. Leo and I were sorting out what time he can collect Harry tomorrow.'

'Harry? And why should *Leo* be making arrangements to collect him?' Penny demanded, emphasising Mia's use of Leo's first name.

'Because Harry and Noah are friends and they want to spend the morning together,' Mia explained, deciding it was easier to ignore the unspoken question. She would only dig herself an even deeper hole if she tried to explain how she happened to be on first-name terms with one of the consultants.

'Friends? How come?' Penny followed her into the office, making it clear that she wasn't about to give up. 'I mean, how did they meet? I know for a fact that Mr Forester's son goes to a private school so it can't have been there.'

'Of course not. Harry and I happened to bump into him and Noah at a fast-food place on Monday.' Mia shrugged. 'We ended up going to the cinema together to see a film. Harry and Noah just seemed to hit it off, so Leo invited Harry round to play with him tomorrow.'

'Fancy that. Maybe the Ice Man is human after all.'

Penny shrugged and Mia was relieved to see that her friend had accepted her explanation. When Penny turned her attention to the reason for her visit—a time-table glitch—she breathed easier. Although she hated misleading Penny, it was vital that nobody found out what was going on. The last thing she wanted was the boys overhearing something they shouldn't.

Mia sat down to update David Rimmer's notes after Penny left, wondering if it was possible to stop people finding out. At some point, she and Leo would have to tell the boys what had happened and there was no know-ing how they would react. It could be that they would have to inform their schools too and the thought of more people knowing that Harry was actually Leo's son and Noah was hers filled her with dread. The more people who knew, the harder it would be to keep it a secret.

It was early when Leo got up on Saturday morning. Mrs Davies didn't come in at the weekend unless he was seeing patients at his rooms in Harley Street. Since Noah's accident, he had tried to keep Saturdays free. Although he was aware that several of his colleagues weren't happy with the arrangement, helping Noah over-come whatever was troubling him took precedence.

Once breakfast was over, he sent Noah upstairs for his coat. Although they were far too early to collect Harry, he couldn't see any point in them waiting around. He sighed, aware that he was as eager to see Mia as Noah was to see his new friend. He was acting like a teenager in the throes of his first crush…except he hadn't acted this way when he *had* been a teenager! It was worrying to realise that Mia had this effect on him, especially when he knew it couldn't lead anywhere.

It was just after nine when he drew up outside her house. He helped Noah out of the car and ushered him up the path. Mia must have heard them because she opened the door before he could knock.

'I take it that Noah couldn't wait either,' she said, smiling at him. 'Harry was dressed and all ready to go by seven!'

'Was he?' Leo smiled back, trying to ignore the leap his pulse had given when she'd opened the door. Maybe he was having some sort of mid-life crisis, he mused, and that explained why he was acting so out of character. He tested out the theory as he followed her inside but he wasn't convinced. He sighed. Maybe he should stop trying to analyse what was happening and just get on with it. 'Good. I don't feel as guilty now for landing on your doorstep at this hour of the morning.'

'Oh, there's no need to feel guilty. We've been up for ages. Still, at least it meant you didn't catch me in my pyjamas.'

'Er…no.' Leo managed to hold his smile but all of a sudden his mind was awash with pictures of Mia in her nightclothes or, more accurately, out of them. He cleared his throat. 'I'll give Harry his lunch if that's all right with you and bring him back around four?'

'That's fine.' She looked round when Harry and Noah came racing into the room. 'Did you hear that, darling? Leo says you can have lunch with Noah.'

Her tone was bright and breezy, so why did Leo

have the feeling that she knew exactly what he'd been thinking? He turned to the boys, eager to hide his confusion. He preferred to keep his feelings under wraps. He had always been highly successful at doing so too and it worried him to know that Mia could slip past his defences so easily.

'Right, guys, let's get going. Say goodbye to your mummy, Harry.'

He waited while Harry gave Mia a hug, somewhat surprised when Noah hugged her as well. Noah had been so withdrawn lately, shying away whenever Leo had tried to hug him, but obviously he felt comfortable about hugging Mia.

It was something he knew he would take on board. As he led the boys out to the car, he couldn't help wondering if this was the turning point he'd been hoping for. Having Mia around could be exactly what Noah needed, even though the child had no idea who she really was. He sighed as he started the engine. It made it more imperative than ever that he keep a rein on his feelings. He couldn't afford to do anything that might harm Noah's relationship with Mia.

Mia set to after Leo left and got all the jobs that needed doing finished in record time. She looked around the pristine kitchen and sighed. Maybe it was easier to get the housework done without Harry constantly interrupting her but she did miss him. She glanced at the clock and grimaced: it was only eleven a.m. Leo had promised to have Harry home by four. which meant she had five hours to kill. How on earth was she going to fill in the time?

She made herself a cup of coffee and sat down at the table to drink it. When she had been in the children's home, she had longed for time on her own, she remembered wryly. Once she had left care, she had found a flat—a bedsit really—and revelled in the fact that she had her own space at last. She had lived on her own until she had married, in fact, and had enjoyed it, but not any longer. She couldn't bear to imagine how lonely her life would be if she didn't have Harry.

She stood up, refusing to sit there and think depressing thoughts. Leo had promised that he wouldn't try to take Harry away from her and she believed him. She went upstairs to her bedroom and opened the wardrobe. She had been meaning to sort through Chris's clothes and give them to a local charity shop and now was the perfect time to do it.

Mia set to work, not even stopping for lunch. She hadn't realised just how much there was of Chris's belongings but by the time she heard a car drawing up outside, she had everything sorted. She ran downstairs, smiling as she opened the front door. 'Hello, sweetheart. Have you had a lovely time?'

'It was brilliant!' Harry declared. 'Noah has this *huge* garage and a hundred million cars. We played with them for ages!'

'How wonderful.' Mia turned to Noah. Leo hadn't made it up the path yet as he was on his phone. It was obviously an important call because he looked very grave. She smiled at the little boy, her heart turning over when once again she was struck by his resemblance to Chris. Maybe it was the fact that she had spent the afternoon sorting through Chris's belongings but she felt very emotional all of a sudden. 'Did you enjoy it too, Noah?'

'Yes.' He smiled shyly up at her. 'Harry's my best friend and he said he wants to come and play with me again if you'll let him.'

'Of course he can,' Mia assured him, giving him a hug. 'And you can come and play with him too, if you want to.'

She straightened up as Noah nodded, feeling her pulse leap when she found herself staring into Leo's eyes. 'Noah was just telling me what a lovely time he and Harry have had,' she explained, trying not to read too much into the way he was looking at her, but it was impossible. To know that Leo wanted her this much was both scary and exciting.

She hurried on, terrified that she would do something stupid. She and Leo could never be more than friends. She had to remember that and not be tempted to put her own needs ahead of the boys'. 'Thank you for inviting Harry. He enjoyed every minute.'

'It was my pleasure, Mia.'

His voice sounded so deep as he said her name that she shivered. She turned away, her heart racing. She knew so little about desire yet that was what she was feeling. She wanted Leo, wanted him to say her name again as he kissed her, caressed her, made love to her, and the strength of her feelings shocked her. She had never wanted any man like this, had never felt this need growing inside her, consuming her. So why did she feel this way about Leo? Why did the sound of his voice saying her name fill her with such longing? She had no idea. What she did know was that she and Leo could never be lovers.

CHAPTER ELEVEN

LEO'S CHEST FELT tight as he followed Mia inside. He took a deep breath but no amount of oxygen could ease the restriction. His hands clenched as he struggled to contain the feelings that were running riot inside him. Maybe she did want him every bit as much as he wanted her but nothing was going to come of it.

He followed her into the sitting room and looked around. He had no idea what she had been doing but she'd obviously been busy because there was a smudge of dirt on her cheek. His hand half lifted to wipe it away before he thought better of it. He didn't dare touch her, couldn't take that risk. One touch wouldn't be enough—he'd want more and more, he'd want it all.

His vision blurred as pictures danced before his eyes, pictures of him stroking and caressing every inch of her satin-smooth skin, and a groan broke from his lips. How the hell was he going to cope when the mere thought of making love to her could push him to the edge?

'Leo? Are you all right?'

The question broke into his thoughts and he rallied. 'Sorry. I was just trying to work out what to do.'

'Why? What's happened? Can I help in any way?'

Definitely, Leo thought wryly, although he managed not to say so. 'Not really. One of my patients has been rushed into hospital. He was due to have bypass surgery but he's been putting it off for months now. There's no way we can delay any longer, though. It needs sorting out a.s.a.p.'

'Surely Dr Wilson can deal with him?' Mia suggested, frowning.

Leo's hands clenched once again as he fought to control the urge to smooth away the tiny lines puckering her brow. He had never wanted to touch a woman as much as he yearned to touch her and it was hard to accept that he was no longer in full control of himself. 'He could, only the patient has requested that I perform the surgery. He's one of my private patients,' he added by way of explanation.

'Oh, I see.' Mia grimaced. 'That makes a difference, doesn't it?'

'It does.' He sighed as he glanced at Noah. Maybe it was a shock to find himself responding this way but he would deal with it. He didn't have a choice. 'I've no idea what I'm going to do about Noah. Normally, I'd ask my housekeeper to mind him but she's away for the weekend. The only thing I can think of is to contact an agency and hire a nanny for the night.'

'There's no need to do that!' Mia exclaimed. 'Noah can stay here. In fact, he can have a sleepover with Harry.'

'Are you sure?' Leo said in surprise.

'Of course I'm sure.' She laughed. 'Although I should warn you that it's doubtful if there'll be very much sleeping done!'

Leo laughed too. 'If today is anything to go by then you could be right. The two of them have never stopped chattering all day long.'

'It's great that they get on so well, isn't it?' Mia glanced at the boys, who were busily engaged in building a tower out of some plastic blocks. She sighed. 'Hopefully, it will make it that much easier when we tell them what's happened.'

'Let's hope so,' Leo agreed quietly. That Mia was as worried as he was by the thought of how the boys were going to react when they found out the truth was obvious. Reaching out, he squeezed her hand, wanting to offer whatever reassurance he could. 'They'll both be in the same boat and that's bound to help.'

He removed his hand before he was tempted to let it linger. Turning to Noah, he quickly explained that he had to go to the hospital to see someone who was very sick but that Mia had invited him to stay with Harry for a sleepover. Both boys let out a huge cheer at the news, making it clear that they loved the idea. They went thundering up the stairs, leaving him and Mia alone. Leo summoned a smile.

'That seemed to meet with everyone's approval. You're sure you don't mind, though? It seems a bit rich to put on you like this.'

'You're not putting on me. I'm only too happy to help, especially when it means I'll have the chance to get to know Noah a bit better. Is there anything I need to know—food he's allergic to or hates, things like that?'

'No, nothing. He's not keen on cheese but apart from

that he eats most things.' He glanced at his watch and grimaced. 'I'll have to go. If you need me then phone. OK?'

'Of course, but there's no need to worry. Noah will be perfectly fine.'

'I know he will.' He headed out to the hall then paused. Mia had followed him and all of a sudden he couldn't contain his feelings any longer. Bending, he brushed her cheek with his lips, feeling a rush of sensations flow through his body. It was all he could do to draw back but he had a patient waiting and he couldn't waste any time. 'I trust you to look after Noah not because he's your son, Mia, but because you're you. You'd never let anything bad happen to him.'

'Thank you.'

Leo heard the catch in her voice and knew that his words had touched her. He opened the door, knowing that if he didn't leave now, he might not leave at all. He drove straight to the hospital, forcing himself to concentrate on what lay ahead. It was easier that way, less stressful to think about the complexities of the surgery he was about to perform than his own feelings. Maybe a time would come when he would have to face up to how he felt but not right now. Right now he was going to save a man's life. That took precedence over everything else.

By ten o'clock the house was quiet at last. Mia made herself a cup of tea and took it into the sitting room. Sinking down onto a chair, she sighed wearily. Harry and Noah had had the most wonderful time. She'd made a makeshift tent for them out of an old clothes airer covered with a sheet and they had played in it all evening. They'd even had their tea in there, wolfing down fish fingers and chips followed by ice cream. It had taken all her ingenuity to persuade them to vacate it for their bath but they had finally given in and spent the next hour splashing about. Now they were tucked up in bed and, hopefully, asleep.

A light knock on the front door roused her. Mia went to answer it, surprised to find Leo outside. 'I didn't realise you were coming back!' she exclaimed as she let him in.

'I wasn't planning to but I felt like some company. I hope you don't mind?'

'Of course not.' She led him into the sitting room. 'Sit down. You look worn out.'

'I feel it.' He rested his head against the cushions and sighed. 'It's not been the best of evenings. The patient I was operating on died in Theatre.'

'Oh, I'm so sorry. What happened?'

'We'd not even started when he had a massive infarct. James and I did everything we could but it was no use.' He ran his hands through his hair. 'I keep going over it, wondering if there was something we missed.'

'I doubt it. If you and Dr Wilson did all you could then there was nothing anyone could have done.' She shook her head when he went to speak. 'I mean it, Leo. You did your best and it didn't work. You can't go blaming yourself when it wasn't your fault.'

'I suppose you're right. It's just hard when you lose a patient like that.'

'It must be.' She stood up. 'How about a cup of tea?

Or something stronger? I've a bottle of wine if you'd like a glass.'

'I'd love one but I'm driving.'

'You can always leave your car here and call a cab,' she suggested, trying not to think about the other alternative. Inviting him to spend the night on her sofa would be asking for trouble.

'I could, couldn't I?' He smiled up at her. 'All right, you've talked me into it. I would love a glass of wine, please.'

'Coming right up.'

Mia hurried into the kitchen, refusing to think about what she had seen in his eyes. There was no point wondering if the same thought had occurred to him as had occurred to her. She poured them both some wine and took the glasses back to the sitting room. Leo had his eyes closed when she went in; he looked exhausted and her heart filled with tenderness. Maybe he did present a detached front to the world but there was no doubt in her mind that he genuinely cared about his patients.

'Is that the wine?' He opened one eye a crack and peered up at her. 'Would you mind putting it on the table? I'm not sure if I have the energy to drink it just yet.'

'Just try a sip,' she said persuasively, offering him the glass. 'It might give you the boost you need.'

'You could be right.' He sat up and went to take the glass from her. Mia wasn't sure what happened but the next second the glass tipped over, showering red wine all down the front of his sweatshirt.

Leo shot to his feet. 'What a mess! At least it didn't go on your sofa, Mia.'

'I don't think there was much left after you had a soaking,' she observed ruefully.

'Hmm, I did seem to get most of it,' he agreed, staring down at his sweatshirt.

'Here, let me have it.' She held out her hand. 'If you let it dry, you'll never get the stain out. I'll pop it in the washer for you.'

'There's no need to go to all that trouble. It's only a sweatshirt.'

'It's no trouble,' she insisted.

Leo shrugged as he dragged it over his head and handed it to her. 'Then thank you.'

'No problem.' Mia summoned a smile but it was an effort. Maybe it didn't bother him that he was standing there naked to the waist but it most certainly bothered her.

She took the sweatshirt into the kitchen and filled the sink with cold water, deciding to wash out some of the wine before she put it into the machine. She heard footsteps behind her but didn't look round, not sure if she could maintain her composure if she was treated to another glimpse of that broad tanned chest with its dusting of crisp black hair...

'Is it coming out?'

Leo's voice rumbled softly in her ear as he peered over her shoulder and Mia felt a wave of desire wash over her. She nodded, keeping her eyes on the water, which was slowly turning pink.

'Looks like it. I'll let it soak for a few minutes before I put it in the machine.' She took a deep breath then turned, trying not to look at him as she picked up the wine bottle. 'How about a top-up seeing as you never got chance to taste the first glass?'

'If you think I can be trusted not to cause more mayhem I'd love one.'

His tone was light but she could hear the undercurrent it held and the feelings inside her intensified. Her hand was shaking as she took a clean glass off the shelf and poured some wine into it. It was harder than ever to deal with how she felt when it was obvious that Leo felt the same way, but she had to try. Maybe she did want him and maybe he wanted her too but they both knew it would be wrong to act upon their feelings. They had to think about the effect it could have on the boys when their relationship ended, as it undoubtedly would.

Mia picked up the glass and took it into the sitting room, putting it down carefully on the table. Leo had followed her and she glanced at him as she made for the door. 'I'll find you something to wear.'

'Thank you.' He stepped aside, making sure she had room to pass. He knew as well as she did how dangerous it would be if they touched one another.

Mia ran upstairs and opened one of the bags she had filled to take to the charity shop. Although Chris had been a lot smaller than Leo, there were a couple of his T-shirts that might fit him. She felt her breath catch as she imagined how Leo would look wearing them, his muscular body filling out the fabric in a way that Chris's had never done.

Tears sprang to her eyes because it felt wrong to think such thoughts, *wrong* to compare the two men this way. She had loved Chris and he had loved her. He had given her so much, taught her to trust and made her see how good life could be if you had the right person to share it with. Their marriage had been a success despite the problems they had faced and she didn't regret a minute of the time they had spent together. However, she couldn't pretend that she had wanted Chris the way she wanted Leo.

Leo sat down on the sofa. If he hadn't been half-naked he would have left. It would have been the sensible thing to do, far more sensible than sitting here and waiting for Mia to come back. What was the point of torturing himself? He and Mia could never be anything more than Harry's and Noah's parents. He understood that so why did he find it so hard to do the right thing? Was he really so weak-willed that he could no longer take charge of his actions, even for the sake of his son?

He stood up abruptly and went to the door, stopping when he saw Mia coming down the stairs. She paused when she spotted him standing in the doorway.

'Everything all right?'

'Fine.' He drummed up a laugh, his heart pounding when he realised he had missed his chance. Now he would have to stay and simply pray that he didn't make a complete hash of things. 'I've managed not to spill the wine again, you'll be pleased to hear.'

'Good. One soaking per night is enough for anyone.' She came the rest of the way down the stairs and showed him the T-shirts. 'These might fit, although they're bound to be on the snug side. Chris wasn't as big as you.'

'Thanks.' Leo reluctantly took them from her. He went back into the sitting room, wondering why he hated the idea of wearing her late husband's clothes so much. Picking up one of the T-shirts, he dragged it over his head. It was a tight fit, as she'd said, but it was better than nothing.

'I can try to find something else if you prefer,' she said softly.

Leo grimaced when he realised that he had made his distaste rather too obvious. 'No, this is fine. I only need to wear it to get home after all.'

'Well, if you're sure?' She left the question open and he shook his head, feeling worse when he saw the hurt in her eyes. It wasn't her fault that he felt this way after all.

'Quite sure.'

He picked up his glass, calling himself all kinds of unflattering names. He had never considered himself to be the male equivalent of a prima donna. Having been sent away to boarding school at a very early age, he had learned to ignore his finer feelings. However, the thought of wearing the other man's clothes made him feel very odd. It was as though he was trying to step into his shoes: first he'd laid claim to his son; now he was wearing his clothes; and, to cap it all, he wanted his wife!

A little wine shot down the wrong way and he coughed. Mia looked at him in concern. 'Are you all right?'

'Uh-huh,' Leo grunted. His lungs had gone into spasm and all he could do was grunt.

Mia hurried over and patted him on the back. 'Try to relax, that's it.'

She patted his back again and Leo felt all sorts of things happen inside him as his lungs started functioning again. He sucked in a much-needed breath of air, trying to ignore the fact that his pulse was racing, his heart was beating out a tattoo, whilst other bits of him were reacting in time-honoured fashion. It was as though every cell was firing out signals, telling him what to do, and all of a sudden he couldn't hold out any longer.

Turning, he pulled her into his arms and kissed her, kissed her as he had been longing to do for what seemed like an eternity. He knew it was madness, knew he would regret it, *knew* he shouldn't be doing it, but it didn't make any difference. As soon as he felt her mouth under his, he was lost.

CHAPTER TWELVE

MIA COULD HEAR the blood drumming in her ears. Leo's mouth was so hot, so hungry as it plundered hers that there was no way she could resist. Closing her eyes, she gave herself up to the sensations that were flooding through her. It was as though every cell was on fire, burning up, consuming her, and she groaned. Desire was even more powerful than she had imagined.

He drew back at last, his grey eyes pinning her with a look that made her tremble. 'I won't apologise, Mia. It was what we both wanted.'

His arrogance would have annoyed her at any other time but she knew it was true. She had wanted his kiss as much as he had wanted to kiss her. She bit her lip, feeling a shiver run through her when she discovered how tender her mouth felt. Leo hadn't held back. He had kissed her with a raw, unchecked passion and her mouth bore the evidence of it.

'I don't want you to apologise,' she said quietly, stepping out of his arms. She picked up her glass, hoping the wine would help her focus on what needed to be done. Although she had wanted his kiss, she couldn't afford to see it as the start of something more. She had to think about Harry and Noah, and how it could impact on them. They had enough to face in the coming months without her and Leo disrupting their lives any further. She also needed to think about herself. She didn't want to end up with her heart broken when their affair had run its course.

'We both know it was merely a matter of time before something happened,' she said flatly. 'However, now that it has, we can forget about it and focus on the main issue.'

'Namely the boys.'

His tone was cool, far cooler than hers, and Mia felt pain pierce her heart. It had been hard for her to strike the right note but Leo didn't appear to find it nearly as difficult.

'Exactly.' She dredged up a smile, refusing to let him see how hurt she felt. So what if kissing her hadn't been the mind-blowing experience for him that it had been for her? He was a lot more experienced and it was only to be expected that he could deal with his emotions better than she could do. Leo definitely wasn't going to feel as though the bottom had dropped out of his world just because of a kiss!

'We can't afford to do anything that might upset them, Leo. The situation is difficult enough without the added complication of us getting involved.'

'I agree. It will only confuse them even more and that's the last thing we want.'

He shrugged, his broad shoulders rising and falling beneath the overly tight T-shirt. Mia looked away, not proof against the feelings that flooded through her. It would be only too easy to change her mind and tell him that they *could* have a relationship so long as they made sure the boys didn't find out. Whilst she didn't doubt that Leo would be able to handle it, could she? Could she live a double life, pretend that she and Leo were merely friends in front of the boys and be his lover the rest of the time? She didn't think so. Desire was still so new to her that she would never be able to hide her feelings; somehow they would slip out. It was a risk she couldn't take and not only for the sake of the children either. She didn't want Leo to know how vulnerable she was where he was concerned.

'Precisely.' She shrugged. 'I suggest we forget what happened. After all, it hasn't been the best of evenings for you, has it?'

'Definitely not.' He smiled thinly. 'Despite what my colleagues think, losing a patient does affect me.'

It was on the tip of her tongue to assure him that it wasn't what she thought but she managed to hold back. Maybe most people viewed him as a very cold fish, but she didn't, not after tonight. Heat flowed through her again. There had been nothing cold about the way Leo had kissed her.

'I'd better go.' He went to the door, pausing briefly to look at her. 'Thanks for the drink, Mia, and for having Noah. I really appreciate it.'

'It's my pleasure,' she murmured as she followed him out of the room. 'Do you want me to call a taxi for you?'

'There's no need. I only managed a sip or two of the wine after I poured the first glass all over me.'

He laughed and Mia did her best to join in, knowing it was expected. Leo was as keen as she was to put what had happened behind them. She saw him out then went back inside, trying not to think about the fact that he probably regretted it. After all, he could have his pick of women, women who were far more beautiful and socially acceptable than her. Maybe he had wanted to kiss her but it hadn't meant anything to him. Not really. Certainly not as much as it had meant to her.

The next week flew past. Between his NHS commitments and his private work, Leo was hard pressed to keep up. Normally, he had no difficulty fitting everything in but, for some reason, he found himself struggling. Maybe it was the fact that he wanted to spend as much time as possible with Noah before he had to tell him about the mix-up, but there didn't seem to be enough hours in a day. He knew that he was fast reaching a point where he would have to do something about it but he kept putting it off. Too much was happening in his private life without him making changes to the way he worked as well.

Mia was no longer covering the cardiology unit. Sister Thomas was back, briskly efficient as she took charge once more. Leo had always valued her no-nonsense approach yet he found himself missing Mia's gentle kindness. Ward rounds were back to being slickly efficient affairs, carried out with the minimum fuss and the maximum speed, and he reacted accordingly. He could feel himself slipping back into his old ways, becoming cold and distant once more with the patients and the staff, and he hated it. However, without Mia there to strike the right balance, there was little he could do.

The fact that Mia had such power over him was very hard to accept. Although he longed to see her, he didn't make any attempt to contact her. He needed time to get over what had happened, time to allow the memory of that kiss to fade. What he mustn't do was put himself in the same position again. Mia had made it clear how she felt about them becoming involved and he agreed with her.

The weekend rolled around and Noah seemed particularly restless. It was the start of the half-term holiday and Leo had managed to book a week off work so he could spend some time with him. He had been planning to take Noah to their cottage in Sussex. Noah loved it there, although they hadn't been able to go very often because of the pressure of work. Leo decided to make it a surprise and tell him on the Saturday morning but the child woke several times on Friday night, screaming after he'd had a nightmare.

Although Leo did his best to find out what was wrong, Noah refused to tell him. He was tired and listless on Saturday morning, and shook his head when Leo mentioned going to the cottage. After the recent improvement in his behaviour, it was extremely worrying, so much so that he set aside his misgivings and phoned Mia. If she could suggest a way to help Noah, that was all that mattered.

She listened carefully as he explained what had gone on. 'And nothing's upset him at school?'

'Not as far as I know.' Leo heard the concern in her voice and immediately felt better. Knowing that he could share his anxieties with her helped. 'The problem is that Noah won't tell me what's wrong. He just shakes his head when I ask him.'

'It must be very difficult for you,' she said softly,

and he allowed himself the rare luxury of basking in her sympathy for a moment.

'It's not me who matters, it's Noah,' he said shortly, guiltily aware that he was doing what he had sworn he wouldn't do. This wasn't about him and how he felt: it was about Noah.

'Of course. But you're bound to be upset, Leo. I would be if it was Harry having nightmares and I had no idea what was causing them.'

Leo sighed, realising that it was pointless trying to present an indifferent front. Mia understood him far better than anyone else had ever done. 'You're right, of course,' he admitted, trying not to dwell on that unsettling thought. 'I hate it that he's upset and that I can't do anything about it.'

'Would it help if he spent some time with Harry, do you think?'

'It might do, although it doesn't seem fair to land you with this problem, Mia.'

'Rubbish! I want to help and not just because of who Noah is. He's such a lovely little boy and it's a real shame that he's having to go through something like this.'

'That's what hurts so much, the thought that he's unhappy and yet I have no idea what's causing it.'

'Then let's make arrangements for him and Harry to get together. They get on so well, don't they, and it might help to take Noah's mind off whatever's troubling him. When would suit you best? I'm off work next week because it's the half-term holiday so you choose whichever day is best for you. I take it that Noah's off school as well?'

'He is,' Leo said, his mind racing. Mia was right because the two boys did get on extremely well. It was rather surprising really as Noah hadn't made any friends since he'd started school. However, there seemed to be a definite connection between him and Harry.

He came to a swift decision, pushing aside any doubts he had about the wisdom of what he was about to suggest. This wasn't about him but Noah, he reminded himself. And he would do anything to help him.

'Actually, I was planning to take Noah to our cottage in Sussex. It's right next to a farm and he loves seeing the animals. I mentioned it to him this morning but he shook his head. However, I'm sure he'd change his mind if Harry came as well.'

'Oh. I'm not sure…' Mia tailed off and Leo immediately realised what the problem was.

'Obviously, you're invited too, Mia! Sorry. I should have made that clear.'

He took a deep breath, trying to control the thunderous beating of his heart. This was all completely above board, he told himself firmly. He had invited Harry purely because having him around might help Noah. It certainly wasn't some sort of cunning plan to spend time with Mia! He hurried on, not wanting to examine his motives too closely in case he discovered they were flawed.

'It's got three bedrooms. One for you, one for me and the boys can share. Please say you'll come, Mia. It'll make the world of difference to Noah to spend some time with you and Harry.'

The cottage was chocolate-box-perfect. Tiny mullioned windows, a thatched roof, roses—or rather the remains of roses—around the door. Mia sighed with pleasure as Leo drew up outside.

'It's beautiful. I didn't think places like this actually existed.'

'It belonged to my godmother. She left it to me in her will.' Leo switched off the engine and turned to smile at her. 'I used to love coming here when I was a child. My parents travelled a lot and I spent a lot of school holidays here with Deborah.'

'It must have helped make up for the fact that you couldn't spend them with your parents,' Mia suggested, and he shrugged.

'It never bothered me, to be honest. I was sent away to school when I was seven so I was used to not seeing very much of them.'

He got out of the car and after a moment's hesitation Mia followed him. She helped Noah and Harry out of the back, thinking about what he had said. She couldn't imagine sending Harry away to school and not seeing him every day, although Leo seemed to think it was completely normal. It worried her that their views were diametrically opposed. There was no way that she would agree if Leo planned to send either Harry *or* Noah away to boarding school.

Mia squared her shoulders as she herded the children up the path. This was something they obviously needed to discuss, although there was no way that she would change her mind. Harry and Noah were not going to be sent away to school, no matter what Leo said.

Leo unlocked the door, ducking his head as he passed beneath the lintel. Mia stepped inside and looked around, loving the inside as much as she loved the outside.

A tiny vestibule led straight into a sitting room packed with original features. A low ceiling complete with old oak beams, a huge fireplace set with logs. The floor was made from what she assumed was local stone, softened by an eclectic mix of rugs in shades of red, green and gold. A huge squashy sofa and a couple of armchairs bore the hallmarks of many years of use but that merely added to the charm of the place and she smiled in delight.

'It's absolutely gorgeous, Leo! If I owned a place like this I couldn't bear not to live here permanently.'

'It is lovely,' he agreed, looking around. 'I haven't changed anything since Deborah died. I suppose it's silly but I wanted Noah to be able to enjoy the cottage the way it was when I was a child.'

'It's not silly at all,' Mia said, touched by the sentiment. She ran her hand over a faded chintz cushion. 'If you'd bought new furniture you might have been tempted to nag Noah about not damaging things.'

'That's it exactly.' He smiled at her, his grey eyes holding a warmth that made her heart race. 'I was always getting told off for doing something or other when I was at home—spilling a drink on some priceless rug or scuffing an antique chair-leg. However, life here was far more relaxed.'

'It sounds as though it was a real haven for you,' Mia said quietly, and he sighed.

'It was. This was the one place where I always felt completely happy.'

It was such a sad thing to say that tears came to her eyes. She blinked them away but not quickly enough to stop Leo noticing.

'What's wrong?' he said in concern, coming over to her.

'Nothing. I'm just being silly.' She turned to the boys and smiled. 'Why don't you two go on upstairs? Can you show Harry your bedroom, Noah? If it's big enough maybe you two can share it.'

The idea was met with whoops of delight. Mia laughed as the two boys went thundering up the stairs. 'I hope you haven't spent a fortune redecorating the bedrooms. That pair are obviously going to make the most of being here.'

'I haven't changed a thing upstairs or down,' Leo assured her, and she shivered when she heard the grating note in his voice. Had he guessed that her tears had been for him, because she hated to think that he had been unhappy as a child? Mia knew it was true, knew also that he was deeply moved by the idea. Maybe they had agreed to focus on the boys but they couldn't pretend that they didn't feel anything for one another.

'Good. Now, how about a cup of tea? I don't know about you but I'm parched.'

'Lovely. I'll leave you to make it while I bring in the bags,' he said smoothly.

Mia went into the kitchen and filled the kettle with water. She placed it on the hob then looked round, taking determined stock of the sunny yellow-painted cupboards and blue and white crockery arranged on the old dresser, but no matter how hard she tried she couldn't blank out the thought that she and Leo had a lot in common. Her childhood had been less than perfect too and it seemed to forge an even stronger bond between them. She sighed. It was going to make it that much harder to keep her distance.

* * *

Leo took the cases upstairs, not allowing himself to linger as he closed the door to the room Mia would use. It was a pretty room with a wonderful view over the garden to the river but there was no point thinking about how much he would love to wake up and enjoy it with her. He and Mia weren't going to share the room. They weresn't going to be lovers. If he said it often enough then maybe—just maybe—the thought would imprint itself in his head.

Mia had the tea made by the time he went downstairs. She looked round as he went into the kitchen and he felt his heart give a funny little jolt. It was as though it had momentarily forgotten how to work properly, which would have been a worrying thought in other circumstances. However, Leo was aware that the temporary arrhythmia was due to something other than cardiac malfunction.

'I've left your case in your room,' he told her, sitting down at the table because his legs felt decidedly shaky all of a sudden. He cleared his throat, determined to get a grip on himself. 'I've given you the room at the back. You have a wonderful view down to the river from there.'

'It sounds lovely.' Mia poured the tea. She brought the cups over to the table and sat down. 'I couldn't remember if you took sugar.'

'Not for me, thanks.' He got up to fetch the sugar basin, pushing it towards her.

'No, thanks. I take sugar in coffee but not in tea.'

She took a sip of her tea and he looked away, not wanting to put his heart through any more workouts by watching her beautiful lips purse around the rim of the cup. He added a heaped spoonful of suger to his tea, almost gagging when he discovered how sweet it tasted. He pushed the cup aside, suddenly conscious of the silence. Normally, he wouldn't have given it a second thought; in truth, he would have relished the fact that he didn't have to make conversation. However, it was different when he was with Mia. He was afraid that if *he* didn't occupy his thoughts, they would find something to occupy themselves!

'Fingers crossed the weather forecast is wrong,' he said hastily. 'It's supposed to rain for the next few days, heavily too.'

'Let's hope they've got it wrong,' she agreed, glancing out of the window.

Leo's hands clenched as he found himself admiring her profile. How had he ever thought she was ordinary looking? he wondered in amazement as his gaze travelled from the smooth sweep of her brow to the delicate curve of her chin. Although he had known many women who were far more noticeably beautiful, Mia's beauty stemmed not just from how she looked but from who she was. She was beautiful inside as well as out, and the combination touched something inside him, a part of him that he had never been aware of before.

'Still, if it does rain, we'll make the best of it. I expect your godmother kept a stock of board games to entertain you when you stayed with her.'

She turned and Leo hurriedly smoothed his face into what he hoped was a suitable expression, although he couldn't be sure he had hit the mark. 'She did. All the old favourites too—snakes and ladders, Ludo, tiddlywinks,' he said, his voice grating just a little because it was impossible to get every tiny bit of himself under control.

'Tiddlywinks? Oh, Harry will be pleased. He loves tiddlywinks. In fact, he's a bit of demon at it and usually wins!'

Her laughter was overly bright and Leo felt his heart lurch again. Could she feel it too, feel the tension that filled the air? He hoped she could yet also prayed she couldn't because it would only complicate matters. If he knew that Mia felt the same as he did then how would he stop himself doing what he wanted and take her to his bed?

His head began to pound at the thought so it was a relief when the boys reappeared. They were starving, they declared, and needed something to eat. Mia laughed as she got up and went to sort out some lunch for them. Leo watched them, listening to the interplay between her and the children as they helped her make a mound of sandwiches. Although Harry did most of the talking, Noah wasn't shy about making his views known. He looked so animated and happy, so different from how he had been at home that Leo felt his heart suddenly ache.

He loved Noah with every scrap of his being but he couldn't draw a response from him like Mia could. It made him wonder if he was right to hold onto him. Maybe Noah would be better off living with her. Not only would he be with his real mother but he'd have Harry too, the brother he would never have if he stayed with Leo.

Leo felt a knifing pain run through him. He had

sworn he would do whatever it took to make Noah happy but could he keep that promise if it meant he would have to give him up?

CHAPTER THIRTEEN

'Now, you are to stay well away from the river. Understand?'

Mia waited until both Harry and Noah had promised that they would do as she said then opened the back door, smiling as she watched them race down the garden. Although the day was very overcast, the promised rain hadn't materialised yet so the children may as well run off some steam. At least they'd have had some exercise if they did end up playing more board games later on.

She went back to the stove and added more bacon to the pan. From the sounds coming from upstairs, Leo was in the shower so she would get breakfast ready for him. He appeared a few minutes later, pausing in the doorway as though taken aback by the scene that met him. Mia felt a little colour run up her cheeks when it struck her that he might not appreciate her taking over. After all, it was his cottage and she was merely a guest.

'I hope you don't mind,' she said quickly. 'The boys were hungry so I made them breakfast.' She shrugged. 'It seemed silly not to make some for you as well.'

'Of course I don't mind,' he declared, grinning at

her. 'I may be a dab hand with a scalpel but I'm no great shakes when it comes to wielding a knife for the culinary arts. I'm truly grateful that I won't have to eat my own cooking!'

Mia laughed, feeling her unease melt away. 'Ah, so that's your one failing, is it? You can't cook?'

'One failing?' He crooked a brow as he helped himself to coffee. 'You're far too kind, Mia. I've a lot more failings than that, believe me.'

His grey eyes met hers and she looked away when she felt her heartbeat quicken. She busied herself with their breakfast, trying not to think about what other faults he could lay claim to. Even if she tried her hardest, she couldn't think of any herself and it was worrying to know that she held him in such esteem.

She finished cooking and took the plate over to the table. 'I hope you're hungry. I may have overdone it on the bacon.'

'I'm famished,' he assured her, tucking in. He chewed and swallowed, rolling his eyes in pleasure. 'Delicious! My compliments to the chef.'

'Thank you.' Mia laughed as she poured herself a cup of coffee. She sat down and helped herself to a slice of toast. 'All compliments gratefully received. It's not often I get the chance to cook for someone who actually *notices* what he's eating.'

'It sounds as though Harry's view on food is much like Noah's. So long as it's something he likes, that's fine.'

He gave her a quick smile then carried on eating. He seemed to be really enjoying the meal and Mia couldn't help feeling a little glow of satisfaction spring up inside her. She was one of life's carers and enjoyed looking after the people she loved.

The thought hit home and she put down her toast, afraid that she would choke if she tried to eat it. She didn't love Leo. The idea was ridiculous…

Wasn't it?

Panic rose up inside her as she studied his downbent head. That she was attracted to him wasn't in question but it was a huge leap from attraction to love. She'd only ever loved one man and that had been Chris, and her feelings for Chris had been very different from how she felt about Leo. Her love for Chris had made her feel safe and secure. For the first time in her life she'd had someone to rely on, someone who wouldn't let her down.

It wasn't like that with Leo, though. There was an edginess to her feelings for him, an air of excitement and danger that sprang from the fact that she found him sexually attractive. She hadn't wanted Chris that way and she wouldn't demean their marriage by pretending that she had.

Maybe it was the fact that she had known from the outset that they couldn't have a full physical relationship that had tempered her feelings—she wasn't sure. However, the truth was that not once had she felt for Chris even a fraction of the desire she felt for Leo. She bit her lip. Adding it all up, what did it mean? Was it love? Or was it something far less demanding?

Leo wasn't sure what Mia was thinking. It was obviously something profound because she seemed to be lost in thought. He carried on eating even though his appetite had disappeared. There was no point speculating about what was going through her mind, definitely no point asking her either. He couldn't afford to go down that route, didn't dare try to find out anything more about how she thought or felt. It was far too risky, especially when they were both here in the cottage, the one place where he had always been able to relax and be himself.

He sighed. They had managed so well up to now too. Even though he had found it a strain being around her the previous evening, having the boys there had helped. However, the boys weren't here now and he was very aware that his emotions could easily get the better of him. He had sworn after his divorce that he wouldn't get involved again. Although he hadn't loved Amanda, their break-up had been taxing. He didn't intend to put himself through that experience again, especially now he had Noah and Harry to consider. He needed to concentrate on them and forget all these crazy ideas that kept invading his mind.

He forced down the last morsel of food and placed his knife and fork neatly on the plate. 'That was delicious. Thanks again for making it, Mia, although I didn't invite you along so you could be chief cook and bottle-washer.'

The jocular note he'd been aiming for didn't quite ring true but she seemed not to notice. Leo felt his heart lurch when she looked up and he saw the awareness in her eyes. He knew then that whatever she'd been thinking had concerned him and it was both intriguing and scary to wonder how he had featured in her thoughts.

'I'm glad you enjoyed it.' She gave a little shrug and he had the distinct impression that she was trying to shrug off whatever had been bothering her. 'As for doing the cooking while we're here, well, it's no hardship. I'm more than happy to sort out the meals.'

'Careful! I may take you up on that offer,' he warned her in the same falsely jovial tone that filled him with impatience. Why on earth didn't he just ask her what was wrong and be done with it? It was on the tip of his tongue to do that when she pushed back her chair and he knew—he just knew!—that she had read his mind and taken steps to forestall him.

'The boys are in the garden. I think they're hoping you'll play football with them.'

'Ah, right. I suppose I'd better go and show willing, although after that breakfast I doubt I'll have much of a chance against the two of them.'

Leo drummed up a laugh as he went to fetch a sweater. Harry and Noah came rushing over when he went outside, demanding that he played with them. They formed a makeshift goal out of a couple of logs and Leo acted as goalkeeper, letting as many balls slip into the 'net' as he stopped. He didn't believe in being too hard on them, unlike his own father had been. On the rare occasions his father had played with him, he'd been treated as an adult and never allowed to win. His father believed it was character forming to make a child face up to the realities of life at an early age, but Leo could remember how dispiriting it had been and refused to adopt that approach with Noah and Harry. They would find out how difficult life could be all in good time.

He sighed as he glanced towards the cottage. He was only just discovering exactly how hard it was himself.

* * *

The rain started after lunch. Mia had packed a couple of Harry's favourite DVDs so once the boys were settled in front of the television, she went up to her room to find the book she had brought with her. Rain was beating against the bedroom window and she paused to watch the raindrops racing down the glass. Whilst she loved the cottage, she couldn't help hoping that it wouldn't rain the whole time they were here. The thought of being shut up inside with Leo was enough to cause her more than a few misgivings.

'Seems the forecast was spot on after all.'

She swung round, her heart lurching when she saw him standing in the doorway. He had changed out of his muddy clothes after the game of football and was wearing a black tracksuit with a pair of old trainers. It was the first time she had seen him wearing such casual clothing and she couldn't help thinking how much it suited him, the soft cotton top emphasising the width of his shoulders and his dark good looks.

'So it seems.' She dredged up a smile as she showed him the novel. 'Good job I brought this along, just in case.'

'Oh, there are plenty of things to entertain you,' he said softly, and her heart went into overdrive as she found herself picturing all the things she could do. With Leo.

'That's good to know.'

Her voice sounded more than a little husky and she cleared her throat. Had he said that deliberately or, rather, said it in *that* way? She hurried to the door, refusing to work out the answer because it was too dangerous. To allow herself even to *think* about all the things they could do to pass a rainy afternoon was asking for trouble!

'Deborah was a keen reader so there's a stack of books if you run out of reading matter.' Leo led the way along the landing, pausing when he reached his room. He swept a hand towards the open door. 'Here, have a look and see if there's anything you fancy.'

Mia hesitated, unsure why she was so loath to enter his bedroom. With the boys downstairs, Leo was unlikely to pounce on her even if he'd been the pouncing sort, which he wasn't. She poked her head round the door, taking rapid stock of the old oak furniture and half-tester bed, a bed that was definitely big enough for two people to enjoy…

'I've added to the collection over the last few years.' Leo went over to the bookcase. Lifting down a couple of paperbacks, he offered them to her. 'Have you read these? I really enjoyed them.'

'I…ehm… No. I don't think I have.' Mia reluctantly stepped into the room, realising how ridiculous it would appear if she remained hovering in the doorway like a nervous virgin. Colour rushed up her throat at the thought and she hastily took the books from him, making a great show of reading the back blurbs although she had no idea what they said.

'You should read this one first so you get a feel for the characters.'

He took one of the books from her and she froze when his fingers brushed against hers. There was a moment when neither of them moved, when even the air seemed to freeze, and then slowly, so very slowly, he placed the book on the bed and turned to her.

'I'm going to kiss you, Mia. If you don't want me to then say so.'

Mia tried her best. She really did. The refusal was hovering in her throat, one tiny word that just needed to be forced out and yet somehow she couldn't seem to do it. She saw his eyes darken, watched the question in them melt away and be replaced by a hunger that awoke an answering hunger inside her. When he reached for her, she was already moving towards him so that it took minimal effort for their mouths to meet.

His lips settled over hers, softly, warmly and so familiarly that she sighed. It shouldn't feel so good to have him kiss her. It shouldn't feel so right when they both knew it was wrong. However, there was no point lying. She wanted his kiss. She wanted him.

Mia closed her eyes, giving herself up to the sensations that filled her. She'd had a taste of desire the last time they had kissed and this was just as potent. She could feel her breathing quicken, feel her body heat, feel all sorts of things she had never felt before, and it was all Leo's doing. He seemed to be able to tap into her emotions in a way that no man had ever done before.

He drew back, tilting her face so that he could look into her eyes and whatever he saw there obviously reassured him because his expression lightened. Bending, he rested his forehead against hers and Mia felt the tremor that passed through him.

'I don't know why this is happening, Mia. But I've never felt this way with anyone before.'

'Me neither,' she whispered, deeply moved by the

confession. She cupped his cheek with her hand, shuddering when he turned his head and pressed his lips to her palm. 'I had no idea that desire felt like this.'

He drew her to him and enfolded her in his arms, and she knew that he was as affected by her admission as she'd been by his. When he bent and kissed her again there was a tenderness about the kiss that brought tears to her eyes. The fact that he was making allowances for her inexperience simply proved that she had been right about him. Beneath that cold hard exterior he presented to the world, there was someone very different. A man she could very easily love.

Mia wasn't sure what might have happened next. However, a sudden crash from the sitting room brought them both back down to earth. Leo sighed as he gently set her away from him.

'I'd better go and see what's happening.'

'Yes.' Mia dredged up a smile, wondering where they went from here. Although they had agreed to forget what had happened the last time they had kissed, it didn't seem feasible to do so again.

'It'll be fine, Mia. I promise you that.'

He tilted her face and she shivered when she saw the hunger in his eyes. That he wanted her as much as she wanted him was clear and it made the situation even more difficult. Could she do the right thing, the *sensible* thing, when she knew that Leo wanted her this much?

'Will it?' she whispered anxiously. 'Are you sure about that?'

'As sure as I can be.' He ran the pad of his thumb over her throbbing lips. 'We'll work something out, Mia. We have to.'

The desperation in his voice was an aphrodisiac in itself. Mia's heart was pounding as he let her go and hurried from the room. Sitting down on the bed, she took a shaky breath. Was it the fact that it was her first real taste of desire that made it so difficult to control her feelings? If she'd been more experienced then she might be able to deal with what was happening with equanimity, but there was no way that she could do that. Leo had awakened feelings she'd not known existed before and it was impossible to behave calmly and dispassionately.

She shivered as a rush of fear assailed her. If she weren't careful her feelings for Leo would take over and that was something she couldn't allow to happen. She had to think about the harm it could cause to Harry and Noah if she and Leo had an affair and it all went wrong. She also had to think about the harm it could do to her too. If she fell in love with Leo and lost him, she might never recover. She had to protect the children and herself, and if that meant steering clear of Leo, that was what she would have to do.

The day seemed never-ending. As Leo played one board game after another, he could barely contain his frustration. He didn't want to play snakes and ladders. He had far more adult games in mind, games that involved him and Mia and a bed. He could have happily passed the afternoon *and* the evening playing with her!

'Daddy! You've just gone *up* a snake!'

Leo dragged his mind back to what was happening when he heard the disgust in Noah's voice. 'Sorry. I wasn't concentrating.' He placed his counter on the correct square and handed the dice to Harry, trying not to look at Mia. He had a feeling that she knew only too well why he was so distracted.

His gaze slid sideways and he felt his heart leap when he saw the colour in her cheeks. It was rare that women in his circle blushed and he found Mia's propensity to do so all the more erotic. That she'd admitted to being an innocent had both surprised and touched him. Even though he had guessed that she and her husband hadn't been able to have a full physical relationship, most women her age had had love affairs and he had assumed she had too. However, from what she had said, her experience of lovemaking, of passion, was limited.

The thought struck deep. It was an effort to focus on the game rather than on the thoughts that filled his head, thoughts of how much he would enjoy teaching her about making love. Would she be as sweetly responsive in his bed as she'd been in his arms? he wondered, and groaned because the thought was too much to deal with. He took the dice from Harry, summoning up a suitable show of enthusiasm when he scored a six. However, he couldn't help thinking that if he did make love to Mia it would be like scoring a dozen sixes all in a row.

The game finally ended and Noah was declared the winner, much to his delight. As Leo watched him and Harry go racing out of the room, he realised that no matter what else happened this week, he had achieved his objective. Being here with Harry and Mia had made a huge difference to Noah. He seemed so much happier, more like he'd been before the accident. Once again the thought that he might have to let Noah go if it was in his best interests crossed his mind but he pushed it aside, not wanting it to ruin the day. He would deal with it if and when it became necessary, although, please, heaven it wouldn't come to that.

'Tea?'

Mia finished stowing the counters in the box and stood up. She smiled at him and Leo felt warmth envelop him. All of a sudden it struck him what had been missing from his life. Maybe he did have wealth and professional standing. He might even move in the highest social circles and be accepted by princes and lords, but none of that mattered. For the first time ever, he'd been accepted for who he was, not what he had. Mia saw him as a man first and everything else second. Reaching out, he caught hold of her hand and pulled her towards him.

'I can think of something I'd like more than tea,' he growled.

He kissed her swiftly on the lips then let her go, not wanting to run the risk of the boys bursting in on them. Mia didn't say anything as she hurried into the kitchen but he had felt her response and knew that she felt the same as he did. One kiss wasn't enough for her either. She needed more and not just more kisses either.

Leo closed his eyes, feeling excitement rippling along his veins. Tonight they were going to have everything they wanted.

CHAPTER FOURTEEN

IT WAS GONE nine before Harry and Noah finally fell asleep. Mia switched off the light and tiptoed from the room. With a bit of luck they would sleep through till morning so she and Leo could have some time on their own.

Colour rushed up her face as she found herself imagining how they would spend that time. That they would make love wasn't in question. They both knew it was going to happen and there was no point pretending that it wouldn't. She wanted Leo to make love to her and she wouldn't cheapen the experience by dissembling.

She wanted to lie in his arms and discover how it felt to be a woman. She wanted to feel the power of passion as it carried her away, allow her mind as well as her body to be consumed by desire. Although she'd had a child, the fact that Harry hadn't been conceived naturally had robbed her of that experience and she intended to make up for it. If she knew how desire felt, she would feel complete and not as though something was missing.

Mia frowned, surprised to discover she felt that way. After her one and only foray into a sexual relationship had turned out so badly, she had shied away from any more such experiences. Although Chris had fretted about the fact that they couldn't make love, she had been secretly relieved. Now she was going to put it all behind her and move on, and the fact that it was Leo—Harry's real father—who would help her make the transition seemed fitting. No matter what happened afterwards, she would never regret this night.

'I've opened a bottle of wine.' Leo was waiting for her when she went downstairs. He held out his hand and smiled. 'Can I tempt you to a glass?'

'You can.' Mia slid her hand into his, feeling her skin tingle as his fingers closed around hers. Her skin seemed unusually sensitive and the slightly abrasive touch of his fingertips made her shiver.

'You're shivering. Are you cold?'

He paused to look at her, a frown drawing his elegant brows together, and she shivered again. Did he have any idea how sexy he was? Did he realise that a look or even a frown could set light to her feelings? Even now she could feel the tingles spreading to other parts of her, places she had never been aware of before she had met him. She bit her lip, wondering if it was normal to be so responsive. Did all women feel this way prior to making love or was there something wrong with her?

'Stop it.'

The order was softly given but it brought her up short. Mia's eyes refocused and she saw him shake his head. 'Whatever crazy thoughts you're harbouring, forget them, Mia. There's nothing to be frightened of. You and I are going to make love but only if you want to. OK?'

His bluntness might have embarrassed her before but not now. Not tonight. Mia nodded. 'All right.'

'Good.' He squeezed her hand then let her go so he could pour the wine. Mia was a little surprised that he hadn't kissed her, although she didn't say anything. Leo knew what he was doing and she would be guided by him.

The thought set loose another volley of thoughts and she took a gulp of the wine in the hope that it would calm her. She mustn't spoil things by panicking. It would be such a shame. Leo dropped down onto the sofa and raised his glass aloft.

'A toast. To the boys and us. May we all get what we want.'

'To the boys and us,' Mia repeated, wondering if it was possible for all of them to get what they wanted. Harry and Noah took priority, of course; she would do whatever was necessary to make sure they were happy. If it meant that she and Leo couldn't have a proper re-lationship, she would accept it. It meant that tonight would be even more special. Precious. This one night might be all she had.

It was a sobering thought but she refused to dwell on it. She drank a little more wine then put her glass on the table. 'I've had enough wine,' she said quietly.

'Me too.' Leo put his glass next to hers and stood up. His eyes were very dark as he searched her face. 'Are you sure this is what you want, Mia?'

'Yes.'

Mia turned and headed from the room. She made her way upstairs, hearing the soft tread of Leo's foot-steps behind her. The landing floorboards creaked and she paused, half expecting that Harry or Noah would wake up, but there was no sound from their bedroom and she carried on to her room. She had left the bedside lamp on and it cast a soft glow over the room. When Leo followed her inside and closed the door, it felt as though they were the only two people in the world. Whatever happened in this room tonight was between them, no one else.

'Mia.'

He said her name softly and with great tenderness. Mia turned to him, feeling the last tiny doubt melt away when she saw the expression on his face. That he wanted this as much as she did was clear. She moved towards him, emboldened by the thought. She had never initiated physical contact before, yet it was *her* arms that reached for him, *her* hands that drew his head down so *she* could kiss him. Their mouths met and she sighed as she felt his lips immediately shape themselves to hers. This was even easier than she had hoped it would be.

They kissed for a long time, a kiss that was filled with so many emotions that she felt dizzy when they broke apart. When Leo had kissed her before, he had kissed her with hunger and with passion, but this kiss had been very different. It was as though he had stripped himself bare, allowed his real self to shine through, and the thought made her feel very humble. He had lowered his defences because he trusted her and now she must trust him too.

She sank down onto the bed and held out her hand. 'Make love with me, Leo. It's what I want more than anything.'

He didn't say a word as he took her hand and sat

down beside her but she had seen the flare of emotion in his eyes and knew how much it had meant to him to hear her say that. When he bent and kissed her again, she closed her eyes, savouring the feel of his mouth on hers. This was just the beginning and there would be so much more to come, so many new experiences to enjoy and treasure. If they were to have just this one night, it would be a night to remember.

Leo could feel his heart pounding. The taste of Mia's lips was pure seduction and he was more than willing to be seduced. He gathered her into his arms, groaning when he felt her breasts pressing against his chest. Her nipples were already hard but he didn't intend to rush her. She'd admitted how inexperienced she was and he couldn't bear it if he ruined things by going too fast. He had to take his time no matter how difficult it was. Mia needed to be loved gently, slowly, and with the utmost care.

Tenderness washed over him as he kissed her again, letting his tongue slide between her lips this time. His heart jerked when he felt her respond but he managed to control the desire that surged through him. Lifting his hand, he smoothed her hair away from her face, his fingers tangling in the silky fine threads at her temple. Her hair smelled of lemons, clean and fresh, and he drank in its scent, amazed that such a simple aroma could be so erotic. Forget all the expensive perfumes, he thought. This was far more seductive!

His hand moved from her hair to her cheek, his fingers exploring the velvet softness of her skin. It felt so warm to the touch, so smooth, that he could have sat there and stroked it all night long, only he knew there were more delights to enjoy. His fingers glided down her cheek and across her jaw then moved to her neck, following the line of her throat until they reached the tiny pulse that was beating so frantically at its base. He could feel it tapping away, feel its rhythm imprinting itself on his flesh and shuddered. If he needed proof that she wanted him then here it was, here where this tiny reflection of her feelings was making itself known.

Bending, he pressed his mouth to the spot, letting the tip of his tongue rest on the tiny pulse point as though in some way he could absorb the evidence of her desire for him. She gave a soft little moan as she tipped back her head to allow him easier access and he felt his own desire spiral out of control.

He wanted her so much! Wanted to lie her down on the bed and cover her body with kisses, seek out the source of her heat and kiss her there as well. He had made love to many women over the years but he knew that making love to Mia would be unlike anything he had experienced before. In that respect they were very much alike. All his experience amounted to nothing when it came to loving her.

The thought was just too much to deal with, way too much to soothe and calm him as he needed to be calmed. He knew he shouldn't rush her yet his hands seemed to possess a life of their own as they stripped off her clothes. Mia helped him, wriggling out of her jeans, shrugging off her shirt, and he realised that she was as eager as him to take things to the next stage. It stopped him feeling so guilty. Maybe it wasn't wrong to allow passion to dictate the speed of their lovemaking after all.

He stood up and stripped off his own clothes, feeling her eyes on him as he stood naked beside the bed. Did she like what she saw? he wondered in a rare fit of self-doubt. He had never worried about his appearance before and it shocked him to discover how vulnerable he was. He cared what she thought, cared far more than he had ever cared about anyone's opinion.

'You're beautiful.'

Her voice was husky, filled with a wonder that swept away his fears. Leo laughed as he lay down on the bed and gathered her to him. 'I don't think men can be classed as beautiful, sweetheart.'

'Well, you can.' She drew back and looked at him and he could see the desire in her eyes smouldering away, and shuddered again. Maybe she lacked experience but by heaven she turned him on! 'You're beautiful, Leo, and there's no other word to describe you.'

'Then thank you.'

He kissed her hungrily, unable to hold back a second longer, but there again he didn't need to. Mia was as eager for him as he was for her. Her heart was racing as he let his lips glide down her body, following the full, lush curves of her breasts, the dip of her waist, the gentle swell of her hips. She had never felt more like a woman than she did right then as Leo paid homage to her.

Everywhere his mouth touched, it seemed that he discovered a fresh delight to explore, a new discovery to savour, like the tiny mole on the top of her hip bone or the dusting of freckles on her arms. She ran her hands down his back, feeling the smoothness of his skin, the hardness of his muscles as they slid beneath her palms. She had never felt so aroused before, wouldn't have believed that just the feel of his body could set light to her desire like this. Every inch of him was so perfect that she was overcome with greed. She wanted to stroke and caress him for the rest of her life!

The thought pushed her to the edge and beyond. 'Make love to me, Leo,' she said urgently. 'Now!'

There was a moment when he paused, the tiniest hesitation, and then he entered her in one strong, fluid thrust. Mia felt her body resist for a second and then it opened to him, warm and eager as it welcomed him inside. Mia felt the blood start to drum along her veins, felt her passion gather momentum until she was totally consumed by its heat and Leo's desire for her. Then all of a sudden she was crying out and clinging to him and he was clinging to her as the world dissolved around them. Nothing existed any more. Nothing except her and Leo and the magic they were creating together.

It was after midnight when Mia awoke. She stared at the ceiling, listening to the steady sound of Leo's breathing as he lay beside her. Reaching out, she ran her hand down his arm, shivering when she felt the silky dark hair slide beneath her palm. Making love with him had been so much more than she had hoped it would be. Not only had he shown her how passion felt, he had proved that she was capable of arousing passion in someone else. His need for her had been every bit as consuming as hers had been for him.

'Are you all right?'

His voice was soft and deep but she heard the concern it held and felt warmed to her core. That he cared how she felt, cared about *her*, wasn't in doubt. Rolling onto her side, she smiled at him, surprised and yet unsurprised by how comfortable she felt. Maybe she should feel awkward or ill at ease but she didn't. It had felt right to make love to him, just as it felt right to wake up beside him.

'Fine. In fact, I feel better than I've felt in ages.'

'Really?' His brows quirked as he propped himself up on one elbow. 'And why is that, do you think?'

'Oh, I'm not sure. It could be the nice little nap I've had. Or maybe it's being here at the cottage and having some time to myself for a change.' She grinned wickedly. 'What do you think?'

'Hmm, I'm not sure either. Maybe it's a combination of the two.' He trailed the tip of his finger across her mouth, smiling smugly when she gasped. 'It may even have something to do with the fact that we just made love.'

'Th-that's another theory,' she murmured because it was hard to form the words when her lips felt as though they were on fire.

'It is, isn't it? And like all theories it needs testing.' He bent and kissed her, drawing back before she could respond, and she could see the mischief in his eyes. 'Although it's rather late to be carrying out a proper scientific experiment, don't you think?'

He kissed her again, his mouth lingering a fraction longer this time before he pulled away. Mia sucked in her breath, determined that she wasn't going to beg. He either kissed her properly or he didn't…

Her resolve lasted no longer than a heartbeat. Leaning forward, she pressed her mouth to his, sighing in pleasure when he immediately took charge, kissing her with a hunger that allowed no room for any more questions. If this was an experiment, she thought in the moment before passion swept her away, it would prove one thing: she now understood *exactly* how desire felt!

They made love again and it was so beautiful that she cried afterwards. Leo drew her into his arms and held her, not asking her what was wrong because he knew. Her tears weren't a sign of unhappiness but of joy. She had found the last bit of herself that had been missing, discovered how it really felt to be a woman. It was a moment she would remember all her life, a moment she would treasure no matter what happened.

It was a sobering thought because it brought all the old doubts flooding back. Mia sighed as she reached for a tissue and wiped her eyes. There was no point pretending when Leo knew how volatile the situation was.

'Tonight has been everything I dreamt it would be, Leo, but I'm terrified in case it causes complications.'

'Me too.' He sat up, packing a pillow behind his back. Drawing her into his arms, he cradled her against his bare chest. 'Tonight was wonderful for me as well, Mia. There's no point lying—I've had a lot more experience than you, but tonight was special. I only wish we could make this a permanent arrangement, but at the moment it would be wrong.'

'It would,' she agreed, her heart aching with a mixture of pleasure and pain. The fact that it had meant so much to him thrilled her; however, what he'd said merely confirmed her own view. They couldn't get involved because of the harm it might cause to the boys.

'So I suppose what we're really saying is that this has to be a one-off.' He tilted her face and looked into her eyes. 'It's not what I want and I don't think it's what you want either but our feelings have to come second to Harry's and Noah's. They'd find it too confusing if we started seeing one another and then they found out we aren't their real parents.'

'They would. It'll be difficult enough for them to understand the situation without that as well.' She bit her lip, determined that she wasn't going to cry. She didn't want to put any pressure on him, didn't want to try to change his mind. They knew what had to be done and they must do it.

Leo didn't try to stop her as she got out of bed. Taking her robe off the chair, she slipped it on and made her way to the bathroom. She switched on the light then stood and stared at her reflection in the mirror over the basin. Although it was the same face she saw every day, she looked different. Making love with Leo had left its mark; she looked more aware, more alive even. However, it was the changes she couldn't see that she would have to live with.

Closing her eyes, she allowed herself to recall the passion that had swept her away, the hunger that had filled her, the feeling of peace and completion that had enveloped her afterwards. She had discovered who she was at last, found the last link that had been missing, and she was a different person because of it. Because of Leo. Because she loved him.

Mia opened her eyes and stared at the face that was

staring back at her. She could see the truth in her eyes, see it so clearly that there was no point pretending any more. She was in love with Leo.

CHAPTER FIFTEEN

THE RAIN HAD stopped the following morning so Mia sent the boys outside to play. Going over to the stove, she turned on the gas so she could make a start on breakfast. Although she wasn't hungry, it would help to take her mind off the events of the night. She sighed as she cracked eggs into a bowl. It was doubtful if scrambling eggs would alleviate this sadness she felt.

'Good morning.'

She hadn't heard Leo coming in and jumped so that some of the egg mixture slopped over the side of the bowl. He frowned as he picked up a dishcloth and mopped up the mess.

'Sorry. I didn't mean to startle you.'

'It wasn't your fault. I didn't hear you,' she countered politely, picking up a fork and beating the eggs to within an inch of their life. Reaching over, he took the fork off her and tossed it into the sink.

'Don't, Mia. I couldn't bear it if we started pussy-footing around one another. The situation is difficult enough without that.'

'You're right, it is.'

She turned to him, seeing the shadows under his

eyes, proof that he too had had a sleepless night. It was a small sop to her feelings to know that he was suffering as well. By the time she had got back from the bathroom, Leo had gone. Maybe he had wanted to make it easier for her, but she wished he had stayed. Although she doubted if they would have made love again, at least he could have held her in his arms, made her feel less lonely, less lost. Now she dredged up a smile, knowing she was being unreasonable. Leo had done what he had to do and she should be grateful.

'Scrambled eggs all right? We've run out of bacon, I'm afraid.'

'Nothing for me, thanks. I'm not hungry.'

He poured himself a cup of coffee and took it over to the window. Mia looked at the bowl then tipped the eggs down the sink. There was no point cooking them when she wasn't hungry either. She filled a mug with coffee and sat down, wondering what to do. Would it be better if she and Harry left or would Leo think she was abandoning him and Noah? After all, this break had been arranged for Noah's sake, so surely she should stay.

'What do you want me to do?' she said, deciding it was simpler to ask him. 'If you want me and Harry to leave then say so.'

'Do you want to leave?'

He swung round and her heart ached when she saw the misery in his eyes. It was all she could do to sit there and not go to him but it would wrong to start something they both knew could only end in more confusion for the boys.

'I'm not sure. That's the honest answer.' She shrugged.

'I love it here and it's obvious that Harry loves being here too, but…'

'But it will be a strain,' he finished for her.

'Yes.' She sighed. 'It might be better if we left, Leo.'

'Maybe.' He drank some coffee then put the cup on the window sill. 'It's up to you, Mia. You must do whatever you think is best.'

He opened the back door but there was no way she was letting him toss the ball into her court. She stood up and glared at him.

'It isn't up to me, though. This is something we both need to decide, the same as we need to decide how we intend to handle things from here on. Harry and Noah need to see one another when we get home…*we* need to see *them*! Which means that whether we like the idea or not, we're going to have to see each other.'

'I realise that. However, you'll have to forgive me if I don't feel up to working out the practicalities at the moment.' He pinned her with a cold-eyed stare. 'What happened last night is still very much on my mind even if you've managed to dismiss it.'

It was so unfair to accuse her of doing that that she couldn't speak. He was halfway out of the door before she found her voice. 'How dare you say that? Just because I'm trying to be sensible, it doesn't mean that I've forgotten what happened.'

'No? I'm flattered.' His smile was sardonic. 'It's good to know that I'm not instantly forgettable.'

'Why are you saying these things?' she demanded, bitterly hurt by the way he was behaving. 'We both agreed that we had to call a halt, Leo. It isn't what I want, but it's not my feelings that matter.'

'Are you sure about that? Sure you don't regret what we did?' He shrugged. 'From the length of time you spent in the bathroom last night, I got the distinct impression that you were having serious doubts.'

'Then you were wrong. Yes, I was thinking about what had happened, but I wasn't regretting it.' Her voice caught. 'The only thing I regret is that we can't risk being together again.'

'I got it wrong, didn't I?' His voice echoed with pain. 'When you took so long to come back I assumed it was because you were having second thoughts and couldn't face me.'

'And that's why you left?'

'Yes. I thought it would be less embarrassing for you if I wasn't there when you came back.' He sighed. 'Obviously, I was mistaken.'

'You were. If you want the truth, I wish you'd stayed. I could have done with a hug.'

'Oh, sweetheart!'

He took a step towards her then stopped when there was a scream from the garden. Mia was hard on his heels as he raced out of the door, her heart turning over when she saw Noah standing on the far side of the fence next to the river. There was no sign of Harry and she could barely contain her fear as she ran across the grass.

Leo scooped Noah up and swung him back over the fence. 'Where's Harry, Noah? Tell me!'

The little boy pointed to the river and Mia went cold as she turned and stared at the water rushing past the end of the garden. With all the rain they'd had, the water level was extremely high, lapping at the bank as it swirled past.

'He went to fetch the ball and fell into the water,' Noah choked out through his sobs.

Leo didn't hesitate as he vaulted over the fence. Kicking off his shoes, he waded into the water. 'I can see him! He's caught up in some bushes.'

Mia clapped a hand to her mouth as he dived into the river. The current was very strong and within seconds he was swept away. She could just make out his head bobbing above the water, although she couldn't see Harry from where she was standing. Noah was shivering with cold and fright so she put her arms around him and hugged him. She wanted to jump into the river herself and help but she knew it was the wrong thing to do. If Leo couldn't reach Harry, she would have to summon help.

The next few minutes were a nightmare. Leaving Noah safely on the far side of the fence, she made her way to the edge of the bank. She could see Harry's red jumper snagged on some bushes and just make out the dark shape of Leo's head as he struggled to reach him. When he finally managed to grab hold of Harry and lifted him out of the water, she felt tears pour down her face. She'd been so terrified that she would lose them both.

Leo made his way back along the river bank. He was carrying Harry, who was shivering violently. 'I don't think he's hurt, just very cold and scared. Let's get him inside and see how he is then.'

Mia hurried on ahead with Noah while he carried Harry back to the house. He took him straight into the sitting room, setting him down in front of the fire and stripping off his sodden clothes. Mia ran upstairs to fetch a towel and wrapped Harry in it. His teeth were chattering and he was crying but he didn't appear to be injured.

'Are you hurt anywhere, darling?' she asked, cuddling him close.

'I've hurt my hand,' Harry told her, holding up his hand so she could see the angry red scratch on his palm.

'I'll put a plaster on it,' she assured him, giving him a kiss. She gave Noah a kiss as well then stood up. Recriminations could wait till later; for now all that mattered was that Harry was safe thanks to Leo. She turned to him, overcome with gratitude. He had risked his own life to save Harry.

'Thank you. I don't know how I can ever repay you for what you've done.'

'It doesn't matter. The only thing that matters is that Harry is safe. I don't know what I'd have done if anything had happened to him.'

His voice grated and Mia felt tears fill her eyes once more. That Leo cared about Harry was obvious. Harry was his son after all, and he must love him just as much as she loved Noah.

It was the first time that she had admitted how she felt about Noah and it filled her with warmth. Holding out her hand, she drew him to her and hugged him, her heart overflowing with love for this child she and Chris had created. Noah was her son just as Harry was Leo's, and somehow they had to make this situation work for all of them. No matter how hard it was, or what sacrifices it took, she and Leo would make sure the boys didn't suffer.

* * *

Leo made his way upstairs, aware that what had happened had brought the situation into sharp focus. He shuddered as he recalled his fear as he had tried to get to Harry. He'd been terrified that the child would be swept away before he could reach him. Harry's life had been hanging, quite literally, by a thread and those endless minutes he had spent struggling to reach him were imprinted on his mind. He didn't know how he would have been able to bear it if he had lost Harry.

He sank down onto the bed, uncaring that his wet clothes were soaking the quilt. Finding out that Noah wasn't his child had been the worst thing that had ever happened to him but if he had lost Harry today, it would have been equally as bad. He loved the boy, loved him not only because Harry was his biological son but because of Mia. She had given birth to Harry, brought him up, loved and cared for him, and it was thanks to her that Harry had turned out the way he had. He loved Harry and he loved Mia. They were both unassailable facts.

'Are you all right?'

He looked up, his heart racing when he saw Mia standing in the doorway. Her face was very pale thanks to the shock she'd had but she was still the most beautiful woman he had ever known. If he could be granted just one wish, it would be the chance to spend his life with her but he couldn't see it happening. Mia may have enjoyed making love with him but she didn't see him as a permanent part of her future.

'Fine. Just a bit shocked, I suppose.' He summoned a smile, refusing to let her see how devastated the thought made him feel. 'Kids certainly know how to put you through the mill, don't they?'

'They do indeed.'

She returned his smile but he could see the sadness in her eyes and realised that she found the situation as difficult as he did. Maybe she was waiting for him to make the first move, he mused, needed his assurances that it could work, as indeed it could. After all, Harry and Noah got on extremely well; surely they would be thrilled at the idea of them all living together as a family?

Leo's head reeled as the full impact of that thought hit him. He didn't just want to have an affair with Mia. He wanted to spend his life with her. But was he *sure* it was what he wanted? Or was it merely the result of all the emotional turmoil he'd been through that day? Although he loved her, he had no idea if his feelings would last.

How long *did* love last? A lifetime? A couple of years? He had never been in love before and had nothing to measure it by, so what if it was like desire and faded with time? How would it affect Noah and Harry if he discovered that he no longer loved her? He could end up doing the very thing he had wanted to avoid and ruin the boys' lives.

Mia could see a range of emotions racing across Leo's face and she frowned. She had no idea what he was thinking but it was clear that there was something troubling him. She was on the point of asking him when she heard Harry shouting for her.

'I'd better go and see what he wants,' she said, turning away. 'I've put the kettle on so come down once you've changed and have a hot drink. You must need it after the soaking you've had.'

'Thanks. I won't be long.' Leo smiled but there was a reserve about it that made her heart ache. She had a feeling that he was deliberately distancing himself and it hurt after their closeness of the previous night.

She didn't say anything, however. She merely returned his smile and went downstairs. Harry wanted to know if he and Noah could watch a DVD and she immediately agreed. It was good to know that Harry seemed to have got over his fright, she thought as she went into the kitchen to make them a drink. He was a resilient little boy and seemed to cope with most things. It made her wonder if she was being too cautious. Maybe Harry would cope better than she feared if she told him the truth about Leo being his father?

Mia sighed as she poured milk into a pan. It was far too soon to tell Harry the truth, especially when it would mean them having to tell Noah as well. She had to wait until she and Leo had worked out all the details and what it would entail. There would need to be a lot of changes made if they were to amalgamate the two families, always assuming that was what Leo wanted, of course. Just for a second the thought of them all living together as a proper family filled her head before she dismissed it. Maybe she and Leo were sexually compatible but he had given no indication that he wanted anything more from her than that.

The boys were fast asleep by seven o'clock that night. Maybe it was all the excitement they'd had but neither of them objected when Leo suggested they go to bed.

He gave them a bath and read them a story, thinking how much he enjoyed doing it. He made a point of being home in time to put Noah to bed and having Harry there simply doubled his pleasure. As he made his way downstairs, he found himself imagining how it would be if it became a permanent part of his nightly routine. Tucking the boys up in bed each night would be a joy, especially when Mia would be waiting for him afterwards.

He sighed as he made his way to the kitchen, where Mia was cooking dinner for them. He needed to take off the rose-tinted spectacles and see the situation in its true light. Family life wasn't all baths and stories—it was so much more. It might be fine for a while but how long would it last? When would the daily routine become a chore? When would the thought of Mia waiting for him become boring rather than exciting? Although he couldn't imagine it happening at this moment, it could do. It happened to lots of people and there was no guarantee that it wouldn't happen to them too.

'All settled?'

Mia looked round when he went in and Leo did his best to respond in a fitting manner. He didn't want to upset her, especially not after last night. The thought of what had happened the previous night made him go hot and cold and he shook his head to clear it of the images that had invaded it. Mia frowned in concern.

'Why? What's wrong? Is Harry upset about falling into the river?' She put down the spoon she'd been using to stir the gravy and hurried to the door. 'I'd better go up and see him.'

'There's no need. He's fine.'

Leo laid his hand on her arm, flinching when he

felt every cell in his body fire off a veritable volley of signals. He could feel his skin tingling where his hand rested on her arm and quickly removed it. Last night had been a one-off and there wasn't going to be a repeat tonight despite what his libido hoped.

'Oh. I thought something had happened,' she said, sounding confused, which was understandable.

'No. Everything's fine. They're both fast asleep.' Leo treated her to another smile because it was impossible to explain. Admitting that he'd been trying to clear his head, and of what, wouldn't help. 'Something smells good,' he said, changing the subject to a less stressful topic.

'Lamb chops and new potatoes,' she said briskly, going back to the stove.

'Lovely. How about a glass of wine? I've a rather good red that I've been saving. Let's open it tonight, shall we?'

Leo gritted his teeth when he realised that he had adopted his 'social' tone, the one he used when dealing with a particularly difficult guest. That Mia had noticed it too was obvious from her clipped reply.

'Don't open it for me. Save it for something special.'

'I can't think of anything more special than having you and Harry here,' he said quietly as he went to fetch the bottle.

He sighed as he lifted it off the rack. He was out of his depth and it was worrying to know that he had no idea what to do. He was used to making difficult decisions but he couldn't decide what to do in this instance.

He loved Mia and he wanted to be with her with all that it entailed, but would it work? Or would it turn out to be a disaster? He had sworn he wouldn't get involved again after Amanda yet here he was, thinking about doing that very thing. If it were only him who might suffer, he wouldn't hesitate; he would tell Mia how he felt and be done with it. However, it wasn't only him, it was the boys too. How could he do what he so desperately wanted when it could impact badly on Harry and Noah?

CHAPTER SIXTEEN

DINNER WAS A stilted affair. Although they talked, Mia sensed that Leo was merely going through the motions for the sake of politeness. She wasn't sure what was wrong and didn't want to ask him either. However, the thought that he was no longer interested in her now that they had made love refused to go away. It was a relief when they finished. She shook her head when he offered to do the washing up.

'I'll do it. You go and relax. You deserve a rest after what you did this morning.'

He didn't argue, simply turned and left, and that in itself seemed to prove her suspicions were correct. Leo had got what he wanted and now he had no more use for her. Tears filled her eyes and she dashed them away. She wouldn't cry, wouldn't embarrass herself or him. Within the circles Leo frequented affairs must be commonplace and she refused to make a fool of herself by letting him see how upset she felt.

Once the dishes were done, she went up to bed, unable to face making any more stilted conversation. She checked on the boys, who were fast asleep, then went to her room. She heard Leo come upstairs a short time later and held her breath but he passed by her door without pausing. One night had obviously been enough for him, she thought bitterly.

She must have drifted off to sleep only to be woken by the sound of screaming. Leaping out of bed, she ran along the landing, fully expecting it to be Harry after what had happened that morning. However, when she went into the boys' room she discovered it was Noah screaming. Rushing over to the bed, she gathered him into her arms.

'It's all right, darling. You're quite safe. You've had a bad dream, that's all,' she said, rocking him to and fro. She looked up when Leo appeared at her side, feeling her heart turn over when she was presented by the sight of his naked torso. Her mind swooped back to the previous night before she brought it back to the present. There was no point thinking about that, no point at all.

'Is he all right?' Leo crouched down beside her and stroked Noah's hair. 'Hey, what's wrong, tiger? Did you have a bad dream?'

'Go 'way!' Noah pushed Leo's hand away and buried his face in Mia's shoulder.

Leo drew back, an expression of pain crossing his face. 'He obviously doesn't want me so will you try and find out what's wrong with him?'

'Of course.' Mia felt a wave of sympathy rise up inside her. She knew how she would have felt if Harry had reacted that way when she'd tried to comfort him. 'He doesn't really know what he's saying right now. Give him a few minutes to calm down.'

'Of course.' Leo stood up and glanced over at Harry's bed, forcing a smile when he saw that the little boy was watching them. 'Noah's had a bad dream and your mummy's going to give him a cuddle. Shall we go downstairs and have a drink until Noah feels better?'

Harry shot out of bed, obviously excited at the thought of getting up in the middle of the night. Leo took hold of his hand and led him to the door, pausing briefly to glance back.

'Noah will be fine,' Mia said, knowing how hard it must be for him to leave the child with her.

'I know he will. He couldn't be in better hands,' he replied roughly.

Mia bit her lip as he and Harry left the room. Had she been wrong to assume that he had tired of her so quickly? There had been something in his voice just now that seemed to disprove that idea.

Noah gave a little moan and she cuddled him close. What Leo did or didn't feel wasn't the issue. It was Noah who mattered. She needed to find out what had upset him.

She stroked his hair and gradually the tension started to leave him. A wave of motherly love washed over her as she felt the thinness of his little body pressing against her. She loved him so much even though she had never expected to feel this way. He was her son and no matter what happened between her and Leo, she intended to play a role in his life. Once his sobs had abated, she gently set him away from her.

'Can you tell me what frightened you, sweetheart? Was it a bad dream?'

'Yes,' he whispered. He looked so solemn that she was tempted to tell him that it didn't matter, only she knew that she had to get to the bottom of this.

'Do you remember what you dreamt about?' she asked softly, and felt him stiffen. 'If you tell me then it might make it less scary.'

'I was dreaming about Harry falling into the water,' he muttered.

'Oh, that was scary,' she said, giving him another cuddle. She smiled at him. 'But Harry's fine now. Your daddy got him out of the water and he's promised not to go near it ever again.'

'It was my fault he fell in,' Noah said in a rush. 'I didn't catch the ball and it landed in the water and Harry had to get it.'

'It wasn't your fault,' she said firmly. 'Harry knew he shouldn't go near the river.'

Noah considered that for a second. 'It was my fault that Mummy crashed her car.'

Mia managed to hide her surprise, although she had a feeling that this was the real root of the problem. 'I'm sure that isn't true, darling. It was an accident.'

'No, it was my fault. I started crying and Mummy got angry and didn't see the bus coming.' Tears filled his eyes. 'I don't want a new daddy. You won't let Mummy make me live with her and my new daddy, will you, Mia? She said that my old daddy doesn't want me any more so can I live with you and Harry?'

Mia didn't know what to say. It was worse than she had imagined, far, far worse, and not just because of what Noah must have been going through for all these months. All of a sudden she was overwhelmed by doubts, by thoughts so dark that she felt sick. Had Leo known that his ex-wife had been planning to take Noah away from him? Was that why once he'd discovered that Noah wasn't his real son, he had set out to find the child who was? Was Harry to be some sort of trade-off, offered in Noah's place?

She didn't want to believe that Leo would do such a terrible thing but she knew how much he loved Noah and how desperate he was to keep him. He had been so ambiguous about his ex-wife's involvement, too. She had put it down to the fact that he had little time for Amanda after the way she had abandoned Noah as a baby, but maybe there was another explanation. Had he deliberately played down Amanda's involvement so that she wouldn't become suspicious?

Mia's head reeled as thoughts rushed this way and that. It was only the fact that Noah needed reassuring that helped her hold it together. She tilted his face and looked into his eyes so that he would see that she meant every word.

'No one is going to take you away from your daddy, my love. Mummy was wrong when she said that Daddy doesn't want you any more because he does. He loves you an awful lot and he'll do everything he can to make sure you stay with him. Do you understand?'

Noah nodded, his face relaxing into a smile as he put his arms around her and hugged her. Mia hugged him back, although her heart felt like lead. Was she right to suspect that Leo had had an ulterior motive all along? Had he been lulling her into a false sense of security, playing on her emotions to get what he wanted, which was Noah living with him? Even sleeping with her could have been part of his plan and that was the worst thought of all, to wonder if he had used her that way too.

Mia took a deep breath, forcing back the tears that threatened to overwhelm her. She didn't want to believe that Leo could have done such a thing but after everything that had happened to her as a child, she couldn't rule it out. The fact that she might have put Harry at risk by her gullibility was very hard to accept but she had to face it. Even if Leo hadn't planned this, there was still Amanda to consider.

Although Amanda hadn't wanted Noah initially, people changed and she could have changed too. Maybe she had found it difficult to bond with him, somehow sensing that he wasn't hers.

Mia's heart filled with dread. It would definitely explain Amanda's past behaviour. She'd always found it hard to believe that any woman could reject her own child but there may have been a reason for it, a good one too. Now, if Amanda was so desperate for a child, she could very well try to claim Harry, her real son. And Leo might help her if it meant he could retain custody of Noah.

Leo could barely contain his anxiety. Mia seemed to be taking an inordinately long time, he thought as he made Harry a mug of hot chocolate. He added cold milk to cool it down then placed it on the table, forcing himself to smile. He didn't want Harry to know how worried he felt.

'Here you go. Drink this up and then we'll see if Noah is feeling better.'

Harry buried his face in the mug, gulping down the treat with obvious pleasure. When he asked if he could have a biscuit, Leo nodded. He found the tin and let the child choose what he wanted, glancing at the clock while Harry debated. How much longer was Mia going to be?

He put the tin away, looking round in relief when he heard her footsteps. She smiled as she came into the kitchen but Leo could see the strain in her eyes and his heart turned over. It was obvious that something had happened. However, with Harry there he couldn't ask her what it was. It was another ten minutes before Mia took Harry back to bed. Leo waited with mounting impatience for her to return. He needed to know what was going on and needed to know it soon! She came in and sat down, her face set as she looked at him.

'I expect you're anxious to know what was wrong with Noah,' she said in a cold little voice he had never heard her use before. It struck fear into his heart so that he had to sit down as well.

'Obviously,' he replied equally coldly, because he didn't want her to know how scared he felt.

'It appears that Noah believed he was responsible for that accident he and his mother had.'

She didn't try to dress it up and Leo realised that there was more to it than that. It was an effort to reply calmly when it felt as though his insides were churning.

'That's ridiculous. It wasn't Noah's fault and I'll make sure he understands that.'

'Good. And while you're doing that, I suggest you make sure he understands that you still want him.' She shrugged, ignoring his stunned gasp. 'It appears that your ex-wife told him he was going to live with her and his new daddy because you no longer wanted him.

When he started crying, she got angry and crashed into the bus.'

'I don't believe it!' Leo leapt to his feet, unable to sit there and listen to such rubbish. 'Amanda actually told him that I didn't want him?'

'So it seems.' She shrugged again. 'Are you saying you didn't know?'

'Of course I didn't know!' he exploded, stunned that she would think he'd had any inkling. 'If I'd known Amanda had told him that, I'd have done something about it.'

'Maybe you did.' Her expression was glacial. It matched her tone and Leo felt his blood run cold.

'And what's that supposed to mean? Come on, spit it out. Something is obviously bothering you.'

'You're right. It is.'

She stood up as well and he realised that she was trembling. It was hard to stand there and not go to her, but he knew that it wasn't what she wanted. Leo steeled himself because he also knew that whatever she said was going to hurt. A lot.

'You found out what your ex-wife was planning and took steps to avoid it. That's why you were so keen to find Harry, Amanda's *real* son.' She gave a broken laugh. 'What was the plan, Leo? Was Harry to be a trade-off—you'd get to keep Noah while she had Harry, and both of you would be happy?

'Maybe you two planned it together—who knows? Well, even if you did, I'm sorry to have to tell you that it isn't going to happen. I shall fight you through every court in the land if either of you tries to take Harry away from me. He's my son and he always will be mine!'

She spun round but Leo didn't move. He couldn't. He was so stunned by the accusation that he couldn't move a muscle. Did Mia honestly believe he would do that? Sink so low as to take her child so he could give him to another woman? He couldn't begin to explain how it made him feel to know that she thought him capable of that kind of deception.

He sank down onto a chair and put his head in his hands. Last night he had reached previously unknown heights of pleasure, of happiness, of joy. And tonight he had sunk to the very depths of despair.

It was raining again the following morning. Mia carried her case downstairs and placed it by the door. The taxi was due shortly and she wanted to be ready to leave as soon as it arrived. Harry trailed after her, looking mutinous as he placed his bag next to hers.

'Why do we have to go, Mummy? Noah's staying so why can't I stay with him?'

'It's just not possible, sweetie.' Mia tried to smile but her lips refused to obey her. 'Noah and his daddy want to spend some time on their own.'

'Don't they want me to stay with them?' Harry asked, looking puzzled.

'Yes, we'd love you to stay, Harry. But your mummy has things to do and that's why you have to go home.'

Mia glanced round when Leo came to join them. His face was set and it was impossible to guess how he was feeling. He smiled at Harry and her heart filled with pain when she realised what a good actor he was. Nobody could tell from looking at him how devastated he must feel that his plans had been scuppered. It made her wonder if his so-called delight in their lovemaking had been an act too. If it had, it had certainly convinced her.

Her eyes swam with tears so it was a relief when the taxi sounded its horn. Picking up her case, she shooed Harry out of the door. Leo followed her out, laying a detaining hand on her shoulder.

'I'll be in touch as soon as I get back, Mia.'

Mia didn't say a word as she shook him off. She helped Harry into the cab and fastened his seat belt then fastened her own. She didn't look back as the driver pulled away and had no idea if Leo was waiting to wave them off. Whatever they'd had…whatever she'd *thought* they'd had…was over.

Mia was relieved when the half-term holiday ended and Harry went back to school. He'd been sulky and out of sorts ever since they'd got back from the cottage, obviously blaming her for cutting short the treat. He cheered up on the Monday morning, though, waving happily as she saw him into his classroom, and she breathed a sigh of relief. Although the worst certainly wasn't over, at least Harry was back to his old self and that was something to be grateful for.

She went into work to find that Penny had put her down for the cardiology unit again. Sister Thomas had booked a week's leave and Penny wanted her to cover. Mia shook her head.

'No, I'm sorry. You'll have to find someone else.'

'There isn't anyone else, or at least no one who can handle the redoubtable Leo Forester,' Penny told her with a grin. 'All the staff agree that he's a changed person when you're on the unit, Mia. Obviously, you know how to bring him to heel!'

It was just too much on top of all the sleepless nights she'd spent worrying about what Leo intended to do about Harry. Tears poured down her face and Penny leapt up in alarm.

'Hey, what's the matter, love? If it was what I said, then I'm sorry. I was only teasing.'

'It isn't that. It's everything. Leo and Noah and Harry and me.'

Mia knew she wasn't making sense but there was nothing she could do. When Penny sat her down, she didn't protest. What if Leo used his vast resources to take Harry from her; what would she do?

'Come on, tell me what's wrong.' Penny patted her shoulder. 'I'm the soul of discretion and I won't repeat a word of what you say.'

It was too tempting. Mia let it all pour out, all her fears, her hopes and her devastation. It was good to be able to tell someone and she felt much better afterwards, although Penny was open-mouthed with shock.

'I don't know what to say. I had no idea...' Penny stopped and gulped. 'What a mess, Mia. But are you sure that Leo was planning to take Harry off you so he could trade him for Noah?'

'No. But it's possible and that's enough.' Mia dried her eyes. 'I won't risk anything happening to Harry.'

'I understand, really I do. But I can't see any judge countenancing such an action.'

'Not even if he was to be handed over to his real mother?'

'With her track record?' Penny shook her head. 'No, I honestly can't see it happening.'

'But what if Leo and Amanda got back together? They might do, even on a temporary basis if it meant they would get what they wanted.'

'Highly unlikely.' Penny dismissed the idea. 'Anyway, the papers are always banging on about the fact that courts try to keep a child with its mother even when they should be removed for their own safety.'

'But that's just it. I'm not Harry's mother. Harry is Leo and Amanda's son. Noah is mine and Chris's.'

'Then you'd have equal rights, I imagine, to sue for custody of Noah.' Penny held up her hand when Mia went to speak. 'I'm not saying you should do it, merely pointing out that you're in the same position as Leo.'

'Except I don't have his money so I can't hire a fancy lawyer to fight my case.'

'There's help available. Anyway, it's not all down to money. Harry loves you. You're his mum. Noah loves Leo. He's his dad. There has to be a way to work this out and the only way to do that is by talking to Leo.'

Mia summoned a watery smile. 'Which is your very clever way of getting me to cover Cardiology.'

'Yep!' Penny gave her a hug. 'You can do this, Mia. You can sort it out. I'm sure of that.'

Mia hoped her friend was right, although she doubted it. She couldn't imagine that Leo would want to invest too much time talking after the way they'd parted. She made her way to the cardio unit and started work, checking the theatre list to see who was scheduled for surgery that day. Leo's name wasn't on the list as one

of the attending surgeons and she breathed a sigh of
relief. At least she wouldn't have to face him just yet.

Leo had spent the remainder of the week trying to get
in contact with Amanda. She had changed her mobile
number and he had to phone everyone he knew to find
out where she was. In the end he tracked her down to a
villa in the south of France where she was staying with
friends. He kept it brief, explaining that Noah had told
him about her plans and that if she thought she was
going to take Noah from him, she could think again.

He didn't mention Mia or Harry; he couldn't bear to.
He simply made it clear that Amanda would regret it
if she attempted to put her plan into action. Although
it might not be the last he heard from her, at least she
knew that she'd have a fight on her hands, and if there
was one thing Amanda loathed it was doing anything
that would upset her pampered life.

With one problem if not solved at least addressed,
he realised that he had to deal with an even bigger one.
He still hadn't got over his hurt and anger at Mia's ac-
cusations but he knew he couldn't leave it as it was. He
was going to have to speak to her, assuming she would
speak to him, of course.

He drove to her house first thing on Monday morning, wanting to talk to her without Harry being there,
but there was no reply when he knocked on the door.
She must have gone into work, he decided, turning the
car round. Although it wasn't ideal to have an in-depth
discussion in working time, he needed to get this sorted
out. He couldn't bear it if they were at loggerheads,
couldn't bear to imagine how worried she must be. He

had to reassure her that he didn't intend to take Harry away from her, no matter what happened.

Maybe it was the fact that he was so distracted but he didn't notice the van that suddenly pulled out of a side road until it was right in front of him. He slammed on the brakes but there was no way he could avoid it. There was a horrible crunching sound of metal striking metal and a roar as the airbag deployed and then silence, broken by the anxious voices of passers-by.

Leo sat in the driving seat, feeling breathless and disorientated from the force of the airbag hitting his chest. He knew the car was quite badly damaged but that didn't matter. What mattered more was that it would delay him speaking to Mia.

Mia was getting into the lift after accompanying a patient to Theatre when she heard a couple of nurses talking. They were saying something about one of the consultants being brought into ED following an RTA but it was only when she heard Leo's name that she started listening.

'Excuse me, but did you say that Mr Forester was in ED?' she asked, feeling a trickle of fear run down her spine.

'Yes. Seems he crashed into a van,' one of the nurses explained. Both women got out at the next floor so she didn't have time to question them further but she knew that she couldn't leave it at that. If Leo was injured she needed to know how bad he was.

Her heart contracted as she pressed the button again, bypassing the cardio unit and heading to ED. There was a queue at the reception desk and she waited with mounting impatience for her turn. 'I believe you have Mr Forester here?' she said, trying to sound as cool and composed as possible, no mean feat when her heart was hammering away.

'That's right.' The receptionist took note of her badge and grinned. 'Checking to see if we'll be keeping him here so you can have an easy ride today?'

'Something like that,' Mia agreed, dredging up a smile.

'I don't blame you. Anyway, Rob's looking after him—he's over there, the tall guy with the bald head.'

Mia nodded her thanks and hurried over to the registrar. He shrugged when she asked him if Leo was badly injured.

'We're still running tests—CT scan, X-rays, bloods—so I can't give you a definite answer. However, from the fuss he's making, I doubt he's on his way to meet the Grim Reaper today.'

'Oh, right. Thank you,' Mia murmured, feeling faint with relief. She went and sat down on a chair, wondering what to do.

Despite the registrar's assurances, she would have liked to see for herself that Leo was all right but would that be wise? She could be playing into his hands by showing her vulnerability, couldn't she? For all she knew, he could have been plotting away, working with his ex-wife to take Harry off her…only she didn't really believe that, did she? Not in her heart. Not where it truly mattered.

Mia stood up, her legs trembling as she went over to the desk where the registrar was talking to one of the nurses. It was a question of trust, wasn't it? Quite simply: did she trust Leo enough to believe that he would never try to hurt her and Harry?

'Excuse me,' she said, feeling a rush of warmth run through her and chase away the chill that had invaded her for the past few days. She did trust him, trusted him to do what was right for Harry, trusted him to do what was right for her too. It was hard to speak when there were so many emotions welling up inside her. 'C-can I see Mr Forester?'

'If you want to, although I warn you he's not in the best of tempers, although I expect you're used to that.' The registrar grinned. 'I never believed the stories about him before but I do now. I'm only glad I don't work for him!'

Mia didn't say anything as he led her to the end cubicle and left her there. The curtains were drawn and she took a quick breath before pushing them aside. She was probably the last person Leo wanted to see but tough. She needed to make sure he was all right and then…

What?

What did she intend to do? Talk to him? But would he want to talk to her? Leo would be well within his rights to refuse to have anything to do with her after what she'd said to him. She could, in fact, make the situation worse by attempting to discuss what had happened and that was the last thing she wanted. Although she wasn't foolish enough to think that they could pick up where they had left off, she wanted them to be friends at the very least. But would Leo want to be her friend? That was the big question.

Mia stood there, gripping the curtain as she debated the idea. Could a man and a woman ever be just friends after they'd been lovers?

Leo swung his legs over the side of the bed. He'd had enough of hanging around. Maybe that young registrar was only following procedure but *he* knew he was fine.

He slipped his feet into his shoes, groaning when his ribs gave him gyp. No doubt he'd have a mass of bruises from the combined force of the seat belt locking and the airbag deploying but what was a bit of physical discomfort compared to this inner agony he felt? He had to see Mia and convince her that she could trust him!

He thrust back the curtain and came to a dead stop when he was confronted by the very person he longed to see. Whether it was shock or relief, he had no idea, but there was no way that he could play it cool. That was the old him, the man he'd been pre-Mia, and he was a completely different person now.

He hauled her into his arms and kissed her right there in the middle of ED, uncaring that there were people watching them. He loved her, he wanted her, and by heaven he was going to make her understand that if he had to stand here all day and kiss her!

There was a moment's hesitation and then she was kissing him back and Leo knew it was going to be all right, that miraculously they could sort out this whole stupid mess. Mia loved him as much as he loved her and they could take on the world and win so long as they took it on together.

He drew back, his breath coming in spurts that were only partly the result of his bruised ribs. 'I had no idea what Amanda was planning. You have to believe me, my darling. I would never have tried to trick you and take Harry from you.'

'I know you wouldn't.' Her breathing sounded strained too and he smiled as some much-needed confidence came roaring back.

'Good.' He rewarded her with another kiss then looked round, grimacing as he realised the attention they were attracting. 'Shall we take this somewhere a little more private?'

'Please.'

She didn't protest as he caught hold of her hand and led her from ED. They passed Rob on the way out but he was too stunned to object when Leo informed him that he would come back later for the results of the tests. It took just a few minutes to reach the consultants' lounge, which was mercifully empty. Leo closed the door and leant against it.

'So where do we go from here?'

'Where do you want to go?' she countered, looking at him with so much love in her eyes that he trembled.

'Nowhere that you won't be,' he growled, pulling her into his arms and kissing her with undisguised hunger. He leant his forehead against hers, feeling uncharacteristically bashful about revealing the true depth of his feelings, although maybe it was understandable. After all, it would be the first time he had told a woman that he loved her.

'I love you, Mia. I want to spend my life with you and build a future for us and the boys, if it's what you want too. Do you?'

'Yes. It's what I want more than anything. If we can do it and not harm the boys in any way.'

He stroked her cheek, understanding her fear. 'There's no reason to think they'll be unhappy about it. We've seen how well they get on and I'm sure they'll be thrilled to be part of a family.' He looked into her eyes. 'But we'll take it slowly, make sure they're completely comfortable with all that we have to tell them, make sure they understand how much we love them too. OK?'

'Yes. It's more than OK,' she murmured, reaching up on tiptoe to kiss him.

The kiss lasted several minutes and only ended when Leo's pager bleeped. He sighed as he checked the display. 'Theatre's paging me. I'll have to phone and cancel. It wouldn't be a good idea to operate at the moment.'

'Because of your accident?' she said anxiously.

'No, because admitting how much I love you has left me with very shaky hands.'

He held them out for her inspection and she laughed, loving the fact that he could admit to his vulnerability, simply loving *him*. He made the call then arranged to go back to ED and meet her later, once all the results were back, not that he expected there to be a problem, he assured her.

Mia went back to the cardio unit and spent the rest of the morning feeling as though she was floating several inches above the ground. Leo loved her and, in time, they would be together: him, her and their boys. Maybe a mistake had brought them together, but the result couldn't be more perfect.

Two years later...

'Now take turns. And don't push the swing too high. We don't want Grace falling off.'

Leo waited until he was sure that Harry and Noah understood then went and sat down on the grass. They were spending a week at the cottage and the weather had been perfect. Long sunny days followed by gloriously warm nights. Taking hold of Mia's hand, he sighed in contentment. Life was wonderful and it was all thanks to her. Raising her hand to his lips, he smiled up at her.

'Have I told you lately how much I love you?'

'Oh, not since about eight o'clock this morning.'

'Very remiss of me. It's enough to make you instigate divorce proceedings.'

He laughed as he kissed the inside of her wrist, sure enough of their relationship to joke about it. They had married a year ago, as soon as they had discovered that she was expecting Grace. It had been right for many reasons, the main one being that Harry and Noah were comfortable with their relationship.

The DNA tests had confirmed what they had already known, that Harry was his child and Noah was Mia's, so once the time had felt right they had sat the boys down and explained what had happened, answered their questions and assured them that even though they had different mums and dads than they'd thought, it made no difference. He and Mia loved them both and amazingly the boys had accepted it.

It had been so much simpler than he'd feared, but then most things were simpler now that he had Mia there, loving and supporting him. When little Grace had been born some eight months later it had been the icing on the cake and the boys had been as thrilled as them. Harry and Noah loved their little sister to bits.

As for Amanda, either she had taken his warning

to heart or, more likely, changed her mind again about being a mother. Rumour had it that she had split up from the man who she had been hoping would become Noah's new daddy. Apparently, he'd been very keen to be a father and Amanda had hoped that providing him with a ready-made son would satisfy his longings.

Leo had no idea what had really happened and didn't care. He was simply glad that he hadn't heard from her, although as a precaution he had taken legal advice if she did try to sue for custody of Harry or Noah in the future and he was confident that she wouldn't win if it came to a court case. Now he lay back on the grass, feeling the warmth of the sun seeping into his pores.

This was how his life felt every day, filled with warmth and love. He had Mia and their family. He had it all.

* * * * *

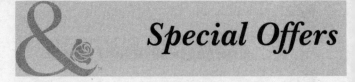